P9-DGI-549

HELPLESS TO REFUSE

"Callie, I . . ." The words ended as he lowered his head toward hers, his arm sweeping around her waist, pulling her close, the clean, musky scent of him overwhelming any last, niggling bits of reason that might have stopped her. It wasn't gratitude that burned in those smoldering brown eyes. Not this time. His lips were just as she remembered them—warm, soft. But his body was hard, fierce as he crushed her to him. And if he hadn't held her, she would have crumpled to the floor, so stunned was she by the raging tide of emotions that swept through her.

Callie flung her arms around him, her hands clinging to the back of his neck, exploring the fever-hot touch of his flesh, then furrowing upward into the thick strands of his tawny hair.

What was happening to her? She couldn't allow this. With a sheer effort of will, she tore her lips from his. "Please, Trace . . ." she whispered. "This isn't . . . I can't . . ."

But the more he touched her, the more she knew it *was* what she wanted—and what she *could* let herself do . . .

MORE TANTALIZING ROMANCES

SATIN SURRENDER   (1861, $3.95)
by Carol Finch

Dante Fowler found innocent Erica Bennett in his bed in the most fashionable whorehouse in New Orleans. Expecting a woman of experience, Dante instead stole the innocence of the most magnificent creature he'd ever seen. He would forever make her succumb to . . . *Satin Surrender.*

CAPTIVE BRIDE   (1984, $3.95)
by Carol Finch

Feisty Rozalyn DuBois had to pretend affection for roguish Dominic Baudelair; her only wish was to trick him into falling in love and then drop him cold. But Dominic had his own plans: To become the richest trapper in the territory by making Rozalyn his *Captive Bride.*

MOONLIT SPLENDOR   (2008, $3.95)
by Wanda Owen

When the handsome stranger emerged from the shadows and pulled Charmaine Lamoureux into his strong embrace, she knew she should scream, but instead she sighed with pleasure at his seductive caresses. She would be wed against her will on the morrow—but tonight she would succumb to this passionate MOONLIT SPLENDOR.

UNTAMED CAPTIVE   (2159, $3.95)
by Elaine Barbieri

Cheyenne warrior Black Wolf fully intended to make Faith Durham, the lily-skinned white woman he'd captured, pay for her people's crimes against the Indians. Then he looked into her sky-blue eyes and it was impossible to stem his desire . . . he was compelled to make her surrender as his UNTAMED CAPTIVE.

WILD FOR LOVE   (2161, $3.95)
by Linda Benjamin

All Callandra wanted was to go to Yellowstone and hunt for buried treasure. Then her wagon broke down and she had no choice but to get mixed up with that arrogant golden-haired cowboy, Trace McCord. But before she knew it, the only treasure she wanted was to make him hers forever.

Available wherever paperbacks are sold, or order direct from the Publisher. Send cover price plus 50¢ per copy for mailing and handling to Zebra Books, Dept. 2161, 475 Park Avenue South, New York, N.Y. 10016. Residents of New York, New Jersey and Pennsylvania must include sales tax. DO NOT SEND CASH.

Wild for Love

LINDA BENJAMIN

ZEBRA BOOKS
KENSINGTON PUBLISHING CORP.

ZEBRA BOOKS

are published by

Kensington Publishing Corp.
475 Park Avenue South
New York, NY 10016

First printing: September 1987

Printed in the United States of America

To My Editor,
Pesha Finkelstein

For believing in me,
even when I didn't.

Chapter One

Callandra Callaghan slapped a fist against the iron rim of the Conestoga's left rear wheel, trying in vain to draw rein on her rapidly disintegrating temper. But it was too late. Far too late. She stood ankle deep in muck, cursing her own foolhardiness that she had dared risk a shortcut through this boulder-studded hollow. The three-hour downpour that had begun at dawn threatened more and more to give birth to Wyoming's newest white water rapids. Even the Tetons rising abruptly from the valley floor six miles to the west seemed suddenly hostile, forbidding, distorting her initial impression three days ago that they had somehow stumbled upon the gateway to the Garden of Eden.

Callie swiped at her dripping hair, its normally spun copper hue dulled by wet and wind. Her simple gray cotton day dress clung heavily, cloyingly to her slender frame, its hem swirling in the tumbling water funneling past her feet.

Earning every inch of forward progress, she sloshed

7

her way toward the four-horse team dancing nervously in its harness. Just short of the left front bay's rear flank she paused, her stomach tightening as the grinding sound of straining wood rose above the crack of thunder. She glanced back, squinting to better see through the pelting rain. The lower wheel spokes seemed to bow outward now, the wheel approaching the outer limits of its tolerance. Yet still the wagon listed, shifting to bear more and more of its over-balanced load toward the sinking left rear.

"Aunt Deirdre!" she yelled, banging on the white oak slats of the driver's boot. "What's happening in there? You've got to keep the equipment from moving . . ."

The canvas flap behind the wagon seat snapped aside, water spraying off in all directions. Arms folded across her chest, seemingly oblivious to the storm, Deirdre Callaghan glared at Callie, the disapproval furrowing the brows above her coffee-brown eyes masking their more familiar and well-loved laugh lines. Callie swallowed a groan. Her forty-year-old aunt was primed for her third lecture of the morning, the rain seeming to bring out the best in neither one of them.

"Don't say it," Callie warned, holding up a hand as if to ward off the expected verbal barrage. "I don't want to hear . . ."

With a sudden jerk the horses lunged against their harness, just as abruptly halting when the wagon held fast to the mire that trapped it. Off balance, Deirdre grabbed for the support of the wagon seat, Callie gesturing instinctively toward the scraping sound of some unseen shifting cargo. Her aunt made no attempt to reach it.

Deirdre's lips thinned. "I wager you care more about those danged crates than you do your own life."

"That's because there's nowhere in five hundred miles I can replace what's in those crates, and you know it."

"And all the better if you don't. It'd end all this gloried nonsense about journals and picture-taking, Yellowstone and buried treasure."

"It is *not* buried treasure!" Callie hissed, slamming down her heel only to feel the squish of mud sucking at her high-button shoe. Cursing, she yanked the foot free. Hands on her hips she stared upward at her aunt, knowing even as she did so the ridiculous picture they must both present railing at each other in the pouring rain. "This is not some blasted pirate adventure. The *treasure,* as you persist in calling it, is only part of why . . ." She clamped her jaw shut as a short, wiry figure slogged into view from around the rear of the wagon.

"More secrets, Miss Callie?" Riley Smith grinned, rubbing a hand over his scraggly bearded jaw. The water runneling off the edges of the scout's droop-brimmed Stetson, coupled with the dripping fringe of his trail-stained buckskins made him look every bit the image of a half-drowned buffalo. "I swear I never seen a woman so close-mouthed. Ain't natural, if'n you ask me."

"Speaking of natural," Callie gritted, "when is this rain going to cease?"

"I tol' ya not to come through the hollow." He waved a hand toward the mile-long forest of aspen that skirted the ravine. "A hollow's no place to be in a gulley washer. But little Miss Callie knows more'n poor dumb

9

Riley Smith. I only trailed grizzlies with Jim Bridger, trapped beaver with the Sublettes . . ."

"And no doubt would have single-handedly defended the Alamo," Callie sneered, "if Misters Bowie and Crockett had only had the foresight to summon you back in '36. Never mind the fact that you were maybe five years old at the time, and that in the intervening forty-six years you've managed to cultivate a taste for tall tales that far outdistances any passing acquaintance with the truth."

Riley bent double, roaring with laughter. "I do love it when you get riled, Miss Callie. I never heard anybody talk as purty as you, when you get plumb red-in-the-face mad." He slapped his knee, sending up a tiny geyser of water. "I don't know why you had ta come so far to show up your daddy. Sure as shootin' alls you woulda had to do was get him in a talking match, and the man woulda screamed for mercy in a minute flat."

Callie whirled on her aunt, who immediately ducked behind the canvas curtain. "What have you been telling this . . . this stranger, Aunt Deirdre?" Callie demanded, astonishment vying with outrage. "Just how much does he know about Da?"

"Now don't go gettin' yer Irish up," Deirdre scolded, peeping out, her face flushing crimson with embarrassment. "After all, you're the one who hired Mr. Smith. He was just naturally curious about why two women . . ."

Callie's rush of Gaelic invectives should have cleared the gray-black skies, so pristinely blue were each and every one of them.

"Now that's no way for a lady to talk, Miss Callie,"

Riley cajoled mockingly. "You'll scare the horses."

Callie glared him into silence, then squared her shoulders, turning to stare belligerently at her aunt. "I love you, Aunt Deirdre," she grated, "but until now I guess I didn't realize just how much your agreeing to come along on this trip was meant to humor me. You don't believe for a minute I'm going to succeed, do you?"

She didn't wait for an answer, twisting again to face the scout. "As for you, Riley Smith, you need only remember one thing about this entire expedition. You're here because you're paid to be here. Neither you nor my aunt has to believe a damn in what I'm doing." She jabbed a finger at her chest for emphasis. "Because I believe in it. I've dreamed it, lived it, wanted it, since I was fourteen years old. And nothing and no one is going to stop me from having it. Not when I'm this close."

"Even if it kills you?" Deirdre asked quietly.

Callie's lips compressed in a grim line, but she didn't respond. Instead she marched toward the skittish gelding. "Let's get out of here." Catching up the bay's bridle, she attempted to soothe the horse, while her own pulses throbbed with hurt and frustration. At least the rain was slackening, diminishing to a mistlike drizzle.

Of all people in the world, she would have thought Deirdre would understand, if only because Deirdre had always been there to understand. Or almost always. It was Deirdre who had been midwife to Callie's mother when Callie was born twenty-three years ago.

Sarah Callaghan had adored her sister-in-law, and for Callie it had been like having two mothers. In fact, the bleakest years of her life had been those between the ages of four and eight when Deirdre had returned to Ireland. It was during that time that Callie's mother sickened and died. With the War Between the States in full force, her father was off on the battlefields, taking pictures, writing stories, building a reputation for himself that had yet to see its end. Fletcher Callaghan returned after Appomattox, retrieving Callie from kindly neighbors, but it was another two years before Deirdre came back into her life to stay.

It was to Deirdre Callie turned for sympathy about her iron-willed father. Deirdre to whom she turned to see her through her first tentative outings with members of the opposite sex. Deirdre who kept her from making the mistake of her life with Nicolas.

Nicolas.

No. She would not depress herself further. She would give no thought this day to Count Nicolas von Endenberg.

She peered around the gelding at the scout. "I said let's get out of here."

Riley sludged his way over to the rear wheel. With extreme redundance he spit on his wet hands, then curled his fingers around an upper spoke. Hunching his shoulder to the wheel, he nodded at Callie. "Git up!" he yelled, adding, "You watch yourself, Miss Callie. If this wheel pulls free them horses are liable to bolt."

Maintaining her grip on the bridle, she shifted her position so that she was no longer in front of the horse, but alongside it. "I'll manage my end. You just . . ." Her eyes narrowed. "That lower spoke . . . does it look solid?" She let go of the horse and took a step back, studying what looked to be a hairline fracture. "Riley."

12

Her voice rose anxiously, "Riley, get away from . . ." The words weren't out of her mouth before she heard the sound. The thunderous crack of splintering wood. As if in slow motion, the wheel split apart, collapsing sideways, the wagon heaving downward. A sharp pained cry was abruptly cut off.

Callie had visions of the axle cutting Riley in two. Horrified, she lunged toward him. The axle of the wheel lay across his left leg. The strain on the man's face told more than any words could. He was in agony. Still he said nothing, concentrating instead, Callie was certain, on maintaining his hard-bitten male image. She dropped to her knees, grateful to see that the mud had cushioned some of the impact. "Aunt Deirdre, get out here! Hurry!"

The woman scrambled out the front of the wagon. Even as the blood drained from her face, Deirdre Callaghan didn't flinch. Her only concession to her fear was a murmured, "My God."

"I'll be just fine, Miss Deirdre," Riley said. "Don't you worry now." He sucked in a breath through clenched teeth.

Deirdre sagged beside him in the three inches of water that still coursed along the floor of the ravine. "Does it hurt very badly, Mr. Smith?"

"Some," he managed.

Callie pushed, shoved, strained, lifted, but the massive wagon wouldn't budge. Shoulders slumping, she sagged to the ground beside her aunt.

"We'll have to empty the wagon," Deirdre said.

Callie's head jerked up. "No."

"Callie, for the love of heaven, we're talking about a man's leg here."

13

"Putting my cameras in the rain won't lower the poundage enough to matter." Even knowing she was right, Callie still had to fight off a twinge of conscience as she struggled to regain her feet. She didn't look at her aunt as she spoke. "I'll dig under the leg. You be ready to pull him out."

Callie reached inside the wagon and grabbed a spade, then, hunching low, she crawled under the wagon's sloping rear. For a dangerous minute she dared study the sharp angle of the axle as it cut across Riley's leg to settle into the sodden earth to his left. But the ominous creak of wood warned her speed now counted more than caution. She set herself to the task at once, digging at the muddy turf with the steel bladed shovel. Any minute she feared the axle itself would split, sending the corner of the wagon straight down onto Riley's pinned leg. Callie swallowed the bile in her throat. If that happened, the weight would surely sever the man's leg from his body.

She was barely cognizant now of anything but the shovel, the mud, and Riley's leg. If the man was permanently injured she knew she would blame herself. It was her fault they were in this wilderness in the first place. Her dream, no one else's.

Deirdre's murmured prayers and Riley's stoic silence only added to Callie's resolve. Scraping, digging, tearing at whole handfuls of mud with her bare hands, she tunneled a small water-filled trench beneath the man's leg.

"Get ready, Aunt Deirdre," she rasped, settling back on her haunches. "We've got to do this just right."

"Callie, get out from under there."

"Never mind me. Just get under his arms and pull

when I tell you." Callie scooped away another shovelful of mud. More and more the axle rested on the ground, instead of Riley's leg. As the circulation returned to the limb, the man couldn't suppress a groan. Callie shut her mind to it, scrambling out from under the wagon. "Pull, Aunt Deirdre! Now!"

The woman jerked back. Callie skittered over to help her, gripping Riley's buckskin collar and heaving back with all her strength. Slipping, tripping, she fell, both women sprawled in the mud and water, Riley on top of them. In the next breath the wagon crashed sideways, the axle disintegrating, the end corner of the wagon crashing down where Riley's leg had been the instant before.

It was a long minute before any of them moved. Trembling so hard her teeth chattered, Callie forced herself to her hands and knees. "Can you stand, Mr. Smith?"

He shook his head. "Leg's broke."

Callie looked at the leg, at the blood that stained his buckskins. Her stomach churned. It was worse than broken. Quickly she motioned to Deirdre. "I want to get him to the trees. Maybe it's at least a little drier in there." Callie got under Riley's right arm, Deirdre his left. With the scout hopping painfully, they managed to maneuver him to the sheltering aspens.

Using a tree for support, Riley lowered himself to the ground, then sagged against it in a sitting position, his head lolling to one side. Callie sank to her knees, her hands shaking. She stared at the bloodied buckskin just below his left knee. Swallowing hard, she tugged the semiconscious scout's knife free of the scabbard on his belt. She would have to cut away the pant leg to check the wound.

Her fingers trembled harder still as she tried to hold the bloody material away from the leg. She didn't want to stab flesh as well as deerhide. It occurred to her that she had no idea what she would do with the wound once it was exposed. Nor did she know that she sat there holding the knife for a full minute without moving.

"Let me do that," Deirdre commanded gently, prying the knife free of Callie's numbed hand.

Callie watched in silent awe as Deirdre deftly sliced away the buckskin, sure but gentle hands unfalteringly tending a wound the sight of which made Callie gag and turn away. Severed bone showed grotesquely white against a six-inch crimson gash.

"It's a clean break, Mr. Smith," she heard her aunt say. Callie forced herself to look again at the wound. "But I'm going to have to set it so the bones can knit properly. Then I'll make a poultice for . . ."

"Aunt Deirdre," Callie blurted, continuing to gape at her, "since when do you know anything about broken legs?" Could this truly be her aunt? Deirdre Callaghan, the woman who fussed and fumed if she so much as pricked her finger on a rosebush? Deirdre Callaghan, who considered it a mortal sin to be any less than impeccably groomed at all times. Deirdre Callaghan, who was tending Riley Smith's gruesome wound as though it were no more than a sprained thumb?

"There was a time in the war when I was a volunteer nurse," Deirdre murmured, almost to herself.

Callie sat back on her heels. "You were what?"

16

Deirdre seemed to shake herself. "Nothing. Never mind."

Callie's brow furrowed. "But . . ."

"Not now." She took Callie's hand and clamped it on the bandage she had fashioned for Riley's leg. She spoke in short, measured tones. "You hold onto him, while I pull. We've got to set the bone."

Her aunt was all business now, as though she regretted her cryptic revelation. Abruptly, Callie shook off an unsettling curiosity. She had always been told her aunt had gone back to Ireland during the war. But her questions would have to wait.

Deirdre was on her feet, gently lifting Riley's injured leg at the ankle. She gave neither Riley nor Callie any time to dwell on what needed to be done. Closing her eyes and gritting her teeth, Callie curled her arm around Riley's leg at the knee. She sucked in a deep breath and tightened her grip, just as Deirdre pulled hard.

For an instant the scout's whole body went rigid, then he relaxed, an involuntary shudder coursing through him. Sweat beaded his surprisingly unlined forehead, but the glaze of pain that had been in his eyes was already receding.

"Done," Deirdre said, a trace of a satisfied smile curving her lips. "Your bones were quite cooperative, Mr. Smith."

"My pleasure, Miss Deirdre," the scout said weakly.

Callie shook her head in amazement, threading a hand through her bedraggled hair. "You two are unbelievable," she said. At the same time she felt herself shrugging back a surge of guilt. If Deirdre had

17

not intervened when she had, Callie had to wonder if she would still be holding the knife over Riley's injured leg, unable to move. It was that inability to act that galled her. A squeamish stomach she could accept as natural. But her impulsive nature gave no quarter for indecisiveness.

Dwelling on it only made her feel worse. Hoping to divert her thoughts, she focused her attention elsewhere. "We should build a fire," she said, "keep him warm." She scanned the soaking groundcover. "It's too wet here."

"Show you how," Riley gritted, starting to rise. "Show you where to find dry kindling in wet weather."

"Stay down," Deirdre said, coming over to place a hand on his chest, which she just as quickly withdrew. Clearing her throat self-consciously, she admonished him, "You're not to move, understand?"

"Yes, ma'am, Miss Deirdre." He lay back, oddly quiescent under Deirdre's hand.

Callie pulled her aunt aside. "He needs a doctor. I'm going to take one of the horses and ride for help."

"Alone?" Deirdre cried. "Callie, what are you thinking of? You're not going anywhere in this wilderness by yourself. I can't allow it."

"Then who will go?" Callie reasoned gently, knowing her aunt's terror was grounded in love. "You? Riley?" Callie squeezed Deirdre's hand. "I'm the only one who can go and we both know it."

Deirdre's voice remained as anxious as her eyes. "But where . . ."

"You remember that valley we bypassed yesterday . . . the one with the ranch house on the far side of it? I'll go there. I'm sure there'll be some able-bodied men about."

"Who knows who lives on that ranch. Outlaws . . ."

"I doubt outlaws build such structures. Besides, it had that wonderful name burned into the signpost, remember? Shadow's Way. How could anyone with such a poetic soul be an outlaw?"

"Your late Uncle Sean was a poet back in Eire. Though he may not have been an outlaw in the legal sense, I'm certain a few husbands would have liked to see him in jail."

Callie grinned.

"I didn't say that to be amusing."

"I know. I just don't want you to worry so much, that's all."

"What're you two plottin' over there?" Riley grumbled. "It'd best not be what I think it is."

"You just rest easy, Mr. Smith," Callie said. "And remember who's in charge of this outfit."

Riley swore, then stammered an apology when Deirdre blushed. Still, it was she who rushed to his side when he again attempted to rise.

"You'll only aggravate your injury, Mr. Smith."

He caught her wrist. "You can't let your niece go off by herself, Miss Deirdre. She might be quicker'n a crooked politician when it comes to words, but she's a lamb in a wolfpack out there alone."

"I'm only going to that ranch we saw yesterday," Callie interjected. "It can't be more than ten miles back."

"Ten miles for you to get turned around in."

"Don't be absurd," Callie said. "Besides, you're in no position to argue. If by some impossible circumstance I can't find the ranch, I'll just come back here."

"This ain't no city park. No streetlamps, no numbered avenues, no neighbors to ask directions. We been takin' a shortcut to the Yellowstone, little lady. There ain't even a wagon road to follow."

"He's right, Callie," Deirdre said. "It's too big a risk."

"No bigger than the one I took coming out here in the first place." She strode toward the wagon. Riley's curse this time was not accompanied by any sign of contrition.

Reaching the team, standing placidly now in the aftermath of the storm, Callie unharnessed the bay. Tugging on its bridle, she led it to the rear of the wagon. She hadn't been able to face looking inside since the wheel broke. If her cameras were damaged . . . Taking a deep breath, she peered into the shadowed interior.

Deirdre marched up to her. "The cameras again! I might have known. They're what you really want rescued, aren't they?"

"I just wanted to make sure they weren't broken." She ran a hand caressingly across the black box with its meticulously packed glass photographic plates. "Maybe I care so much about them because the pictures they take will outlive us all."

"If anything happens to you . . ."

"The responsibility will be mine," Callie finished. "And mine alone. It was my choice to come out here, remember? You saved me from marrying Nicolas, but you hardly did it with the notion that I would board the next train for Chicago."

"And who was it who forced this whole insane notion into your head at all, child? With a cold stone in his breast where his heart should be! It's Finley who put

20

us all here. Finley, who'll never feel a twinge of guilt over any of our graves." The sudden rush of anger in Deirdre's voice faded as abruptly as it began. "I'm sorry, Callie. I didn't mean . . ." She turned away. "Your da loves ye. He just . . ."

"He just wants to control my life, like he controls everything else." Callie knew she shouldn't press her aunt, especially when Deirdre was upset enough to call Fletcher Callaghan by the birth name he had shed the moment he had set foot on American soil. She recalled tales of how brother and sister had clashed over Finley O'Callaghan's decision to alter the family name in hopes of softening the impact of Irish prejudice that had been everywhere in 1850's New York. But nothing had softened Fletcher Callaghan's drive for absolute control of his family. And Deirdre had spent a lifetime deferring to that control. Or so Callie had always believed.

Such thoughts only sparked a new curiosity about Deirdre's softly spoken thunderbolt of a few minutes ago—that she had once been a nurse. Fingering the bay's reins, Callie cast a sidelong glance toward her aunt. "Why did Da tell Mama and me that you went back to Ireland during the war?"

Deirdre's gaze shifted from Callie to a dozing Riley Smith. "This isn't the time."

Memories of a dim, sick-smelling bedchamber washed over Callie. "I was five years old, and I was sitting beside Mama's bed holding her hand. Her hand was so cold and I was so frightened. I begged her to let me go find you. But she told me Ireland was too far away. She told me you were where you had to be."

"I was," Deirdre said quietly.

Callie stared at her aunt, at the range of emotions that skated across her face. "Mama knew, didn't she? About your being a nurse. And about the real reason you left us."

Deirdre nodded.

"Then that's all the reason I need."

Deirdre blinked rapidly, her eyes overbright. Shaking herself, she said quickly, "I think you were about to go for help?"

Callie gave her aunt a swift hug. "Whatever it was, I know you did what you had to do."

"I'll tell you the whole of it one day. I promise."

Callie grabbed up the reins. "I'd best get going. I want to find that ranch before dark." But before she could mount, Deirdre caught her arm. "For my peace of mind if nothing else, I want you to talk to Ri— Mr. Smith before you go. Make sure you're headed in the right direction."

Callie sighed, then relented, leading the gelding back to the trees.

Riley's eyes opened at the sound of their approach. "I don't believe it," he croaked, his gaze shifting from Callie to the bay. "I thought you had a brain in that head of yours, girl, but now I think the good Lord may 'ave forgot to pack any. You're really goin' off in this wilderness like that? Just the clothes on your back? No weapon, no food, no idea on God's green earth where the hell . . ."

"Mr. Smith!" Deirdre chided, "you really must have a care with your language."

"Have a care for your niece, Miss Deirdre!" Riley shouted, waving his arm toward Callie, then twisting in pain as the movement aggravated his leg. He took a

22

long, steadying breath, his gaze shifting from Callie to Deirdre, then back again.

"The ranch is only ten miles . . ." Callie said.

"I don't care if'n it's ten yards. Ain't you learned nothin' in the two months we been travelin' out here? You heard the wolves at night, seen the track of a grizzly, heard me tell about renegade Injuns . . ."

"The only Indians I've seen were at Fort Laramie, and they were quite friendly."

"I'm tellin' ya what *can* happen, Miss Callie. I thought you wanted to live to write that book of yours, to take your pictures. Well, you ain't gonna live five minutes, if'n you go off like a newborn calf to a puma's cave the first chance you get to show what I learned ya."

Callie felt her cheeks heat. He was right. Every word he said, the man was absolutely right. She would have been a fool to ride off unprepared. "I'm sorry," she said, and meant it.

Riley's anger softened. "I'll give ya one thing, Miss Callie, you're never afraid to say that word. You make a mistake, you admit it. That don't come easy to most folks."

"It don't . . . doesn't come easy to me, either, Mr. Smith. Believe me." She straightened. "But even you have to admit I'm the logical one to go for help."

"I admit that, yes. But it won't do me'n Miss Deirdre a lick o' good, if you end up needin' more help than we do."

She sat down beside him. "Agreed."

He went through a litany of warnings, reiterating things he'd told her since he'd hired on in Omaha—how to follow the sun even in cloudcover, keeping off ridge

23

tops to avoid being skylined, checking her backtrail to memorize where she'd been as well as where she was going.

"The same trail can look like a different world from the opposite direction," he said. "Sun position, landmarks, everything matters. You look and look, then look again. Make a map in your mind."

He told her to hand him his rifle, then while Deirdre scowled, he reminded Callie how to load and unload it. When he finished with the gun, he said, "You'd best take my sorrel, instead of that harness animal. That bay's too high-strung."

Callie rose to her feet and returned the rifle to its scabbard. "If I haven't mentioned it before, you're a damned fine trailblazer, Mr. Smith."

He blushed and Callie grinned. Threading her fingers through the sorrel's shaggy mane, she climbed into the saddle. "I'll try to be back by nightfall, but please don't fret if this ranch family makes me wait 'til morning." She flipped open Riley's saddlebags and handed Deirdre his extra six-gun. "You may need a little extra protection of your own."

"Just be careful," Deirdre said. "Please."

"I promise." Callie dug her heels into the gelding's sides. The sun had made an appearance, and her damp clothing soon made her feel as if steam were rising from her body. Again and again she checked behind her, noting oddly shaped trees, peculiar boulder formations, taking pride in how easily she would make the return trip to the ravine. Thanks to Riley Smith.

She rode on, the stillness of the tree-bristled landscape broken only by the steady thumping of the gelding's hooves on the grassy turf. When she'd been in the saddle for nearly two hours, she pulled up, dismounting to stretch her legs. She groundtied the horse, then ambled several yards away, drinking in the combined scents of the wildflower dappled meadow and the heady mountain air.

It was then that it struck her.

The silence.

The absolute silence.

Born and bred in the city of New York, Callie had spent a childhood immersed in sound, her nightly lullabies orchestrated in the streets—jangling harness and neighing horses, shouting street vendors and clanging paddy wagons. She was twelve when her father moved the family to a Victorian mansion on the city's outskirts. The sounds changed, but the activity level did not. Her father's position as owner and editor of *The Sentinel,* one of the city's most powerful newspapers, meant a never-ending stream of parties, dinners, and business meetings with scores of influential people.

People.

Above all New York meant people.

So many people.

This was the first time in her life Callie had ever been totally alone.

She stood there, at once reveling in it and wary of it. The urge to lie beneath one of those magnificent trees and pour her feelings into her journal was almost overwhelming. But her conscience would permit no such luxury. Riley deserved a warm bed tonight. She would do her best to see to it that he had one.

And just that suddenly she was eager to hurry on. As beautiful as the land was, she sensed also its capacity to be savage, even cruel. She needed the company and comfort of a fellow human being. She needed to meet the poetic soul who owned a ranch named Shadow's Way.

Hurrying now, she remounted and kneed the horse into a gallop.

Chapter Two

Callie felt at home on the smooth gaited sorrel, the animal's long strides devouring the distance to Shadow's Way in an easy, measured rhythm. Only the urgency she felt about bringing aid to Deirdre and Riley kept her from enjoying the ride. Easing off the pace, allowing the horse to blow, she pushed her stiff, straggling hair away from her face, noting wryly its unmistakable haystack texture. Once Deirdre and Riley were safe, if she did nothing else in her life, she was going to take a steaming hot bath, preferably for three hours straight.

For now the slower pace of the horse allowed her mind to drift. Normally resistant to thinking about the early years of her life, the seductive beauty of the snow-splashed Teton peaks all but compelled her to be reflective. Again and again Callie thought of Deirdre's pronouncement that she had been a nurse during the war. That fact alone was astonishing enough, but for Callie never to have heard it mentioned before could only mean Deirdre's nursing activities had been deliberately concealed. Why?

Had Fletcher Callaghan been embarrassed by his sister's decision to tend wounded soldiers? It would be just like him to invent a return trip to Ireland rather than admit Deirdre had done anything against his wishes. Deirdre was Fletcher's sole surviving relative from the famine years. Losing so much of his family to typhus and starvation in Ireland left him fanatical about keeping his remaining family together. Any rebellion on Deirdre's part would most certainly have incurred her brother's wrath.

Still, it didn't explain why Deirdre would have kept silent about it all these years. Surely there had been some point where her aunt had at least alluded to having once been a nurse. Callie had been so young when it all happened, she supposed the memory could be partially obscured by a child's fanciful thinking.

One fact was irrefutable, though. For four years Deirdre had cut herself off from Fletcher Callaghan, and thus from Sarah and Callie. And wherever she had gone, Ireland or elsewhere, the reason for her leaving centered around her brother's last visit home during the war.

Callie shivered, reining the sorel to a halt, guessing she was still a good two miles from Shadow's Way. Even with nineteen years' distance she fought against reliving that most painful part of her life. But at last she gave in to it. Gigging the horse into a ground-eating canter, she allowed her memories to sift over her.

It was late November 1862. Ignoring Deirdre's pleas, Sarah Callaghan had risen from her sickbed. Fletcher had sent word he was coming home for a visit. "This is only the second time he's been able to get away from the war," Sarah argued. "I can't have him finding me ill."

Callie had been playing with a toy camera her father had had specially made for her. She paused at the foot of her mother's bed to peer anxiously at the two women who were her whole world.

"His second visit in near three years," Deirdre said, the disgust in her voice evident even to a four-year-old. "I can scarce believe how important we must all be to him."

"Deirdre, please," Sarah said, "he can stay only a short time, surely the two of you can put aside your differences."

"You're saying you don't think he's going to bring up my wantin' to leave?" Deirdre shook her head sadly. "It's likely why he's come back."

"Yes, I daresay he'll bring that up all right. But you stick to your guns. You've a right to live your own life."

"Ah, Sarah, you're too good for him." She scooped Callie into her arms. "Your mama's a very special lady, *ma chroi,*" she said, tickling her under the chin. "You remember that, you hear?"

"Mama's special!" Callie giggled. "Very special. Like Aunt Dee-Dee." She wrapped her arms around her aunt's neck, then sobered. "Mama doesn't feel good, Aunt Dee-Dee."

"Now, Callie," her mother admonished gently, coming over to take her from Deirdre's arms, "we mustn't say anything about that to your da. We wouldn't want to worry him. He's got so much on his mind, and he wants to make things good for us after the war."

"But, Mama, it would be good for us for Da to

be home."

"Hush, child. A man has to do what he thinks best."

"But he's doin' what he wants to be doin', while we do Mrs. Periwinkle's laundry!"

Her mother had smiled, the first glimmer of light Callie had seen in her usually pallid face in weeks. Then she had made Callie promise not to make Da sad. Callie would keep mama's "secret."

She remembered thinking that she should ask Aunt Dee-Dee not to make Da sad, either, when actually it was Callie who was sad . . . and scared. Soon after Da's arrival, Callie was crying herself to sleep to the sounds of shouting matches between her father and her aunt.

The shouting matches ended the night Deirdre had come to Callie's room. She'd sat down on the edge of the bed and smoothed Callie's tangle of coppery tresses away from her face.

"Aunt Dee-Dee," Callie mumbled sleepily.

"Hush, sweet love," Deirdre said, bending down to kiss her forehead. "Aunt Dee-Dee couldn't leave without saying good-bye to her favorite little girl."

"Leave?" Callie's lower lip began to tremble. "Can I go with you? And Mama?"

"No, love. You have to stay here. But don't you worry, everything will be just fine."

Callie had never seen her aunt cry before. It frightened her more than anything ever had. "Aunt Dee-Dee, hug me!" Callie had stretched out her small arms. Her aunt had squeezed her close. And then she was gone.

The next day Fletcher Callaghan shouted that his sister had gone back to Ireland on holiday—a very long holiday—and her name was never to be mentioned in the household again. Then he, too, was gone. Back to war, back to laying the foundation of the Callaghan empire.

Callie had never forgiven him for sending Deirdre away. No matter where she'd gone, it was his fault. His fault, too, for not seeing how ill her mother was. To her mind he hadn't cared.

"Any more than you care about me now," she heard herself say aloud. She sawed back on the reins, startled to realize she had forced the tiring horse into a hard gallop. Dismounting, she gulped in long, steadying breaths.

"I imagine it would pleasure you greatly to see my grand venture end, wouldn't it, Da?" she mused, straightening. "Your little Callie was disobedient, so she shouldn't get what she wants. Not unless her father wants it for her." She kicked at a small rock settled amidst a patch of pungent sagebrush. "Damn. Quit feeling sorry for yourself, Callandra. I don't like it." She caught up the trailing reins and started walking.

It had been nearly three months since she and Deirdre had left New York. Two months since they'd been outfitted in Omaha and hired on Riley Smith. In all that time she had seen no evidence that her father was on her trail, but she had not the slightest doubt that he or one of his hirelings was out there.

Worse, what if he'd sent Nicolas? The prideful count, who had regaled her for hours about his royal Prussian lineage, was not the sort of man to be left at the altar and go meekly off to lick his wounds. She had often wondered what sort of satisfaction he had demanded of her father for his injured dignity that day. Had the

31

count sworn to find her? Bring her back to New York on her knees, begging forgiveness? Her father would have approved of such a plan. In fact, he might even have suggested it himself.

"Well, it's not going to happen, Da," she vowed. "No matter how this turns out, I'll never be sorry I tried." She stooped to pluck a tiny yellow flower, running her fingertips across its spidery petals. "Besides, maybe Aunt Deirdre is right. Maybe I am a pirate at heart." She smiled. She wouldn't be the first lured by the legend of a half million dollars in missing gold. But for Callie the treasure wouldn't be in the gold itself, it would be in the finding of it when so many others had failed, including Fletcher Callaghan.

Leading the gelding, she crested a small hillock. It had been four hours since she'd left the ravine. Thoughts of the gold, the pictures, the book dissipated as she focused on her more immediate goal and gave out a triumphant whoop of joy.

Abutting a rocky bluff on the far western end of a wide green valley stood a one-story clapboard-sheathed house. To the right of it lay a sprawling series of corrals and outbuildings, a setting which had instantly appealed to her photographic sense when first she'd seen it yesterday. She regretted now not having taken the time to set up a shot. Just below her on the valley floor was the isolated wooden archway that she fancied proclaimed the ranch the home of a poet.

SHADOW'S WAY

An odd sense of exhilaration swept over her, which she tried to attribute to Deirdre and Riley's rescue being so near at hand. But it was more than that. There was something about this place. She had felt it yesterday, too. It was why she hadn't lingered to take the pictures. She had wanted to get away. Not because of any feeling of unease, but more the opposite. She felt too comfortable here. Content. And she shied away from the feeling as surely as a wild mare shies from the bit.

She clambered back into the saddle and nudged the horse forward. It wasn't long before she was clutching the pommel for balance, the ride growing steeper as she neared the valley floor. Her lips twisted derisively as she hitched up the lower edges of her skirt to find the fabric still damp, stiff with caked mud. Her bodice, though largely dry, felt clammy and uncomfortable as though the rainwater had deposited a layer of silt between it and her flesh.

She straightened resolutely, a trace of a smile on her lips. If she looked as much the victim of some apocalyptic mudslide as she felt, she prayed whoever lived in the house had a stout heart. A feeble one would likely be shocked into its grave.

Riding toward the house, Callie couldn't help but notice the direction of the afternoon shadows. Formed by the bluffs, they would drift inexorably across the verdant meadow, until by early evening the entire ranchyard would be enveloped in shade. Shadow's Way indeed.

Several horses milled about in the various corrals, but she spied no human inhabitants, and so continued toward the main house. Dismounting, she tied the gelding to a huge brass ring secured to a hitching post staked to the left of the front porch. She took a deep breath, unconsciously reaching up to smooth back her snarled hair. It was hopeless. With a rueful grimace she knocked on the door.

No response.

Her brows furrowed. She heard definite sounds of people moving about inside. She knocked louder, her fist still raised when the heavy oak door whipped inward. Her hand remained frozen in midair as her neck tilted back, her eyes locking on the glowering countenance that seemed to fill the entire doorway.

The impact was both instantaneous and devastating. Her photographic instincts took it all in—thunderous brown eyes, tawny gold hair that fell in unruly waves to skim the collar of his shirt, full, sensuous lips slashed in a grim line. She guessed his age at twenty-seven, twenty-eight, maybe, with squint lines around his eyes to attest to a life on the open range. His denim shirt was unbuttoned to the navel, and Callie felt her cheeks heat as she caught a hint of the sun-bronzed flesh it barely concealed. A straight nose and stone-carved jawline added an air of subtle arrogance, an arrogance she discerned at once would put people off, though the aloofness would be in their perception not in fact.

She started to stammer something, anything, but before the words would form, a short, waspish woman carrying a satchel darted past the man and through the doorway, nearly capsizing Callie in her wake. A gaunt, sour-faced man matching the woman in height scurried after her.

"Stay away from that one, miss," the woman offered, though Callie said nothing. "Pure hellion he is. Spawn of the dark world itself."

Callie gave the glowering man a sidelong glance. She noted no horns, no tail. She decided she could be magnanimous and give this imposing man the benefit

34

of the doubt. At least until they'd actually spoken to each other.

"I believe you and your husband know the way to Rock Springs, Mrs. Yates," the man said, his voice deep and steady. His dark eyes did not stray from the couple until they had climbed into the buckboard in front of the house. "I don't expect to see you on Shadow's Way land again."

Callie watched the buckboard tear out of the yard and was almost sorry. She was now alone with the man in the doorway. His eyes flicked to her, coolly assessing her from the top of her head to tip of her toes. "You're a mess," he pronounced. "Dry off by the fire. Then go back to wherever it is you came from."

For once Callie suppressed her mercurial temper. She had Riley and Deirdre to consider. Telling this ill-mannered rancher what she thought of his behavior would do neither her aunt nor the injured scout any good.

Instead she straightened her spine and stuck out her right hand. "And a good morning to you, too, sir. My name's . . ."

"What is it you want?"

She pulled her hand back, twisting her fingers in the rain-stiffened material of her skirts. *Calm,* she reminded herself. She must remain calm for Deirdre and Riley's sake. She forced a too bright smile. "I'm in need of a wagon, sir. If you would be so kind. You see, my guide is . . ."

"There's a wagon in the barn. Take it. Bring it back." He shut the door in her face.

Callie stood there, openmouthed, trying to decide which she felt more strongly—incredulity or fury. Of all the . . . The only person on earth who'd ever even attempted to be so highhanded with her was her father, and the mere fact that she was standing in Wyoming instead of at the altar about to marry Count Nicolas von Endenberg as her father had dictated proved how much good that had done *him*.

"I appreciate that this is your ranch, sir," she called through the door, no longer attempting to disguise the anger in her voice. "But I don't appreciate being treated in such a disgraceful manner. You could at least have the courtesy to hear me out." She paused, hoping for full effect. "A man's life may depend on it. Surely I could have five minutes of your time."

Only the fact that she truly believed Riley was in no immediate danger kept her from slamming her way into the house.

She heard the beginnings of a cry from a young child. Whimpering soon turned into a full-blown wail. The man stormed to the door, carrying the distraught youngster. "A man's life?" he gritted, his eyes searching the trail from which she'd come, clearly skeptical. "As you can hear, Miss Whoever-you-are, I don't have five minutes. I don't have five seconds."

His voice wasn't so much angry now, as exasperated. Callie suppressed a smile. His initial explosive impact on her senses was being severely tempered by the squalling toddler, who was struggling to be free of his father's restraining arms. He looked to be about three years old and was obviously feeling sorely neglected.

"It's as I said. My guide has broken his leg."

"I told you where the wagon is."

"You're not going to help?"

His brown eyes were cold, implacable. "No, I'm not."

For a full ten seconds Callie stood there, glaring at him. Nothing in him gave her the slightest hint that he gave a damn about a man lying injured out in the middle of nowhere. The oddest thing was not that she was surprised that there were such callous human beings in the world, but that this man was one of them. For in that single assessing moment, when all of her photographic instincts had come into play, she could have sworn that underneath all of the surface hardness lay something vulnerable and hidden. Now she dismissed the notion to fanciful nonsense. She had been out in the rain too long.

"Fine," she snapped, "I'll take care of everything myself. And, of course, I'll bring back your precious wagon. Please forgive Riley if he bleeds a little on the floorboards." With that she whirled and stalked toward the barn.

She found the wagon there just as he'd said, but the stalls were empty. Did he expect her to round up a team of horses from his corrals? Muttering a steady stream of Gaelic epithets she first struggled with the heavy harness she found slung over one of the stall sides, then nearly tripped on the trailing leather as she hauled it across the hay-strewn floor and flung it down beside the wagon. Her insides roiling, she hefted a rope hanging from a peg on the barn wall. She was not going back to that house to ask him which horses she could take. She would take whichever two she could catch.

Slinging the rope over her right shoulder, she stomped out of the barn. She stopped dead, surprised to see the man striding toward her. He was carrying the boy, who was snuffling now, rubbing red-rimmed eyes.

"Wait, don't tell me," she said, "let me guess. You told me I could use the wagon, but you didn't say anything about supplying the horses that go with it, right?"

If he thought anything of her sarcasm, one way or the other, it did not show in his eyes. Without a word, he handed her the boy, took the rope, and headed for the corral adjacent to the barn. Callie watched him put a booted foot on the lowest railing, then vault over the upper two. As he shook out the rope and headed toward a big bay, her attention was diverted by the child, who was tugging on a handful of her bedraggled locks. He was giggling merrily.

"It is pretty funny-looking, isn't it?" Callie laughed, brushing tousled blond curls away from his forehead to peer into lake-blue eyes. Her gaze narrowed on a small, purpling bruise above the boy's left eye. It didn't look serious, but it could easily have accounted for his tears earlier. "How did you hurt your head, huh?"

"Bump head," he said, patting the bruise. "Ouch."

"That's too bad. I guess you'll have to be more careful."

"Careful," he repeated solemnly.

Callie smiled. "You must have your mother's eyes," she mused. "But you've got your papa's chin—stubborn." She tickled his neck. "What's your name, huh? Can you tell me your name?"

"Cris-toe-fer," he said, exaggerating each syllable.

"Christopher?"

He grinned.

"Well, Christopher, let me tell you your father's a

real charmer. Your mother must have a wonderful time giving parties for the neighbors. Nobody comes."

The boy's puzzled look ended her churlish monologue.

"I'm sorry," she said. "It's not your fault he's a sourpuss. I mean . . ." She rolled her eyes heavenward. "Callie, you'd better stop while you're ahead."

In minutes the man returned leading two bay geldings. She started to thank him, but swallowed the words as he trudged past her into the barn. She followed, frowning, as he went about hitching up the team. Some poet, she thought grimly.

Finishing up, he looped the ends of the reins around the brake handle, then took a step toward her. Maybe now we'll get down to a few of the social amenities, Callie thought hopefully. But he only held out his hands. She was at first confused, then startled, as the boy all but jumped out of her arms.

"Papa!" he cried happily, wrapping his arms around the man's neck and giving him a wet kiss on the cheek.

For that small breath of time the man's brown eyes softened, shining with an inner warmth that made her heart give an odd leap inside her chest. And then he smiled, and for the most foolish instant she was stunned by how irresistibly appealing it made him look. He gave the boy a gentle hug, then set him on the floor to watch him trundle over to a stack of hay bales. When the man looked again at her, it was as though the softness, the gentleness had never been.

"Can you manage the wagon now?" he mocked. "Or do I have to lift you into the driver's seat?"

She stamped her foot. "Who taught you your manners? Your mother . . ."

"Died when I was born."

"Obviously!" Callie shot back, even as she was horrified to hear herself say such a thing. "Christopher has better manners than . . ."

His eyes narrowed ominously. "How do you know his name?"

"He told me," she said, taking an unconscious step back.

His hand snaked out and caught her arm, his fingers digging cruelly in the tender flesh. "The Marlowes sent you, didn't they?"

"Who? What are you . . ." She jerked back. "Let go of me!"

"Don't lie to me. A woman alone shows up on my doorstep at the exact moment I've had to dismiss my housekeeper. Isn't that stretching coincidence just a little too far?"

"I have no idea what you're talking about, Mr.—?"

"You know my name."

"I do?" Callie was incredulous. "Listen, mister, I have no idea who you are or what you think of me or anything else. Nor do I have the time or inclination to find out." She started to climb onto the wagon.

He studied her for a long minute. "You really would go by yourself, wouldn't you?"

"I told you I have a man injured." She flicked the reins, clucking at the horses.

He caught the reins. "Get down."

"I beg your pardon?"

"I'll go."

"Then I'll go with you."

"No. I don't want Christopher out in this weather. It might storm again."

40

"Surely your wife can watch the child . . ."

His look now was positively thunderous. "I don't have a wife."

Callie flushed. "I'm sorry . . . I mean . . ." Good heavens, the poor man was a widower. No wonder he seemed so frazzled, a man alone, raising a young child. She took a calming breath. "You don't even know where . . ."

"This is my ranch. For more square miles than you can count. You describe to me where they are, I'll know."

He helped her down from the wagon, his hands touching her waist no longer than absolutely necessary. In fact, it seemed he wouldn't have touched her at all if he could have avoided it. He took her place on the wagon seat, his appraising look still weighing some unknown question. Then he seemed to shake it off, nodded toward the boy, "He hasn't had his lunch."

"I'll make him something."

He took the reins in his hands, listening as she told him where she'd left Riley and Deirdre. "I know the place," he said. "It was stupid to go into that ravine during a storm. We're not above flash floods around here."

"I made a mistake. I admit it. So shoot me—later."

"Don't tempt me."

Holding tight to the child, she slogged alongside the wagon. "When you get there," she blurted, "please, if you could bring back some of the things that were in the wagon. Deirdre will show you . . ."

He looked down at her. "A clean dress?"

She glowered at him. "I'll wash this one, thanks. What I want are my things. My aunt Deirdre will

41

show you."

"Sounds like you're as concerned about your possessions as you are this man Riley."

"You don't happen to know my Aunt Deirdre personally, do you?" she grumbled, then reluctantly checked her temper. "I would really appreciate whatever you can do."

He pulled the team to a halt. Arms on his knees, he let the reins dangle between his strong tanned fingers. "What did you say your name was again?"

"I didn't. Since you didn't see fit to mention your own."

"Well?"

"Well indeed."

He smiled slightly. "Trace. Trace McCord."

"Callie Callaghan."

"Irish?"

She stiffened. "And if I am?"

He shrugged. "Then I doubt I have to worry about the Marlowes. They're fairly narrow-minded about their Anglo-Saxon heritage."

"And you?"

He shrugged again. "To me a man proves what he is by what he does. I suppose the same goes for a woman. But if you're not here with Chris when I get back, there won't be a rock big enough for you or the Marlowes to crawl under."

"I wish I knew who . . ."

"If you don't know, you don't need to."

"Please, Mr. McCord, I assure you Riley is . . ."

He cut her off. "He'd better be. He'd just better be." He snapped the reins and set the horses into a fast trot.

"Your father is a brute," she stated calmly, chucking

the boy under his chin. "But I think he has to work hard at it." That brought a smile to her lips, and an answering one from the child. "What say we rustle you up something to eat? And rustle up a bath for yours truly."

"Eat!" he squealed.

As she walked toward the house, her mood grew thoughtful. She remembered the frequent wary look in Trace McCord's eyes—a trapped look. And she was left to wonder what or who had made him that way.

Chapter Three

Trace McCord cursed under his breath. He had just left Christopher in the care of a total stranger, based solely on her word that she needed his help. What if the woman was lying? What if the Marlowes... Damn!

Callie Callaghan. What kind of a name was that anyway? He snapped the reins urging the bays into a faster trot. He would be gone no longer than absolutely necessary. He cursed again. The solitude of the foothills, which has so often offered him sanctuary in the troubled, rebellious days of his youth, now proved as disquieting as his thoughts. What if the woman had played him for a fool? He likely wouldn't be her first. He had detected a certain, no doubt deceptive appeal under all that muck and mud, a trait that might distract a more gullible man.

But had he been just that? Gullible. To believe her. What if there was no wagon accident? No injured Riley Smith? His stomach knotted. What if Christopher was gone when he got back?

Trace rubbed a hand across the back of his neck. The

44

boy would be there. He had to be. Even the Marlowes weren't that stupid. With the hearing just two months away, they would never take the risk.

Despite the afternoon's warming temperature he felt a shudder pass through him. Damn, how empty his life would be without that boy. If he lost him . . .

He forced the thoughts away. Brooding had never gotten him anywhere. He wasn't going to indulge in it now. He was glad to reach the crest of the ravine Callie Callaghan had described to him. Handling whatever had to be taken care of down there would be the perfect distraction.

"Whoa, boys!" he called out, drawing back on the reins. He leaped off the buckboard and stood at the lip of the hollow. The disabled wagon sat precisely where Callie had said it would. He had to give the woman credit. He'd had no trouble at all pinpointing this spot from the information she'd given him. He breathed a little easier. Even the Marlowes wouldn't go to this much trouble.

He led his horses down the hillside. When he reached the Conestoga, a trim woman of about forty stepped out of the trees, eyeing him warily. For the briefest moment he had the impression the woman was on guard, protecting something.

"My name's Trace McCord," he said. "A Miss Callie Callaghan sent me. I take it you're her aunt?"

The woman relaxed. "Thank God. Callie's all right, then?"

He nodded.

The suspicion was back. "Then where is she?"

"She stayed at the ranch with my son." God, how easily he said the word, savored it, believed it. "He's only three years old, and I didn't want to chance another storm."

The suspicion remained, but her anxiety overrode it. She gestured toward the trees. "Mr. Smith is in considerable pain. I'd like to get him settled in a bed before nightfall. I mean, I . . ."

"Yes, ma'am." Trace stepped over to her. "Lead me to him."

Twisting her hands in the folds of her skirts, Deirdre turned and headed into the timber. She led him to a scruffy-looking man half propped against a tree. The man was studying him with an easy caution, though there was a definite strain on his craggy features.

Trace's gaze shifted between the scout and the woman. Riley Smith seemed as much a part of the forest as the aspen under which he lay—world-weary and trailwise. Deirdre Callaghan, on the other hand, was as out of place in these mountains as a doe in a tea room. Frowning, he shoved off a rising, and thoroughly unwelcome, curiosity about Callie Callaghan's peculiar assemblage of pioneers. Instead he introduced himself to the scout.

"McCord?" Riley mused, struggling to sit up further. "Any relation to Jeb McCord?"

The question caught Trace off guard. He stiffened, then shifted to seem as if he were merely working out a kink in his back. The woman took no notice, but he knew the scout had not missed it. "He was my father," Trace said quietly.

"Helped 'im trail horses north from Mexico back in '52," Riley said, his eyes locked on Trace's. "Said he was gonna start him a ranch in Wyoming. Guess he did."

46

"We'd best get moving. It's going to be dark before we get back as it is." Trace reached out a hand. "I'll get you over to the wagon."

"Jeb had him a wife and a boy at the time," Riley went on, sucking in his breath as Trace helped him to his feet. "Boy was eight then."

Trace's jaw clenched. The man was rattling on now to stave off the pain, but just how much did he know?

"Boy couldn't 'ave been you. You ain't hit thirty yet. A brother?"

"Seth," Trace gritted. "He's dead. So is my father."

They reached the buckboard. Trace eased the man into the back. Riley stretched out, unable to stifle a groan. "Sorry," he managed. "Don't know what got into me. 'Tweren't my business."

"Forget it." But Trace had the feeling the scout would forget none of it.

Deirdre scrambled into the wagon beside Smith, tucking the blankets around him. "Can we go now?"

"Nothing I'd like better, ma'am," Trace said. "But I'm afraid your niece mentioned something about bringing back some of her things."

"Oh, for the love of heaven," Deirdre exclaimed. "I'm not surprised. Did she ask you to rescue them before Mr. Smith and myself?"

Trace swallowed a smile. "No, ma'am. She distinctly put it third on her list. A high third, but third."

Trace assisted Deirdre from the buckboard, then followed her over to the Conestoga. He grimaced as she pointed out several crates. "Travels light, doesn't she? What's in here?"

"Cameras. Film plates. Journals."

Trace expelled a long breath, remembering the

47

almost desperate glint in Callie Callaghan's eyes when she asked him to bring her things back with him. He had thought it would be a trunk full of clothes and other female fripperies. Now he seriously considered leaving the stuff here. He could come back for it tomorrow. But that look in her eyes wouldn't let him. With a grudging resentment he hefted the crates from the Conestoga.

Callie paced anxiously in front of the massive fieldstone fireplace that dominated the main room of the Shadow's Way ranch house. The sun had dipped below the horizon well over an hour ago, and still there was no sign of McCord's wagon. What if he hadn't been able to find them? What if Riley had worsened . . . died?

"Stop it, Callie!" she snapped. "You're being a fool. The trip merely takes longer by wagon than it does on horseback."

She forced herself to sit on the horsehair settee that faced the fireplace. Watching the dancing light of the flames calmed her, if only a little. Her eyes flicked to the deerskin shield that hung above the mantel. Bordered with eagle feathers, she was taken with the primitive buffalo drawing in its center. It was similar in style to other oak-framed paintings hung throughout the house.

Her gaze roved across the rest of the room. Most of the furnishings—the ladder-back chairs, the straight-legged oak writing desk, the bearskin rug in front of the hearth—were stark, practical, contributing to the overall masculine feel of the house. The single exception was the exquisitely carved cedar chest nestled under the window seat. She found herself wondering if it had belonged to McCord's wife, then chided herself for wondering.

She paced to the window, her restlessness returning. Where were they? She almost wished the child hadn't fallen asleep so early. Christopher would be just the distraction her overactive imagination needed right now. But the child had had an exhausting day. She sank onto the window seat, a slow smile curving her lips. The *child* had had an exhausting day? There had been times this afternoon when she would have gladly considered trading places with Riley and his broken leg, rather than maintain the frenetic pace of the three-year-old.

After Trace left, she'd settled Christopher at the kitchen table for his lunch, then dared explore the various rooms of the house, hoping to find at least a washbasin and a cake of lye soap. She could tolerate her grit-covered body no longer.

At the rear of the house she peered into a room across the hall from two adjoining bedrooms. She thought it would be a guest bedroom, or a workroom of some sort. Instead, she stepped into a bathing room that would have put some of the finer hotels in New York to shame. In one corner stood a Franklin stove for heating water. In the center of the room, complete with water pump, was a genuine claw-footed porcelain tub.

"I take back all the nasty things I've thought about you, Trace McCord," she murmured, running her fingers caressingly along the tub's outer rim.

If she'd felt at all guilty about making herself so at

home in a stranger's house, the idea of immersing herself in that porcelain testament to civilization banished the thought from her mind. Quickly, she readied the water.

"Callie take a bath?" came the small voice.

She turned to see Christopher toddle into the room.

"Yes," she said, "Callie is most certainly going to take a bath." She smiled at the boy, reaching for a washcloth to wipe the remains of his lunch from his mouth. "I think it may well be the longest bath in the history of the world." Her smile widened as the boy gave her a baffled look. "Never mind," she said, maneuvering a dressing screen in front of the tub. "You just play nicely for a little while, all right?" She stepped behind the screen and quickly shed her clothes.

She had one leg in the water, when she heard Christopher start out of the room. "Wait!" she called. "I won't know what you're doing if . . ." He was out the door.

Grabbing up a towel, she threw it around her body and scurried after him, one foot making wet prints across the oak floor. She was halfway down the hall before it occurred to her to call out to make certain she was still alone. She'd seen no one else on the ranch as yet, but she doubted McCord ran the spread without hired help.

"Outside!" Christopher screeched as she caught up with him and scooped him into her arms just shy of the front door.

"Later," she assured him, but he wasn't listening. Tightening her hold, she carried the struggling child back to the bathing room. Inside, he streaked for the door the instant she set him down, but this time she was ready. She darted in front of him and slid the bolt into place. "Outside! Outside!" he wailed again and again.

Grimly, Callie climbed into the tub. She had heard a pack of wolves howling in the distance her first night in Wyoming. As she sat in the water scrubbing furiously at her hair and body, she considered ruefully that the animals made substantially less racket than one sorely displeased three-year-old. Her dream of a lengthy soak ended in two minutes flat.

Again wrapped in the towel, she unbolted the door, freeing the affronted youngster. "It's nice to know you have your father's patience as well as his chin," she drawled, too pleased at feeling clean again to be annoyed for long.

Peering into the hallway, she assured herself she and the child were still alone. It had only just occurred to her that she had nothing to wear. Her dress was a disaster and the rest of her clothes were still with the Conestoga. She would have to find something, anything, to put on until McCord returned with her things.

She considered donning a pair of his jeans and a shirt, but somehow found the thought of wearing his clothes strangely intimate—too intimate, no matter what the circumstances. Feeling decidedly ill at ease she made a quick check of McCord's and Christopher's wardrobes, plus the more stylish armoire she found in an apparent guest room on the opposite side of the house. Somewhere in the back of her mind she supposed she hoped the quick exiting Mrs. Yates might have left something behind.

But it wasn't until she opened the cedar chest that she found anything remotely feminine. Shifting aside two sunbonnets and a camisole, she spied a pale yellow gingham dress that had been carefully stored near the bottom of the chest. With a cry of delight, she allowed the towel to slip to the floor, then held the dress against her. It would be a near perfect fit.

Quickly she settled it over her head, then paused before fastening the button front. What was she doing? The dress might well have belonged to McCord's deceased wife. Not only that, but he would have to know she had opened the chest to find it. It was bad enough that she look through a wardrobe, but the cedar chest was a much more private thing. What would he think of her?

"Well, it's the dress, or stay in the towel," she reasoned desperately, then buttoned the dress before she changed her mind. Pantalets and a pair of doeskin moccasins completed her plunder of the trunk.

"Mama," Christopher said, patting the smooth material of the skirt.

Callie gasped, startled. She had been so busy worrying about Trace McCord's reaction to the dress, she hadn't even considered the effect it might have on the child. The sad look on his small face nearly broke her heart. She sat on the cedar chest and lifted him onto her lap.

The boy did not pull away, snuggling against her breasts, seeming contented by the contact with her body and perhaps the pleasant scent of the cedar. Callie's arms circled him, held him. She had never had much experience with small children, but sitting there, rocking him, rocking them both, she was startled by the feelings, warm and deep, that swept through her.

She thought he might have dozed off, when suddenly

52

he tilted his head back, as if remembering something of extreme importance. "Outside!" he pronounced, clambering down and heading toward the front door. Callie followed, trying to shake the odd melancholy that had settled over her.

Perhaps it was just the afternoon shadows mingling with a shifting cloud cover, but once outside her gaze was immediately drawn to the bunkhouse some one hundred yards distant. She could have sworn she saw the door closing.

A ranchhand? Then why hadn't McCord told her, or more to the point, sent the ranchhand in his place, since McCord had been so reluctant to leave Christopher in her care?

She took the boy's hand, hunkering down so that she could talk to him at nearly eye level. "Do you think there's someone in the bunkhouse, Christopher?"

He nodded. "Reese."

"Reese?" Rising, she kept a firm hold on the child's hand and headed toward the squarish clapboard structure that she was certain housed McCord's hired help. She was about to knock when she heard an odd, almost moaning noise coming from inside.

"Reese," the boy repeated, grinning. He pounded his small palm against the door.

Callie's confusion ended as the door swung inward. She took an involuntary step back, instinctively placing herself between the giant of a man who filled the doorway and the child, who was now struggling to be free of her restraining hand. The man had to be six feet, his weight pushing two hundred fifty pounds. His dark hair hung in unkempt snarls framing a pug-nosed, puff-cheeked face that split into an open-mouthed grin as he gazed down at Christopher. Wideset bovine eyes shone with the uncomplicated affection of the simple-minded.

"Reese!" Christopher gurgled.

"Chrissy." The man clapped his bearpaw hands together, then took a playful swipe at the boy. Christopher shrieked merrily and ducked behind Callie's skirts. "Where's yer papa, Chrissy?" The man's eyes squinted nearly shut as he noticed Callie for the first time. "Who're you? What'd you do with the boss?"

"Boss?" Callie stammered, still disconcerted by this huge man's childlike manner. "You mean Mr. McCord?"

The man's head bobbed up and down. "He's the boss."

"He . . . he's gone. That is, he'll be back." She was backing down the bunkhouse steps, Christopher in tow. "Very soon now, I'm sure. My . . . my guide injured his leg. He . . . Mr. McCord went to rescue him. I . . ."

"You scared of Reese?"

"Of course not," she said, flushing hotly, as she halted her backward flight. "Why would I be scared?"

He lumbered down the steps, scooping the boy into his big arms and twirling him over his head. Christopher squealed with delight. Callie relaxed a little. Obviously Christopher trusted this man. And she knew Trace McCord wouldn't keep a dangerous person on his ranch, not with the child here.

Abruptly, Reese set the boy down. "Got to check the fence up north aways," he said. "Somethin's been spookin' some of the mares." The man marched toward the barn.

"Bye, Reese." The boy waved after him.

Callie was not sorry to see him go.

"Come on, Christopher," she said, once again taking up his hand, "how about your showing me around this wonderful homestead of yours?"

The child's small brow furrowed.

Callie laughed. "You want to pet the horses?" she amended, laughing again when he emphatically nodded his head.

They spent nearly an hour petting one of the gentler mares in the near corral. Only then did Christopher finally seem to wear down a little.

"I'm hungry," he said, rubbing his eyes tiredly, then plopping himself down beside a hay bale in front of the barn.

"I'm with you," Callie said, lifting him up to carry him back into the house. But before she could finish preparing supper, he'd fallen asleep on the bearskin rug. Rather than wake him, she carried him to the room in the back of the house she had earlier discovered to be his. That is, unless Trace McCord was given to sitting on rocking horses and playing with rag-stuffed, flop-eared puppies.

The last brought a sarcastic smile to her lips. Given the man's temperament maybe he did play with the toys of a three-year-old—since he *acted* like one.

"Enough, Callie," she chided. "He did go after Deirdre and Riley, didn't he?"

Yes, he went after them, she mused, as she sat on the window seat three hours later, but when was he going to bring them back? She stood, striding impatiently to the door, then stepped outside. Shivering, she rubbed her hands along her arms, her body reacting with less

55

tolerance to the night temperature having just come from the warmth of the fire. Standing there, she gazed out at the shadowed vastness of the Grand Tetons, looming like jagged sentinels to the west. It struck her then just how glad she was that she had dared take the chance, that she had dared leave New York, Nicolas, her father—no matter what the consequences. For consequences there would be. No one defied the almighty Fletcher Callaghan, not even his daughter.

"You won't forgive me for this one, will you, Da?" she murmured. She had done more than simply go against his wishes. By not marrying Nicolas she had embarrassed her father in front of people whose respect he had spent a lifetime cultivating. Respect, grudgingly won, easily lost. On the surface her father boasted his well-deserved reputation as one of the most ruthless businessmen in the country. But underneath the facade Callie had long ago discovered his almost desperate need for the respect, even fear, of his contemporaries in the business world. It was as if their approval, however contemptuously given, could make up for the one stigma Fletcher Callaghan could never fully erase from his life—the fact that he had been born Irish.

Callie sighed, pushing away the unpleasant thoughts. For as long as she could remember her father had tried to impose his singleminded self-bigotry on her. But she would have none of it, Not then. Not now. If there were people who didn't like the Irish, it was their problem, not hers. In fact, when she finished her photographic essay of Yellowstone, she fully intended to have it published under what she considered her true name: Callandra O'Callaghan.

And if she should manage to upstage the United States Army and some of the best treasure seekers in the country, including several hired by her father to find the lost Yellowstone gold . . . all the better.

In the light of the half-risen moon she caught the barest outline of a moving silhouette on the western lip of the hillock. The sounds of turning wheels, jangling harness, and hoofbeats drifted toward her. Her heart beat faster. McCord.

Chapter Four

As the buckboard pulled into the ranchyard and Callie heard Trace McCord shout "Whoa!" to his tired geldings, she experienced a most peculiar flush of warmth and pleasure. Somehow it felt good just standing there watching this man come home. She admonished herself at once for such frightful fantasy, but she needn't have bothered. McCord quashed her mood the minute he opened his mouth.

"Where's Christopher?" he demanded, his eyes glinting with the same wary suspicion she had seen in them when he had driven off eight hours ago.

"Asleep," she said, struggling to keep her voice even. "In the rear bedroom. There were toys in it, so I assumed it was his room. Of course, I may have been mistaken."

Her sarcasm was lost on him as he skirted past her and strode into the house. "He doesn't believe me," Callie said wonderingly, staring at his retreating back. "He honestly doesn't believe me." She turned to face Deirdre, who was still seated in the back of the wagon

58

with Riley. "Did you see that?" she asked. "What does he think I did with his son?"

"Never mind Mr. McCord," Deirdre said. "I'm more concerned about Mr. Smith at the moment. The poor man has been through quite an ordeal."

Callie climbed into the back of the wagon, eyeing the apparently sleeping scout. "How can he sleep? That leg must hurt terribly."

"Exhaustion, I imagine. He didn't doze off until just about an hour ago. Mr. McCord drove slowly—to spare him, but . . ." Her voice caught. "Mr. Smith was so brave."

"It hasn't exactly been a day at the symphony for you either, Aunt Deirdre. Are you all right?"

"I'm fine. Please, I just want to get him to bed."

Callie could not make out her aunt's features in the darkness. Perhaps Deirdre's conscience was nudging her, where Riley was concerned. Callie could well remember the shouting matches between her aunt and the scout—scores of them—since they'd left Omaha. But ever since the man had injured himself . . .

"We'll get him over to the bunkhouse," Callie said. She thought about mentioning Reese, but decided against it. The man had not yet returned from his inspection of the fence. Likely, he would have camped out for the night, rather than come back to the ranch at this late hour. At least for Deirdre's sake Callie hoped so. Her aunt had had enough unsettling experiences for one day.

Together they assisted a groggy Riley Smith over to the squarish building. Inside, Callie turned back the wool blankets on one of the lower bunks, then helped Deirdre ease the man onto the bed. Riley's craggy

59

features twisted, but he made no sound as Deirdre maneuvered a pillow under his splint-encased leg.

"I'll stay with him," she said, straightening, "until he falls asleep again. Though I think he could do with some warm broth . . ."

"You don't need to keep fussin' after me, Miss Deirdre," Riley said. "Just leave me lay here for a spell. I'll be fine." A thin film of sweat had broken out on the man's forehead.

"You'll do as I say, Mr. Smith," Deirdre admonished gently.

A half smile played on the scout's beard-framed lips. "Yes, ma'am."

"How about if I bring you both some supper in a little while," Callie suggested. "I wasn't certain when you'd be back, but I have soup simmering in the kitchen." She hesitated, studying her aunt. "You're sure you'll be all right out here?"

"I'll be fine. I just want to see that he's settled comfortably. What about you?"

"What do you mean?"

"Where are you planning to sleep tonight?"

"Mr. McCord has a guest room." Callie didn't miss the flash of concern that skittered across her aunt's features. Quickly, she added, "I'll wait up for you, of course."

Deirdre fingered her chin thoughtfully. "You probably think I'm being foolish. But there was something about Mr. McCord . . ."

"You don't like him?" Callie couldn't have said why the thought disturbed her.

"No . . . no it isn't that. He's just . . ." She faltered. "I'm not certain what it is. Maybe it's just that I see him as a man alone. No. More than a man alone. A man who's lonely. Deep down. A man missing something important in his life."

"What on earth did you two talk about on your way back to the ranch?" Callie asked, trying and failing to make her voice sound light, casual, as though something in Trace McCord had not already touched her as well.

"Nothing in particular," Deirdre said. "Maybe it was how openly and easily he talked about his young Christopher, but whenever the subject shifted to anything else . . ." She didn't finish. "Ach, never mind. I'm just tired. You go and get yourself ready for bed and I'll be there in a little while."

"I'll be fine," Callie assured her again, as much for her own sake as for Deirdre's. "You take as long as you need with Riley." Outside, she wondered if she was as perplexed about Deirdre's interest in Riley Smith as she was about her own with the moody Trace McCord. Angry at this newfound preoccupation of hers, she shoved open the front door and stomped inside.

She stopped dead in her tracks. McCord was standing in front of the fireplace, his right forearm resting on the mantel as he stared into the flames. She was certain he hadn't missed her melodramatic entrance, but he did not look at her. Her heart thudded against her ribs. Her earlier thought that she would request the luxury of that long, hot bath lodged in her throat. She couldn't seem to say anything at all.

"The dress fits." His voice was unreadable.

Nervously Callie fingered the buttons on the dress front. In all the excitement of Deirdre's return, she had forgotten about its significance. Nothing in McCord's tone gave any hint as to what was going through his mind. Was he angry? Hurt? Indifferent? To see his wife's clothing being worn by someone else. "I . . . there was nothing else," she said, then stopped. Blast the man, couldn't he at least look at her?

"It doesn't matter," he said. This time his tone left no doubt that it mattered very much indeed.

"I'm sorry," she murmured, feeling a rare flush of shame. She had had no right to go through his things. "I should have put my own dress back on."

"I saw it in the back room. It doesn't look salvageable." He sighed, pushing away from the mantel. "You're welcome to the dress. It was just hard for me to see someone wearing Jenny's things."

"Jenny? That was her name . . . your wife?"

His eyes hardened. "I told you, I don't have a wife. Jenny was my sister-in-law. She died three months ago."

Callie was as confused by his anger, as she was by this new bit of information. Christopher had clung to the dress, calling for his mother. Trace McCord's *sister-in-law* was Christopher's mother? But the boy called Trace "Papa." Callie swallowed hard. Trace and his sister-in-law . . .

"I'm sorry," she said, "I thought . . . I mean . . ." What did she think?

"If it's any of your business, which it isn't, Christopher is actually my brother's son. Seth and Jenny's son." His gaze shifted back to the fire. "Seth is dead. He died while Jenny was still carrying Christopher. It was Jenny who encouraged the boy to think of me as . . ." He didn't finish.

Callie sank onto one of the ladder-back chairs.

Seldom in her life had she felt so awkward. She wished to heaven she'd never seen the dress. In spite of McCord's grudging assurance that it was all right that she wear it, it was obvious the sight of it distressed him terribly. Jenny McCord had encouraged her brother-in-law to take her husband's place with her child. Had she come to wish Trace would take Seth's place with her as well? Or had it been Trace who wished . . .

He strode over to her. She was instantly, disturbingly, reminded that she wore no chemise beneath the bodice of the dress. Unconsciously, she crossed her arms in front of her. His eyes caught and held hers. For the longest minute he simply stared at her, and she had the disconcerting image of a man weighing the pros and cons of an important purchase. Then, for the barest instant, she could have sworn she saw a cold, calculating light glint in those brown eyes. But just as suddenly it was gone. A decision made? His next words drove the vague image from her mind.

"I'm the one who should be apologizing. I haven't exactly been a gracious host." He held out a hand, palm upward. "I've had a lot on my mind lately. I know it's not much of an excuse, but it's all I've got."

Mesmerized, she slipped her hand in his, rising to her feet.

"You're welcome to the dress," he said. "It's yours."

As subtly as she could manage, she tried to extricate her hand from his, but just as subtly the pressure of his fingers increased. "Can we start over?" he murmured.

"Start over?" Her heart was threatening to leap from her chest. Never had a man so affected her. His touch ignited a heat that seemed to sear along her arm to envelope her entire body, and she was achingly afraid that he was all too aware of it.

"My name's Trace McCord," he said, lifting her hand to his mouth, pressing his lips to her fingers. "What's yours?"

She stared at her hand as though it were no longer a part of her body. "Callandra Callaghan," she responded, her voice hoarse.

"I'm very happy to meet you, Callandra." His breath was hot against her flesh.

"Callie."

"I think perhaps your arrival here today was more fortuitous than I originally thought." He let go of her hand, but did not break the contact of his eyes.

"Fortuitous?"

"It occurs to me that we could be mutually beneficial to each other."

A hint of alarm shot through her. Was this the same man who had slammed the door in her face when she'd told him she needed his help? He was making no sense. But the very nearness of him continued to play havoc with her senses. Unwillingly, she recalled Deirdre's warning of a man alone—lonely. "Really, Mr. McCord . . ."

"Trace."

"I'm very tired. I think . . . I think I'd best be getting to bed. That is . . . the guest room . . . I mean . . ."

"Of course. Forgive me. We can talk in the morning." He straightened, his manner more formal all at once. "I shouldn't have said anything. If I've offended you . . ."

"No, no, of course not. I . . ."

A muffled cry drifted down the hallway.

Trace cocked his head toward the sound. "Sometimes he'll go back to sleep right away."

The cry grew louder.

He grinned. "And sometimes he won't." He headed toward the rear of the house, holding up a restraining hand, when she made a move to follow. "I'll take care of him. You've done enough. Besides, he might be a bit grumpy toward a stranger this time of the night."

"I'm a little grumpy when I wake up myself." She wished the words back at once. His eyes snapped toward her, his heated gaze suggesting he would like to see her awaken from sleep. But then the look was gone, and she was left to wonder if it was just something about Shadow's Way that made her feel so fanciful.

In minutes Trace returned to the room, carrying the sleepy-eyed youngster.

"Hungry," the child whimpered, rubbing his eyes.

"He had his lunch, didn't he?" Trace asked.

"Of course. You told me he hadn't eaten. But then he fell asleep before I could give him any supper."

He nodded his approval. Evidently he, too, felt it wise to let sleeping children lie.

The child's fussing grew louder as Trace carried him into the kitchen. Callie followed.

"Hungry!" he cried.

Trace opened a cupboard, shifting several cans of tin goods about, apparently searching for something the child would eat. He seemed ill at ease, awkward all at once, as if he were out of his element. Then, Callie guessed more rightly that he was awkward having her watch him with the child.

"Sit down and comfort him. I'll make him something to eat," she said, amazed at the tone of command in her voice. To her further surprise Trace did as she asked, settling the child in his lap.

Callie stroked Christopher's tousled locks, her hand inadvertently brushing Trace's arm. She turned away quickly, lest he see in her eyes the evidence of what that simple touch had done to her. The exposed flesh of his forearm had seemed to pulse with heat under the sensitive tips of her fingers.

What on earth was wrong with her? She wasn't some silly schoolgirl to have her heart flutter in the presence of a handsome stranger.

Coolly, deliberately, she reasoned that her response was a purely artistic one. He was indeed a handsome man, photographically speaking. She found herself wondering if he would pose for her, then blushed heatedly, shoving the thought away.

Rather than shout at Trace over the noise of the child, she made a quick perusal of the cupboard and decided to boil some oatmeal. While it was simmering, she sent Trace out to the bunkhouse with soup and cornbread for Deirdre and Riley. The oatmeal was just about ready when he returned.

She sat down in the chair opposite Trace at the kitchen table. The boy was beginning to wind down already. Without a lot of cajoling to stop what he was doing, he had no reason to continue. When he'd reached the snuffling stage, Callie knelt beside him on the floor with a piece of bread in her hand.

"I don't know about you, Christopher," she said, "but I am starving." She began to munch absently on the piece of bread. The boy looked at her, a trifle curious to find an adult sitting on the floor beside him.

"Hungry," he whimpered.

"I know you are," Callie assured him. "And it's just

terrible that you missed your supper. But we can take care of that right now."

"Want some," he said, sticking out his hand.

Callie broke off a piece and gave it to him. The boy began to chomp contentedly.

"How about the rest of your dinner?" Callie asked.

Christopher stood up and ambled toward it. He let Callie lift him onto a chair and adjust a bib under his chin. When she set the bowl of food in front of him, he went to work on it at once.

"Tank you," the child said.

"You're welcome," Callie answered. His smile gave her heart an unexpected lurch. She wished suddenly she had her camera. Christopher was a natural subject—beautiful, animated, open. Thoughts of the camera only brought everything else rushing back to her. She forced herself to again sit in the chair opposite Trace.

"Well?" He prodded at her silence. "I'm surprised you haven't asked me if I rescued your equipment?"

"I saw it in the back of the wagon. Thank you. And thank you for rescuing Aunt Deirdre and Riley, too."

"You're welcome."

Her heart pounded faster. How could just being in the same room with this man continue to affect her so?

"You take pictures?" he asked.

She nodded. "I'm working on a book . . . about Yellowstone. That's where we were headed before Riley's accident. But now it'll be weeks before . . ." Her eyes widened as the realization hit her—a man who lived on this land, knew it well enough to find one ravine out of hundreds, might well know the lands outside his ranch's borders. Then, just that quickly, she dismissed the outrageous thought. She could never ask Trace McCord to ride with her to Yellowstone.

But it was as if he read her mind. "You're going to need a new guide."

"I suppose," she conceded slowly. His eyes settled on the rise and fall of her full breasts. She felt the heat in her cheeks as her nipples pouted perceptibly, responding to that look as surely as if it were a caress. He was deliberately baiting her. Why? "Do you know of anyone who could take Riley's place?"

"I might."

"Well?"

"Let me think about it."

In spite of the fact that she hadn't asked the man to be her guide, she experienced a swift rush of disappointment. Without someone who knew the territory, she would have to give up, return home. Or at the least lose precious time returning to civilization to hire someone else. Not wanting him to see her frustration, she glanced at Christopher. The boy had finished what he wanted of his meal and was now merrily thumping the table with his spoon.

She stood up and walked over to the sink, where she picked up a small cloth and moistened it with water from the pump.

"You don't have to do that," Trace protested, stepping up beside her.

His masculine presence so near to her was becoming almost as comfortably familiar as it was overwhelming. She had to consciously will her hands to stop shaking.

"It's all right, really," she assured him. "He's a sweet boy." She wiped the child's face and hands, then helped him down. He sauntered off happily.

"I tell you what, Callie," Trace said, "I may be able to arrange for that guide you need if you can do me a favor in return."

Her suspicions were immediately aroused, reminding her of the assessing glint she thought she detected in his eyes earlier. But she said only, "What sort of favor, Mr. McCord?"

"I'd like you to watch Christopher for me."

"Now?"

"Until I can find someone to be my housekeeper."

"What?" she cried, wide-eyed. "Mr. McCord, I am a writer, a photographer—not a nanny . . ."

"It would only be a temporary situation, I assure you. Until I could arrange for someone permanent."

"And how long would that take?" she asked shakily. Where would he find someone in the middle of nowhere? How could she stay here? Work for this man? Damn, she could almost sense he knew how desperate she was for her project to succeed. Yet her every instinct screamed at her to say no.

"Exactly how long would be pretty hard to predict, don't you think?"

"I've never cared for a child full time," she hedged.

"You seem to have a knack for it."

He was not mocking her, and she warmed to the unexpected compliment. It made her all the more wary. There was something dangerously compelling about this man, tugging at a part of her she had long held under tight rein. But instead of doing the sensible thing and telling him she couldn't possibly agree to such a situation, she heard herself say, "Why didn't you keep the woman you threw off your ranch this afternoon, until you found a replacement?"

"She was unsuitable."

"How do you know I won't be?"

"I don't. At the first sign you are, you'll be gone, too."

Of all the insufferable . . . Callie felt her temper nudge her. This man certainly wouldn't win any tact contests. "I'm sorry," she said at last. "I suppose I won't be suitable, either."

"What does that mean?"

"I mean I have to have time for myself, Mr. McCord. I have to take my pictures, write in my journal. I can't watch Christopher twenty-four hours a day."

"I don't expect you to be his mother," he snapped.

Callie started at the bitterness in his voice. "I didn't think you did," she managed.

"You'll be expected to care for him during the day, while I'm working on the ranch."

"Where would I stay?"

"We have a guest room. You and your aunt are welcome to it."

She straightened. Even with Deirdre a most effective chaperone she was curiously ill at ease at the thought of sleeping under the same roof with this man. One night she could have managed, but indefinitely? She hoped the telltale blush creeping up her neck didn't betray the direction of her thoughts.

"I . . . I should discuss it with my aunt first."

"I expected you would."

Expected? As though this entire conversation had come as no surprise to him. "I don't imagine she would have any real objections. I know she's worried about Riley. This would give him a chance to heal . . ."

"It's settled then?" he pressed.

She looked at him, a feeling of bemused acceptance rippling through her. "For now anyway," she hedged. "I guess you've got yourself a nanny."

Christopher chose that moment to wander over to her. He held a book in his hands. "Read the book," he said, poking at her.

Trace said nothing, obviously waiting for her reaction. He was testing her already! Did he doubt she was capable of reading a book to a child? She picked up Christopher, who maintained a firm grip on the leatherbound book, and headed into the outer room. She settled herself on the settee, the boy comfortably ensconced on her lap.

"My, this is quite a book you've got here," she said, reading the title aloud. *"Aesop's Fables."* She opened the book to the middle. "Ah, the fox and the grapes. Let's see if that silly old fox learns his lesson this time, shall we?" She felt a little silly herself and self-conscious all at once, as Trace made no move to leave.

He should be as exhausted as she was, after a long day dealing with unplanned crises.

Christopher yawned broadly, his head nodding forward. "I don't think we're going to make it to the end of this story." Callie smiled, barely stifling a yawn herself. In seconds he was fast asleep.

Trace stepped up behind the settee, bending his long legs so that his face was even with the back of her neck. "He likes to sleep with his puff-puppy. It's in his room."

Callie nodded, suddenly incapable of speech. Hearing that deep male voice talking about puff-puppies was doing strange things to her. *Please go away,* her mind begged. *I don't know what you do to me, but please go away.*

"Callie." His voice was low, husky, the one word a gentle command that she turn and face him.

She turned. He leaned closer. His lips—such full, passionate lips—were barely three inches from her own.

"I want to thank you," he said. Feather-light, his lips brushed hers. In that tiny instant she memorized their texture, their shape, their taste. His masculine scent filled her nostrils. Her heart seemed destined to burst from her chest.

"You're . . . you're welcome," she stammered, because she couldn't think of anything else to say. She should have been outraged, appalled that he dare . . . Instead, a soothing lethargy crept through her body.

He rose, a smile quirking one corner of his mouth. "If you can put him to bed, I'll go in to check on him after I take a bath. I've got a little too much grit on me to face clean sheets." With that he headed down the darkened hallway toward the bathing room.

For long minutes Callie stared after him, wondering when she'd remembered to start breathing again. What must he think of her? He'd kissed her as a show of gratitude for agreeing to care for his son, and she had accepted it like some sort of affection-starved spinster.

With shaking knees she carried the child to his bed. Her gaze involuntarily fell on the closed door to the bathing room. Try as she might to shut her mind to it, she did not mistake the sounds of water splashing into the porcelain tub. Had he already shed his clothes?

Shocked to her toes at her wanton thoughts, she hurried back out to the main room. This was never going to work. She would have to insist Trace find someone for Christopher as soon as possible. No matter how she tried to escape the notion, she was becoming more and more convinced that she had not imagined the near cunning in his eyes tonight. His mood had shifted—consciously, deliberately—from hostile to friendly, more than friendly.

Why?

And why did she know that it had everything in the world to do with her?

Chapter Five

Even standing in front of the crackling fire, Callie could hear the muffled sounds of Trace McCord sloshing around in his bath. Her cheeks flushed as she conjured up the image of that lean, well-muscled body without the encumbrance of clothing. Quickly, she busied herself straightening tumbled pillows and twisted antimacassars, the day's evidence of a child at play.

She smiled, picking up the rag-stuffed dog. Christopher must have dropped it when she carried him back to bed. She started down the hallway to the boy's room, her eyes again pulled toward the closed door to the bath. Abashed, she averted her gaze. Deirdre would have her head if she even knew she was in the same house with a man in such a state, let alone standing outside his door.

Giving herself a mental shake, Callie stepped into Christopher's room and snuggled the toy next to him. She smiled as he reflexively curled his small arm around the dog, cuddling it under his chin.

She was still smiling when she left the room, the rasping of the latch on the bathing room door catching her ear. Automatically she turned toward it. The door swung open, Trace framed in the doorway arch, that lean, well-muscled body she'd been trying so hard not to think about standing barely two feet away from her.

He was holding a towel, head tilted downward, rubbing his thick, wet hair.

He was stark naked.

Callie's shocked gasp stopped him in midstride. His head jerked up, his gaze locking with hers. In his eyes she saw startled confusion; her own must have registered horrified disbelief. No more than a heartbeat of time passed.

He moved first, scrambling back into the room and slamming the door. Callie took several seconds even to remember to breathe, as the image burned through her brain—lantern light glowing from within the room silhouetting the man, emphasizing the tautly honed perfection of muscles used to hard work.

Her face suffused with heat, Callie staggered down the hallway as if in a daze. In the front room she gripped the top slat of one of the ladder-back chairs, still unable to quell the memory of lean hips and a dark nest of hair . . .

"I'm sorry." The deep male voice was directly behind her.

She whirled, startled. She had been so absorbed by her thoughts she hadn't even heard his approach. It was obvious he had thrown himself into his clothes. He was barefoot, the towel still draped across the back of his neck to check the dampness of his hair, but faded denim jeans now hugged his hips, a gray chambray shirt hanging loose, unbuttoned.

"I am sorry, Callie," he repeated. "I guess I'm not used to house guests." His eyes pleaded with her to understand. He was genuinely mortified. "It's late. I'm tired." He whipped the towel from his neck in exasperation. "Damn. I forgot you were in the house."

Callie grimaced, ridiculously annoyed. She'd made that much of an impression? Two seconds after she was out of his sight, he forgot her existence? Still, she could tell his embarrassment was real. No doubt he was exhausted from the trip to rescue Deirdre and Riley. Christopher's belated bedtime hadn't helped, either. It was well past midnight, a long physical day for a man who had likely risen before dawn yesterday.

"I guess I was just going through the motions," he went on, when she said nothing. "I take a bath; I go to bed. I never wear anything when I . . ." He blew out an exasperated breath. "I'm making this worse."

"It's all right," Callie murmured, finding her voice at last. "I . . . I should have made some sort of noise or something."

He stepped closer to her, his right hand making tentative contact with her left shoulder. She told herself she should back away, but she couldn't summon the will to move. All she could do was stare up at him, her eyes unwillingly focusing on the full, sensuous lips that had so recently brushed her own. With no conscious thought her own lips parted slightly, her breathing growing more shallow, her heart pounding.

"Callie, I . . ." The words ended as he lowered his head toward hers, his arm sweeping around her waist, pulling her close, the clean, musky scent of him overwhelming any last, niggling bits of reason that might have stopped her. It wasn't gratitude that burned in those smoldering brown eyes. Not this time. His lips were just as she remembered them—warm, soft. But his body was hard, fierce as he crushed her to him. And if he hadn't held her, she would have crumpled to the floor, so stunned was she by the raging tide of emotions that swept through her.

She felt the first flick of his hot, moist tongue against her closed lips and shuddered, a tremble of delight. Shyly, she responded in kind. Trace groaned deep in his throat, his whole body seeming to ignite. She flung her arms around him, her hands clinging to the back of his neck, exploring the fever-hot touch of his flesh, then furrowing upward into the thick damp strands of his tawny hair.

What was happening to her? She couldn't allow this. With a sheer effort of will, she tore her lips from his. "Please, Trace . . ." she whispered. "This isn't . . . I can't . . . What are we doing?"

His breathing was ragged, his eyes reflecting the passion he was belatedly seeking to master. But there seemed a bewilderment in him, too—or did she see it only because she wished it so, because she was so confused herself. Over and over the thought drummed through her head—she had only just met this man this morning. She hadn't even permitted Nicolas to kiss her until their fourth evening out, and that kiss had kindled nothing like this.

Trace started to release her. "I didn't mean . . ." They both twisted toward the sound of the front door opening, Callie jumping guiltily back. Deirdre!

Callie suppressed a groan, her eyes flicking anxiously to McCord's open shirt, his bootless feet. "Mr.

McCord just finished his bath," she stammered, furious at how falsely light her voice sounded even in her own ears. "He was . . . I mean . . ."

Her brows furrowed as McCord's gaze dropped meaningfully to her bosom. She looked down, horrified. The fabric clung provocatively to the tips of her breasts, the dress's entire bodice moistened by its intimate contact with the man's still-damp chest. Dismayed, she crossed her arms in front of her, but it was too late.

Deirdre stood in the entryway taking it all in, her gaze shifting from Callie to McCord and back again. More than censure, Callie saw disappointment in her aunt's face. And it hurt more than any anger could.

"Mr. McCord," Deirdre began, her quiet tone only serving to magnify Callie's distress, "I'm afraid I find your manner of dress in the presence of my niece most inappropriate."

Trace said nothing, accepting Deirdre's reprimand with an almost gracious silence. Callie had the strange perception that he did so, because he had decided he deserved it. The regret in his eyes was the only thing sparing her from total misery.

"Things may be a bit less formal out here," Deirdre went on, "but . . ." She paused, seeming to search for the right words. "But I doubt a young woman's reputation is any less important in Wyoming than it would be in a more . . . civilized setting."

"Aunt Deirdre!" Callie cried, upset by her aunt's none-too-subtle insult, "I'm as much at fault here as . . ."

"Your aunt is right," Trace cut in. "This was no way for me to be dressed in front of a lady." He buttoned the shirt, then stuffed the tail into his pants. "Things may be a bit different in the West out of necessity—there aren't too many debutante balls, for example. But out here more than anywhere a man shows respect to a woman. If I've compromised you in any way at all, I apologize."

Any way at all? Callie thought wonderingly, unable to quell the memory of hard, muscled arms crushing her against a hard, muscled body. She stood there, speechless. While she didn't doubt the sincerity of his words, there was something, *something* about the way he said them. An obsequiousness that seemed totally foreign to the man, yet designed to win Deirdre's good graces.

Though she'd known Trace McCord less than twenty-four hours, Callie was finding him much more complex than the boorish oaf she had at first categorized him to be. Already she'd witnessed his anger with Mrs. Yates, his tenderness with Christopher, his embarrassment—as much for her sake as his own, for his bathing indiscretion—and his compelling sensuality in the touch of his mouth on hers.

What were his motives? Why did he seem to be going out of his way to have Deirdre forgive his momentary lack of propriety?

Callie frowned. Whatever his motives, his methods were working perfectly. Deirdre let out a sympathetic sigh. "It's been a dreadful day. I suppose the best thing for all of us would be to get some sleep."

"Yes, sleep," Callie said too quickly. "That's what we need all right. We'll all climb into bed."

Trace rolled his eyes.

"Oh, you know perfectly well what I meant," Callie

snapped, wondering how long she was going to allow Trace McCord to fluster her. Abruptly, she turned to her aunt. "How is Riley, by the way?" She wanted the subject changed and right now.

"He's resting comfortably," Deirdre said, her manner growing constrained. She was evidently wrestling with some guilt of her own. "Perhaps I should have stayed with him, but . . . well, I decided I would be more comfortable in Mr. McCord's guest room."

Callie knew at once her aunt was skirting the truth. Deirdre didn't want to be here; she wanted to be in the bunkhouse. Her nursing experience would have made the arrangement entirely acceptable, but her aunt had another worry that took priority even over Riley's injury.

Trace McCord was the reason Deirdre would be spending the night in the mainhouse. Callie stared at the floor. Deirdre had made up her mind. Callie had herself a chaperone. At least for tonight. And after her experience with Trace here in front of the fire, maybe it was just as well.

"Come along, Callie," Deirdre said, "we'd best be getting to bed. It's going to be an early day for both of us come morning."

Callie recognized the look in her aunt's eyes. There would be a long mother/daughter talk before either one of them would be going to sleep this night. But before Callie headed toward the guest room, she looked toward Trace who was again leaning against the mantel, his back to her, staring into the flames. "Good night, Mr. McCord."

He turned around, his eyes hooded, unreadable. "Good night . . . Miss Callaghan. Sleep well."

Deirdre hustled over to Callie. "To bed, young lady," she said, hurrying Callie out of the room. Over her shoulder she called back, "You know, you really should lock your door, Mr. McCord. It might save you all sorts of trouble." She hurried to add, "I mean with marauding Indians, outlaws . . ."

"The only thing marauding in these parts at the moment, Miss Callaghan, is a rogue bear down from the high country. I doubt he can open the door—locked or unlocked."

"Bears! What next!" Deirdre said.

Callie shot McCord an acid look. He had just given her aunt one more round of ammunition in her arsenal of excuses as to why they should return to New York. Muttering to herself, Callie led the way to the guest room.

"Oh, my, this is lovely!" Deirdre exclaimed, lighting the room's kerosene lamp.

Callie had made only a cursory check of the room earlier in the day in her search for something to wear. Now, coupled with the information she'd gleaned from her conversation with Trace, she was certain that this room had been Jenny McCord's. The furnishings here were in sharp contrast to the more practical pieces in the rest of the house.

Embellished with Gothic traceries, an ornately carved Chippendale dressing table abutted the wall to her left. A similarly wrought armoire sat against the opposite wall. But it was to the rear of the room that her exhausted body drew her.

She stood at the foot of the brass bed, idly caressing one of the cool brass balls that sat atop each of the bed's corner posts. "Do you think we could postpone our little talk until morning, Aunt Deirdre? I'm very tired."

"What talk is that, dear?" her aunt asked with feigned innocence, as she turned back the bedcovers, pausing to run a hand admiringly over the exquisite quilted coverlet.

"You know perfectly well . . ."

"The mattress is feather-ticked," Deirdre beamed. "Can you imagine? Out here?"

"Aunt Deirdre . . ."

Her aunt sat down on the bed. "Mr. McCord's quite handsome, don't you think?"

Callie couldn't look at her, her gaze flitting nervously about the room. "I hadn't noticed," she lied.

"Notice or not, you and I had best have a little chat."

But Callie was hardly listening. She let out a surprised gasp to see her trunk shoved against the wall just off the door. Trace must have brought it in after he'd taken Deirdre and Riley their supper. She had been thinking she was going to have to sleep in Jenny's dress, but now . . . Quickly, she retrieved her nightrail, tossing an extra one to her aunt. Unfolding the privacy screen, she ducked behind it and exchanged the dress for her nightclothes.

"Oh, this is so much better," she said, pirouetting across the room to the bed. "I'll be asleep in two minutes."

"Callie, this is your Aunt Deirdre you're talkin' to, not your father." Deirdre was in no mood to be put off.

Callie yawned broadly. "I'm going to sleep." She lay down, jerking the covers up to her chin.

Deirdre shifted to face her, though she remained sitting atop the quilt. "Callie, it's you I'm thinkin' of. You're young, you're pretty. A man like Mr. McCord,

82

livin' so isolated, could well take advantage of an impressionable young woman."

"I think I am well able to take care of myself where men are concerned."

"And how many men have you ever met that are like Trace McCord?"

"Men are men."

Deirdre chuckled. "You think I'm just an old spinster you can fool with that kind of talk, don't you?"

"Of course not."

"Then why was a man you met only this morning standing beside you half dressed when I walked into this house? Lookin' for all the world like he was about to kiss you?" She paused meaningfully. "Or maybe he just did? And you're tellin' me you were treatin' him no different than you would any other man?"

"It was not what you think!" Callie gritted, struggling to a sitting position. "He was merely apologizing for . . . for . . ." Dear heavens, she couldn't possibly tell Deirdre of her hallway encounter with McCord, "for being rude to me when I first came to the ranch for help this morning," she finished lamely.

"A gentleman doesn't compromise a lady."

"And a lady doesn't allow herself to be compromised, right?"

"Callie, I love you. I don't want you hurt."

"You make it sound like Trace can hurt me. I scarcely know the man."

"Trace, is it? I noticed you calling him Mr. McCord whenever I was about."

"Aunt Deirdre, please. I am very tired. I promised him I would look out for his son. I need to get some

83

sleep, if I'm going to keep up with a three-year-old." She told her aunt of her arrangement with McCord to look after the child.

"At least that should make for an interesting few days," Deirdre mused. "Until Mr. Smith's leg heals enough so that we can head back East. Watchin' you care for a youngster . . ."

"East? Aunt Deirdre, we're not going back. At least *I'm* not! I didn't come all this way to give up now."

"Don't tell me you're planning on taking on Yellowstone alone?"

"Of course not. I may have a bit o' wanderlust, but I'm no fool. Why do you think I agreed to watch Mr. McCord's son?"

"Oh, Callandra, surely not . . ."

"Trace promised to be my guide . . . or at least find me someone who will."

"You and that man? Callie . . ."

"Riley rode with you and me. What's the difference if it's Trace?"

"There's something about the man, Callie. You must see it. He's just so close-mouthed about anything but Christopher."

"Don't you think that's understandable? From what I gather, except for the child, Trace's family is dead. Memories like that can be quite painful."

"I suppose so. Still . . ."

"You're being fanciful." And yet Deirdre's perceptions of Trace came strikingly close to her own. There was something disturbingly mysterious about him. This morning he had all but thrown her bodily off his ranch and then minutes ago . . . She swallowed nervously. Trace McCord was no shallow dandy out after her inheritance. She knew how to handle men like that. She had done so often enough. No, McCord didn't even know she was the daughter of one of the wealthiest men in the country. Nor was she so wide-eyed and innocent to think that he had fallen head over heels in love with her on first sight. Something else was driving him.

"Just be careful, Callie. Please."

"I will. I promise."

Deirdre blew out the lantern, then quickly dressed in Callie's extra nightrail. "Good night, dear," she said, settling into bed beside her niece.

"Good night, Aunt Deirdre." Callie lay awake long after the sounds of Deirdre's deep, even breathing told her her aunt had fallen asleep.

Again and again her thoughts drifted back to the moment Riley first halted the wagon atop the ridge overlooking the Shadow's Way valley two days ago. Even Deirdre had urged her to take a picture. But Callie refused, wanting only to leave at once. She hadn't been able to explain it then, she couldn't explain it now.

There was nothing of fear or foreboding that compelled her to be on her way. It was the opposite. It was the overwhelming need to stay, to know. But that couldn't be, she wouldn't let it be. Yellowstone was her destiny. Not some middle of nowhere ranch with a poetic name.

Yet even the mystery of her attraction to this place, and undeniably to its owner, intrigued that part of her that had always been drawn to the unknown. Part of the lure of Yellowstone was the chance to find a lost half million dollars in gold.

Lost or hidden.

Like parts of Trace McCord.

McCord. How different he was from Nicolas. Callie grimaced into the darkness. Count Nicolas von Endenberg was the last person she wanted intruding on her thoughts before she drifted off to sleep.

Count Nicolas von Endenberg—and her wedding day.

Chapter Six

Callie sat on the brocaded bench seat in the opulently furnished reserve vestry of St. Patrick's Cathedral, fingering the Brussels lace skirts of her wedding gown. The room, normally restricted to visiting clergy, had been set aside by the bishop himself three months ago when Fletcher Callaghan announced the impending marriage of his daughter, Callandra, to one of Europe's most preeminent bachelors.

In less than an hour Callie would be the bride of Count Nicolas von Endenberg, a nobleman of Prussian extraction who claimed a lineage traceable to Alexander the Great himself. Her father would be pleased. Nicolas would be pleased. And she . . . She didn't want to think about it.

Callie studied her reflection in the mirror, her copper tresses done up in a becoming twist, tiny curls framing her oval face. But it was her eyes that held her, their normally emerald hue dulled to match the drab green of frost-nipped grass.

"Too bad I don't have a camera," she mused with

acid sarcasm. "I could forever capture the jubilant mood of my wedding day."

All that was left for her to do was put on her veil. Deirdre would be back shortly to help her with that. Her aunt had excused herself ten minutes ago, claiming to have some urgent errand to run. Callie hadn't missed the dark circles hovering around Deirdre's eyes, either. She knew her aunt wanted desperately to talk her out of going through with this farce, but Deirdre's long, unswerving loyalty to Fletcher Callaghan had prevented her from saying the words.

Rising to her feet, Callie paced to the thick oak door. Easing it open she peered into the wide corridor that led to the main body of the church beyond. Fury snapped through her. Edmont Simmons still stood with his back to the wall, precisely where her father had left him. The portly old typesetter from *The Sentinel* rocked rhythmically back and forth from the balls of his feet to his heels and back again, as if privy to some unheard band of musicians. Her father told her Simmons was there so that she could "send for anything or anyone she might need right up until the moment the organist began playing 'The Wedding March.'"

Did her father really think her so stupid that she couldn't see what he was doing? He had posted Simmons in the corridor like a sentry guarding a prisoner.

Silently, Callie closed the door, unable to stop the first trickle of tears she had shed all morning. She had sworn, after crying herself to sleep last night, that she would shed no more. She would accept her fate with

88

dignity. Not unlike Anne Boleyn came the unwelcome comparison.

"Why, Da, why is it so important that I marry Nicolas? Marry any man of your choosing, instead of my own?" Her father had arranged everything, from her first meeting with the Count when he'd been indulging a secret passion to be on the stage, to their first evening together at a performance of Mozart's *Don Giovanni,* even to the exact place and time of Nicolas's proposal. But then she could scarcely be surprised. Her father had done his best to arrange her whole life.

Angrily, she wiped away her tears, but she couldn't wipe away the lost feeling in her soul. No. More than lost . . . defeated.

All of her life her father had checked her at every turn, just as he'd checked her mother, and, but for a four-year aberration, Deirdre. But unlike her mother and Deirdre, Callie had continued to defy him time and time again. Everything was fine as long as she played the precocious ingenue, but let her have an original thought, an unacceptable goal—and her father went off like a Fourth of July skyrocket.

His distaste for her dreams had started in earnest nine years ago, when she was fourteen. The irony was that it had been a story in his own *Sentinel* that set the course she would take for her life, leaving her and her father destined it seemed to remain forever at loggerheads.

The article spoke of a photographic exhibit by William Henry Jackson that would be on display for two weeks at the Metropolitan Museum. It had been

89

Jackson, two years previously in 1871, who had been a part of the Hayden Geological Survey of the Western Territories. His photographs presented to Congress last year had been instrumental in the passage of a law setting aside two million wilderness acres—primarily in northwestern Wyoming—as the nation's first national park. Yellowstone.

Callie found the whole idea of Jackson's adventure irrepressibly exciting. Interrupting Deirdre's teatime in the parlor of the Callaghan mansion, Callie waved the paper under her aunt's nose. "I simply must meet him," she sighed breathlessly. "If I don't I'll absolutely die." She pointed at the article. "Just read this. He saw bears and elk and buffalo and hot springs and geysers and even . . . please, Aunt Deirdre, look at this! Even some poor men who survived the ambush of their army troop by some villainous brigands."

"I hardly think that is the sort of man your father would approve of your talking to."

"Father wouldn't approve of me talkin' to Saint Patrick himself, unless the poor saint could prove he had access to the papal fortune."

"Callandra! I'll not have such talk." Callie could see that her aunt was having a hard time holding back a smile. Finally, she gave in to it. "All right, you can blaspheme your father, but never poor dear Saint Patrick."

Callie giggled, then grew serious. "Will you take me to meet Mr. Jackson?"

"I'll be sorry I did, I'm sure. But, yes, we'll do it."

At the museum Jackson was so taken with Callie's genuine enthusiasm, he invited her and Deirdre to a private screening of some of his more precious photographs back at his hotel.

In near reverence, Callie ran her fingers along the outer edges of the heavy photographic paper. The prints were wondrous. Black and white stills of mountains, streams, rock formations, animals, hot springs, fumaroles.

"The pictures don't even do them justice," Jackson said sadly.

"One day we'll be able to capture everything on film just like our eyes do," Callie said. "I've seen the photographers' work at the paper. It's so cumbersome. But a hundred years ago, it was only a dream. A hundred years from now . . . They'll be able to take pictures of a single raindrop falling from the sky."

Jackson smiled approvingly, charmed by her spirit. "Too bad you're not a man, Miss Callie," he said.

For the first time in her young life, Callie was not offended by such a remark. Jackson recognized her love for what she saw in his pictures, but he knew how much harder than any man she would have to fight for the same freedom he took for granted.

She strolled around the hotel suite, studying the various pictures he'd set up on easels for display. "Yellowstone. It even sounds majestic."

"It's from a Minnetaree Indian word *mi tsi a-da-zi*. It means Yellow Rock River."

"That's beautiful."

"Not nearly so beautiful as the place itself. And now with the law and the people behind it, Yellowstone will stay just as I saw it forever."

"I'm going to go there and see for myself," Callie announced, taking a quick glance at her aunt who was much too vigorously stirring her tea. "But first I'm going to take pictures right here. Of the Adirondacks, of the city, and . . . and I'll write important stories that touch people's lives." Her aunt was still stirring. "What do you think, Aunt Deirdre? Can't you see me standing beside a geyser?"

"I think your da would hardly approve of your meeting Mr. Jackson. I doubt he'll want you traipsin' in the wilderness."

"What Da wants doesn't matter. This is my life we're talking about. Not his. You may bow to his every wish, but I won't. Ever." Callie wished the words back at once as her aunt winced, her hand trembling now as she swirled her spoon in the teacup. "Aunt Deirdre, I'm sorry. I didn't mean . . ."

"It's all right, dear. Truly."

"No, it is not all right. That was horrid of me. I know how contrary Da is with you, much more than he's ever been to me." She slapped her right fist into the palm of her left hand. "I know what. You and I will both go to Yellowstone. That will really get Da's goat!"

Jackson laughed. "Maybe you'll make it there after all, young lady. You've got gumption. But it takes more than courage. You'll need careful planning, the right equipment . . ."

"I can get all that. Da has lots of money."

"Callie!" Deirdre chided, "that isn't the sort of thing a lady discusses in public."

"Lady. Bosh and nonsense. I don't want to be a lady, I want to be a writer."

"Maybe you could write about finding the Yellowstone treasure," Jackson put in. "The Fort Ellis gold."

Callie's eyes lit up. "Treasure? Gold? But that's wonderful. Da would surely let me go then. He's always giving money to gold hunters."

Deirdre harrumphed. "The one peculiar trait of Finley I have failed utterly to understand. How the man can be so tight-fisted with a penny, then squander thousands of dollars to finance expeditions to uncover lost Spanish galleons, lost gold mines, and the like. It makes no sense."

"But his people have found two Spanish galleons and one gold mine," Callie reminded her. "He's made ten times his investments back." Her gaze shifted to Jackson. "But if Yellowstone is protected, how can anyone be mining gold?"

"It's not that kind of gold. Well, it was once, but not anymore. This gold was packed in crates, army crates. But for my money it's gone forever."

"Oooh, tell me about it!" Callie pleaded.

The man spread his arms wide, gesturing eerily like some sort of spectral apparition. Callie smiled. She was going to get the full treatment.

"Dark and spooky, it was," Jackson began. "The soldiers marching through the wilderness all the way from Fort Ellis in Montana. They had a fortune in gold with them. Paper money, too. The gold was from the Montana mines. They were heading to Fort Laramie with it. The paper money was for the troopers' payroll and to buy supplies from ranchers—horses, cattle, that sort of thing. None of it ever got through."

Callie scooted a Queen Anne corner chair across the floral carpet and sat down in front of Jackson. She was mesmerized.

"There were thirteen troopers. Some say that's what made them unlucky. Others tell me it was Indian spirits that made them go mad."

"Madness?" Callie was more intrigued than ever.

"I was there."

Callie gasped.

"Well, not exactly. The Hayden Expedition was in Yellowstone at the same time the gold wagon was coming through. We didn't cross paths, though, until it was too late for most of them."

"Too late?"

"There were only two troopers still alive when we found them. A Private Burns and a Lieutenant Mason. The lieutenant was shot bad."

"Dear God. What happened? An ambush?"

"Would that it were. The lieutenant told us it was one of their own. A Sergeant Hogan decided he wanted the money for himself."

"A traitor!" Callie gasped.

"He was posted as guard one night and, while the others slept, he started slitting throats."

"Mr. Jackson!" Deirdre exclaimed, leaping to her feet, and nearly spilling her tea. "I'll not have my niece subjected to such gruesome tales."

"Hush, Aunt Deirdre!" Callie caught herself. "Please?"

Jackson waited. Finally Deirdre shook her head, sinking back into her chair. "All right, if you want to have nightmares for a month, who am I to stop you?"

Callie squirmed in her chair. "So what happened then? Did Sergeant Hogan get away?"

"I'm coming to that. Just hold your horses." It was obvious Jackson relished the telling of the tale. His voice was appropriately mysterious as he went on. "It seems Private Burns came awake while Hogan was prowling through the troops doing his devil's work.

Burns's shouting alerted those who were still alive, including Lieutenant Mason. But even then most of the poor bastards . . ." He stopped, looking guiltily at Deirdre. "Begging your pardon, ma'am."

"Never mind manners!" Callie said. "Please, go on."

Deirdre grimaced, but gave Jackson a forgiving nod.

"Anyway," Jackson continued, "Hogan pulled a pistol and started shooting. That's when the lieutenant was hurt. Private Burns risked his own life pulling the lieutenant to safety in the rocks."

"Oh, this is so exciting."

"Worrying about the lieutenant like he was, Burns didn't think to grab a weapon. He had to watch while Hogan started throwing bodies into a mud hole."

"Mud hole?"

"Scalding hot pools of water and mud. Yellowstone's got scores of them."

Callie shuddered.

"It gets worse. It seems one of the soldiers was still alive. He started screaming when Hogan tossed him in the hole." He paused meaningfully. "The man was Private Burns's brother."

Callie's heart caught.

"The lieutenant told us Burns just plain went mad. He charged down the hill, grabbed up a dead soldier's gun, and started firing at Hogan. Hogan scrambled onto the gold wagon and took off."

"He got away?"

"For the moment. The lieutenant limped down the hill and managed to bring Burns back to his senses a bit, telling him the wagon would be easy to track. So they caught up a couple of the horses Hogan had scattered, then went after him. But Hogan must have

95

figured he couldn't get away in the wagon. When they caught up to him, he was riding one of the harness team."

"So he hid the money?"

Jackson nodded. "Intending to go back for it later. But Private Burns was in a frenzy of grief and rage. The lieutenant was too weak by then to control him. He tried to stop him, but after they got the drop on Hogan, Burns shot him dead."

"Good enough for him!" Callie pronounced, then winced expecting Deirdre's censure. But none was forthcoming. Her aunt seemed as absorbed in the story now as she was. Deirdre had stopped drinking her tea and was listening to Jackson with rapt attention.

"So the money . . ." Callie began.

"Has never been found," Jackson finished. "Burns killed the only man who knew where it was."

"But surely Mason or Burns . . ."

"Mason was too badly hurt. We happened upon them the day after Hogan was killed. We'd been a little shaken up ourselves the day before by an earth tremor. We tried to find the gold ourselves, but it was gone. Vanished, as if it never was. The lieutenant was delirious with fever by day's end. Private Burns, well, there was no talking to him. He was in another world. Out of his mind, poor devil."

"How awful. What ever happened to them?"

"Burns tried to hang himself that first night."

Involuntarily, Callie reached for her throat.

"We cut him down in time, but the rope being around his neck like that . . . well, I think it finished off what was left of his senses. We took him and Lieutenant Mason on to Fort Laramie where we reported the attack. A troop of soldiers was dispatched back to the area, but no one ever came up with the gold. I heard later Mason died of infection from his wounds."

"And poor Private Burns?"

"He disappeared." Jackson leaned forward, whispering conspiratorially. "Just between you and me, ladies, there are those who say he's out there right now. In Yellowstone. Wandering the hills and valleys looking for his dead brother, looking for Hogan, looking for the money."

"It's all so horrible," Callie said, "and yet, I can't help thinking how exciting it would be to find the money, maybe even see a ghost or two . . ." She knew she would never forget a single detail of Jackson's story. This was the one. This was her dream. She would go to Yellowstone. Take pictures as good or better than Jackson, and find the stolen payroll. Even her father couldn't turn down such a story.

"We've taken enough of your time," Deirdre said, rising.

"It was my pleasure." Smiling, Jackson picked up one of the photographs lying on his desk. With a fountain pen he signed the back of it and gave it to Callie. "With my compliments, young lady."

Callie looked at the twisting, burbling stream with its rushing waterfall. To the left stood a motley assortment of men, including the blurred image of a soldier.

"Private Burns," Jackson pronounced. "He was too jittery to stand still for the time I needed to take the picture."

Callie held the picture to her bosom. "I'll treasure it always. And I'll go there one day, Mr. Jackson.

You'll see."

"I don't doubt you will, Callie Callaghan," he said. "I don't doubt you will at all."

Callie shook herself, driving away memories too painful to bear, as she paced the confines of St. Patrick's vestry. She was throwing it all away. Every dream, every goal she'd ever set for herself, to follow the dictates of Fletcher Callaghan, just as she'd accused Deirdre of doing those many years ago in William Jackson's hotel suite.

"No! No, I can't do it. I can't." She started to tug at the hooks that bound her into the wedding dress. A knock sounded at the vestry door.

"Who is it?" she called, trying to keep the tremor out of her voice.

"Your father."

She stiffened, then quickly refastened the two hooks she'd managed to free. "The door's unlocked."

Fletcher Callaghan strode into the room as he strode through life, as if he owned everything and everyone in it. His impeccably tailored ebony frock coat and dark brocade vest emphasized the trim lines of his short, compact frame. At fifty-four he could easily pass for a man ten years younger. His carrot-hued hair was streaked with silver at the temples, giving an added arrogance to ruddy features too rugged to ever be considered handsome.

"Did your guard need to make a visit to the necessary?" she asked, her mood such that she made no attempt to mask how miserable she was.

"Callandra, don't start again. You know why I have Mr. Simmons standing by. In case you . . ."

"In case I *need* anything. Yes, I heard. Too bad *you*

never have. Heard *me,* that is. What I need, Father, what I've always needed is just to live my own life."

"Callandra." His voice was stern, a warning that he would not permit this particular battle of words to escalate as they so often did. "The wedding starts in twenty minutes. Everyone is in place." He took a step closer to her, but made no attempt to touch her. "Nicolas looks dashing. I'm sure you'll be very happy together."

"Good breeding stock. Wasn't that the term I overheard in the study one night when you were discussing the match with Nicolas." She drew in a long, steadying breath. "I know I'm only your daughter. I just wish you didn't find the relationship so burdensome."

"Don't say that. You're my family, Callandra. Everything I do, I do for you."

Callie calmed her own whirling emotions long enough to really look at her father. It was the first time she ever remembered seeing him unsure of himself. He was here looking for her reassurance. She found herself almost feeling sorry for him. Cold, ruthless Fletcher Callaghan. Merciless in business, a man with no friends, commanding the respect of those around him through fear and money.

"He'll be good to you, Callie."

"Were you and mother ever happy?"

"I don't want to talk about . . ."

"No, you've never wanted to talk about Mother, have you? Why? A guilty conscience? Didn't you love her?"

"Don't ever say that? I worshiped your mother, I . . ." He stopped, taking on an air of cool detachment

99

once again. "Her parents never approved of the Irish scum she married. They disowned her. She never said so, but I know it broke her heart over time."

"She loved you."

"It wasn't enough. Love isn't what makes a marriage, Callie. When emotions are involved, people don't think clearly." He seemed to want to say more, but finished with, "The ceremony starts in fifteen minutes. Be ready." Then he turned and abruptly left the room.

The door opened again almost immediately. "I saw your father leave," Deirdre said quietly. "I didn't want to interrupt."

"No, one must never interrupt Fletcher Callaghan. A mortal sin." Her voice shook.

"Callie, for the love of heaven, talk to me. Before it's too late."

"What is there left to say?"

"That you're in love with Nicolas von Endenberg."

"Love has nothing to do with marriage, Aunt Deirdre. Da assured me of that." Tears slipped from her eyes.

"So," Deirdre shook her head, "after a lifetime of fighting him, you give up. Just like that. You'll spend the rest of your life with a man you don't give a fig about. Abandon your pictures, your writing." She paused. "Yourself."

"You of all people know how he is."

"Yes. I know."

Callie looked at Deirdre and saw her own pain reflected in her aunt's eyes. "Oh, God," she whispered. "What am I doing, Aunt Deirdre. I can't go through with this."

"I know."

Callie sank onto the brocaded seat. "Da will never listen. He'll have me bound and gagged and dragged to the altar if he has to."

"Not if you're not here, he can't."

"What . . ."

"I have a carriage waiting for us in the alley." Deirdre tore at the wrapping of the package she'd brought back with her. "And a change of clothes for us both."

Callie stared at the two nuns' habits, then threw her arms around her aunt. "Oh, Deirdre, you saved my life."

Quickly they donned the garments. Callie stared at herself in the mirror. "Oh, how I'd love to see Nicolas's face, if he saw me dressed like this."

"Come on. We haven't a minute to waste."

Callie hugged her again. "I love you."

No one, not even Edmont Simmons, paid them any mind as they walked down the corridor, arms folded prayerfully, heads bowed. But as they neared the rear door, Callie's head jerked up at the sound of Deirdre's sharp intake of breath. Just ahead of them, pacing with obvious irritation, was Nicolas.

He did look dashing, Callie conceded, his gold-trimmed red uniform jacket making a striking contrast to the white of his trousers. Cornsilk hair skimmed his jacket collar, and though she could not see them, she guessed his pale-blue eyes mirrored his agitation.

Even knowing she was about to humiliate the man by leaving him at the altar, Callie felt nothing. Had never felt anything for Nicolas von Endenberg, not even the passion of hate.

"Keep your head down," Deirdre hissed.

Hardly daring to breathe, they skirted past him,

101

nearly collapsing with relief when he didn't give them so much as a cursory glance. Hurrying out the cathedral's rear door, they clambered into the rig Deirdre had hired, giggling, as much in relief as amusement at the driver's startled look. Inside the carriage, Callie noticed a valise packed with some of her own clothes. She looked at her aunt. "You intended to talk me out of it all along, didn't you?"

"I intended to be ready, when you talked yourself out of it."

Tears pricked Callie's eyes. "You are so special to me."

"Hush, child," her aunt said, obviously battling her own emotions. "What's important now is keeping us both out of your father's sight for a while." She called to the driver to take them to a downtown hotel. "We'll register under false names and wait out the worst of your father's temper."

Callie sat for a minute, thinking about the turn her life had almost made, thinking further about the direction she had so long wanted to go. "No," she said quietly. "Not a hotel. Home. I want my cameras. It's time to see if I have it in me to follow my dreams, instead of just talking about them."

"Callie . . ."

"I have to do this, Aunt Deirdre. Please understand."

At home she and Deirdre changed clothes and packed as quickly as they could, but the driver was still loading the last of her equipment when her father's coach thundered up the drive. The coachman nearly set the matching Morgans on their haunches as he hauled back on the reins.

Fletcher Callaghan leaped from the coach even before it came to a complete stop. "How dare you?" he ranted, his gaze shooting from Deirdre to Callie. "How dare both of you humiliate me like this?" To Deirdre he snarled, "I should have known not to trust her with you. You put her up to this disobedience, didn't you?"

Deirdre faced her brother squarely, something Callie had never seen her do in her life. At least not in front of witnesses. "Don't stop us, Finley."

"Don't call me that."

"She doesn't love him."

"She doesn't know what she wants. She's my daughter. I'll decide what's best for her."

"Like you did for me?"

"Oh, please, not that old . . ."

"You ruined my life, Finley. I'll not let you destroy Callie's." She gave Callie a gentle nudge. "Get in the carriage."

Callie held back, looking from her aunt to her father. It was the first clue she'd ever had to the pain that had so long lain between them. But she knew neither one would speak further of it now. "I'm sorry, Da. But you just wouldn't listen."

"All right," her father shouted. "Go! But you'll be back. Both of you. And you'll apologize to Nicolas. I just pray he'll still have you, Callandra."

Inside the carriage Callie drew a shaky breath. "What's crazy is I love him, Aunt Deirdre. I really do. Why couldn't he ever just listen?"

Deirdre didn't answer, but then Callie hadn't expected her to. They rode in silence to the train station. Once there Callie bought two tickets, heading west.

"He'll come after us, you know," Deirdre cautioned as they settled into their berths on the Pullman car.

Callie leaned back, allowed the clacking of the wheels on the rails to lull her. "I know. But I won't go back. I won't. Not until I'm finished."

"I should never have gone along with this. Not marrying Nicolas was one thing. But two women alone . . ."

"I told you we'll hire a guide when we reach Omaha. He'll get us outfitted. I've been waiting for this moment ever since that day in William Henry Jackson's hotel suite. I'm going to Yellowstone. I'll write my book, take my pictures, and find that gold. It'll be the story of the century, and even Da will have to run it in his paper—under my name."

"An army troop died over that money."

"A dozen others have died trying to find it since."

"The money's cursed, Callie. Leave it be."

"No, not cursed. Just lost. And I'm going to find it." She lay back, snuggling under the woolen bedcovers. The gentle swaying of the train soothed her as it glided down the track, urged her to sleep, to dream.

Dream. Her dream. She was going to Yellowstone at last. She would show her father she was as good as any reporter on his staff.

The money's cursed, Callie. Leave it be.

She shivered, feeling for all the world as if someone had just walked over her grave.

Chapter Seven

Naked, Trace padded over to the window of his bedroom, staring out at the light of the half moon filtering across the bluffs that abutted the rear of the house. He couldn't sleep. Though lately that was hardly unusual, tonight his restlessness stemmed from more than the sword's edge of fear he'd been fighting for weeks. Now . . . now . . . Damn! Things were more complicated than ever. More complicated than he had ever imagined they could be.

And in more ways.

He grimaced, recalling how he had almost dug out a pair of long johns to wear to bed tonight. "I doubt Miss Callaghan will be making an appearance in your bedroom," he grumbled aloud. Still, his mind prodded him that there could always be a fire, or Christopher could call out in the night bringing both himself and the fiery-haired woman to the boy's bedside.

Swearing, he tromped across the room and threw open the door to his wardrobe. Rummaging in the dark he found a pair of knee-length drawers. He shoved into them, cinching the drawstring tight with another quiet oath.

What was the woman driving him to? Or, more to the point, where was he driving himself because of her? He still couldn't believe he'd stepped buck naked from his bath into the hallway not once thinking that Callie was still in the house. Some part of him had to wonder if his memory lapse had been deliberate.

Even here, alone in his room, his thoughts about her remained half formed, elusive. He refused to consciously confront what deep down he knew had already been decided.

She was here. She was convenient. Perhaps even providential. Why not take advantage of such a perfectly timed gift from the gods?

But to use her? Use any woman, no matter what his motives. How could he live with it? Live with himself after the deed was done.

"Damn!" He clenched a fist, wishing none of it were necessary. If only Jenny had trusted him.

But she did, came the annoying thought. Even if it didn't seem so to him now. She had only done what she thought was right. What was best for Christopher.

He strode back across the room, lying down atop the covers of his bed. He considered the irony. That his sister-in-law had put such faith in him, when his own blood family . . . He closed his eyes, conjuring the image of his iron-fisted father, white-haired, red-faced with fury, a man to whom only one side of a story mattered—his own side. And Seth, as tall and formidable as Jeb, but whose emotions were balanced by an innate sense of justice, a trait that often forced him into the role of mediator.

"Thief!" Jeb McCord raged, stalking the width and breadth of his study like some affronted deity.

Seth tried to restrain his father, but the old man again cracked sixteen-year-old Trace hard across the side of his face.

Trace tasted blood, but held his ground. "Don't waste your breath on him, Seth. He has his mind made up. He always has his mind made up. He knows everything."

"Shut up, Trace," Seth snapped, wedging himself between his father and his brother. "Being a jackass and a thief gives you no say in any of this."

Trace stiffened. "You may have ten years and thirty pounds on me, Seth, but I'll take you both on."

"That's your answer to everything, isn't it?"

"Just butt out of this Seth," the elder McCord seethed. "He's gone too far even for him. I caught him in my safe with a hundred dollars of my money in his pockets."

"I wasn't going to spend any of it."

Jeb drew his arm back again, but didn't follow through with the blow. "Liar! Thief! Nothing like your brother since the day you were born. Always daydreamin'. Me forever kickin' your butt to get a lick o' worth out of ya. Well, this is the last straw. I won't put up with your stealin' from me or anybody. I'm sendin' for the law."

Trace whirled away from them both, storming to the study door. "You try it. You just try it, old man. I don't need you, I don't need either one of you. I know you wished it was me who woulda died instead of Ma."

"Damned right!" Jeb roared.

Trace froze, aware in that instant that some lost,

aching part of him had at last challenged his father to deny what Trace had believed all of his life. He'd given his father one last chance to *be* his father. Jeb McCord had responded by wishing him dead. He told himself it didn't matter, told himself he didn't care, told himself he didn't feel the searing pain that ripped through him. But with a bitter oath, he bolted from the room.

"Pa, you had no right!" he heard Seth yell. "Stay here. Cool off. Let me talk to him."

"If he shows his face on my land again, I won't just have the law on him, I'll have a gun."

Trace ran to the barn. He was saddling his gray stallion, when Seth stomped up to him. "Well, you've really done it this time, Trace," he said, his voice more bewildered than angry.

Trace tightened the cinch, then slapped the stirrup into place. "He hates me. I hate him. Simple."

"No. He's your father. A son doesn't hate his father."

"I hate him!"

"Why'd you take the money?"

Trace stared at the ground, then shrugged. "He hadn't spoken to me in three months. I thought maybe it would get his attention."

Seth swore. "I don't pretend to understand him. How he treats you isn't right. But you don't give him much of a chance to . . ."

"I don't give *him* a chance!" Trace exploded. "My God, Seth! He'd put me in jail! He wishes I was never born."

"Ma's death twisted him. He was hard before that. But . . ."

"Yeah, and he blames me for her dyin'. He doesn't blame himself for puttin' me inside her . . ."

Seth gripped Trace's shirt front. "Don't talk like that. Dammit, Trace, don't let his sickness destroy your whole life. I know if you really tried you could straighten yourself out."

"Yeah, if I really tried."

Seth held the reins to the gray, as Trace mounted. "Go on up to the mountains for a few days. Let him calm down. I'll talk to him."

"I ain't comin' back this time, Seth. I'm old enough to make it on my own. Besides, you've got Jenny to think of. You're getting married. You don't have time to bother about your stupid kid brother."

"Jenny doesn't think you're stupid. She keeps after me, tellin' me you just need a steady hand. She likes you, Trace." He grinned. "So you can't be all bad."

Trace managed a half smile. "Thanks." He offered Seth his hand.

Seth shook it. "I'll send for you when it's okay to come back."

"Sure."

"Take care of yourself, kid."

Trace stayed away for four months, but when he'd gotten word that it was all right to come home, he had. In the darkness of his bedroom, Trace shuddered. That had been one of the bigger mistakes of his life.

He shut his mind to what followed. It was over. Done. What worried him was whether or not the Marlowes had dug too far into his past. They would be here soon. He had little doubt of that. Vultures circling, waiting . . . He slapped a hand against the mattress. He had so little time.

In all of it one thing held true. Christopher. God, how he loved that boy. He knew, conscience or no, he would use anything, *anyone,* to keep him. And that included Callandra Callaghan.

Callie had the vaguest impression someone was calling her name. But she was certain she had only just shut her eyes, so she ignored the summons and snuggled back under the bedcovers in Trace McCord's guest room.

"Callandra," the voice persisted, "if you've agreed to care for Mr. McCord's son, I suggest you get yourself out of that bed at once. The child has already been up for half an hour."

The mock chagrin in Deirdre's voice broke through Callie's grogginess. With an effort, she forced her eyes open. "What time is it?"

"Six A.M."

"Shouldn't a three-year-old child sleep until at least noon?" she grumped.

"Not in your lifetime, dear," her aunt chuckled.

Yawning broadly, Callie struggled to a sitting position, her eyes widening when her feet came in contact with the chilled oak floor. She shivered, coming more grudgingly awake. "It's freezing in here."

"All the more incentive for you to make your way to the kitchen," Deirdre said. "I've already started breakfast for everyone."

Callie pulled a calico dress from her trunk. "How's Riley this morning?"

"He had a peaceful night. No fever. But it'll be at least three months before he's as good as new."

"Such as that might be," Callie muttered.

"I won't have you talking against him," Deirdre said

too sharply.

"I was only kidding." Callie looked at her aunt. "Aunt Deirdre, is there something . . ."

"You'd better get out there and see to the child."

Callie frowned, then decided it was just as well that Deirdre was in no mood for any involved discussions. Callie didn't have the energy to sort through any emotional tangles at the moment anyway, not when faced with her own current bewildering assortment of feelings. "Is, uh, is Mr. McCord having breakfast with us?"

"I couldn't say. But I know he hasn't eaten. He was up feeding the stock when I went out to check on Mr. Smith. Mr. McCord was kind enough to accompany me." Deirdre's hand fluttered to her chest. "And thank heavens he did. A positively enormous man came lumbering into the bunkhouse just after I'd begun to check the dressing on Mr. Smith's injury."

"Reese?"

"You've met him?"

"Yesterday."

"He's very . . . peculiar."

"He made me a little nervous, too. But obviously Tra . . . Mr. McCord trusts him, or he wouldn't have him around Christopher."

"Why don't you just give in and call him Trace, dear? You're going to fracture your tongue if you continue to stumble over his name that way."

Callie had to laugh. "I guess you're right. But just keep in mind that my using his first name doesn't mean anything."

"Did I say it did?"

Callie finished getting dressed, then as an afterthought retrieved her latest journal from her trunk. If she found the time, she would have some interesting entries to make. The storm, the wagon accident . . . Blood rose in her cheeks as she thought of last night in front of the fireplace. Perhaps there were some incidents best left only to memory.

As she headed toward the kitchen a sound from Christopher's room distracted her. She found the boy playing contentedly on his bed. "You like that dog of yours, don't you?"

He held the raggedy mutt out to her. "Friday. That's his name."

"Somebody's been telling you about Robinson Crusoe, I'll bet," she said, coming over to sit beside him. "Do you remember my name?"

"Callie."

"Very good." She was thoroughly flattered. "Would you like some breakfast?"

"Eggs."

"Sounds good to me."

"I'm glad to see you two getting along so well," came the already painfully familiar voice from the open doorway.

She kept her attention on the child. Unbidden, the image of the man as she had seen him last night in the hallway skittered through her mind. Her hands were trembling. "Have you . . . have you had your breakfast?"

"No. But don't worry about it."

She lifted Christopher off of the bed. "It wouldn't be any trouble." How could a man look so good in scruffy blue jeans? His tousled brown-gold hair gave him a warm, seductive look every bit as inviting as a rumpled

112

bed, a scandalous thought that she immediately banished from her mind.

"I've taken care of myself for a long time. You just see to Christopher." He hadn't budged from the doorway. It almost seemed that he wanted her to press past him.

"Papa!" Christopher cried, stretching out his small arms. "Papa, carry me!"

Trace scooped the child from her. She used the opportunity to scoot past them both and hurry toward the kitchen, where she welcomed the aroma of frying bacon and baking cornbread, not because she was particularly hungry, but because the food effectively masked the musky male scent of the man who padded close behind her carrying his son.

"There you all are," Deirdre said. "Well, help yourself. I'm going to take something out to Mr. Smith."

"Everything smells wonderful," Callie said, stepping up to the stove. Quickly, she prepared a plate for Christopher, who settled eagerly at his place at the table and went to work on his eggs. She then filled another plate and handed it to Trace.

"Thank you." He sat down next to Christopher, but kept his eyes on Callie. "Aren't you going to eat?"

"Of course." She continued to bustle around the kitchen.

"When?"

She skewered a couple of slices of bacon, then added a portion of scrambled eggs and sat down opposite him at the table. "Happy now?"

"Ecstatic. Sleep well?"

"Perfectly. You?"

113

He hadn't expected that, and she derived some measure of satisfaction from seeing him momentarily disconcerted. "Just fine," he said at last.

She started eating, awkward to have him watching her. Determined, she slapped open her journal. "Excuse me, I know I'm being rude, but I need to make a few notes. I'm keeping a full record of my journey out West."

"Of course." After a moment of watching her write, he said, "That's McCord with two c's, a little one and a big one. Trace. T-r-a-c-e."

She slammed down her pen. "Why on earth would you be harboring the delusion that you are part of my entry?"

He grinned. "If I were keeping a journal, you'd be part of mine."

She rose to her feet, careful to keep her voice calm, so as not to disturb the child who was still engrossed in his meal. "If you'll excuse me . . ."

He held up a hand. "Don't be ridiculous. Sit. Besides, I'm the one who's leaving." The chair scraped back as he stood up. "You stay with Christopher." He ruffled the boy's hair. "You be good for Callie, hear?"

The boy grinned.

Trace started to leave, then hesitated, turning to look at her. Again Callie had the oddest feeling that he wanted to tell her something, but, for whatever reason, couldn't bring himself to do so. Maybe if she gave him a little nudge . . . "Is everything all right?"

"What do you mean?"

She bristled at how defensive he sounded. So much for nudging. "If you're worried about my taking care

114

of Christopher . . ."

"No. Not at all. I . . . Damn!" He reached toward her, then let the hand drop back to his side. "I'm sorry." Abruptly he turned and left.

Sorry for what? she wondered, leaning back in her chair. Perhaps she was being ridiculous, suspecting hidden motives where there were none. In any event she wasn't going to waste any more time thinking about it right now. While Christopher finished his breakfast, she pulled out a fresh sheet of paper and began to compose the rough draft of an essay on how wonderstruck she'd been yesterday alone in that clearing. Once she had the words precisely the way she wanted them, she would transfer them to her journal. When she finished sketching her thoughts, she left the paper on the table, then cleared away the dishes.

"Done," Christopher said, climbing down from his chair.

"And just in time," Callie said, catching up his hand. She was feeling much too full of energy to stay in the house this morning. "You and I are going to take some pictures."

"Pitchurs?" Christopher repeated.

A half an hour later she'd loaded one of her cameras in the rear of the buckboard, hitched up the team, and was about to head out when Deirdre called to her from the bunkhouse porch. Callie guided the buckboard over to where her aunt stood.

"And just where are you going, young lady?"

"Not far." Callie gestured toward the stand of trees just beyond the hillock that bordered the western edge of the valley. "I want to make sure the camera survived the jolt it took when the Conestoga collapsed."

"You're going out there all alone? Just you and Christopher?"

"We'll be fine."

"What will Mr. McCord think of your taking the child away from the ranch?"

Callie fingered the reins. She'd thought about that, especially after the none-too-subtle threat Trace had made yesterday morning about someone named Marlowe. But he'd given her no instructions about keeping Christopher cooped up in the house all day. If he trusted her to watch the boy, he would have to trust her judgment about his care. "I'm sure he won't mind," she said, though she wasn't sure at all.

"Well, you be careful."

"We'll be back before lunch." Callie snapped the reins, gigging the horses forward. Away from the barns, she reveled in the crisp, clean scent of the wildflowers that grew in such profusion all along the valley floor. She smiled up at the perfect blue of the cloudless sky, glad that she had decided to get away for a while. "There's a lot to be said for being a pioneer, Christopher."

"Pi-neer." He nodded solemnly. "Callie is a pi-neer."

"Callie's trying hard to be a pioneer." She grinned, and the child giggled.

An hour later she pulled into a copse of trees and began setting up the camera. "I'm going to take your picture, Christopher. Have you ever had your picture taken?"

He shook his head uncertainly.

"It'll be fun. You'll see."

She made an elaborate display of showing him how

116

to load the film plates, then played peek-a-boo with him from underneath the black linen cloth she had draped over the back of the camera.

"All right, it's picture time." He was the epitome of cooperation while she perched him atop a two-foot high boulder, then backed away.

"Be very, very still now," she cautioned gently. "Very still. That's it. I'm going to count to three very slowly. Watch my hand. Don't move."

He grinned. She took the picture, yanking out the exposed plate and sliding it into the holder at the rear of the camera. "I think your papa's going to like that. Now how about if we take one over—" She whirled at the sound of a twig snapping in the underbrush twenty yards to her left.

Nothing moved.

"I hope it wasn't anything with teeth," she mumbled, keeping her eye on the grove of trees, even as she positioned Christopher amidst a circle of wildflowers. When nothing came charging toward her, she decided whatever sort of animal it was must have been harmless. "I probably startled it, more than it startled me."

She returned her full attention to her camera, taking a second picture of the child. Christopher clapped his hands gleefully afterward. But after the third shot, he tired of the game and she let him frolic about in the tall grass.

Keeping him well in sight, she sank to her knees, then settled back to make another entry in her journal. It was then the feeling came over her. Nothing definite, but real nonetheless. She was being watched.

She again looked toward the brush where she'd

heard the twig snap. Only the branches of the towering pines shifted in the slight breeze. "You're being foolish, Callandra," she chided herself. "This is hardly any way for an adventurous pioneer to behave."

Still the feeling persisted, until at last she gave into it, telling herself she did so for Christopher's sake. There was no sense taking chances as long as the child was with her. Slapping the journal shut, she gathered up the child, who had fallen blissfully asleep beside her. She settled him atop the blankets in the back of the wagon. Again and again her gaze was drawn to the tangled underbrush. Whatever the presence was, it seemed not merely curious, but menacing.

Allowing her agitation to get the better of her, she scrambled onto the wagon seat and slapped the horses into a quick gallop. It was only when she'd left the clearing well behind that she began to relax. Drawing back on the reins, she drew in a long, steadying breath. "That was stupid. You're probably running away from a raccoon, not to mention the fact that your driving is likely more dangerous than anything that was in that brush."

By the time she reached the ranchyard, the mountain air had soothed her jangled nerves enough so that she'd all but forgotten the clearing incident. She unhitched the horses, letting Christopher sleep, then carried him toward the house. Crossing the yard, she looked back toward the sound of approaching hoofbeats. As she reached the front door, the black buggy careened to a halt inches from the porch. The sleek lathered chestnut pulling it snorted, pawing the earth, peering back at its driver as if to question which of them should more sensibly hold the reins.

A thin, bespectacled man whose dark frock suit overwhelmed his scrawny frame hopped from the carriage and scurried up the steps. He all but barreled into Callie, sidestepping at the last instant to keep from catapulting her through the open door.

He then spared himself a headlong tumble only by catching himself against the doorframe. With a less than dignified snort, he straightened, taking a step back. Grumbling, he whipped off his glasses, rubbing furiously at them with the silk kerchief he yanked from his vest pocket. "And who are you, pray tell?" he demanded, his gaze darting between her and the sleeping child.

"I might ask you the same, sir."

The man's eyebrows quirked upward. "Lyle Morton," he announced, settling his spectacles back into place on his hawkish nose. "Trace McCord's attorney."

"Callie Callaghan. I'm . . ."

A horse thundered into the yard. Trace leaped from the back of the gray stallion, hurrying toward them with long, measured strides. She didn't miss the apprehensive look in his brown eyes, though his voice was carefully neutral. "I wasn't expecting you until next week, Lyle."

The men shook hands. "I think we'd better talk privately, Trace."

Callie followed them into the house, but took the hint, excusing herself. "I was just going to put Christopher down for a nap. We've both had a lot of fresh air this morning."

The men ignored her, disappearing at once into the study. Before the door was fully closed Morton's voice was already raised. "I stayed at the Bar W last night.

119

They had some unexpected guests. A Mr. and Mrs. Yates."

"So?"

"So the woman said you fired her. Your third housekeeper since Jenny died."

"Like I said—so?"

Callie imagined the epithet that followed was not typical of the lawyer's every day speech. As she readied Christopher for bed, she recalled the Bar W, a small cattle ranch run by a large, friendly family named Watson, some thirty miles to the south. She, Deirdre, and Riley had spent the night there three days before their wagon broke down. As far as she knew, Shadow's Way and the Bar W were the only homesteads between Yellowstone and Rock Springs. Yet the Watsons had boasted of hosting dozens of visitors over the years since Yellowstone had been established.

Trace's less than amiable greeting the other morning might have explained why Shadow's Way had not been similarly approached by travelers, but she decided to be generous and give the man the benefit of the doubt. The Bar W was visible for miles, setting on an open plain. To find Shadow's Way one had to be looking hard for it, or do as she had done, discover it by accident.

Accident.

Or fate.

She had not felt drawn to the Bar W.

She had never felt so drawn to any place in her life as she did to Shadow's Way.

She expelled a weary sigh. Such musings only exacerbated her unease. As Christopher snuggled tiredly into bed, Callie tried and failed not to hear parts of the shouted conversation taking place in the next room.

"The Yates woman was working for the Marlowes," Trace said. He was angry. And something else. It took Callie a moment to sort through what seemed so out of place in his voice. And then it came to her. Fear.

What on earth would Trace McCord be afraid of?

"You can't know that, Trace," Morton was saying. "Everyone in the world is not working for the Marlowes."

Trace's voice lowered slightly, though it sounded now as if he were speaking through clenched teeth. "Chris had taken a tumble off of his bed. I heard him crying when I came in. Only then did Mrs. Yates get up from the desk in the front room. I saw her shove something under the blotter. After I checked on Chris I took a look. It was a letter—addressed to the Marlowes."

"I don't much give a damn if Mrs. Yates turns out to be Edna Marlowe's mother. Get this through that hard head of yours. You cannot be going off half-cocked right now." Morton sounded more frustrated than angry. "If you're to stay in Judge Lancaster's good graces it's imperative that you be the model of exemplary behavior. He's the only one whose opinion counts."

Callie rose to leave Christopher's room. This was none of her business. But then the subject of their conversation shifted. She stilled.

"And where, may I ask, did this Callie Callaghan come from? Are you out of your mind having an unmarried woman staying here? Even Lancaster will nail your hide to the barn door." There was a slight

121

pause, then an equally agitated, "Wait a minute, you're not thinking what I think you're thinking about this young woman, are you?"

She couldn't make out Trace's quiet reply.

"It becomes my business if it affects your case," the lawyer exploded. "Dammit, Trace, I know what that boy means to you."

The study door slammed open, Trace stomping out into the front room. "If you know what he means to me, then you'll know why . . ."

Callie stepped out of Christopher's room. The two men exchanged looks, Trace shrugging, then stalking off to stare out the window.

"It was a pleasure to meet you, Miss Callaghan," Morton said, doing a commendable job of hiding his exasperation. His sidelong glare at Trace was not nearly so subtle.

"Likewise," Callie managed. She didn't mistake the strange tension that crackled in the air between the two men.

When it became obvious Trace had nothing more to say, Morton sighed and headed out the door.

"Allow me to see you out," Callie said too quickly, nearly tripping over the man as she followed after him. Nothing was going to keep her in that room alone with Trace. Morton merely bid her a cordial good-day, then climbed into his carriage and drove off.

She looked back at the house. Trace was no longer visible through the window. She guessed he'd gone in to see Christopher. Now she had to resist the urge to go inside and confront him. Her suspicion that he was somehow involving her in whatever problem he faced had only been confirmed by his cryptic conversation with Morton. She grimaced. It was useless to speculate. Besides, thinking about confronting Trace and actually doing it were two entirely different matters.

Instead she headed toward the bunkhouse. Maybe a talk with Deirdre would help.

When she walked into the small structure, Riley was half sitting, half reclining on a lower bunk, his leg propped up by several pillows. Deirdre quickly snapped shut the book she'd been reading and lay it aside. "Callie, I hadn't heard the wagon . . ."

"I got back a little while ago." She crossed to Riley's bedside, her gaze surreptitiously sliding over to the small leatherbound book. She smiled to herself. *Sonnets by Shakespeare.* "Christopher's sleeping. Trace is with him."

"I'm real sorry about getting myself stove up like this," Riley said. "I know you had your heart set on seein' Yellowstone."

"I'll get there." She glanced about the room. "Reese is gone again?"

"Went back out on the range," Riley said. "Something about settin' bear traps. He sure is an odd one. I wonder why McCord keeps him on."

"Maybe he feels sorry for him."

"Maybe." It was obvious he was unconvinced. "If you ask me, there's somethin' odd about a lot of things around here."

"Why would you say that?" Callie sat at the foot of the bed, being careful not to disturb the scout's injured leg. "Do you know something, you're not telling me?"

"Don't *know* it. *Feel* it."

So Riley, too, sensed something out of sync on Shadow's Way. Oddly, the thought gave her no comfort, instead adding to her mounting sense of foreboding. To divert her thoughts, she said, "Aunt Deirdre told me you knew Trace's father."

"Not real good. Rode north with him once. Real hard case. Got the feeling he wouldn't have forgive his own mother if she crossed him."

"Do you think Trace ever . . ."

The door swung open without a knock. Trace. Callie glanced guiltily at Riley, then back at Trace, but apparently the man had overheard nothing. "I'm riding out to check the herd," he told her. "Chris is still asleep."

"I'll go in."

He nodded, then rode out without another word.

It was long past dusk when Trace returned. Deirdre was already asleep in the guest room. Christopher, too, was down for the night. Callie sat in front of the fire, reading through her journal.

Trace strode in, slapping his gloves and hat down on the desk. He started down the darkened hallway, then turned abruptly, only just noticing her.

"Forget I was in the house again?" she asked softly, setting her journal to one side.

"I guess I thought you'd be asleep."

"Thought or hoped?"

He'd carried in his rifle from the scabbard on his saddle and now he returned it to the gun rack on the wall. "What's that supposed to mean?"

"You tell me." She had been doing quite a bit of thinking tonight. It was time some things were out in the open.

He raked a hand through his hair. "It's late. I'm tired. I guess I'll just turn in." He didn't move.

She waited.

A light burned in the depths of his brown eyes. She could almost feel him take a step toward her, though he remained rigidly still across the room. A minute passed, then another, the only sound in the room the sharp snap of burning wood in the fireplace. Then, ever so slightly, he straightened, striding over to the edge of the settee. "The air's cooler outside," he suggested quietly.

The temperature had nothing to do with his veiled invitation, and they both knew it. It was more than curiosity that goaded her as she rose to follow him outside into the late-evening stillness. She wanted to be with him, needed it, for reasons she had not yet dared examine.

On the porch he seated himself on the bench swing, the chains that secured it to the roof creaking softly. He touched the empty space beside him, looking at her. When she stayed by the door, he added, "Please?"

She sank down beside him, determined that his nearness would not muddle her thoughts. He flexed his legs slightly, setting the swing into a gentle, rocking rhythm. The soothing motion relaxed her. Her thigh brushed against his tautly muscled one. She stiffened abruptly, unintentionally jerking the swing to a stop.

"I don't bite," he growled softly.

"I had a cramp in my leg!"

"Of course," he demurred. "Can we start again?"

"Start what?"

"Swinging."

"Maybe I should work on my journal."

"You wanted me to tell you . . ."

Trembling, she leaned back into the swing. She had

125

asked for this.

"It's just that I don't know where to start."

She waited, not saying anything more. Whatever it was, he would have to tell it in his own way.

"I told you Christopher isn't my son . . . my blood son," he said, his voice now flat, expressionless. A defense against revealing too much of himself? "Jenny—his mother—died four months ago. She was always frail, sickly. I think her being in Wyoming is the only thing that kept her alive as long as . . ." He stopped, shifting in the seat, shifting the direction of his thoughts. "I'm in the process of legally adopting Christopher."

"But that's wonderful. He adores you . . ."

"There's a problem," he said, not looking at her. A muscle in his jaw flexed. He muttered an epithet, then apologized for doing so. Setting his feet, he brought the swing to a halt. "This is crazy. I can't . . ."

"Trace, please, I know there's something wrong. Is there some way you could lose Christopher?"

He twisted toward her, his face, his mouth, just inches from her own.

"I can't lose him, Callie. I can't."

"Then you won't."

"But you don't understand. There's no time. I need . . ."

"Need what? Tell me. Maybe I could help. I have . . . resources."

His eyes searched hers. "No. If you knew the truth, all of it, you'd be gone, just like . . ." He slapped a hand against his knee. "Never mind. Go back inside. Go to bed."

Her hand slid over his. "No."

126

He twined his fingers with hers, leaning toward her. With a low groan his mouth claimed hers. She was astonished at the heat that fired her blood. His kisses were fierce, hungry, almost desperate, as Callie gave herself up to the warmth of his embrace.

She knew nothing of this man, only that some primitive part of her had been jolted to the core ever since she first set eyes on him.

The fine stubble of a day's growth of beard brushed against her cheek as he nuzzled her ear, her neck.

"This shouldn't be happening," he whispered hoarsely, his breath warm and wet against her throat. "God knows, it's not what I wanted to happen. If I had a choice . . ."

Even so, his mouth moved over hers once again. This time his tongue traced the outline of her lips until she moaned involuntarily from the exquisite pleasure of it. Her lips parted to welcome his thrusting tongue into her mouth. Her arms circled his neck of their own accord.

When her own tongue mated with his, she felt the convulsive shudder that swept through him. And just that abruptly, he pulled away. With suppressed violence he bolted from the swing to stand on the edge of the porch, his breathing harsh, erratic.

She could feel the wild beating of his heart because its rhythm matched her own. He didn't turn, didn't look at her as he spoke, the sentences fragmented, their meaning unclear.

"If there was any other way . . . If I thought you would understand . . . It wasn't supposed to be like this."

She stood, coming up behind him, not touching him,

though she longed to touch him. As before, his torment was real, genuine, but this time she detected no undercurrent of deceit. For what she suspected was a heartbreakingly rare moment, the path to the deepest, most vulnerable part of him lay unguarded, exposed. And it was up to her to find a way to reach it.

Chapter Eight

"Take a walk with me?" Trace asked, holding out his hand. Her heart hammering against her ribs, Callie linked her hand to his, curving her fingers into the calloused warmth of his palm. She allowed him to lead her from the porch steps, out past nickering horses in the corrals, out into the lush grasses that carpeted the valley floor. They'd walked nearly half a mile before he released her.

"It's so beautiful here," she sighed, turning a slow pirouette in the moonlight.

"Damned beautiful." He tugged his gaze away from her, angry at himself for allowing her to distract him. There was no room in this for anything but cold hard reality. Yet just being near her muddled his thoughts, clouded his motives just enough . . . Hunkering down, he tugged a blade of grass loose and threaded it through his fingers. "Beautiful as it is, I used to run away from this place a lot, when I was a boy."

"Run away?"

"Maybe escape is a better word. My father and I

didn't see eye to eye."

She knelt in the grass beside him, smiling thoughtfully.

"You find that amusing?"

"Not the way you think. It just seems we have something in common. My father has spent his life trying to dictate mine. I wish I would have had mountains like yours to escape into."

He regarded her silently for a long minute. Callie tried hard to gauge what might be in his mind at that moment, but he was on guard again, aware of how keenly she studied him.

"Have you been to Yellowstone often?" she asked when she could bear the quiet no longer.

"A dozen times. Maybe more. I'm afraid your pictures won't be able to do it justice." He paused, then added, "But maybe your words can."

She straightened, startled. "How can you know that?"

"I saw the essay you left on the desk earlier. I hope you don't mind. It didn't look personal." He looked away, then back again. "I read it." His eyes held hers. "You're a fine writer, Callie."

Her throat tightened. If he was playing a game, setting her up for something, he most certainly knew the right strings to pull. "Thank you."

"You're welcome." His voice was low, husky, with a seductive warmth that sent tiny brush fires sparking along her flesh.

"What do you want from me, Trace?" she asked, her own voice trembling. "What is it you're trying so hard to tell me . . . or not to tell me?"

He twirled a finger around another blade of grass.

"Your aunt said you were out taking pictures with Christopher today."

"That's not an answer."

"I'd appreciate it if you wouldn't take him away from the house again without checking with me first."

"Trace . . ."

"I know, I know . . ." he sighed. "But, damn, you don't know how hard this is for me."

"How hard *what* is?"

He stood up, stalking off several paces. "I love that boy, Callie. I love him like I wish my fa—" He stopped, drawing in a long breath.

Shy, hesitant, she stepped up behind him. "I realize we haven't known each other very long, but . . ."

"Maybe you should go back to the house, Callie. Now." His voice was a plea, as if he feared what would happen if she stayed.

"You can tell me, Trace. Whatever it is, you can tell me. If there's a problem, maybe a fresh eye . . ."

"You're a very perceptive woman."

She twisted her hands together. "You make it sound like you wish I weren't."

"It would be a lot easier, believe me."

She didn't say anything. He was going to have to make up his own mind.

"What do you suppose your aunt would think about your being out here alone with me?"

Callie gave him a wry smile, even as she continued to wonder where this was all leading. "Let's be glad she's asleep."

"I don't want to make trouble between you."

"Trace . . ."

"I love my son. I love him, Callie. I can't . . ."

"Can't what?"

He looked at her, his eyes for an instant twin mirrors to his soul. She was almost undone by the torment she saw reflected there.

"He's my son as surely as if he were of my own body. No one is going to take him away from me."

Callie blushed hotly. She could imagine that body in the throes of passion. "Take him? These Marlowes you spoke of? You're afraid they're going to steal him away?"

He raked a hand through his thick, sand-colored hair, knowing he was making this worse for both of them. But to put it in words, to tell her . . . It was one thing to rehearse, to imagine, but to actually go through with it. What if she refused?

"My sister-in-law's will had a certain condition attached to it. A condition that on the surface might seem reasonable . . ." He paused, glancing in her direction, his eyes pained. "She and Seth seemed to take turns being my protector, whether I needed one or not. Seth with an iron hand, Jenny with butterfly softness." He shook himself. "If the condition of the will isn't met, Christopher's custody reverts to Jenny's relatives—an aunt and uncle, Edna and Edgar Marlowe."

Callie gasped. It wasn't fair that Trace should lose the boy. They had established a relationship that would harm them both if it were severed. Chris had already lost his parents.

"The Marlowes don't give a damn about him."

"Then why would Jenny allow them any chance at her son?" she pressed, not sure why she'd opted for the role of devil's advocate, except that she wanted the whole truth, not just Trace's version of it.

"Jenny had a blind spot where the Marlowes are concerned. They were responsible for her after her parents died."

Callie suspected there was more to it than Trace let on, but she didn't feel comfortable enough to probe further. She had to let him do the talking. Too, she didn't think Trace made a very objective judge about whether or not the Marlowes could love Christopher as much as he did, but she admitted she was already biased in Trace's favor.

"What does all of this have to do with me?" Her voice was barely above a whisper.

He didn't answer. His whole body was tense. Even in the dimness of the cloud-shrouded moon, she could see the rippling muscles tighten beneath the flesh of his forearms. Talking to her like this was taking a toll on his pride, that much she knew. He was holding himself so still, she felt if she touched him he would explode.

His hands balled into fists at his sides. But the anger in his body was not reflected in his eyes. There was a sadness there, a despair that made her want to pull him close and comfort him. She forced herself to remain where she stood, not knowing how he would react to any show of sympathy.

"Callie," he started, then stopped. "Damn, this is impossible."

She longed to help him, but didn't know how. It had something to do with Christopher's custody, but what could she do to help with that? He wanted to say more, but apparently, as earlier on the porch, he could not bring himself to do so. Finally, timidly, Callie sought to bridge the gap between them. "This condition in the will you spoke of, the one Christopher's custody seems to hinge on . . . just what is it?"

His eyes bored into hers, a strange light in their brown depths. There was a fierce pride in that gaze, but there was also an inescapable trace of fear—fear of losing Christopher. And she suddenly knew he would do anything to keep him. Her heart pounded as she awaited Trace's reply.

"I get custody of Christopher," he said, biting out the words one at a time, "permanent custody, only if . . . I have a wife."

Callie's throat went dry. He couldn't possibly . . .

"I had six months to find a wife." The words poured out of him. "If after that time there was no wife, Chris's custody would be turned over to Jenny's guardians. Four of those six months are gone." He continued relentlessly. "Since there seems little hope that I'm going to meet someone and fall madly and passionately in love with her in such a short amount of time, you can imagine how . . . concerned I'm becoming."

She was certain he had substituted the word concerned for scared.

"In any event, I'm not the marrying kind. I tried it once, it didn't work out."

Callie's eyes widened at this new bit of information. "You're divorced?"

He ignored the question. "So now I need a wife."

"Why are you telling *me* all this?"

"I should think that would be obvious, Callie," he said. "We can be mutually helpful to each other. I can solve your problem. You can solve mine."

"My problem?" she quavered.

"You need a guide."

"My God," she gasped, "I can find a guide anywhere."

"None that know Yellowstone as well as I do. And none," he added meaningfully, "who would do it for nothing, as I would."

She stared at the ground.

"I would also arrange for a special room for your photographic equipment, your writing . . ."

"And just what is all of this generosity going to cost me?" she asked softly, already knowing the answer, yet not willing to believe it.

"I need a wife," he said simply. "I need a wife within forty-six days."

"And you expect me . . ."

"To be my wife."

Callie couldn't breathe for a full minute. He had actually put it into words. This was what had been in his mind from nearly the first moment. "I need a guide for two weeks, Mr. McCord. A wife is a much more long-term arrangement. I scarcely see where the trade would be equitable."

"I need a wife only for a short time. After Christopher's adoption is final, nothing, not even divorce, could take him away from me."

Callie was shaking. It was all she could do to remain on her feet. His wife? Was that what the kiss had been about? She recoiled inwardly. Had he been testing the goods?

"Certainly you know some woman of whom you are fond," she heard herself stammering. "Someone who would be more suited to this . . . this arrangement."

He shifted, not looking at her. "I know of more than one woman who would like to marry me," he said

135

without expression. "I even considered one or two. But a divorce from any of them would be a messy affair. They might fight it once they got their legal hooks in me."

Of all the conceited . . . she thought wildly. "You could be certain that I would not fight it, Mr. McCord." Then she considered the import of what she had said. She hadn't meant . . .

"Then you'll marry me," he asked, watching her hopefully. She knew from where the hope stemmed. His love for Christopher was unquestioned. He wanted the boy, even to the point of fulfilling an impossible wish in his sister-in-law's will.

"I . . . I'd have to think about this, Mr. McCord," she whispered, reverting to addressing him formally because calling him by his first name suddenly seemed much too intimate.

"My name is Trace."

His nearness was once again exerting a strange power on her senses. She couldn't seem to think rationally. She no longer denied the physical attraction she had felt for him from the first moment. And she had to admit she felt a great deal of sympathy for him, too. Jenny had no right to make such a condition. A man should marry for love. In a way, she thought it would be for love—the love of his little boy.

Perhaps she could consider it. He'd agreed to be her guide for nothing. She was growing short of money. And she certainly couldn't wire her father for more. Then she realized what she was doing. Marriage for money? The idea was abhorrent.

"I know this is all a shock to you," he said. "I won't press you on it anymore tonight. But I need an answer as soon as possible. If you won't do it, I'll have to find someone else who will."

Trace cupped her chin with his bronzed hand, caressing the line of her jaw with his work-roughened thumb. "I can't lose him, Callie, I can't."

"I know."

He headed toward the house. He never once looked back. Callie never once took her eyes off him. Her thoughts tumbled one over the other. Marriage to a man she scarcely knew. Marriage to save his child. Why did she know that no matter what he risked—she would risk more. That try as she might to deny it, the price she could pay would be her heart.

Chapter Nine

For long minutes Callie stayed behind in the meadow, staring after Trace, scarcely able to comprehend what he had just asked of her. Marriage! It was impossible! An act of desperation by a desperate man. Trace wanted Christopher above anything else. He would do anything to keep him. Even marry a woman he didn't love. But could she be party to such a plan? Marriage was not a thing to be taken lightly.

If she gave no care to whom she was married she could have gone through with her father's dictum that she marry Nicolas.

"What am I going to do?" If she said no, Trace could lose Christopher. "But that's not my responsibility," she reasoned. Wouldn't it be better for him to choose a woman he knew?

She grimaced, recalling his words. *A divorce from any of them would be a messy affair.* Did he really have such a low opinion of his women friends? Her gaze swept the majestic landscape. Or was it more likely in this beautiful but isolated land that a man had few if any choices for selecting a mate?

"Do you really know so many women who would like to marry you, Trace McCord?" she murmured. "Or is that you're too full of your male pride to tell me you've already been turned down by the one or two available females in the Wyoming territory?" The last brought a smile to her lips, which just as quickly vanished. What mattered wasn't whether Trace had women beating a path to his door, what mattered was how very much he wanted to keep Christopher. And whether or not she was willing to pay the price to help him.

She hugged her arms tight against her, considering, then dismissing, going in and waking Deirdre. She needed someone to talk to. But morning would be soon enough. Paying no particular attention to where she was going, she soon found herself near the bunkhouse. She knew Reese wasn't around, so on an impulse she opened the door and went inside.

Riley lay propped against two pillows on the single bunk against the far wall. The kerosene lantern on his bedside table cast a dim light, flickering shadows dancing across the spartan furnishings of the room. The scout looked up from the book he was reading, sliding it almost guiltily beneath him.

"What in the world are you doing out this time of night, Miss Callie?"

"Is your leg bothering you?"

"Believe I asked the first question."

She scraped a straight-back chair across the pine floor and sat down beside the bed. "Couldn't sleep," she shrugged.

"Uh huh."

She stood up. "I'm sorry. I didn't mean to disturb you."

"Sometimes talkin' helps."

"Talk about what?" She fidgeted, starting to back away. Why had she come in here? She and the scout had been at odds from the first. And yet . . . she did trust him. There was an unassuming honesty about him, and it was more than evident that Deirdre trusted him, liked him even. She sighed. She did so need someone to be calm and logical about all this. And for once, she didn't think she would find that with her aunt.

Drawing in a deep breath she sat back down again. There seemed no reason to mince words. Very bluntly she said, "Trace McCord just asked me to marry him."

She waited for the scout's shocked reaction. Instead the scraggly-bearded man hardly raised an eyebrow. "Love can do peculiar things to a man's mind."

"I am not talking about love, for heaven's sake!" she snapped. Quickly she told him what McCord had told her. "How can I even mention such an outrageous proposal to Aunt Deirdre?"

Riley chuckled. "That woman has more to her than you or I ever imagined, Miss Callie."

"This isn't funny."

"Didn't say it was. I knew the boy had somethin' in his craw, but I couldn't 'uv guessed it was anything like this."

"What do you think I should do?"

His lips curved amidst the whiskers that framed his mouth. "You don't much care what I think, Miss Callie. What you're doin' is usin' me to talk to yourself

140

about all this. Then you'll do what you always do—you'll make up your own mind."

"Why would he ask *me?* Why not some woman he already knows?"

"Maybe he only knows married women. The West ain't exactly crawlin' with single ladies. 'Specially none too many as purty as you."

Callie blushed. "Mr. McCord doesn't give a care what I look like."

"Ain't just your looks, Miss Callie. It's in your eyes." The scout's own eyes softened, grew warm. "Like with your aunt. There's a spirit in the both of ya that shines out, makes a man look twice even when you're lookin' like a drowned pup."

Any other time Callie would never have diverted the subject from the scout's openly admiring comments about her aunt. But she was too nervous about her own situation. "What he thinks of my looks hardly explains why he would choose to marry someone he only just met."

Riley chewed thoughtfully on his lower lip. "Maybe there's some other reason he'd be wantin' a stranger."

"Something he's not telling me?"

He gave her a half shrug. "Couldn't say."

"But it's what you think."

"Ain't really fair of me to think nothin', not without talkin' to McCord, gettin' his side of it."

Callie planted her hands on her hips. "Don't you dare tell him I said anything to you!"

He grinned. "I coulda guessed that, Miss Callie. What I'm sayin' is that I still think there's somethin' eatin' at 'im. Maybe it's just that sometimes the acorn doesn't fall too far from the tree."

"Now what in heaven's name is that supposed to mean?"

"If Trace McCord is like his pa . . ."

Callie shook her head. "I doubt that. They didn't get along too well."

"Which don't mean nothin'. In fact, it could mean he was so much like his pa, his pa couldn't stand 'im for just that reason alone."

"What exactly do you know about his father?"

Riley shifted uncomfortably. "It ain't my place to speak ill of the dead."

"Riley, please, any tiny piece of information can help. I have to know what I might be getting myself into . . ."

The scout was silent for a long minute, then slowly he nodded. "All right, I'll tell ya what I know. But you ain't gonna like it."

"Just tell me."

"It was when me and Jeb McCord were trailin' horses together back in '52. One night the herd was gettin' spooked. Jeb went to check on the noise and found two young Cheyenne bucks tryin' to cut a couple ponies for themselves. Well, nobody took anything that belonged to Jeb McCord. He was plum loco mad, yellin' how he was gonna make an example of 'em, so's none of their tribe would get the same idea."

Though Callie was certain she didn't want to know, she asked anyway, "What did he do to those men?"

Riley grimaced, the memory obviously as painful now as it was when it happened. "He hanged 'em."

Callie knew her face must be gray. "Just like that? For trying to steal horses?"

"It's a hangin' offense out here, but . . ."

"But they didn't succeed!" Callie rose to her feet. "And even if they had you're talking about two horses from an entire herd! Why didn't you stop him?"

Riley winced, but his gaze remained steady. "I tried to. He shot me."

"My God," Callie gasped, "what kind of a monster was he?"

"The kind that don't take no truck with anyone about anything. He had his own code. After he shot me and hanged them Indian boys, he stayed put, nursed me till I was on my feet again, even though it cost him a week's travelin' time."

"Does Trace know any of this?"

He shrugged. "Maybe. Maybe not. I could just about hear Jeb McCord drummin' his sense o' justice into his sons' heads, though. So it wouldn't surprise me if Trace knew."

"What am I going to do? He loves Christopher. It would break his heart to lose him." She shook her head. "I'm sorry. I'm just rattling on and on. I know it was hard for you to tell me about Jeb. I appreciate it."

"I just hoped it helped ya a little."

"I think it did." She looked at her hands. "Please, don't say anything . . ."

"I won't tell Miss Deirdre. But I think you better."

She nodded. "I will. Thanks, Riley." She walked outside. Her pulses still pounded. She wasn't in the least tired, though it had to be well past midnight. She wondered briefly if Trace had gone to bed. Then she spied him by the corral. Ignoring her better judgment, she crossed over to him.

"Nice night," he said companionably, as though their recent conversation had not taken place.

"Yes, it is."

A sleek chestnut mare trotted over, shoving her head over the top railing. The animal snorted happily, as Callie stroked her velvety muzzle.

"Kachina," Trace told her, by way of introduction.

"What a wonderful name! What does it mean?"

"You saw the Indian figures above the fireplace in the house?"

Callie nodded, remembering the tiny, gaily costumed dolls.

"Kachina dolls," he explained. "Hopi Indian religious symbols. Each kachina has a specific personality, like Tawa, the spirit of the sun, Hohle, the gift-bringer, and Hehea, the woman-chaser."

"Have you been praying to Hehea lately?" she drawled, then caught herself, abashed. How could she have said such a thing?

But he only laughed, and she was warmed by the sound of it.

"She is beautiful," Callie said, patting the mare's neck.

"Good breeding stock."

She felt as if she'd been kicked in the stomach. She had sarcastically applied the same term to herself on her wedding day.

His eyes narrowed. "What's wrong?"

"It's nothing." Then she wondered if she owed him any explanations about Nicolas. She decided it would be all right to simply cut to the particulars. "I, uh, I was engaged once. It didn't work out."

"Were you in love with him?"

Was she imagining it, or was there a new, sharper edge to his voice? "No, I didn't love him." Now she was being absurd. He seemed to visibly relax. But why should he care if she had been in love or not? Then she realized that, in fact, her negative response likely gave him the impression that she was the sort of woman who agreed to marry a man for reasons other than love. Quickly, she added, "It was because I didn't love him that I decided I couldn't marry him."

"Then why did you say yes, when he asked you in the first place?"

"It's a long story."

"Your father?"

She chuckled. "You just shortened the story considerably."

He was so close. In the dim light she could sense more than see the taut muscles of his arms, tense now as though he were deciding something.

She realized with a sudden rush of astonishment that she wanted him to kiss her again. She was grateful for the shadows lest he read the shameless thought in her eyes. Surely she was only playing out some sort of fantasy because of Trace's marriage proposal. Like some besotted fool, she wanted an element of romance, something she'd never wanted, never even considered with Nicolas. And—her mind taunted her—she'd known nothing of Trace's marriage proposal when she'd responded so wantonly to him earlier.

"You're really taken me by surprise with all this," she said shakily. "I . . ."

His arms curved around her. She felt herself being crushed against his hard chest. His breath fanned the heat in her blood as he kissed a trail along her face to find her waiting lips. He kissed her hungrily, like a starving man suddenly set before a banquet. The kiss was alternately tender and savage, as he gauged her response against his own.

"You taste like honey," he whispered hoarsely. "So sweet. God, so sweet."

Callie melted against him, her legs no longer willing to support her. A tiny gasp escaped her as his tongue gently teased her lips apart, then began a searing exploration of the inside of her mouth. She heard his low groan, her arms involuntarily encircling his neck, holding him closer, forcing him to maintain the intimate contact. Not that he seemed in any hurry to end it.

Her pulse thundered in her ears, her knees quivering. With a boldness she didn't know she possessed, she brought her own hands up to tease the open vee of his shirt. She opened the buttons and let her fingers glide across the soft mat of hair. He sucked in his breath as she traced the outline of his nipples, his throaty growl of pleasure adding to the fire that consumed her, as surely as his kiss.

In an instinctive, primal gesture he thrust his hips toward her, nestling himself against her thigh. The rigid flesh of his sex left no doubt as to the extent of his arousal. Rather than jerk away in shock, Callie found the sensation burningly erotic. She rubbed her thigh against the hardness, her female body responding to the mating instincts of the male.

A mindless, wordless sound escaped his lips, his hand slipping urgently to cup her breast. Callie arched upward deliberately to enhance the wondrous magic of his touch. Just when she thought she could bear the separation of her flesh from his no longer, he tugged open the buttons of her dress, pulled free the ribbon binding her chemise. She cried out, as her breast spilled into his eager hand. She wanted nothing more than to give herself up to the raging whirlpool of her emotions, but some tiny fragment of reason held her back.

This would be no love match. If she agreed, it would be a union for the sake of legal necessity. She couldn't, wouldn't let herself be used to quench a transitory lust—not even her own.

"Please, Trace," she murmured brokenly. "Don't . . ."

He released her at once, setting her at arm's length. "I'm sorry," he muttered. "I had no intention of doing that." He twisted away, staring out into the corral. "I hope you won't hold it against me while you're considering our bargain."

His voice was thick with the passion he still felt. Callie was thankful for the darkness as she straightened her clothing. He wouldn't be able to see the scarlet blush she felt in her cheeks. Never had she wanted anything so much as this—to let him hold her, kiss her, touch her. She experienced an unfamiliar ache of frustration and wondered if he felt the same. She struggled to keep the emotion out of her voice. "Believe me, Trace, I had no intention of it happening, either. If you'll excuse me, I think I'd better go inside."

She left before he could voice any protest. Not that she believed he would. He was probably wishing fervently that she had not come near him again tonight. His only goal was legally adopting Christopher, and he had proposed a business arrangement with her to achieve that goal. He didn't want complications any more than she did. She had her book to write, the treasure to find . . .

Inside the house, Callie collapsed onto the settee, her

mind reeling with the day's events. Married? She still couldn't assimilate it. *If you don't do it, I'll find someone who will.* She imagined Trace married to someone else and felt a shaft of jealousy rip through her. Jealousy? *But that's insane! I don't even know the man.* And even if she did marry him—was she truly considering it?—it wouldn't be for very long. In short order he would have his son, and she would again be on her way to Yellowstone.

Unwillingly, she remembered the mastery of his touch, the ease with which he could make her forsake the accepted behavior of a lifetime. If he meant this to be a strictly practical arrangement for them both why did he press what had to be for him a wholly unwelcome physical attraction between them? She stiffened, his all too probable motive rocking her. Maybe it wasn't all that unwelcome. Perhaps he even viewed it as a kind of tawdry bonus for her cooperation.

A hot flush of anger swept through her. She couldn't imagine sleeping with a man to protect a marriage that was all but a mockery. When she gave herself to a man, she wanted it to be for love.

That Trace desired her was obivous. He was a man alone, as Deirdre had already pointedly remarked. Why wouldn't he take advantage of it? No! It would be enough if she gave him a chance to gain permanent custody of Christopher. She could allow no more than that.

Feeling more bewildered than ever, she headed toward the guest room. Quickly she readied herself for bed, making no real attempt to be quiet as she did so. But Deirdre slept on. Whether consciously or unconsciously, Callie slammed her toe into one of the bed's brass posts, cursing loudly. This time Deirdre woke up.

"Where have you been?" her aunt asked. "It's so late."

"Out for a walk. I couldn't sleep." With a rueful grimace in the darkness, she added the appropriately polite lie, "I'm sorry I woke you."

"Nonsense." Deirdre started to sit up.

"No, really, go back to sleep." *Stop it, Callandra,* she muttered inwardly, *or she* will *go back to sleep.*

"But if there's something troubling you . . ."

Callie sank onto the edge of the bed. "Nothing in particular," she said, her voice suddenly trembling. "Except that . . . Trace McCord asked me to marry him."

Deirdre sat bolt upright, turning up the kerosene lantern beside the bed. "I beg your pardon?"

Haltingly, Callie told her aunt the story, only now fully realizing how emotionally draining the events of the evening had been.

"I take it from how upset you are that you haven't turned him down," Deirdre said. "That you're actually considering this madness?"

"I'm not sure any more what I'm thinking."

Deirdre climbed out of bed, crossing the room to pour herself a glass of water from the pitcher on the nightstand. "I knew he was up to something, but this!" She took a sip of the water. "I thought he was just a man too long alone, one you should look out for, but I never imagined." She retraced her steps, sitting next to Callie on the bed. "You said he told you he's been married before. Is he divorced?"

149

"He didn't say exactly. But obviously he's no longer married or else he wouldn't need another woman to fulfill the codicil."

"Callie, this might be a sham, but as a Catholic, for you to even think about marrying a divorced man . . . no matter what the reason . . ."

"I know." She would never have considered it herself once. Odd how the heart could compromise the principles of a lifetime. The heart? That brought her up short, until she reasoned that, of course, her heart would be involved. After all, she felt a great deal of sympathy for the man. He loved his son.

"And just how much of a *marriage* is this man going to be expecting?"

"I didn't ask," Callie hedged. "I assume we'll go on as now, since the marriage most certainly would be for appearance only. I mean we're certainly not in love with each other for heaven's sake. This is a legal convenience so that he can keep Christopher."

"And then your life will go on as though it never happened?"

Marriage to Trace McCord and then go on as though it never happened? It was more likely the moon would fall out of the sky. Still, she found herself considering it over and over.

"Callie, what aren't you telling me in all this?"

"What do you mean?"

"I mean, how do you *feel* about Trace McCord?"

"I barely know the man," she sputtered defensively.

Deirdre only shook her head. "If you didn't like the man at all, and didn't think he deserved the boy, you would have turned him down as soon as the words were out of his mouth. If you found the man to be a decent

150

fellow and thought he deserved Christopher, you would have told him 'Sure, let's get it done.' You would have married him, waited for the custody to be final, had the marriage annulled, and been on your way."

"Just what are you saying, Aunt Deirdre?"

"The fact that you said neither yes nor no leads me to thinking that there's more involved here than Trace McCord's getting custody of Christopher. I think you're afraid to face what you're feeling."

"Why on earth . . ."

"Because your heart's involved, and not with the child's custody."

"Don't be absurd!"

"You don't think I know what I'm talking about? That I can't possibly . . ."

"You understood about Nicolas," Callie interrupted gently, sensing her aunt's hurt.

"I understood you didn't love him. But maybe you think I couldn't have understood if you *did* love him."

Callie sat very still. This suddenly wasn't about her and Trace. The faraway look in her aunt's eyes told her that. "Is it . . . is this about . . . Riley Smith?"

Deirdre smiled. "Not exactly, dear. It goes back a bit farther than that."

"The war," Callie breathed, almost to herself. "When you left Mama and me during the war . . . when you were a nurse . . ." She gripped her aunt's hand. "Tell me. I've waited so long to know. Please, tell me."

Deirdre's eyes misted. "There was a man, a soldier. Sgt. Caleb Trent. English, Rebel, Protestant. Three black marks against him, as far as your father was concerned. Finley could never have forgiven Caleb any one of them."

"You loved him?"

"I loved him."

"You went to him?"

She nodded. "He was wounded in a skirmish near Williamsburg. He was . . . incapacitated. An invalid. He begged me to go back home. He didn't want to chain me to half a man. But half of man was more than any whole man I'd ever known. We were married by a justice of the peace, because no priest would perform the ceremony. The bishop apologized, saying even if Caleb wanted to convert, he could never father a child so there was no sense in our getting married."

"That's outrageous!" Callie muttered.

"Finley was out of his mind when I told him about Caleb. He disowned me. Said he didn't have a sister, never wanted to see me again. I didn't care. I only wanted Caleb."

"What happened?"

"I went to my husband. We had two years. Two years that made it worth living the rest of my life without him."

"Why didn't you ever tell me?"

"I don't know. As much as I loved him, I still think of how I sinned in the eyes of the Church. I guess I didn't want to be a bad example for you."

"You could never be any such thing to me. I wish I would have known. For a long time I felt like you deserted Mama and me when we needed you most. Still, I loved you so much, I blamed Da for your leaving."

"I wouldn't have gone, not even to Caleb, if Sarah had asked me to stay. But she didn't. She wanted me to be happy."

"Thank you for telling me now."

"If you love Trace McCord . . ."

Callie's defenses snapped back into place. "Don't be silly. I don't even *know* him."

"I knew Caleb for five minutes and I knew I wanted to spend my life with him. His leg was broken, yet he was standing beside the bed of another wounded soldier, helping to hold the man down, talking to him, assuring him everything would be all right. His voice was so gentle, and he was so kind. I almost couldn't bear it when his own wound wasn't serious enough and they sent him back to the fighting." She trembled slightly. "His next wound was." She drew in a deep breath, straightening. "Well, enough of the past. It's you and your future we're talking about here."

"And not much of my future at that. The marriage would only be for a little while."

"You're going to say yes?"

"I'm going to talk to Trace again, but . . . Lord help me, I know which way my mind is headed. If I can help him keep his son . . ."

Deirdre gave her a swift hug. "It'll work out for the best, dear. I know it will."

"I'm glad you woke up," Callie said, returning the hug. "Even if I did have to nearly break my toe. Thank you."

Callie lay awake awhile longer, unable to quell the memory of Trace McCord's mouth, his hands, her face heating as she recalled the feel of his arousal pressed against her thigh. She shivered. No, she dared not allow things to go beyond the bounds of a legal arrangement. To do so would be to give him the power to break her heart.

Tomorrow she would talk to him. Tomorrow. Her mind made up, she drifted into a dreamless sleep.

In the front room by the fire, Trace stared long and hard into the flames for another hour before he finally forced himself to bed. There his dreams were filled with a fiery-haired woman, who wrapped her long, silken legs around him as he drove himself inside her, who cried out that she loved him, as he did the same. And then came the inevitable day that she found out the truth about him.

The pain was a knife twisting in his gut as she cursed him, cursed the day she ever set foot on Shadow's Way land.

Chapter Ten

Trace was nowhere to be found when Callie forced herself out of bed the next morning. She had little doubt that he had deliberately absented himself. He had promised to give her time to think things over, and apparently he was doing just that. She spent most of the day catering to Christopher, thoroughly enjoying spoiling him, as more and more he returned her attention with unabashed affection.

"Cal-lee, hide!" the boy commanded merrily as they indulged in an after-supper game of hide-and-seek.

She was just scrunching down behind the settee, when Deirdre returned from the bunkhouse with Riley's empty supper dishes. Her aunt shook her head, laughing. "I can't get over how well you and that child have taken to each other."

"Neither can I," Callie admitted, half bemused, half delighted. She'd never had much experience with young children, nor had she ever been the first to rush toward doting new parents to have a chance at fussing over the babe. For whatever reason, though, Christopher was different. He was special. And she was very glad the feeling was mutual.

Peering around the end of the settee, she watched him scoot from room to room searching for her. "Find Callee," he cried. "I find Callie."

"Where do you suppose she's hiding this time?" Deirdre chuckled, pointing her finger toward the settee.

"Shush, Aunt Deirdre," Callie whispered. "You're cheating!"

Grinning, her aunt set the dishes down and came over to Callie. "I'll hold him off," she intoned with mock bravado. "Christopher? Have you checked your papa's bedroom? Do you think Callie's hiding in there?"

"Papa's room? I find her!"

Callie heard Christopher's advancing steps skid to a halt, then retrace themselves, thumping back down the hallway.

"A moment's respite, at least," Callie giggled, then sobered. She had not missed the anxious look that suddenly clouded her aunt's features. "Is something wrong?"

"Not wrong precisely."

Callie rose to her feet. "Then what?"

"I was just thinking of something Mr. McCord told me this morning."

Callie wasn't certain she wanted to know, but she asked anyway. "What did he say?"

"He was telling me that he had a devil of a time finding a good nanny after the boy's mother died. Christopher just didn't take to any of them."

The child trundled into the room. "Cal-lee, hide," he

said indignantly, pulling on her skirts.

"In a minute, sweetheart," she said, her gaze never shifting from her aunt. "Did Trace say something about Christopher's not taking to me, either? Is that what . . ."

"No, no, dear," Deirdre assured her. "In fact, just the opposite. He's thrilled at how much the child seems to like you."

"Then what . . ."

Christopher yanked more forcefully on her dress. "Callee, hide!"

"Maybe it's me," Deirdre said slowly. "You seem so . . . at home here."

"And that bothers you?" Callie had to raise her voice to be heard above the child's high-pitched demand that she continue the game.

"What bothers me is just what I told Mr. McCord."

Callie straightened, her chest tightening. "Oh, Aunt Deirdre, you didn't say anything about his proposal? Please, tell me you didn't."

"I told him to have a care for your feelings." Deirdre looked at the floor. "I asked him not to hurt you."

"Cal-lee, hide!" Christopher shrilled again and again.

"Not now!" she snapped. To Deirdre she said, "How could you do that? How could you say . . ." She followed Deirdre's gaze to the child. His lower lip trembled, his small face crumpling. A stab of regret ripped through her. She closed her eyes, drawing in a deep breath, then lifted the youngster into her arms. "I'm sorry, Christopher," she murmured. "I didn't mean to shout at you."

He wrapped his arms around her neck. "Hide?" he

said, hopefully, quietly.

Callie's lips curved ruefully. "I give up. I can't battle both of you. All right, Christopher, you go hide." She set him back on the floor. "I'll count to ten, then come find you. All right?"

The child laughed gleefully, then bolted down the hall to his father's room.

Callie turned back to Deirdre. "I know you're worried about me. But Trace isn't going to hurt me. Why would you even think such a thing?"

"You know full well I'm not talking about physical hurt, young lady. I've heard the way your voice softens when you speak of him, the way your eyes sparkle."

"They most certainly do not!" she cried, appalled that Deirdre had so easily picked up on her feelings. She could only hope Trace was not nearly so observant. "I have to go. I have to find Chris, or he'll be right back out here." She gave her aunt a hug. "I'll be fine. Really. Just let me handle it, all right?"

Deirdre shook her head. "Just take care, please. He's not asking you to a church social."

"I'm aware of that."

"You've decided? You're going to marry him?"

"I don't know yet."

"He hasn't got much time."

"I know. I'll talk to him tonight. I promise."

"Cal-lee find me!" Christopher called.

"I've got to go." She hugged her aunt again. "Stop worrying." But as she hurried down the hall, she didn't miss her aunt's softly called warning. "He'll hurt you, Callie. He can't help but hurt you, because he's hurting himself."

Two hours later Callie sat in front of a crackling fire

working on her journal. Her pen stilled, as she caught the sound of hooves thundering in the yard outside.

Trace was home.

She swallowed nervously. "Calm down," she said aloud. "You know he'll bed down Shoshone before he comes in the house." She sat there, waiting, listening to the snapping logs in the hearth.

Christopher was down for the night. Deirdre was in the bunkhouse reading to Riley. The previously companionable solitude only accelerated the sudden pounding of her heart. Fifteen minutes after she heard the stallion pound into the yard, the front door opened and Trace strode into the house.

"I haven't made up my mind yet," she blurted, cutting off his softly spoken, "Good evening."

"I said I wouldn't press you on it." He went through the routine she'd heard the night before—slapping down his gloves and hat, returning his rifle to the gun rack.

"A few more questions have come to mind, though," she ventured.

He ambled over to the settee and sat down, one arm stretched comfortably behind her. It was as though he already knew she would go through with this sham, she thought fiercely. How dare he be so damned sure of himself?

"I'm all ears," he said.

No, he certainly wasn't that. Even the thin dusting of trail dirt that clung to that hard-planed face looked annoyingly sensual on Trace McCord.

"I want to know about . . . about where you and I will be slee— I mean . . ." She stopped, furious at her stammering, yet wondering helplessly how in the world she could ever voice the question uppermost in her mind.

To further fuel her agitation Trace began absently thrumming his fingers on the back of the settee. Was he that impatient to be gone, when he claimed to be so desperate for her help? "If I'm keeping you . . ." she snapped.

His fingers curled guiltily into his palm. "Sorry." He curved his hand over the back of hers. "It's been a long day, and I want a bath. But if you need to talk first . . ."

"Yes, yes, I do." There was no way in the world she was going to let this man take another bath in this house while she sat idly by awaiting his return. She still hadn't recovered from his earlier birthday suit sojourn through the hallway. "What I would like . . . need to know . . . concerns our . . . yours and my . . . that is, if I went through with it . . ."

"You'll have to forgive me," he said, a lazy grin curving one corner of his mouth, "but I'm not quite sure I'm following you."

Who could? she thought wildly, then plunged on. "All right! I want to know about the sleeping arrangements of this . . . this marriage. There. Are you satisfied? Did you follow me that time?"

"What would you like to know?"

He was determined to make this difficult. She would have to put everything into embarrassingly precise words.

"You know what I mean," she grated. "This marriage is simply an arrangement so you can keep Christopher. I would feel uncomfortable if . . . if . . ."

"My kiss was that unpleasant?"

She didn't miss the lightly mocking tone. He knew

160

damned well she had enjoyed the kiss. She blushed heatedly, unable to prevent it, as she remembered her freely given response. But she'd be damned if she was going to admit it to this arrogant cowboy.

"Under the circumstances," she managed to choke out, "I don't think it would be proper if you . . . you . . ."

"Exercised my husbandly rights?" he finished for her.

She nodded, not daring to look at him. Her face was crimson.

"The marriage will be in name only," he stated, standing up and stalking to the other side of the room. "I thought you understood that. This is business, not pleasure."

Callie's heart sank. Even though it was what she had wanted to hear, the words left her strangely bereft. She realized now she had been deluding herself that his male urges meant any more than availing himself of a willing partner. He obviously regarded his attraction to her as an annoying nuisance to be dealt with at once. He would simply promise to keep his hands to himself. And for him it was that easily done, too.

She assured herself his answer was precisely what she had hoped for. If this was business for him, it would have to be doubly so for her. Yet such an arrangement would almost certainly be easier for Trace. His goal was Christopher. Callie was having a harder time justifying this proposed charade for the sake of her expedition to Yellowstone.

She would not let him see how deeply his words had cut. "Well," she sighed. "Business only. That's certainly a relief."

Trace shot her a quick glance, but by then she had forced a look of stony indifference.

"We will, however, sleep in the same room." He paused meaningfully. "My room."

"What?" Callie gasped, leaping to her feet. "But you just said . . ."

"Jenny's guardians are sure to have their lawyer sniffing around. I wouldn't put it past them to look into our sleeping arrangements. I don't want them gleaning any damaging testimony for the custody hearing."

Callie quivered. Sleeping in the same room with this man sent a renewed flush of desire through her that she quickly quashed. She was living in a romantic dream and the sooner she rid herself of the notion the better.

"You only have one bed," she reminded him weakly.

"I'm aware of that."

The same room was one thing. But the same bed? How could she rationalize that? To herself? To Deirdre? "Trace, I . . ."

"Am I to take all of these questions to mean that you're at least leaning in my direction? That you're thinking of agreeing to marrying me?"

"I suppose I am. I don't believe I am, but I am. You and Christopher look so right together. You . . ."

He interrupted, apparently not interested in her opinion of his relationship with his son. "If you decide in the affirmative, the marriage will take place this Saturday."

"But that's impossible! This is Wednesday! I know you want to get things settled for Christopher's adoption, but . . . Saturday?"

"I want it done. Over. So I don't have to worry about it anymore. The ceremony will be small, informal.

Riley and Deirdre could stand up as witnesses."

She frowned. There was more to it than that. She couldn't have said why, but she was again certain he wasn't telling her everything. Was there a reason he didn't want anyone else in attendance? She pushed away questions she knew he wouldn't answer. That wasn't the primary issue anyway. It was his impossible demand that the wedding take place in three days. "I'm sorry. If it has to be Saturday, the bride will just have to be someone else."

"Why?"

"I'm an Irish Catholic, in case you need reminding. There are banns to be announced. A priest to be found. The fastest it could possibly be is a month."

"Dammit, Callie, this isn't a real marriage. Wouldn't it be better if it was legal to satisfy the codicil, but not one religiously binding for you?"

"I couldn't hurt Aunt Deirdre like that. Or even my father, if he should ever find out. Don't worry, we'll still end it somehow."

"But a divorce . . ."

How quickly he brought up the end of the marriage, before it had even had its beginning. "It wouldn't be a divorce," she said. "It would be an annulment, because the marriage will never be . . . consummated." She couldn't look at him when she said that.

He paced the room like a caged lion. "What's it going to look like if I get married with only days to spare before the will's deadline, instead of weeks?"

"Not so much worse than it looks now."

He bit back a low curse. "I can't wait that long, Callie. I can't."

"Why? Legally . . ."

He stalked toward the door. "It has to be Saturday."

Her temper broke. "I don't believe this!" she exploded. "You're the one who has the consummate gall to ask me to be your wife in name only to help you procure custody of your child, and now you're taking offense that I won't kowtow to your timetable!"

His own voice grew mild. "I guess I am being a bit unreasonable."

"A bit."

"I still think . . ."

She waved a hand impatiently. "I have a few more questions."

"I'm listening."

"You said you were married once."

His jaw clenched. He didn't answer. She hurried on. "Is your wife . . . alive?"

"The last I heard."

She sank onto the arm of the settee. "Then you're divorced?"

"Now what the hell difference does that make?"

"As a Catholic, I . . ."

"Can't marry a divorced man. Perfect!" he shouted. "I thought I had this all arranged. I thought . . ."

"There you go again!" she yelled back at him. "I'm the one who would be doing you the favor, and you're making me into some kind of villain. Along with my religious preferences to boot! And I won't have it. Maybe I don't exactly go along with every tiny precept of my religion, but I'll not hurt my family for the sake of a mockery! Maybe it would be different if I was out of my mind in love with you, then they'd just have to understand, but . . ."

He stepped closer to her. "Then tell them that."

164

She blinked, disconcerted. "What?"

"Tell them you're in love with me."

His eyes seared her. She had to will herself to look away. "You'd sink to any depths wouldn't you?"

"To get Christopher? Yes, I would."

Her shoulders sagged. "Why are we fighting?"

"I'm not sure." He gave her a slow smile, the effect of which was to weaken her knees enough so that she was glad she wasn't standing. How could a smile do that?

He stepped closer still. "Does it matter if I didn't exactly divorce Lanie?"

She blanched. "My God, you mean you're still married?"

"Seth didn't approve of my marriage. He said I was too young and hotheaded to know what I was doing. That Lanie led me astray."

"I find that difficult to believe."

His grin broadened. "Thank you. I think. Anyway, he had the marriage annulled. In fact, I'm not even sure if I ever went through with it formally. I was pretty drunk that night."

"Drunk? When you got married?" Her suspicions roused. "Just where did this ceremony take place?"

"In a Cheyenne saloon."

"Oh, my."

"The less you know about me the easier it will be to put up with a marriage for a month or two, don't you think?"

"Perhaps so. You don't know where Lanie is now?"

He shrugged. "I got a letter from her about eight months ago. She was back in Montana. There's a lumber camp up there . . ."

"I get the picture."

"I'm sorry. I don't mean to sound flippant. I cared about her. She was a fine woman in her way."

"I'm sure."

He slid his palm behind the curve of her neck. "I am sorry. I know this is a helluva lot to ask. But I want my son. To keep him, I need a wife. Callie, please, be my wife."

"Even if it takes a month?"

He blew out a long breath. "Even if it takes a month."

She took a step back, deliberately removing herself from the devastating effect of his touch. "Then I guess we've got ourselves a deal."

"Say it. I want to hear you say the words."

She swallowed hard, then looked him square in the eye. "The answer's yes, Trace. I'll be your wife."

Chapter Eleven

No matter how she tried, Callie couldn't concentrate. Deirdre had insisted they use Christopher's nap time to reorganize the ranch house kitchen, but Callie saw through the ploy at once as her aunt's way of keeping her occupied so that she wouldn't spend any idle time worrying herself sick over Trace's proposal. Callie hadn't yet found the words to tell her aunt she had decided to go through with the marriage.

"How do you know Trace isn't going to be furious to find his salt cellars shifted around?" Callie gritted, stretching for the first of six crystal wineglasses maddening inches beyond her reach on the top cupboard shelf.

"Careful," Deirdre warned, holding up a hand as though to ward off disaster.

"If I can just . . ." Callie managed to snag the goblet's stem with the tips of her fingers, attempting to twist it toward her to get a more secure grip. The glass slipped away, twirling ominously before it overbalanced and came tumbling out of the cupboard to shatter into a

glittering shards across the marqueted oak
. It was the second thing this afternoon she'd
broken. Her first victim had been a jar of strawberry
preserves that had taken her half an hour to clean up.

Her aunt ambled over with the broom and a dust
pan. "He won't have to worry about finding our new
hiding places," she grumbled, "because he won't have
anything left to hide. I thought the physical activity
would keep your mind off what the man wants of you.
But you can't stop thinking about it, can you?"

Callie swept up the broken glass. "Could *you?*"

Deirdre shook her head. "I guess not. You can stop
the playacting, too. I was thinking you were upset
because you couldn't make up your mind. But that's
not it, is it? You've decided. You're going to marry
him."

Callie stared at the floor.

Deirdre crossed over to the table and sat down.
"We'd best forget about destroying Mr. McCord's
kitchen, and have us a little talk."

"No."

"Sit."

Callie sat.

Deirdre clasped Callie's hand in hers. "What he's
asking of you isn't an evening at the opera or a church
social or even being nanny to his child."

"I'm well aware of . . ."

"Are you? Are you really? We're talking about
marriage, darling. No matter what kind of marriage it
is, no matter how easily he thinks you'll be able to end it
when the bargain is fully struck, you're going through
with something that will be a part of you for the rest of
your life."

Callie rose to pace back and forth across the room. "I feel sorry for him. He has a right to Christopher. And yet . . ." Her shoe crunched on a splinter of broken glass she'd missed. Stooping, she retrieved it, cursing when the tiny dagger pierced a fingertip. Pinching her thumb against the pinprick wound, she continued to measure the width and breadth of the kitchen in long, agitated strides. "There's something he isn't telling me. I know it; I *feel* it. I wish I could see all this as doing him a grand favor and be done with it. But I can't."

"Maybe it's more than his not telling you something." Deirdre paused, seeming to consider her words before she went on. "How do you feel about the man himself, Callie? How do you feel about Trace McCord?"

"We went through this."

"No. *I* went through it. You never did answer me."

"I most certainly did. He needs help, and I have the power to help him."

"But to marry him?"

Callie sagged back into the chair, swiping brusquely at a stray wisp of coppery hair. "It's so strange, Aunt Deirdre. So very strange. I didn't marry Nicolas because I didn't love him. And now I'm terrified to marry Trace because . . . I think maybe I do. I love him, but I don't know him at all."

Near dusk, Trace reined in Shoshone, gazing down at the herd of some one hundred horses grazing placidly in the valley below. This was the largest of his three herds settled here in the lushest valleys on Shadow's Way land. A flush of pride stole over him,

169

which he quickly shook off. The mares here looked good, damned good. They'd dropped a good crop of foals for the third year in a row. Over the past winter he'd only lost two of his yearlings, none of his two-year-olds. And at least two dozen fine three- and four-year-olds were ready to be culled in the fall. With the standing order he'd closed with the army last spring for new mounts, Shadow's Way could edge into the black for the first time in years.

Dismounting, he busied himself readying a camp for the night. After a meager meal of jerky and beans, he settled back against a small boulder, staring into the flames of his cookfire. He'd found no sign that these horses had been harassed by the rogue grizzly who'd panicked a smaller herd six miles to the north. He hoped the bear had gone back up into the high country.

Bear trouble would have been the least of his worries five years ago, when he'd first come back to the ranch after his father's death. Shadow's Way itself had been on the verge of going under.

He poured himself a cup of coffee, the scalding liquid hot and bitter. Still, it went down easier than the memories. Five years . . .

Seth had been running things alone. Jenny was too frail to be of much help physically, though her moral support sustained them all over the worst times.

"You've overexpanded, Seth," Trace said, wishing they had chosen anywhere but the study to begin their latest shouting match over how best the herds should be managed. "You're going to lose the ranch if you continue to breed more stock than you can hope to sell, breeding with inferior studs just to . . ."

"Don't you tell me how to run this ranch," Seth cut

in. "Shadow's Way is mine. Pa left it to me. Not you."

Trace winced visibly, but Seth took no notice as he raged on. "You work for me. You're here because Jenny thinks you need roots now that Pa's dead. But she wasn't here when we were growing up. She wasn't here to see that you spent more time gone than home. And that the time you did spend home was spent feeling sorry for yourself."

Trace bit back the curse that rose in his throat. He had tried, tried hard since coming back to keep things on level ground between him and Seth. In spite of all the years he'd been gone, he'd never gotten Shadow's Way out of his blood. If he and his father had ever had anything in common, it was a love of this land. Even if it meant working for Seth, he would do his damnedest to make a go of it. Somewhere inside him, he knew, he harbored the hope that one day Seth would recognize him as an equal partner.

"And as for inferior studs," Seth sneered, "your choice of brood mares isn't exactly the highest quality, either. Just take a look at that *wife* you brought back from your week-long drunk in Cheyenne last month. The little tramp has . . ."

Trace backhanded Seth across the mouth. Seth staggered back, looking more startled than hurt.

"When the old man died," Trace hissed, "I thought maybe, just maybe, I'd get a fair shake from you. But I am sick of your reducing our business discussions to personal insults." He paced over to the study window. "If I hadn't gone to Cheyenne for my *drunk,* as you call it, I would've broken your neck. You had no right to sell off that stallion I brought back from Mexico."

"The ranch is mine. We needed the money that horse

171

brought in."

"That horse was mine! He would have been the foundation for . . ."

"Shut up! Just shut up! We've got other stallions."

"None with the bloodlines of that one."

"Right. And you just happened to have him in *your* possession. How do I know you didn't steal him?"

"You son of a—" Trace straightened. "I told you that horse belonged to the don of a ranchero outside of Mexico City. I saved his life. He made the horse a gift."

"I'll just bet he did. One night when he was asleep."

"I don't have to listen to this." Trace stomped toward the door. "I'm going out to check on the foal Better Lady dropped. I'm positive the red stallion is the sire. Maybe some day his colt can make up for your sellout."

"Don't think your walking out of here settles anything. I'm telling you again that I want that little trollop of yours off this ranch. I don't want her around Jenny."

"Jenny? Don't try to put this off on Jenny. She likes Lanie."

"Jenny likes everybody. But I won't have her being exposed to human garbage."

Trace was across the room in three strides. He grabbed Seth's shirt front, his voice all the more deadly because he spoke in scarcely more than a whisper. "No more, Seth. No more. You insult me all you like. I'm used to it. But one more remark about Lanie, and you and I will go at it out in the yard until one of us doesn't get up."

Seth relented. Trace's eyes narrowed, the sudden glint of shame in his brother's features pushing him past his anger. He let go of Seth's shirt and backed off a step. "What the hell is going on anyway? Why are you all but driving me off this ranch? I thought that was always Pa's special pleasure. Never yours."

"I'm sorry." Seth sagged to a sitting position on the corner of the desk. "I am sorry, Trace. I'm no better than he was sometimes. Takin' anything that doesn't go right and puttin' the blame on you."

Trace frowned. "Are you going to tell me what you're talking about?"

Seth expelled a long breath. "I know the stallion was yours. But we had a note due at the bank. I didn't know if we were going to make it or not. Selling that stallion was the only way to be sure there'd still be a Shadow's Way in another year."

Trace studied his brother with a dawning insight. Ten years his senior, Seth had spent his life striving to be the perfect son, the perfect brother, the perfect husband. Not until now had Trace considered the price Seth paid to be the best at everything. In his way, Seth had been as damaged by Jeb McCord's dictatorial self-righteousness as Trace, who had suffered the man's physical and emotional abuse.

"You can never make a mistake, can you?" Trace murmured. "Why the hell didn't you just tell me? I would have understood. Maybe we could have figured something out."

"I took care of it the only way I could." Already Seth seemed to regret his momentary lapse of control. Distractedly, he rifled the papers on his desktop. "As for your wife . . ."

Trace was back on his guard.

"Don't worry. No more insults. I just . . . well, I don't know how else to say this. Lanie is not your wife."

173

"What's in those papers?"

"I had a man do a little checking. You were pretty drunk the night Lanie became Mrs. McCord."

"So? She's still my business."

"The man who performed your wedding ceremony was no more a preacher than I am."

Sheepishly, Trace raked a hand through his hair. "Maybe I'm not all that surprised. She's always been a bit more of a woman than I've ever fancied a wife would be in the bedroom."

"I won't push your putting an end to it right now," Seth said. "But I expect you to take care of it. You can't have your mistress staying at the ranch."

"Just make sure you let *me* take care of it."

That night Trace lay in bed, Lanie straddling his hips, her ebony hair spilling down past her shoulders, curtaining her coral-tipped breasts. He was sated. As usual, she'd been a tigress in bed. But now her brown eyes, normally too cynical for her lovely oval face, grew serious, cold, her words chilling his ardor.

"What do you mean, you're leaving?" he demanded.

"I'm tired of the ranch. It's boring. You had to know I could never stay here for long."

"Seth put you up to this, didn't he?"

"I don't know what you're talking about."

"Dammit, Lanie, if I say you stay, you stay."

"I told you, I'm bored."

"You find this boring?" He nuzzled her throat, nipping along her jawline with his teeth. But she pulled back.

"It's no good anymore, Trace. I'm sorry."

The next morning she was packed and ready to head for Cheyenne. But not before Trace had found two hundred dollars in her valise. He swore. So much for Seth's promise not to interfere.

"We had fun, don't spoil it," she said.

"I don't want you to leave."

"Do you love me?"

"Lanie . . ."

"I know you don't."

"Love is a fairy tale. You and I are good together. It doesn't make sense for you to go back to . . ."

"Back to being a whore?"

"I don't think of you that way."

"It's what I am. Even with you. I don't know how to be anything else. Maybe I don't want to be anything else."

"Will you be all right?"

"I've been takin' care of myself since I was six. I'll be fine."

"Write to me. If you ever need anything . . . *anything* . . ."

"I'll remember. You're a good man, Trace McCord. Too bad your brother's too blind most of the time to see it."

"Seems to be the way of things with my family. Or maybe you're the one who's blind. Maybe Seth and Jeb saw me right."

She curved her hand along his jaw. "No. They saw what they expected to see. Seth sees you as that wild boy you told me about. He doesn't see the man those years made of you. But then you don't see it, either. That's why you figure you deserve a woman like me."

"Don't run yourself down."

"You're sweet. But you deserve better. You're the one who sells himself short. All the time. Like on this ranch. You're pitching in, doing the job of six men, and you still don't feel like you deserve to be a part of it, just because your pa left it to your brother."

He pulled her close. "I'll miss you."

"I'll miss you. I never had anyone better in bed."

"A man's got to have one talent."

She slapped his arm, giggling, then sobered. Wrapping her arms around his neck, she gave him a swift kiss, then climbed onto the buckboard next to Reese.

"That was another one of your mistakes," Seth muttered, coming up behind Trace as the buckboard pulled out of the ranchyard. "We certainly don't need a hulking, dull-witted ranchhand like Reese."

"I've told you. I owe him. He saved my life once."

"I've told you—I don't like him."

Jenny McCord came up beside them, her wispy cornsilk hair making her almost translucent skin more pale still. "I'm sorry, Trace. I tried to get her to stay."

"I know."

Seth shook his head. "Jenny, you'd take in any stray that . . ." He stopped, casting a wary look at Trace. "Sorry."

Trace said nothing.

"I think I'll go mend that harness I've been meaning to get to." Without another word he stalked off.

"He doesn't mean half of what he says to you, Trace," Jenny assured him. "He doesn't want to see you hurt. He knows your father did enough of that."

"Seth has his own ideas of what's right for me. Trouble is, nobody ever asks me."

"I'll always ask."

He smiled. "Seth's a damned lucky man."

She blushed. "Please try to remember he's as hard or

harder on himself than he ever is on you. He feels so much responsibility for Shadow's Way. Your father shouldn't have left it only to Seth."

"It was his. He had a right to do what he wanted with it. As far as he was concerned he only had one son."

"I wish you could have made it home before he died, maybe . . ."

"He would've spit in my face from his death bed, and we both know it."

"Don't let it eat you alive, Trace. You didn't deserve how he treated you."

"Yeah, who knows, maybe if I really tried, I might even straighten myself out."

"Trace . . ."

"I'd better go. I've got chores of my own to finish."

"Trace, wait, please. Before you go I need to . . ."

The anxiety in her voice stayed him. "What is it?"

"It's Seth. He's determined to get that red stallion. He's going to catch that horse or die trying."

"No one'll ever ride that red devil. I've told Seth that before."

"He's stubborn. He won't listen to me."

Trace snorted. "And you think he'll listen to me?"

"I'm just so afraid."

"I'll try again."

She gave him a hug. "He loves you. In his way, he loves you very much."

"Maybe."

Jenny touched her abdomen. "You know, you're going to be an uncle."

Trace grinned. "I like the sound of that. You just make sure you tell that baby you love him. Promise? You tell him that."

177

"I'll tell him," she said quietly. "Or her. I promise."

The sound of nickering horses brought Trace back to the present. He looked up to see Reese riding in. Trace was instantly alert. "The bear?"

Reese shook his head. "Set some traps."

"I don't think that's a good idea. You never know what'll get trapped in 'em. I just want that bear. There's somethin' not right in the head about him. Bears don't stalk horses."

The big man nodded, then rode off.

He was an odd one, Trace admitted. But he owed him.

Try as he might, he couldn't keep his mind where he wanted it. Time and again his thoughts shifted to a flame-haired woman with a temper to match. He'd asked her to marry him, actually gone through with it. He'd had no choice—for Christopher's sake. But her arrival had most certainly spared him the ordeal of asking anyone else. He grimaced, recalling how he had told her there were others all but clambering to be his wife. Hardly. Though he'd asked no other woman, he could well imagine the cutting refusals if he had. Any local woman familiar with Shadow's Way would be equally familiar with the disreputable tales linked to its owner.

All the more reason it was imperative that he get Callie to agree to the wedding taking place as soon as possible. Somehow he had to talk her out of her religious reservations. The longer the delay, the more likely she would learn the truth. Then she would refuse, likely even siding with the Marlowes in Christopher's custody. But if he could marry her before she found out, he would be safe. A wife couldn't give any damaging testimony against her husband, and her Catholic faith would forbid a divorce. He would delay an annulment until it suited his purpose.

He shifted on his blankets, an unwelcome stab of desire coursing through him. She had qualities a man would look for in a woman with whom he wanted to share his life. But this was expediency, he reminded himself fiercely. Not a real marriage. She had only agreed to his proposition because it was short term.

The Marlowes could arrive any time. Lyle Morton had received a letter announcing their plans to travel west from Pennsylvania. They'd given no date, but Trace could afford to take no chances. Callie had to be his wife before they arrived.

"They know," Lyle told him. "They know all about you and your father. That whole business."

"So can anyone who asks around."

"Callie Callaghan hasn't asked."

"Exactly. That's why you have to hold off the Marlowes until after the wedding."

"I'll do my best. But I can't make any guarantees."

"Whatever you can do, Lyle, you know I'll be grateful. I've never even understood why you took me on as a client considering the attitude of most folks in the territory." He said the last with an edge of bitterness.

"You paid a high enough price for what happened."

"Still, you were the fifth lawyer I went to in Rock Springs. If you'd turned me down . . ."

"I liked your brother. Seth was a good friend. He never went along with what your father did. If Seth trusted you, that was good enough for me."

Trust. He wondered if Callie Callaghan trusted him.

"Damn." It didn't matter. Nothing mattered but keeping Christopher. Not his pride. Not his ethics. Not anything. A thought struck him. If Callie were compromised in some way, then the honorable thing would be to marry her . . . at once.

He closed his eyes. No. He wouldn't push her that far. He wouldn't make love to her. Though the prospect was an infinitely pleasant one. She was a damned sensual woman. He swore, an unwelcome current of desire coursing through him. It was a long time before he went to sleep.

He wasn't sure if he was awake or dreaming when the plan came to him, but the next morning he knew what he was going to do. That she would hate him gave his conscience no more than a momentary twinge. She would hate him anyway—eventually. *When* made little difference. All that mattered was that the plan would work. In less than two days Callie would be his wife.

Chapter Twelve

Early-evening shadows laced with wildflower-scented coolness blanketed much of the ranchyard as Trace tied off Shoshone to the hitchrail in front of the bunkhouse. He wanted to talk to Riley Smith. The man's cooperation was essential if his plan tonight with Callie was to succeed. But inside the small building it was not the rough-hewn scout he found, but Callie's aunt expertly working a needlepoint sampler.

"Mr. Smith is out exercising his leg," Deirdre said. "Much against my better judgment. Was there something in particular you wanted to see him about?"

"No, no, nothing," Trace said. "I'll find him, don't worry." Quickly, he excused himself. Chatting face to face with the woman who would be an equal pawn in his plan tonight sent a surge of guilt ripping through him that he repressed at once. His timetable did not allow for the luxury of conscience. He wasted no time in finding Smith. The scout was hobbling about near the barn with the aid of a fork-limbed crutch. "You sure you're up to that?"

"Couldn't stand being cooped up in that shack one more minute. Not even with Miss Deirdre. I'm a man used to living under the sky."

"I know the feeling."

The scout studied Trace with a kind of casual scrutiny for which Trace took no offense. The man also minced no words. "I hear you got yourself a problem adoptin' your boy."

"Deirdre told you?"

"No. It was Miss Callie."

Trace frowned. "I didn't know she confided in you."

"Sometimes it's easier to say things to a stranger than to someone you care about too much."

"You may have a point," Trace conceded. As the man limped alongside, Trace retrieved Shoshone, leading the stallion toward the barn.

"She asked me not to say anything to her aunt," Riley went on, "but she didn't ask me not to talk to you. That little gal and Miss Deirdre mean a good deal to me and I don't want to see 'em hurt. Trouble is if you hurt one, you can't help but hurt the other."

"I don't intend to hurt either one of them. All I ever wanted out of this was Christopher."

"So why Miss Callie? A handsome fella like yerself shouldn't have much trouble gettin' ladies to swoon at yer feet."

Trace stiffened ever so slightly. There was an undercurrent of suspicion in the scout's voice that made him wary. It was almost as if Riley knew . . . But that was impossible. Trace uncinched the saddle, dragging it from the stallion's back, carrying it into the barn. He didn't look at the scout as he said, "I think Callie's arrival here was more than just a lucky accident."

"Meanin'?"

"Meaning she's a very special woman. Christopher is already very fond of her." He settled the saddle atop the sidewall of a nearby stall, the stirrups thudding against either side of the pine slats. "In fact, I'm rather fond of her myself." His pulse quickened. Odd, how he'd worried he couldn't voice the lie, but now said aloud it seemed not a lie at all."

"You tryin' to tell me you love her? That you'd want to marry her even if you didn't have to?"

"Maybe love is too strong a word," he hedged, suddenly unwilling to sort through the myriad of emotions that roiled to life whenever he thought too long and hard about Callie Callaghan. He had to force himself to keep his voice neutral as he continued. "She and I have only known each other a few days. But there is something about her. Something to make me think that over time . . ."

"Why don't you just tell Miss Callie how you feel?"

Trace picked up a curry brush, running a calloused thumb over the hard bristles. "Because I don't think she'd believe me."

"So what is it you want from me?"

He hesitated. Now that his opening had arrived, he was loath to plunge into it. What he wanted Smith to do would seem innocuous enough, but if his plan worked, Callie's reputation would be in ruins. Her only hope of avoiding total disgrace would be to agree to marry him at once. That she would despise him went without saying. What he planned was despicable—

even for a man with a reputation for committing despicable acts. But the specter of a life without Christopher goaded him on. "Can you keep Deirdre away for a while tonight? Say, till midnight. Then bring her to the house."

Riley opened his mouth to protest, but Trace hurried on. "I want—I *need* to have the evening alone with Callie. To talk to her after Christopher's fallen asleep. I have a surprise for her."

Riley scratched his jaw. "I ain't real sure about this. Miss Deirdre won't like her niece bein' alone with you at such an hour."

Trace grabbed the first thought that came to his head. "I want to give Callie an engagement ring. It was my mother's. I want the two of us to be alone when I give it to her. Surely you can understand that." Trace could tell the man was wavering. "Midnight," he emphasized. "Not before. Not after." For good measure he added, "Please."

His reluctance receding into a conspiratorial grin, Riley nodded. "Since Cupid's arrow run me through, who am I to deny the same pleasure to a fellow man? I'll have Miss Deirdre there at midnight."

Trace spent the next half hour brushing down Shoshone. It was as if with each measured stroke, he was layering on his determination, convincing himself there was no other way. The shadows of early evening lengthened, darkened, as dusk settled in. Finally he could put it off no longer. He strode toward the house.

Inside, the only light came from the fire flickering on the hearth. The welcome scent of woodsmoke filled his nostrils as he stood in the entryway. Callie was seated on the settee, her tumbled hair spilling over its back like a copperspun firefall. He knew she was aware of him, but she gave no overt notice. Though the back of the settee blocked his view he could tell by the tilt of her head that Christopher was sitting next to her. He longed to pull the child into his arms and hold him after a day-long absence, but he resisted the urge, mesmerized by the scene before him. He moved closer.

Callie's voice was alternately low and wispy, high and gleeful as she wove an animated tale of childish high adventure populated by dragons, princes, and buried treasure. Though it was apparent she was making up the story as she went along, Trace was awed by the interlocking details that seemed so effortlessly to fall in place. He shook his head in wry amusement to realize he was as anxious as Christopher to find out if the tiny kingdom of Kind n' Fair could be saved by the brave young wizard. For his part Christopher sat enthralled, his wide blue eyes alive with delight.

Several minutes passed while Callie guided Christopher along the trail of a playful dragon, an anthropomorphic toad, and a mischievous troll.

"'Then with a sprinkle of his magic fairy dust the gallant young wizard saved the entire kingdom,'" Callie said. "'The king was ever so grateful.'" Her voice lowered. "And that's when the king let the young wizard sleep in the plushest bedchamber in his castle." Her voice became a whisper. "The oh-so-tired wizard lay his head on his pillow and closed his eyes and . . ." Christopher's head bobbed forward. Callie smiled, leaning over to plant a soft kiss on top of his tousled blond locks.

Trace felt his insides clench, a strange, empty ache searing through him. If only it didn't have to be forced.

For convenience sake. Maybe . . . maybe after time, after the custody was settled . . .

No. He couldn't think that way. Didn't dare think that way.

She would know the truth about him by then. Any attraction between them would die. She would hate him for deceiving her.

Hate him.

She looked up then, mouthing a silent "hello." Her smile of welcome was almost his undoing. "Chris missed you," she said.

"I missed him." He came over and lifted the drowsy child from her, easing him against his broad shoulder. "But I couldn't bear to interrupt. I had to know if the king was going to slay the dragon."

"Not in my stories," she said with mock dismay. "I like dragons. My heroes would never kill one. You'll notice my wizard *tamed* his dragon and they lived happily, if sleepily, ever after."

Trace couldn't help grinning, couldn't help the warmth that stole over him just being near her. To cover his feelings, he said, "You mean your heroes don't win the heart of the fair maiden?"

"Not this time around anyway. The fair maiden has her heart set on someone else."

He carried Christopher down the hallway, ridiculously pleased when Callie followed. "Does the hero *ever* win the fair maiden?" He couldn't have explained why his voice seemed suddenly hoarse.

Callie sank down onto one side of Christopher's bed as Trace tucked a quilted coverlet around the youngster's small body. "The fair maiden isn't looking for a hero," she said softly. "She doesn't believe in them." With the tips of her fingers she smoothed Christopher's hair from his forehead.

"But you did say her heart belonged to someone else."

"Ah, but he's no fantasy hero. He's peevish, self-critical, and secretive. He's tender, passionate, and proud. A real flesh and blood human being. Our fair maiden deserves no less."

Why did her litany of human attributes make his throat tighten? His heart pound? They were discussing a fairy tale! Heroes, villains, dragons, trolls . . . Then why couldn't he concentrate? Why did his senses focus on the slender outline of her silhouette less than an arm's reach away in the darkened room? Why did he catch the vaguest hint of jasmine clinging to the tumbled waves of her fiery hair. He stood abruptly. If he didn't put some distance between them he was going to kiss her right here on his son's bed.

He stalked back to the front room, where he dug his fingers into the back of the settee, fighting down a surge of desire so strong it was physically painful. Damn, what was happening to him? He had to stick to his plan, had to remember this was expedience, not pleasure. He took a deep breath, forcing a calmness he didn't feel, looking up when she came into the room. "Did, uh, did Christopher give you any trouble?"

"None. He's a sweetheart. We were baking bread. He helped me knead the dough. Speaking of which . . . if you're hungry . . ." She started toward the kitchen.

"No," he said too quickly.

She stopped, startled.

"I'm sorry. I . . . you're not cooking anything. It's my turn." He waved a hand toward the settee. You sit.

Just sit and relax. You've done so much for me, I'd like to do something in return."

"That isn't necessary. I was only talking about putting a little butter on a slice of bread."

"You've had dinner?"

"Two hours ago. Besides, it's getting late . . ." She sat down.

"Please, I want to do this. Let me put something together in the kitchen."

"I really think we should just go to bed." Her cheeks flamed as his eyes darkened. "I meant that we both have to get up early ." His gaze continued to hold hers. Exasperated, she slapped a hand on her knee. "Dammit, I mean each of us should go to bed . . . individually. To our individual bedrooms."

He smiled. "I know what you mean. And I appreciate your attention to my sleep requirements, but . . . if you have a few minutes, I think we should talk. We've got a few details we still need to get straight."

"This isn't going to change my mind about announcing the banns and . . ."

"I didn't expect that it would."

She stayed in front of the fire as he busied himself in the kitchen. She wished she could control her mounting nervousness. If she didn't know better, she could have sworn *he* was nervous, too. But then she could hardly consider that unusual. He was still inordinately concerned about setting a wedding date to conform with the parameters of the codicil, even though she'd assured him she would only need thirty of his remaining forty-two days.

Yet perhaps there was more to it than that. The

huskiness of his voice, the deliberate innuendo in their discussion of heroes and fair maidens . . . Almost as if thoughts of legalities and technicalities were suddenly superfluous to him.

No. She had to stop this. She was being ridiculous. The man was looking for a business partner. Period.

Her flights of fancy returned in a rush when Trace padded back into the room. He had removed his boots and was now stocking-footed. In his hands he held a bottle of wine and two glasses. Callie knew she should protest, but instead she accepted one of the crystal goblets, watching his strong tanned fingers as he twisted the corkscrew, pulling the cork free with a resounding *pop*.

He filled her glass, then his own. "I'm not sure if I'm supposed to let this breathe or not . . . Seth was more the connoisseur."

Breathe, she thought wonderingly. She wasn't worried about the wine's breathing. She was worried about her own. Her hand shaking, she passed the burgundy liquid under her nose, noting the heady bouquet. "I shouldn't," she said.

"A toast," he said, his voice silken, throaty. He raised his glass. "To a fair maiden."

Her fingers went numb. She nearly dropped her glass as he clinked hers to his. Where was all this leading? She had to divert the conversation to a less volatile subject and quickly. "I suppose you noticed you're missing one of these goblets," she murmured guiltily. "I, uh, thought I was taller."

To her surprise he gave her a crooked grin. "Actually, there used to be eight of them. I've demolished two myself over time. So I'm still ahead of

189

you in the clumsy department two to one."

Why was he being so pleasant? More than that, why couldn't she take her eyes off him? She forced herself to take a sip of the wine. But she wasn't used to it, wasn't used to the spreading warmth that filtered instantly to every part of her. She held the glass at arm's length, studying the reflected glow of the flames leaping along the finely cut crystal. She took a steadying breath. "Why are you doing all this?"

"I told you."

"If you didn't need a wife in forty odd days, I might believe you. But I'm afraid that little detail makes all of your attention just a bit suspect."

"You can be a very direct woman."

"You can be a very beguiling man."

He quirked a smile at her. "Is that good or bad?"

"I'm not entirely sure."

He smiled, a decidedly *beguiling* smile. "I just thought we should get to know each other, that's all. Since we're going to be married."

"A marriage in name only."

"I'm well aware of the terms," he said.

Callie took another sip of her wine, trying to decide why her reference to their platonic marriage would put such a sharp edge in his voice. After all, he was the one who started this. He was the one who maintained that everything was going to be strictly business. Why the sudden need to get to know each other? Why especially, when she was sitting here so close to him, battling the almost overwhelming need for him to pull her into the circle of those powerful arms? She took another drink of her wine.

"What makes a woman leave what must likely have

190

been a comfortable, thoroughly civilized life in New York to look for buried treasure in Yellowstone?"

She frowned. "Riley Smith talks too much."

"Riley Smith is intrigued by a lady fortune hunter. And so am I."

She studied his hands, the way they curved around the head of the glass. She imagined those same fingers twining through her hair. She didn't object when he poured more wine into her glass. "Deirdre was supposed to keep that part of my itinerary a secret from Mr. Smith." She felt so warm, so light-headed.

"Do you really think the money is still there?"

"Maybe." She was scarcely listening. Her gaze trailed along the corded muscles of his throat, down to the deep vee opening of his chambray shirt. A faint sheen of perspiration glistened across what flesh she could see. She imagined how it must continue along the broad expanse of his chest.

"Personally, I think the money is long gone," Trace said.

"That's nice." She wasn't listening. She finished her wine and held out her empty glass, smiling when he poured her what was left in the bottle.

"It probably disappeared into one of the deeper hot springs."

Callie's thought processes seemed a bit fuzzy all at once. She knew Trace was talking about Yellowstone, and she dearly loved to discuss the legend of the lost payroll. But she was having difficulty concentrating on what he was saying. Determined, she drew back her shoulders, trying to repress what she knew was a perfectly silly grin. "Do you know that you're a very good-looking man?"

He laughed, lifting her wineglass and setting it on the floor. "I think you're tipsy."

Her brows furrowed as she concentrated on what he had just said. Tipsy? Why would he think . . . ? Her eyes widened as she swallowed convulsively. Surely she hadn't said aloud what she'd just been thinking . . . about how good-looking . . . ? She sagged against the back of the settee. "I think you're right. And I think I'm mortified."

He laughed again, a warm, good-natured sound that convinced her he considered the compliment to be the wine talking and nothing more.

"You said you've been to Yellowstone. Have you ever looked for the money?"

He shook his head. "You're talking two million acres."

"But the massacre site can be pinpointed."

"Maybe I just don't believe in treasures. Though, like I said, I'd like to know why you're a treasure hunter. You. Callie Callaghan."

"It's no deep, dark secret. I want to prove something to my father. Show him I'm as good or better than any man he has on his staff at *The Sentinel*."

Trace's brows furrowed. "The *New York Sentinel?*"

She hesitated, then decided there was little use hiding the truth. "Yes. Why?"

"From things I've heard that's a pretty powerful paper. And your father works there?"

She took a deep breath. "My father *owns* the *New York Sentinel.*"

"Oh."

"I suppose you think that answers your next question. About whether or not I'm doing it for the money."

"That wasn't my next question. But if that's the one you want to answer . . ."

She tried to gauge what he was thinking, but found it impossible. She detected neither undue surprise nor particular interest in her revelation that her father was a rich and powerful man. "There is a finder's fee . . . a reward, if you will. And I won't deny that I wouldn't mind claiming it. I've already gone through my savings to outfit this trip. And I absolutely will not accept any financial assistance from my father." She grimaced ruefully. "Not that he'd offer it in the first place. But he will pay for the story, if I find the treasure. A story this big, he would even buy from his own daughter."

"You're a gutsy lady. I admire that."

"From the things you've said, I would think you could empathize with having to prove something to one's father."

He stared into the flames.

"I'm sorry. Maybe I shouldn't have said that. It was worse than with my father, wasn't it? At least I know my father loves me, however misguided he might be about what's best for me."

Trace slammed back the rest of his wine. "I don't want to talk about it."

Tentative, nervous, she reached toward him, but stopped short of touching him. "It's not fair to make me do all the talking, you know."

He stood, striding over to the fireplace. The wine had all too obviously had the effect he had wanted. She was open, vulnerable—just as he'd hoped. Then why wasn't he pressing forward with his plan? Why didn't he take her right here, right now on the bearskin rug as each minute his body more and more insistently demanded? He sucked in a lungful of air, picking up one of the kachina dolls. Hehea. The woman-chaser.

"You don't have to chase this one. She's not going anywhere."

He kept his eyes on the mantel. "Damn. I don't want to hurt you . . ."

"I believe you."

The wine was affecting him, too. Though he was fighting like hell against the sexual tension that fired his blood, he was paradoxically more at ease, relaxed, then he could ever remember being. He frowned, realizing he couldn't give full credit to the wine. It was Callie who put him at ease, being here, talking to her like this. Callie, whom he was enticing, seducing, using . . .

He bit off a curse.

"Trace, what is it?"

He turned, stomping toward the front door. He couldn't go through with it. Whenever the wedding finally took place would have to be all right. Somehow he would make certain that Callie and the Marlowes didn't meet during the couple's upcoming visit. Somehow . . . He slammed a fist against the door. Damn, why did his past have to keep rising up to haunt him? Maybe if he told Callie the truth . . . Maybe she would understand . . .

He closed his eyes. How could anyone understand what he had done?

She was there. Behind him, her hand gliding over his shoulder. He straightened.

"Trace . . ."

"Go to bed, Callie. Go to bed. Now. I'm . . . tired." He jerked the door open, then shut it again. He wanted no moonlit walk tonight. "I think I'll go to bed myself."

The door hadn't caught, and it creaked open. Callie pushed it shut before following him back over to the settee. "You're a hard man to figure out," she said softly.

"What do you mean?"

"You ask a woman to marry you, a woman you met three days ago, so that you can maintain custody of the son you love. The woman agrees. And you're still miserable." She had intended her voice to be light, but didn't quite succeed as she sensed his distress.

He sank onto the settee, then leaned forward, his head in his hands. How he wished he could tell her all of it. But he couldn't take the chance, couldn't risk her backing out of the marriage.

"There's an old proverb," she said, coming over to sit beside him. "The wine goes in, the truth comes out. I think that's what's happening to us both."

Not me, he thought bitterly. *Never the whole truth from Trace McCord.*

"Tell me about Jenny," she asked, not certain why she wanted to know. "Did you love her?"

As short a time ago as this morning, he would have exploded at such a question, even from Callie, even knowing what he needed from her. But now his mood was thoughtful, reflective. "She had to stand up to a lot of gossip—mostly from people in Rock Springs whenever we went in for supplies—because she stayed on at the ranch after Seth died. Living here with me. Yes, I loved her. But not the way you think. She was like a sister to me."

"I'm sorry. I have no right to pry into your life like this."

"No. It's all right. It feels good to talk about it." He

watched her closely as he continued. "Do you know I delivered Christopher?"

Her eyes widened, not with shock or censure, but with wonder. "How special that must have been for you."

"There was no one else around when she went into labor." A deep tenderness glinted in his eyes. "Until then, I hadn't really thought about the reality of the child. But when I held Christopher in my hands, felt the life in him . . . I can't explain it. I never expected my reaction to be so deep, so visceral. God, how I loved him. From that first second."

Her heart thudded. She had thought she loved Trace before, when she'd been drawn to his looks, the animal grace in the way he moved, the loving way he doted on Christopher. But now here tonight she knew it was more than anything physical, it was the man—who he was, what he was. Peevish, self-critical, secretive. Tender, passionate, proud. Trace McCord. Not exactly a mythic hero, but a fully realized dream nonetheless. How could she marry this man and then walk out of his life forever?

"Jenny was the only person in my life who ever just accepted me for being me."

"That doesn't seem so difficult." Her smile was shy, tentative, knowing she was revealing too much, but unable to stop herself. Sensing—or was it hoping?—that he really didn't want her to stop. That he wanted her to care, needed her to care.

"I haven't done many things right in my life. My father hated me for being born. Lanie usually only had one thing on her mind. Seth tried to get me on the straight and narrow by setting the perfect example. He never cut himself any slack. Never. Always had to be perfect. For Pa. For me. I tried to tell him I'd rather have a brother than a saint, but . . ." He shook his head, leaving the thought unfinished.

"How did he die?"

"A horse threw him. A big red horse he'd been after for years, raiding our mares, stealin' himself a herd. We got him. I told Seth he was not a horse ever to be broke. But Seth had to prove me wrong. The stallion rolled over on him. Broke his back. He lived for three days, but there was nothing anyone could do. He asked me to take care of Jenny."

"He didn't tell Jenny to take care of you. He told you to watch out for her. He gave you more credit than you do yourself."

He twisted to look at her. "You're like a dream. It doesn't make sense that you should land on my doorstep when I need . . ."

"I know what you mean. I didn't want to stop here. It's like I knew there would be something to make me stay. Make me want to stay."

He sat there, his shoulders almost too squared, as though he'd had to pick himself up and dust himself off too many times, each time squaring his shoulders more defiantly at life. "I want you to know I really appreciate the fact that you've said yes."

She could actually *feel* how uncomfortable he was to admit that he was grateful, to admit that he was in anyone's debt. "Just when exactly is the custody hearing?"

"Hopefully not too long after we're married."

"The judge just sees that you're married, that you've fulfilled Jenny's wishes, and grants you permanent custody?"

"Lyle Morton seems to think that should do it."

"I know I'm out of line again. But if Jenny truly cared for you . . . why would she impose such a condition on Christopher's custody?"

"Maybe she thought he needed two parents."

"No. You would have been enough."

His eyes burned. He looked at her, really looked at her. The scattering of freckles across her nose, her green eyes, the soft oval of her face, the curtain of silk that was her copper-fire hair. Pleasant features that were suddenly beautiful. Beyond beautiful. Her lips slightly parted, her skin flushed from the wine, her eyes soft, compassionate. There was a resiliency in her, a sense of humor that could see her through the worst life could offer. And he knew even if she were eighty, he would never see her any other way again than as she was at this moment.

Like a thunderbolt, the truth ripped through him. He loved her.

"I think Jenny added the codicil *for you,*" she said, and he was surprised that she hadn't noticed the profound change in him. Surely it must show on his face, in his eyes. But then, she wasn't looking at him. She was watching the embers glow on the logs in the hearth. "You haven't done what she wanted."

"What's that?" he managed, still awestruck by the power of his newfound realization.

"She wanted you to go out and court some wonderful young woman and fall in love and live happily ever after."

"Jenny was a romantic. She loved Seth." He was talking, but he was no longer thinking. All he wanted in the world was to make love to this woman—to show her with his body what his heart had just magically discovered.

Love is a fairy tale.

He'd said it to Lanie, because he'd never felt, never expected to feel in his life, what he felt for Callie Callaghan. As impossible as it seemed, the fates had brought her to him. She was his. She had to be.

"You are still going through with the marriage?" he asked.

"I wouldn't be sitting here like this if I wasn't. This is too important to you for me to be coy . . ."

How could he have even considered using her? Of compromising her in any way? If she ever found out . . . God, he didn't deserve her. He swore inwardly. He didn't have her. She would leave when the custody was decided. She had agreed to this arrangement only for Christopher's sake, the very reason he had been forced to propose the arrangement in the first place. But now it was so much more. Damn, why did the Marlowes have to be involved? Why . . . He squeezed the goblet so tightly it shattered in his hand.

She was at his side in an instant. "Are you all right? Let me see that." She turned his palm over in her own.

"It's all right. It didn't cut me. It . . ." He swept her into his arms, burying his face in her satin-fire hair. "Callie . . . Callie . . . Callie . . . forgive me."

"Forgive you for what?"

He pulled back a little, though he kept her prisoner in his arms. "Nothing. Never mind. I know you're not going to believe this, but . . ." Why did he suddenly feel as if she held his very life in her hands? "I want you to marry me."

She cocked her head to one side, smiling bemusedly. "I know. That's what this is all . . ."

"No. Forget the custody hearing. Forget everything. I want you to marry me, because . . ." he swallowed, "because . . . I love you."

He wished the words back at once when he saw first the puzzlement, then the suspicion dawn in her green eyes. Damn, he had said it all wrong. He shouldn't have blurted it out like that. He should have led up to it gradually, told her . . .

His lips closed on hers, his mouth raining kiss after kiss across her lips, her cheeks, her nose, her eyelids. His hands closed on either side of her head, his fingers threading through her satiny hair. "Don't say anything. Nothing. Just let me love you. Let me prove to you I'm telling the truth."

"You love me?" she whispered, barely able to take in the full import of that tiny phrase, but able to read the aching want in his brown eyes.

His lips pressed against hers. She could feel the warmth of his breath flaring from his nostrils against her cheek. His mouth moved eagerly over her own, his tongue caressing her lips. She felt herself grow warm, hot, weak. Her mouth opened, accepting the thrust of his tongue.

Her hand slid inside his shirt, tracing the outline of his nipples, gliding over hard muscle. He groaned, his hand reaching up to catch the back of her neck, holding her to him, as her hands fumbled with the buttons of his shirt.

She tracked her fingernails across his chest and

down to circle his navel, then charted a course above his beltline. She knew she should stop, but it felt so good to touch him.

He unbuttoned her dress front, then unlaced her chemise, freeing her breasts. He wasn't thinking anymore about weddings or codicils or right or wrong. He only knew his body was on fire and she was the source of the heat and he craved more.

His hands cupped her breasts, his heart hammering. His mouth devouring hers. His loins aching.

He raised up her skirt, his hand gliding beneath the waistband of her pantalets, caressing her, finding her wet, ready. She moaned softly, inviting, needing. The thoughts intruded—she's had too much wine. She's a virgin. It wasn't right. He rationalized—she's going to marry me.

"Trace . . ."

His name on her lips was the delicate shift of butterfly wings on a moonbright night.

He eased her down atop the bearskin rug, the soft fur a tactile delight.

"Callie . . . Callie . . ."

He shoved out of his jeans, feeling the heat of the hearth sear along his naked flesh. He lay back, groaning, achingly, maddeningly aroused. He watched her face, watched her hand skate across his abdomen and down. He sucked in his breath as she circled him, tracked him, held him. "We have to stop this." Each word was a croaking whisper.

Her mind told her how irrational she was being. But she convinced herself that if she let him, if she wanted him as much as he seemed to want her, then maybe she could believe that he loved her. Loved her as she loved him.

"Take me," she pleaded.

"I can't. We shouldn't. Callie, you're . . . you've had too much wine." His body paid the price for his newfound ethics. His sex was rigid with need. But he loved her. He couldn't take advantage of her.

Ten minutes ago he could have forced himself to use her, told himself his having Christopher justified any method at all to get him. That once the custody was settled it wouldn't matter if she hated him, because she'd be gone and he'd never see her again. But it did matter, it mattered more than anything in the world. He couldn't bear for her to hate him. He loved her. Loved her.

"It's all right, Trace," she murmured. "We're going to be married. Please, show me what it's like. Please. I want to know. I want to please you."

"You please me by being here, by being alive in my arms." He positioned himself above her, capturing her eyes, seeing the haze of alcohol, the smile. He teased her with the proof of his desire, and saw her eyes widen. He held himself still, took his mouth to her breasts, groaning, losing his mind to the sheer ecstasy of what was happening between them.

She raked her fingers down his back, reveling in the rippling muscles, the lean, hard body. She was so wanton, abandoned. Never had she felt this way. Part of her knew it was the wine, and yet it felt so good, so good.

She ached for something she didn't understand, but knew instinctively that Trace McCord was both the source and the surcease of her need. She was ready, more than ready. She opened herself to him.

"Callie, we'll have all the time in the world on our wedding night. I want it to be right, to be perfect. I don't want you to feel hurt or angry or . . ."

She reached between them, held him, her throaty whisper driving any last vestiges of good intentions from his brain. With a cry half anguish, half ecstasy he drove himself inside her, linking his body to hers and knowing, *knowing* he would never be whole again without her.

How could a man understand love in an instant? How could his life be turned inside out by one beat of his heart.

He reveled in the feel of her arms around him, holding him to her as he began to move inside her.

"Trace, oh, Trace, it's going to be good between us. I want to stay . . ." There was a sound, a noise, something that didn't belong.

"My God," she cried, "there's someone at the front door." She was up, scrambling, terrified. "Deirdre!"

Trace was on his feet, shoving into his pants. Cursing. Cursing as she'd never heard anyone curse. "It's all right. Get into the guest room. Stay there. I'll keep whoever it is outside."

She pressed herself against the wall, unable to move out of the way in time. She heard voices. Riley. Her heart pounded as she waited to hear Deirdre's as well. Waited to see her aunt sweep into the room. But no one came inside the house. Trace had opened the door only a crack, effectively blocking anyone's entry.

"Sorry I'm late," Riley was saying.

Late? She frowned. What was he talking about? Late for what? Why would Trace have expected Riley to come at all? A sickening ball formed in her stomach and grew larger as she listened.

"So did you give Miss Callie the engagement ring?"

"I, uh, didn't get a chance yet . . ."

"I tried to be here right at midnight with Miss Deirdre like you asked, but she twisted her ankle while we were walking. She's over at the bunkhouse. Actually, I was wondering if you could give me a hand bringing her to the house. With this bum leg . . ."

"Fine. I'll be out in five minutes." He shut the door, cursing softly. He turned, startled to see Callie standing in the shadows barely three feet from him, her face ashen.

"You *told* him to be here at midnight with Aunt Deirdre? *Told* him? Why? Why would you do that?" The realization rocked her. "You wanted them to find us together, didn't you? Didn't you?" she shrieked. "You did it on purpose. You used me! You bastard! You used me!"

"Callie . . ." He took a step toward her, but stopped as she backed away.

"A real marriage? You love me? What a fool I am. What a fool you've made me! You did all this so I would have no choice but to marry you, marry you on your damnable terms."

"Callie, it didn't happen. I stopped him. I . . ." He brushed back his hair, feeling more like something that belonged under a rock.

"Keep talking! Just keep talking, you son of a bitch! You'd say anything, do anything to get me to marry you! Anything! Even destroy me in the eyes of my aunt! I hate you! I hate you!"

"I'm sorry."

"Sorry! You expect me to believe anything you say

204

ever again?" Her eyes narrowed. "The door. My God, you even made sure the door was open. If I hadn't locked it myself . . ." She was trembling, choking back the bile that rose in her throat as the image of what could have been tore through her. "Riley would have found us. Naked in front of this fire! And you planned for Deirdre to be with him! God in heaven, what kind of a monster are you?" She whirled and ran for her room, slamming the door in her wake.

He bolted after her, but did not attempt to open the door. "Callie, Callie, please. It wasn't supposed to be like that. It was never supposed to go so far . . ." Damn. He leaned against the pine, the memory of seeing the hate, the disgust in her eyes more painful than anything he had ever known.

"Liar!" she screamed.

He shoved open the door, but didn't go in.

The hate and disgust were still there.

"Get out!"

She was too angry, too hurt. He knew she would never hear anything more he had to say tonight. Turning away, he stalked outside to give Riley a hand with Deirdre, as he promised he would. He found the woman sitting on a haybale near the barn, Smith clucking around her like a mother hen.

"Don't fuss so," Deirdre was saying as she struggled to her feet. "I already feel foolish enough. Tripping over a silly rock."

"Nothing foolish about it," Smith said. "Now you let Trace and me help you over to the house. You did for me when I was hurting, now it's my turn."

Trace had the feeling the woman was blushing, but his own mood was so grim, he wanted only to get her deposited in the house and be done with it. Without asking, he stepped in and scooped the woman into his arms.

"Mr. McCord," Deirdre exclaimed, "this will never do."

"It's the quickest way, ma'am. You'll just have to forgive me." He shuddered. Asking Deirdre's forgiveness merely seared him anew with what he had done to Callie.

"Is everything all right?" Deirdre asked, her kind eyes studying him too seriously.

"Just fine."

"Is there something wrong with Callie?" The woman was concerned now.

"I wouldn't have any way of knowing . . ." He stopped, weary of his own lies. "You'll just have to talk to her, ma'am."

"I'll do that."

Trace deposited Deirdre in the front room on the settee, allowing Riley to take over from there. "If you'll excuse me, it's been a long night." He headed to his room, stretching out atop the bedcovers, trying to be cold, assessing. At least he doubted Callie would say anything to her aunt about tonight.

Forty-two days. Could he find someone else to marry him?

Someone else? As though there could ever be anyone else in his heart again? He loved her. Loved her! He remembered the feel of her under his hands, his body. The look in her eyes when she'd told him he was all the parent Christopher needed. The joy in her face when he'd thrust himself inside her.

He wasn't supposed to care who it was. He was just

supposed to use her.

He was shaking.

He would talk to her, explain. Explain what? He had been caught in his own trap, and even as he loathed himself for what happened, he knew he would redouble his efforts to persuade her to marry him. Though now their time together would be an endless torment because she hated him, he would seek no other wife.

Callie would fulfill the codicil. As he lay there in the darkness, he considered a way to assure her compliance.

Now more than ever it was imperative that Callie marry him before the Marlowes arrived. He would play his ace tomorrow. It would solidify her hate, but it would also be the leverage he needed to insure that her answer be yes. The marriage would take place tomorrow. The Marlowes could arrive any time now. Once they opened their mouths, his bluff would be called, and if Callie weren't already his wife, she never would be.

Chapter Thirteen

Callie slept fitfully, her dreams filled with grotesque images, nearly all of them of Trace McCord. In each of his guises he would appear at first solicitous and caring, but time and again his face would contort, his features shifting into a vile mask, his heart revealing its true nature, one filled with treachery and deceit.

Though she woke an hour before dawn, she lay still, feigning sleep, waiting for Deirdre to wake and leave the room. Her aunt had come in not long after Callie's final shouted exchange with Trace. Callie had detected her aunt's halting step, recalling Riley's mention of a twisted ankle. She had to fight off a surge of guilt for not inquiring about the severity of the injury. But her mind was too filled with guilt of a different sort to risk a late-night talk with her too perceptive aunt.

At least she could be grateful for one thing: Riley had obviously given Deirdre no hint that anything had been amiss in the house last night when he'd stopped by. If Deirdre had had any inkling at all about what had transpired in front of the fireplace, Callie was certain her aunt would have confronted her at once.

Bone weary, Callie climbed out of bed. Thoughts of confrontations only led to the one she would inevitably face this morning with Trace. With no care to how she looked she dragged a brush through her hair, then pulled on a faded calico dress she had taken to using as a dustcover for one of her cameras. Somehow, facing the morning looking her best would only serve to depress her further.

In the kitchen she found a note from Deirdre. Her aunt and Riley had taken Christopher on a picnic. *The child will keep Mr. Smith on his best behavior,* Deirdre wrote. Even through the mist of her pain Callie could see the joy evident in the happy strokes of Deirdre's pen. They had not spoken of it at all, but Callie was certain her aunt was in love.

She sighed wistfully, glad at least that Deirdre was finding their stay at Shadow's Way to be a pleasant one. Too miserable to eat, too upset to even consider writing in her journal, Callie headed outside, strolling aimlessly. Never had she felt more wretched.

Damn the man! Why had he felt the need to use her? She had been sympathetic to his plight. Sympathetic, hell! She had been stupid enough to think she was in love with him. Her heart lurched painfully as she blinked back tears. At least she had rid herself of that fantasy! Now that she knew the man, knew what he was capable of, she despised him.

She thought about saddling a horse and riding off to be by herself for the day, but couldn't quite summon the energy required for the task. Instead she meandered over to the nearest corral. Trembling, she leaned against a rough-hewn post. "I do despise him," she said, as if hearing the words spoken aloud would sear them more indelibly into her brain.

She lifted her gaze toward the inner circle of the corral, as Kachina nickered a welcome. The mare trotted over, shoving her velvety muzzle over the uppermost railing. "How can such a sweet horse be owned by such a beast?" she murmured, patting the sleek chestnut's neck.

For years she had allowed no unsettling emotions to intrude on her life, even fantasy emotions that might have permitted her to imagine what it would be like to be in love. Such musings had been overshadowed by her dreams of proving herself as a reporter, as a writer, proving herself to Fletcher Callaghan. Now she wished desperately that she had maintained that practiced aloofness, that she had not given herself up to the joy of loving. For in so doing she had discovered that love harbored a darkness in its light—that for all of its wonder, love wielded an awesome power to cripple, to destroy.

How Trace had used her! How he had planned to continue to use her! A marriage in name only, he said. Just words. When she had refused to accede to his wish that they marry at once, he had devised a despicable plot to humiliate her in the eyes of her aunt.

Callie shook her head. She had to give the man credit. He had read Deirdre very well. If her aunt had walked in on their tryst last night, she would have dragged them both to Rock Springs that very moment and pounded on doors until she found a priest to marry them.

The crunch of bootheels crossing the dirt of the ranchyard told her of Trace's approach. She held her ground, but did not turn around. She kept her eyes riveted on Kachina, continuing to stroke the mare's satiny neck.

"You have every right to hate me," he said.

Amazing, she thought. *He even sounds contrite. He must have been up all night practicing.*

"But I'm still desperate enough to ask you to go through with the wedding."

She jerked back, stomping away from the mare so abruptly that the horse shied, bolting to the opposite side of the corral.

"Callie . . . wait!"

She stopped, but still she didn't turn to face him. She wondered why she was even listening, why she didn't just run, get away. But she knew. They would have this conversation sooner or later. She decided it might as well be now. She didn't move as he stalked toward her, coming around to stand in front of her.

"All right," he said. "I'm not asking. I'm telling. You're going through with the wedding."

Before she could give voice to the explosive curse that rose in her throat, he added, "I'll make it worth your while. Financially."

That didn't even deserve the dignity of a curse. "You have forty-one days to find someone else," she said coldly. "I suggest you stop wasting precious time talking to me and begin searching for a female with the warmth and sensitivity of a cobra. That'll be a love match for certain."

"There won't be anyone else."

"Women like that *are* hard to find."

"Lyle Morton will be here at noon. He'll have Father Liam O'Casey with him. You and I will be married."

211

"You're out of your mind!"

"I intend to have Christopher."

"Then you'd best start checking under rocks for a mate! You won't find any cobras nearby, but you could settle for a rattler."

He didn't even wince. Not once.

"It's a shame you found yourself incapable of exercising such restraint last night," she said, hating how her voice shook. "This morning could have been so very different."

His gaze remained steady, determined. "Like I said, I'll compensate you for your time. And I'll be your guide to Yellowstone."

"I wouldn't let you be my guide across the corral."

He drew in a long breath, then let it out slowly. His words sent her heart into her stomach.

"You'll marry me, Callie. Today. Or your aunt will find out precisely what happened on that bearskin rug last night."

She couldn't suppress a gasp of horror. "You wouldn't. Surely even you are not capable of . . ."

"I have tried to impress upon you how desperate I am."

Tears slid from her eyes. "I hate you."

"I'm not asking you to do otherwise. Just be my wife until the hearing is over. We won't talk; we won't even see each other. I'll stay out on the range with my horses as much as possible. But we're getting married today. At noon."

"No."

Anger flicked briefly in his brown eyes, only to be quickly subdued. "I believe your aunt is on the north bluff with Riley and Christopher. It should take me about ten minutes to get there."

He headed for the barn. She stood rooted to the ground, unable to move, unable to breathe. How could she have so totally misjudged this man? Maybe that was what hurt the most. That she had dared imagine herself in love for the first time in her life—only to have the man she thought she loved turn her world to ashes.

A minute later he strode out of the barn leading Shoshone. He hadn't taken the time to saddle the stallion, merely putting on a bridle. "Last chance," he said, his voice infuriatingly even. He gripped the horse's silvery mane and vaulted onto its back.

"Damn you."

"Do I invite her to a wedding? Or tell her her niece might be pregnant out of wedlock?"

She staggered, as though he struck her. "But . . . but you didn't . . . I mean . . ." Tears of shame streamed unheeded down her cheeks.

"Is this your wedding day, Miss Callaghan?" he pressed relentlessly.

She focused on nothing, staring straight ahead.

He slammed his heels into the stallion's sides.

"All right, damn you!" she shrieked. "I'll marry you."

He reined the horse to a stop and dismounted, tromping back over to her. "A wise decision."

"Go to hell."

"The priest will be here at noon. Be ready." He grabbed her and kissed her brutally, savagely, his lips bruising, insulting, his hands roaming insolently along her body.

She held herself rigid in his arms, hating him, hating herself for allowing him to maneuver her into such an untenable situation.

With a sudden, savage profanity he released her. "Believe it or not," he snarled, "that was just a demonstration to remind you that this marriage is in name only. If you have any intentions of making it otherwise, you will be sorely disappointed. I want no entanglements at the end of this farce. None."

She recoiled in horror. "If *I* have any intentions of making it otherwise? Let me tell you where it will snow before you ever touch me like that again, Mr. McCord."

"Just so we understand each other." With that he again mounted the stallion. "I'll tell your aunt that her niece is in need of a maid of honor."

She wiped the back of her hand across her mouth, as she watched him ride out. But try as she might she could not wipe away the feel of his lips on hers.

Married. In less than twenty minutes she would be Mrs. Trace McCord. Callie sank onto the maple fan-back chair in front of the matching vanity in the guest room, unwillingly recalling the last time she had nervously awaited a wedding. Only this time there could be no last-minute escape. This time she must wed the man who paced impatiently in the front of the house awaiting the arrival of the priest who would marry them.

She had felt no love for Nicolas, nor had he seemed to feel any but a casual affection for her. Yet if the fates and her father had succeeded in forcing her to go through with that wedding, she knew somehow she would have made the best of it, throwing herself

214

wholeheartedly into the pursuit of her dream to be a writer.

Nicolas had wanted the power and influence of belonging to the Callaghan family. Fletcher Callaghan had wanted his daughter wed to Nicolas's title and position. With Trace a wedding would involve no social maneuvering. But what it would involve, *did* involve, was imminently more dangerous—to her heart, to her soul. Could she survive a marriage to Trace McCord with her spirit intact? She sighed heavily, curving her fingers around the ivory-handled hairbrush on the vanity. Could she continue to assure herself she didn't love him?

She slapped the brush down, rising to her feet. Of course she didn't love him! She had merely been suffering from an infatuation based on wrong information. Now that she knew the man . . .

God, why did her heart ache so? Was it for what she had lost, no matter how fleeting? Or was it for what could have been had Trace McCord been the man she'd believed him to be?

She studied her reflection in the mirror, the dark circles under her eyes a silent testament to what these past days had cost her. She had been in love. *In love!* And now . . .

She hated him.

She swiped at a vagrant tear. God help her, that wasn't true. She didn't hate him. Not totally, as she thought she should. Some tiny part of her still clung to the notion, however misguided, that he couldn't possibly be as callous as his behavior would have her believe.

She remembered the calculating light in his eyes that

first night when he'd kissed her. But more than that she remembered his lopsided grin and the undercurrent of heat when they'd talked of heroes and fair maidens. There had been more than a touch of insecurity, a disarming vulnerability about him. She couldn't have been that wrong. Perhaps there was something she didn't know, something that could make a difference, maybe even explain, if not excuse, what he had done last night.

She clung to that belief, perhaps stupidly, she admitted, because she couldn't accept that the man would so crushingly hurt her without a reason. Not when her cooperation was essential in his quest to secure permanent custody of his little boy. Otherwise, he could have hired a woman to play the part, paid her off and been done with it. No matter how unbelievable it might seem, there had to be some specific reason he wanted her—Callie Callaghan—to be his wife, and no one else. And if only to stave off her own misery she intended to use these next weeks to find out what that reason was.

"I think you want me more than you know, Trace McCord," she murmured aloud. "That much you couldn't hide, any more than I could hide what I felt for you." She would use his desire to her advantage. Whatever game he had been playing last night, there had been a time, if only for a moment, when the game had been playing him. She had gained the upper hand, only she hadn't known it. Next time she would. No one was that good at pretense. When he'd told her about Jenny and Seth, told her about his father, about Christopher, he'd spoken from his heart. He had shared more than he had intended, and because of it he had lost control.

If she could press him into such a state again, she could twist the game to her rules. She would make him open and vulnerable, make him share his secrets. Perhaps, came the vengeful thought, she could even pay him back just a little for the pain she had suffered from his lies.

She shivered. No, she couldn't think about getting even. To do so was to stoop to Trace's methods. At least he had a motive—securing custody of Christopher. To plot any truly effective revenge against him would mean taking steps to jeopardize that custody. And that she could never do. She had come to love that little boy. No matter how much Trace had hurt her, she would not take it out on Christopher.

Pacing fretfully, she wondered what could be keeping her aunt. True to his word, Trace had ridden out to find Deirdre and Riley, informing them that they were *cordially* invited to a wedding.

Deirdre had been gracious enough not to ask too many questions, confining herself thus far to keeping Christopher entertained while Callie dressed. Trace had balked when Callie volunteered to wear her frumpy calico. Instead he'd retrieved a linen-wrapped garment from Jenny's cedar chest.

"It was her wedding dress," he said, handing it to her.

"I couldn't," she stammered. But Trace would have none of it. Two hours of airing had reduced the sharp scent of cedar, though not eliminated it. Now Callie stood in the center of the guest room, smoothing the lovely silk. How different she must feel today than when Jenny had worn the dress for her own wedding day. From Trace's description, Seth and Jenny had been very much in love. If last night had not ended as it had, Callie had to wonder if she might not have been experiencing that same tender emotion herself.

A knock on the door interrupted her brooding thoughts.

"Who is it?"

"Trace." His voice was unexpectedly soft, like a caress. Callie felt herself grow warm.

"What do you want?"

"To talk."

She said nothing.

"I'd rather not do it through the door."

"Don't you know it's bad luck to see the bride before the wedding." She didn't even try to keep the sarcasm out of her voice.

"Callie, open the door."

She did so, yanking hard, allowing it to swing free to slam with a resounding thud against the wall. "It's open now."

His gaze remained infuriatingly steady. "Do I have to stand in the doorway?"

She stepped back into the room. "It's your house."

He regarded her speculatively, his eyes taking in the soft curves of her body. She blushed as she realized that he was probably thinking of how Jenny had looked in this dress.

"You look lovely. Jenny would be pleased."

So it was back to compliments and game-playing, she thought acidly. Well, she was on to him now. He would not find her naive and trusting again.

"You look passably handsome yourself," she said, coolly appraising the fine cut of his gray frock suit and deep blue silk shirt. The black string tie provided the

218

perfect accent, and had she truly been looking forward to this wedding, she couldn't have imagined a more dashing groom. "If you don't mind, I really would like to be alone until . . ." She stopped.

"Until you have no other choice?"

"Please go."

He stood quietly for another minute before he spoke. It was as though he was choosing each of his words with extreme care. "You know what this wedding means to me."

"You've made it excruciatingly clear."

"I know. I'm sorry."

She waited. As much as she mistrusted him, there was something about the way he was holding himself, almost as though he were about to ward off a physical attack, that made her feel absurdly protective of him.

"I've been thinking . . . about how unfair I've been to you."

"You have a flair for understatement, Mr. McCord." Her voice was hard, and in spite of her best intentions, defensive. She didn't want to feel protective, didn't want to feel anything for this man but hate.

"I've been thinking that there are some things you should know, things that might help you understand . . ."

"Nothing could make me understand what you intended to happen to me last night. Nothing."

"I wouldn't have let it happen . . . I . . ." He closed his eyes. "Damn." When he looked at her again, she was stunned by the anguish she saw mirrored in his gaze. "Just let me say this straight out . . ."

The door swung open, Deirdre bustling in, her ankle injury slight enough so that it no longer hampered her

219

step in the least. "Riley's seein' to the youngster, don't worry." She picked up Callie's hairbrush. "Now, my dear, it's time for those finishing touches . . ."

Callie hadn't taken her eyes from Trace. She had watched him straighten, his gaze grow hooded. Whatever he had been about to say was gone, shuttered away. "Trace . . ."

"It's all right, Callie." He smiled, though it didn't reach his eyes. "It's nothing. Never mind. I'll, uh, see you at the ceremony."

Deirdre looked from one to the other. "I interrupted something . . . Oh, dear."

"No, Miss Callaghan," Trace assured her. "It was nothing. I'll leave you and your niece alone."

When he'd gone, Deirdre turned to Callie. "I'm so sorry."

"It doesn't matter." Callie pressed a hand to her forehead, fighting off the beginnings of a pounding headache. He had been going to tell her. . . . *something she didn't know, something that could make a difference, maybe even explain, if not excuse, what he had done last night.* She sagged onto the edge of the bed. It had taken a lot for him to come in here, to even consider taking her into his confidence. He might never find it in himself again.

"I still don't understand why you have to rush this so," Deirdre was saying.

"You wouldn't want us breaking any commandments now, would you?"

Deirdre blushed. "So it's no longer just a business agreement between you?"

"We just decided to yield to our better judgment and get married, before things get out of hand." Callie's

220

stomach churned as she piled lie upon lie.

"Then why do you seem so . . ." Deirdre seemed to grope for the right word, ". . . sad."

"Oh, you know how I am about weddings. I always panic when the event is close at hand."

"This is no time for bad jokes, young lady. You sit down and tell me what you're about with Mr. McCord."

Callie caught her aunt's hands in her own. "I can't. This one time I can't. I have to work this out for myself, Aunt Deirdre. Please understand."

"No nuns' habits to escape to the hills in?"

Callie managed a weak smile. "No nuns' habits." She stepped over to the window, gazing out at the emerald sea of grasses that blanketed the eastern slope of the Shadow's Way valley.

"I do have to ask you one thing," Deirdre said. "Are you going to be tellin' your father about all this?"

"Maybe he already knows."

"And what do you mean by that?"

"It means I don't believe for a minute that Da doesn't know where we are. I think he's letting the leash out, waiting for me to fail."

"If Fletcher knew where you were, he'd be in this house. He would not be allowing your marriage to a man he would consider a heathen."

That's probably a good word for Trace, Callie thought wickedly, but said only, "Da will make his presence known when it suits him. I'm sure he's not personally on the hunt. He's hired someone. Or sent Nicolas."

"That dandy!" Deirdre scoffed. "The count's pride was likely wounded. But I can't imagine him wrinkling

221

his uniform to traipse across the country after the woman who left him at the altar."

"Maybe not."

"Callie . . ."

Callie straightened, wanting the subject changed. "Everything will be fine. Trace will get custody of Christopher, and then you and I and Riley can continue our grand trek."

"Mr. Smith won't be up to that for weeks yet."

"Well, that settles it then. The custody hearing is still a few weeks off. Things will work out perfectly."

Perfectly.

She trembled. She was going to be married to Trace McCord, a man who had resorted to blackmail to accomplish his goal. Blackmail. The thought splashed over her like an icy spray—what would prevent him from using the same tactic tonight in his bedroom?

Chapter Fourteen

Trace prowled the grounds between the corrals and the main house, wondering what could be keeping Lyle Morton. He'd never known the lawyer to be late. He hoped the man wouldn't choose today to take up new habits. Morton was bringing the priest. Within minutes of the Reverend O'Casey's arrival, Trace intended to make Callie his wife.

Heat surged through his loins as he remembered her in Jenny's wedding dress. Damn, she was so beautiful. If he hadn't been such a fool, maybe tonight could have been a real wedding night between them.

But he had been a fool. And she hadn't listened when he'd tried to explain. After his tactics this morning it was likely she never would. He had spent the night trying to think of some other way to convince her to marry him. But blackmail seemed the only solution. Especially since he intended the marriage to take place today. After his abortive seduction, she wouldn't believe anything he had to say anyway.

Like the fact that he loved her.

God, he really did love her. He had hoped that the cold light of day would have brought him to his senses. That he couldn't possibly be in love with a woman he was being forced to marry to keep Christopher. But seeing her this morning—her hair in sleep-tossed disarray, her eyes puffy, red-rimmed, her dress a shapeless rag—he had been stunned by the effect she had on his senses. It had been all he could do not to pull her into his arms, to beg her to forgive him.

That she had been crying tore him apart. Callie did not seem a woman easily pushed to tears, and that he had driven her to them twice in less than twenty-four hours clawed at his insides like a living thing. Did even assuring Christopher's custody justify hurting her like that?

If there was a way he could undo what happened last night . . . No, there was little use dwelling on the impossible. Getting through the wedding was what he had to focus on now. The Marlowes could be arriving anytime. Even emotional blackmail might not work on Callie once they had a chance to enlighten her on his less than noble past.

Nor did he delude himself that he could make her love him, even if the Marlowes kept their mouths shut. He had hurt her too deeply. Maybe she would find some satisfaction in knowing that he had paid a high enough price for what he had done. And he would pay a higher one still. Though he had come a step closer to securing Christopher's custody, he faced the prospect of being married to Callie, spending night after night in the same bed with her—and never being able to touch her, never making her his.

He swore, kicking viciously at a clod of dirt. It was

what he deserved. When the custody was settled, she would be gone. And with her, she would unknowingly take his heart.

Angrily, he shoved the thoughts away, telling himself it didn't matter. In a very real way he'd been alone all of his life. It wasn't like he wasn't used to it. Besides, he wouldn't actually be alone. Not anymore. He would have his son.

He was grateful when he finally spied Lyle Morton's buggy driving into the ranchyard. If nothing else, the wedding would distract him from any further self-flagellation, at least for the moment.

"You're late, Lyle," Trace said, striding up to the buggy.

"Glad to see you, too," the lawyer said, sticking out his right hand.

Trace accepted the handshake, even as his gaze shifted past the lawyer to the buggy's passenger. The gray-haired, black-suited Reverend Liam O'Casey regarded Trace with the same quiet curiosity with which Trace regarded him.

"I appreciate your coming, Father," Trace said, wondering if it was appropriate to offer his hand to the priest.

Father O'Casey settled the matter by extending his right hand. "Always happy to tighten those bonds of matrimony, my boy."

"You do have a bride for us?" Lyle asked.

"She's inside."

"You realize this is highly irregular, Son," the priest said.

"I know, Father. But I'm very busy at the ranch. We couldn't come to you."

"All well and good, I suppose," Father O'Casey said. "But since this is all happenin' in a bit of a rush, I would appreciate it if I could speak to the bride privately for a few moments before the ceremony."

Trace was instantly wary. "Why?"

"Because she's had no chance to have any prenuptial preparation. I just want to make certain she's aware that this is a lifetime commitment."

Trace stiffened. "She's well aware of what she's doing and why, Father. I assure you."

"Nevertheless, I'll not perform the service until I've spoken to her."

Trace could see he had no choice in the matter. Any further reluctance on his part would only fuel the priest's suspicions. "She's inside. The room in the rear on the right side of the house."

"I'll find it." The priest headed through the door and disappeared inside.

When he was out of earshot, Morton turned to Trace. "You'd best keep things moving along briskly," Lyle said.

"The Marlowes?"

"That's why we were late. They're two hours behind me. At most. They tried to pigeonhole Father O'Casey before we got out of town, but I managed to keep him clear of them."

"They were in Rock Springs?"

"Got there three days ago. You're just lucky Edna Marlowe was too travel-weary to come out to the ranch right away."

Trace swore.

"What's your bride going to think once they get here and have a little talk with her?"

226

"It won't much matter by then."

"Oh, but it will, Trace. The soon-to-be Mrs. McCord may well be called on to testify at the hearing."

"Why?" Trace's voice was more pained than angry. He imagined how easily Callie could use such an opportunity for revenge, how easily she could destroy any chance he had of keeping Christopher. "Surely she can't testify *against* me."

"This isn't a criminal proceeding. In the best interests of Christopher, Judge Lancaster has the right to interpret rather broadly who can and can't testify. If she doesn't have much to say in your favor it could influence him by omission."

"There isn't much I could do about that."

"Maybe you should just tell her the truth. Maybe she'd go through with it anyway. She seems to like the child." Morton's brows furrowed behind his wire-rimmed spectacles. "She has agreed to this, hasn't she?"

"She agreed."

The lawyer continued to look skeptical. "So are you going to tell her about . . ."

Trace cut him off. "I'll run my own life, thanks. I think it's time we went inside."

Morton gripped Trace's arm. "I don't like the sound of that. Miss Callaghan is entering into this union of her own free will, is she not?"

"I said she was."

"Maybe I'd just better ask her myself."

Trace jerked his arm free. "Ask her whatever you like. But remember this, you're my lawyer. That means you work for me."

"Don't threaten me, Trace. You know how long I'd be your lawyer if I didn't believe in your case. Jenny

227

wanted you to have Christopher."

"Then why the hell . . ." Trace slammed a hand against the porch's wooden support post. "Never mind. I don't want to know."

"Jenny had her reasons for doing things this way. I'm not entirely sure I agree with all of them, but . . ." Morton sighed. "She was my client, too. As Seth was."

"Is there something you're not telling me?"

The lawyer didn't meet his gaze.

"Dammit, Lyle . . ."

"I'm sorry. You'll find out soon enough. It's just that . . ."

"That what?"

"That I can't be the one to tell you. Jenny put one or two conditions on me, too."

Trace stared at him. "What the hell are you talking about? And why are you saying things like this to me now?"

"It's nothing."

"Liar," he hissed. "It's the Marlowes, isn't it? There's something . . ." He stiffened, knowing any further badgering would get him nowhere. "Just tell me it won't jeopardize my getting Christopher."

"Your raising Christopher was what Jenny wanted."

Trace stalked the length and breadth of the porch. "That's not a very direct answer. Damn. I'm about to be married. That alone is supposed to ensure my getting Christopher. Now you're suggesting . . ."

"I'm suggesting nothing," Morton snapped. "Nothing." He straightened. "The longer we stand out here jawing, the closer the Marlowes come to Shadow's Way."

228

Unsure whether to be angry or scared, Trace stomped past Morton into the house.

He spotted Callie near the fireplace. She was involved in an obviously intense conversation with the priest. Trace found himself worrying about just how much the clergyman knew about his past. The longer he watched the conversation, the more concerned he became. He was about to interrupt, when Christopher shot out of his bedroom, shrieking at the top of his lungs.

"Bug! Bug on my bed!"

Trace corraled the boy, lifting him into his arms. "Whoa there, pardner," he said, welcoming the distraction. "Let's go see about this varmint, shall we?" With a final anxious glance toward Callie, he carried the child back to his bedroom.

"Bug!" the boy said, pointing warily in the direction of the bed coverlet.

Trace spotted the daddy longlegs spider and smiled. "Come here, Chris," he said, motioning toward the child.

Christopher shook his head.

"It's all right. This little guy can't hurt you." Trace eased his hand under the spider, allowing it to crawl into his palm. "See?"

Christopher's mouth twisted with indecision. "Papa like spider?"

"Spiders have their place. They eat bugs like the flies that bite Shoshone and Kachina."

"Good spider?"

Trace grinned. "Good spider." He held his hand steady and crossed to the open window, where he

229

puffed gently on the spider, watching it fall to the ground and scurry off. "Now he's outside where he belongs."

"Cris-fer love Papa."

Trace gathered the boy in his arms, squeezing him against his chest. "Papa loves Christopher, too. Very much."

He carried the boy back to the front room to find Callie still talking to the priest.

"Papa put good spider outside!" Christopher announced.

The priest chuckled. Callie gave Trace a curious look. Setting the child on the floor, Trace came over and gripped her arm. "I think you've talked to the good Father long enough, dear. It's time to get on with the ceremony."

Her green eyes sparked with outrage, that he would dare interrupt her conversation with the priest. But her voice was as light as goose down. "Whatever you say, darling." She twined her arm with his and gave him a chaste peck on the cheek. Batting her eyes with mock innocence, she also gave him a swift kick in the shin, which he was certain the priest did not notice.

Grunting painfully, Trace smiled down at her. "I'm glad you're as anxious as I am, dear."

"Oh, more so, sweetheart," she cooed angelically. "I've never wanted anything over with more in my life."

Christopher came up to her, tugging on the skirt of her wedding dress. "Cal-lee, hide!"

"I'd love to," she muttered.

Trace glared at her, but managed to keep his voice even. "Where are your aunt and Riley?"

"Maybe they decided not to witness this travesty."

230

"Well, they'd just damned well better get . . ." He straightened, smiling as the priest came up to him. "Can we get on with it, Father?"

"Momentarily, I'm sure, my son. Miss Callaghan has informed me you've agreed to bring up any children the Lord might bless you with in the Catholic faith."

"She informed you of that, did she?" Trace said, still smiling. "Well, that's certainly true, Father. Whatever I have to promise to . . . I mean, I find that a wise choice, to be sure."

"And she tells me that you're thinkin' of convertin' yourself."

Trace continued to smile and nod. "She's sure a talker, isn't she?" He ran a hand over his face, certain his grin would soon crack the stretched taut flesh. "Can we get started?"

"As soon as the witnesses . . ."

The door opened, Riley Smith ambling into the room dressed in his finest buckskins. A beaming Deirdre was at his side, the mauve silk dress she wore rustling softly as she walked. "Hold on a minute, Reverend," the scout said. "I'd like a quick word with ya, if I could?"

Trace grimaced, but did not interfere as Smith herded the priest over to one side. A minute later Father O'Casey faced the small assembly, smiling broadly, "My, my, it seems we're going to have a double ceremony."

Callie gasped. "Oh, Aunt Deirdre . . ."

"I wanted to tell you, dear, but Riley insisted it be a surprise."

Callie grinned through happy tears. "I think that's the very first time I heard you call him Riley." She

231

turned to the scout. "You'd best take very good care of my aunt." She paused. *"Uncle* Riley."

The scout gave her a bashful hug.

"I hate to intrude," Trace said, "but I think we'd best get started." Morton's warning that the Marlowes were within two hours of Shadow's Way was now over an hour old. If the couple put the whip to their horses . . .

A thunderous crash sounded from the kitchen.

"Christopher!" Callie and Trace said the child's name simultaneously, both rushing toward the high-pitched shriek that followed the crash. Their terror that he had been hurt dissipated immediately. The three-year-old was sitting in the middle of the floor surrounded by the remains of the cake Deirdre had been planning to serve following the ceremony.

Callie grabbed up a towel.

"Forget it," Trace said, unable to quell the rising fear that the Marlowes would burst in to halt the wedding just before Callie became his wife. "Leave him. I'll take care of it later."

"I'm not going to leave him in the middle of a mess like this."

He grabbed her arm. "I said leave it."

"I will not! What's the matter with you?"

He released her, trying hard to rein in his temper, even as he watched Lyle Morton check his pocket-watch for the third time in five minutes."

"There, there, Christopher," Callie soothed, wiping at the sticky mess with the towel. "It's all right. We know you didn't mean it."

Trace jammed his hands into his pockets and stomped into the front room. He didn't trust himself to speak.

232

"Nerve wrackin', ain't it?" Riley Smith grinned from his perch on the arm of the settee. "Gettin' married, that is."

Trace gave the scout a curt nod, hardly listening. Blast! He was so close. To have it spoiled now . . . He twisted around to see Callie carrying a subdued Christopher into the room.

"Can we get on with it now?" he gritted.

"Whatever you say, beloved," she shot back. She did not let go of the child, even when the priest began the ceremony. She just prayed she wasn't going to faint.

"Do you take this man to be your beloved husband?" the priest asked. "To love, honor, and . . ."

"Cal-lee, hide!" Christopher shrilled suddenly, tightening his hold on her neck.

She resisted the urge to burst into hysterical laughter, taking instead a sadistic pleasure in watching a muscle in Trace's jaw flex, as the priest was forced to repeat the question. She gave a long, thoughtful pause before finally murmuring, "I do." The relieved sigh that coursed through Trace almost made her feel sorry for him. Almost, but not quite.

"Down!" Christopher demanded, as the rites concluded. Callie obliged, watching him plop onto the settee and curl up beside his puff puppy.

"Thank God that's over," she mumbled to herself, then straightened, startled, as the priest said, "Gentlemen, you may each kiss your bride."

She watched Riley give her aunt a quick but affectionate kiss. She smiled wistfully, then shuddered, recalling Trace's earlier behavior near the corral, when he had so crudely reminded her that the marriage was a business arrangement only. Surely, he wouldn't embarrass her in front of a priest.

She needn't have worried. His lips barely brushed her cheek. Even then she knew he had done it only out of a sense of obligation, a duty he couldn't avoid.

Father O'Casey presented the newlywed couples, each to the other, "Mr. and Mrs. Riley Smith. Mr. and Mrs. Trace McCord."

Callie felt Trace's arm tighten around her waist. She dared a quick glance up at him. The gesture caught him off guard. For just an instant she saw a haunting tenderness that nearly sent her to her knees. But just that quickly it was gone, his gaze smug, confident. And she had to wonder if the tenderness had been only a momentary aberration as he realized that he had now fulfilled the codicil, that Christopher would soon be his.

"Looks like we've given Cupid a real helping hand today," the scout was saying, shaking Trace's hand.

Callie wondered how Trace was going to get out of that one, but the sound of thundering hooves in the ranchyard diverted everyone's attention. She followed Trace to the front door, watching as a small carriage lurched to stop bare inches from the edge of the porch.

"Damn fool," Trace muttered, stiffening perceptibly as the driver leaped to the ground and proceeded to open the carriage door.

A man alighted first, his sharply tailored suit complementing precisely the sharp set of his angular features. He turned at once to assist his traveling companion from the coach. The woman slapped his hand aside, stepping down and somehow managing to arch her chin upward at the same time. Even under a fine layer of inevitable trail dust, the woman exuded an air of contemptuous arrogance that made Callie dislike her instantly, intensely.

Nor did she have to be introduced to the couple to know at once who they were. All she had to do was watch Trace. He had the look of a trapped animal, as if he were going to bolt for the house, grab up Christopher, and run. Then suddenly he straightened, looking cold and formidable.

Callie took an unconscious step back as the man and the woman studied her with an open hostility.

"Edna and Edgar Marlowe," Trace said unnecessarily.

"Trace, dear," Callie said, "you didn't tell me you were expecting other guests for the ceremony." She wasn't sure who she felt more anger toward—the Marlowes or Trace. "We could have waited a few more minutes."

"It must have slipped my mind."

Her teeth ground together. He had known they were coming. That's why he had rushed everything. Could the man be trusted about anything at all?

"Isn't it miraculous," Edna Marlowe was saying, her icy gray-green eyes on Callie. "That you and Trace should meet and fall in love mere weeks before the deadline set by Jenny's will." She made no attempt to mask the cynicism in her voice.

"Love is a miracle," Callie grated. "Fate, kismet, destiny. What can I tell you? It just happened." She couldn't believe she was saying these things, telling a bald-faced lie to this woman.

"Perhaps your love has blinded you to . . ."

Trace gripped Callie's elbow and propelled her toward the door. "Excuse us, Edna. This is our

235

wedding day. Callie and I would like to be alone for a little while."

His hand remained a steel band on her arm until they'd reached the near corral. Only then did he release her.

"You knew they were coming, didn't you?" she demanded, rubbing the circulation back into her abused limb. "Is that what prompted your delicate ultimatum this morning?"

"I don't know what you're talking about."

"You could give lectures on evading the truth." Gathering up her skirts, she tromped toward the barn, Trace keeping pace with her stride for stride.

She didn't have to turn to know what the expression on his face would be. When she did finally look back, she was surprised at how precisely she had pictured him. How could she capture him so well, when she had known him less than a week? His eyes sparked with anger, the planes of his face hardened by the grim set of his jaw.

"Forgive me, *darling,*" she sighed, batting her eyelashes mockingly, "I guess I'm just not as accomplished a liar as you are. I'm certain if we're married long enough you'll do your best to educate me in the art."

His whole body was rigid with rage, but she watched him contain it, subdue it, until he could speak evenly. "You have quite a way with you when you're angry."

She had expected just about anything but that. "You almost make that sound like a compliment."

"I told you once, you're a very direct woman. I like that. I admire it. It's a trait I've not found particularly dominant in myself."

"Do tell." She drew in a deep breath, getting hold of her fury. "Why are those people here?"

"I don't know."

"Maybe they love Christopher, too?"

The anger was instantly back in his eyes. "Don't you ever think about siding with them against me."

She took a step back. "Is that a threat?"

He slapped a hand into the upper railing of the corral, cursing when the gesture drove splinters into his palm. "No, it's not a threat. For God's sake, what do you take me for?"

"I have no idea, Mr. McCord. No idea at all. You're whatever time and circumstance dictates you be."

Muttering under his breath, he picked at the splinter.

Callie grabbed his hand and peered at his palm. "Do you really think the Marlowes stand a chance at the adoption? I mean, you have fulfilled the codicil."

"This is a private hearing. A private matter. Anything can happen, and probably will." He jerked his hand back, unable to bear her touching him another second without telling her how much he loved her, how much he hated what he was doing to her, would continue to do.

"Is there something you're not telling me, something that might color the adoption in the Marlowes' favor?"

"Of course not." He didn't look at her when he said it.

"Dammit, Trace! Don't lie to me. Not anymore. Or all of this will be for nothing. Please, if there's something else . . ."

"There isn't." He stood there, staring at her, the soft curves of her body accentuated by the fine cut of Jenny's wedding gown. His body throbbed with the

237

need to touch her. With a sudden, violent motion, he pulled her to him, wrapping his arms around her, kissing her with an explosive passion. She fought him at first, her fists shoving hard against his chest. But he gave no quarter.

And in the end she wanted none.

His tongue did not gently tease her lips apart, but rather demanded and received entry into her mouth with a powerful mastery that left her weak. His hands roamed expertly along her back, kneading the firmness of her buttocks, before rising to settle in the coppery strands of her hair.

He kissed her eyes, her nose, her cheeks, her neck, then his lips burned into hers once again, seeking, devouring, conquering.

With a tortured groan he filled his hands with her breasts. He teased the aroused tips beneath the confining fabric of her wedding dress. His eyes blazed into hers, one hand coming up to caress the side of her throat as he nuzzled his face against her neck.

"Sweet, Callie . . . so sweet . . ."

Like a masterful predator his invading tongue claimed her mouth once again. She gave herself up to the power of his possession. The persuasive assault of his lips, his body putting the lie to his promise that the marriage would be in name only.

"I don't believe what you do to me," he rasped. "This isn't part of the bargain . . ."

She gasped. "Yes, the bargain."

"Callie . . ."

She whirled away from him, ignoring his plea that she wait. As she neared the house she spied two figures moving away from the window.

The Marlowes.

They had been watching. Had Trace known? Sweet heaven, was his little performance by the corral for their benefit? To convince them that his "love" for her was genuine? She gave a strangled cry. How many times did the point have to be driven home? He really would go to any lengths to keep Christopher. Any lengths at all.

Lyle Morton and Father O'Casey were coming out of the house, just as she reached the front porch.

"Such a lovely ceremony," the priest said. "And you made such a beautiful bride, colleen."

"Thank you, Father," Callie managed, grateful beyond words that the priest and the lawyer seemed to have missed Trace's demonstration of affection. "Will you be leaving now?"

"I'm afraid so, Mrs. McCord," Morton said. "I've got business to attend to back in Rock Springs. We'll be taking the Marlowes' driver back with us, too."

"They're staying over?"

"For a day or two it would seem."

"How nice of them to ask."

"I'm saying Mass tomorrow at the Bar W," the priest interjected gently. "I'll be thinkin' about ye."

Callie had the uncomfortable feeling that the priest was all too aware of the tense undercurrents swirling about Shadow's Way and its occupants. "I'd certainly like to thank you both for coming," she said, because she couldn't think of anything else to say.

"Things will work out," Morton said. "You'll see." He looked at the priest, "If you could allow me a moment, Father?"

"Sure n' I can take a hint, lad." The priest gave Callie

an affectionate hug, then headed toward the buggy.

Callie's brows furrowed, wondering what the lawyer could possibly have to say.

"I want you to know something, Mrs. McCord."

"Please call me Callie," she said, not out of any feeling of familiarity with the lawyer, but because she couldn't abide the continual reference to her new name.

"All right. Callie. It's about Trace."

"I'm not sure I want to hear . . ."

"He's not nearly the bastard he's likely presented himself to be."

"Mr. Morton, I fail to see . . ."

"Give him a chance. I know your marriage isn't a love match. But he's going to need all the help he can get at that custody hearing."

"What are you talking about? All he had to do was get married!" She blushed, grateful the priest was out of hearing range.

"On the surface that would seem to be true. However . . ."

"However? What do you mean—*however?* Trace swore to me . . . ?" She stopped. What good was his word anyway?

"There are certain things I'm not at liberty to discuss that could affect what happens at the hearing."

Callie planted her hands on her hips. "I beg your pardon? You wanted to talk to me, but what you're telling me is that you can't tell me anything."

"Actually, what I most wanted to say was that Trace needs a friend in the courtroom. Someone besides me."

"But you won't tell me why."

"Don't worry. You'll find out. One way or another. But whatever you find out, however you find it out, remember this one thing—Trace may have been a wild kid, but he's a fine man. And he loves that little boy, or I wouldn't be going through all this."

"Mr. Morton..." She stopped as Trace approached. She watched the two men exchange glances. Trace was obviously irritated, but whether at her or the lawyer she couldn't say. In any event, *she* was still enormously irritated at *him*. No matter how hard and long Lyle Morton sang Trace McCord's praises, she was in no mood to either listen or believe a word he said. Turning on her heel, she stomped into the house.

Inside she cringed to see that Deirdre and Riley had departed, likely to take a walk out back. That left her and Christopher alone with the Marlowes.

"Do come sit down with us, dear," Edna Marlowe said, patting the vacant spot next to her on the settee. "We've just been getting to know our little grand-nephew here. He's certainly a darling boy."

Christopher was squirming on Edna's lap, whining grumpily that he wanted to get down.

"It's past his nap time," Callie said tactfully. "Perhaps I should put him down for a little while."

"I wouldn't hear of it," Edna said, rising to her feet. "Just tell me where his room is."

"Edna's so good with children," Edgar Marlowe said, flipping absently through the pages of a feed catalog Trace had left lying on the desk.

"I can see that," Callie murmured as the woman hauled the now crying child down the corridor.

Very slowly, Callie counted to ten. She had to give Edna Marlowe at least a few moments to be alone with Christopher. Children could be fussy with strangers. And, after all, the woman was a relative, no matter how

241

remote—by miles or blood. But when Christopher continued to wail piteously, Callie could bear it no longer. She hurried down the hall to the child's room, halting at the doorway, staring in disbelief.

"I said lie down, young man," Edna intoned. "I'll not tolerate such rude behavior. Not for one instant." She held the child's arms down as he struggled upward, crying all the harder.

"Let go of him!" Callie said, stepping over to the bed.

"Cal-ee!" Christopher shrieked, writhing free and leaping into her arms. Callie cuddled him close.

"Is this how he behaves for you?" Edna demanded. "He's like a wild animal. I'd have that nonsense curbed inside a day." She tried to grab Christopher from Callie's arms. When Callie resisted, the older woman straightened haughtily. "I see your manners aren't much better. No wonder the child is out of control."

"Mrs. Marlowe, you've only just arrived," Callie said, taking great care to keep her voice even. Christopher didn't need any further upset. "And you're obviously out of sorts from your long trip. Perhaps you should lie down for a while, gather your wits . . ."

"My wits!" the woman shouted. "Why you impertinent . . ."

"Don't like you," Christopher pronounced, thrusting out his lower lip at Edna Marlowe.

"You need your mouth washed out with soap, young man," Edna said, waggling her finger at the boy.

"Please go out to the front room. I'll get him settled and be right out."

The woman looked like she was going to protest, but she apparently thought better of it. With a final sniff of disgust she stormed from the room.

Callie spent the next few minutes calming herself, before she could effectively calm the distressed youngster.

"Don't like her," Christopher snuffled again and again.

"I don't blame you," Callie said, then stopped herself. She would not deliberately sabotage the Marlowes' relationship with the child. But that didn't stop her next words. "You lie down, sweetheart, and I'll tell you a story about a nasty old witch who gets what's coming to her." She rolled her eyes, thoroughly ashamed of herself, then launched into a juicy tale of childish vengeance. By the time she'd finished, nearly an hour later, Christopher had fallen asleep, and Callie felt at least a measure of calm returning. The feeling vanished as soon as she rose to her feet and walked back to the front room.

Edgar Marlowe was sitting on Jenny's cedar chest, gazing disinterestedly out the window. But Edna was on her feet and moving toward Callie the instant they caught sight of each other.

"Enjoy it while it lasts, dearie. Your marriage, that is. Trace McCord *is* an attractive man. I suppose one could reap a few side benefits from being his wife, no matter how temporary the arrangement."

Callie refused to rise to the bait. "I'm going to change my clothes, then go riding for a while. You and your husband feel free to make yourselves at home." She paused, then added, "Within reason, of course."

"Don't you care at all what sort of a man he is? What sort of a father he'll be for that child?"

"He loves Christopher."

"So he must tell you. But considering the way you

leap to his defense, I would be willing to wager that there're a few things he hasn't told you. A few things indeed. For example, has he told you why he really wants the boy?"

"I just told you. He loves him."

Edna Marlowe laughed. It was not a pleasant sound. "Jennifer's parents were quite wealthy, miss, uh, Mrs. McCord."

"Very wealthy indeed," Edgar Marlowe put in. "My brother and his wife controlled shipping lines, railroads, property. But they could never control their own daughter. Of course, it was primarily for her health that they allowed her to come west."

"I hardly see what this has to do with . . ."

"They left Jennifer a substantial trust," Edna said, her gaze glittering with pure venom. "But Seth McCord was too prideful to use his wife's money. She never touched a penny of it. The trust is still there. For Jenny, or now, more correctly, for her heirs."

"Just what are you saying?" Callie choked, hardly recognizing her own voice.

"You know exactly what I'm saying, my dear. Whoever has custody of Christopher controls that trust."

Chapter Fifteen

"Trust fund?" Callie echoed. What were the Marlowes talking about? Money was not an issue in Trace's quest to keep Christopher. But the cold, knowing look in Edna Marlowe's eyes sent a chill straight through to Callie's soul.

"Oh, my dear," Edna Marlowe tsked, trying hard to look horrified, "surely you knew. Your husband wouldn't have kept such an important bit of information from his new bride, now would he?"

Callie didn't answer. She had no answer. Any hint of renewed compassion she might have felt for Trace dissolved as her sense of betrayal mounted. A trust fund. Gaining custody of the child gained him custody of the child's money! With a sickening revulsion she recalled a snatch of conversation she'd overheard the first day she'd met Lyle Morton. . . . *you could lose Shadow's Way.* She had presumed Morton's warning grew out of his fear that Trace would center too much energy on Christopher's custody to the detriment of actually running the ranch. But if the reference had been financial . . . If Trace was in danger of losing the ranch unless he secured a ready source of income . . . She bit her lower lip to keep the tears at bay. Edna Marlowe would not see her cry.

"McCord won't get the boy," Edna went on. "Our attorney will see to that. The man isn't fit to raise a child. He's not fit to raise livestock."

As unconscionable as Trace's deceit appeared to be, Edna Marlowe's cloying superiority antagonized Callie more. The woman seemed to glory in each twist of the knife. She continued relentlessly. "Of course, if you didn't know about the trust fund, I don't suppose you'd know about all of the other choice tales in the man's sordid past, either now, would you? Maybe he married you for your ignorance."

Callie didn't trust herself to respond. Her jaws clamped shut so tight it hurt, she headed toward the guest room. The Marlowe woman stepped deliberately into her path. A spiteful smile played along her full lips as she spoke. "But then if you are familiar with his *exploits,* that makes you no better than he is. The judge won't think much of a woman who would marry a man like Trace McCord."

Callie took a long, steadying breath. Her voice was almost unnaturally even. "Why don't I let you and your husband settle in, get comfortable. I was just going to change clothes, maybe go out, get a little fresh air. Do a little riding." She didn't wait for a response.

Hurrying to the guest room, Callie threw off the wedding gown in favor of a pair of trousers and a blue cotton shirt. She turned to go, then stopped. Moving back over to the bed, she sank down, gently caressing the material of Jenny's gown.

My God, she thought, *I'm married. I'm Mrs. Trace McCord. I'm the man's wife!* She shook her head, the full impact of this afternoon's events still barely registering.

He's going to need a friend in that courtroom, Lyle Morton had said. And the lawyer expected her to be that friend. *He's not nearly the bastard he's likely presented himself to be.*

She sighed heavily. Morton couldn't know just how far Trace had gone. In fact, she had to wonder how far he would yet go. Be Trace's friend? The man scarcely tolerated her. He had proven last night just how unimportant her feelings were in this entire matter.

She rose to her feet, squaring her shoulders with sudden resolve. She would have this trust fund thing out with Trace right away. Certainly she had nothing to lose by risking a confrontation.

This time she made no effort to speak to the Marlowes as she headed out of the house. She was inordinately pleased, though, that her choice of attire left them staring after her, thoroughly scandalized.

Outside, she considered calling back to them and asking that they let her know if Christopher should awaken. But she decided against it, certain her request would be ignored. She would just have to make sure her talk with Trace didn't take too long.

She found him in the barn, still dressed in the dark gray suit he'd worn for the wedding. He was straddling a bale of hay, mending a frayed harness. It gave her heart an odd lurch to see him looking so casually handsome while tending to something so mundane. She had to suppress what she suspected was a very wifely urge to scold him soundly for not getting into his

247

work clothes, suppress, too, the very real urge to nestle up behind him on that hay bale and hold him close in spite of everything he had said and done to her over the past twenty-four hours. Some foolish part of her still held onto a flicker of hope that there had been a reason for his callousness. That given any other option he wouldn't have acted as he had.

Drawing a deep breath, she approached him with a deliberate, measured stride.

"The Marlowes and I just had a little talk," she said, watching carefully to see what his response would be.

He continued to work the harness, seeming not in the least interested. But she had seen the barely perceptible movement of his shoulders, as though once again he was girding himself for battle. "And just what exactly did they tell you?" he asked, his voice betraying no emotion whatsoever.

"I think you know."

He didn't look at her. "So . . . your already low opinion of me has been sent plummeting."

"You would expect it to rise?"

"No."

"Then you admit it?"

"What good would it do to deny it?"

"You son of a bitch," she murmured. "Don't you even have a conscience? How can you sit there so calm, so smug . . . ?" Her voice rose along with her fury. "To take advantage of a child who loves you!"

He swung one leg over the hay bale, rising to his full height. "Whatever I am, whatever I've been, Christopher is my son. And I'll do whatever I have to do to keep him."

"Keep his money you mean!"

BUSINESS REPLY MAIL
FIRST CLASS   PERMIT NO. 276   CLIFTON, NJ

POSTAGE WILL BE PAID BY ADDRESSEE

ZEBRA HOME SUBSCRIPTION SERVICE
P.O. Box 5214
120 Brighton Road
Clifton, New Jersey 07015

NO POSTAGE
NECESSARY
IF MAILED
IN THE
UNITED STATES

"Just because I was . . ." He stopped cold, his eyes narrowing. "What did you say? What money?"

"Don't plead ignorance now. It's too late. You just admitted . . ."

He cut her off. "You just said the Marlowes told you about me."

"Yes. About your despicable deceit! That the reason you want Christopher is so you can control the trust fund left to him by Jenny."

He gripped her arms. "What the hell are you talking about? What trust fund? Jenny didn't have any money."

"Not *her* money, her parents' money. The money they left her when they died. She never touched it, so it was left to Christopher." She watched the varying degrees of astonishment that skated across his features. "You *didn't* know?" she said, her heart leaping. He didn't know! No one could be that good at pretense. She felt almost giddy. But just that quickly she sobered. "What in the world did you think they told me?"

He was paying no attention to her. "A trust fund." He swore. "Did Lyle know about this?"

"How would I . . . ?" But he was already brushing past her, saddling Shoshone.

"Even Jenny," he muttered, cinching down the saddle. "Even Jenny . . ."

"Trace, what is going on? What is all this? For the love of heaven, please . . ."

"Tell me exactly what the Marlowes said."

"That Christopher has a trust fund that will be controlled by whoever has custody of him."

He leaned heavily against the horse, looking for all the world as if he had just absorbed a severe beating.

249

Then abruptly he straightened, vaulting into the saddle. "Don't wait up for me."

"Trace . . ." She was suddenly frightened. "Trace, don't do anything stupid."

But he wasn't listening. He slammed his heels into Shoshone's sides, thundering out of the barn.

She drew in a shaky breath. It wasn't likely he would throttle his own lawyer. She grimaced. At least, she hoped not.

Part of her couldn't help rejoicing that Trace had known nothing of the trust fund. But she was now certain he was hiding something he considered even more loathsome. *Whatever I am, whatever I've been, Christopher is my son.*

Whatever he'd *been?* He had expected the Marlowes to tell her what he'd been. He had known they were coming. And in his own mind he had been certain that whatever they could tell her would immediately abrogate her promise to marry him.

She shook her head. She'd exonerated him from one despicable motive. When he returned, it might well be to confront him about another.

For now she put it out of her mind. She returned to the house, where the Marlowes thankfully ignored her. She didn't have the energy for any more verbal sparring.

Instead she went in to check on Christopher. She found him awake and sitting up in bed. "Why didn't you come out to find me, Christopher?" she asked.

He made a face. "Don't like her," he pouted, pointing in the general direction of the front room.

"Sometimes you have to get to know people better before you like them," she said.

"No." He crossed his small arms in front of him, his chin thrusting stubbornly, reminding her at once of Trace. She suppressed a smile.

"How would you like to go outside and play hide-and-seek?"

Christopher squealed with delight. "Hide! Chris-fer hide from Cal-ee! You find me." He tugged on her hand, and she happily allowed him to pull her through the house.

Outside in the yard, Callie covered her eyes, making an exaggerated display of counting to ten. "Six . . . seven. You'd better hide really well," she called. "Eight . . . nine. Ready or not. Ten!"

Scanning the yard, she spotted the child easily, his little behind sticking out from in back of a hay bale beside the barn. Still she searched loud and long. "I just can't find that boy anywhere! Maybe I'll have to give up!"

She padded over to the barn and swooped down on him, tickling his tummy. He twisted in her arms, shrieking happily. "Cal-lee find me. Now you hide."

She laughed, then hurried off, making sure not to hide herself too well. As she sat in the small shed behind the bunkhouse, she couldn't help but think that playing hide-and-seek was certainly a novel way to spend one's wedding day. She deliberately kept her thoughts light. Whenever her mind drifted to the night ahead with Trace, she shivered. The man was totally unpredictable.

She couldn't even be certain he would be back tonight. His reluctance to face the Marlowes might keep him away until the couple had returned to Rock Springs, leaving her to face their insinuations alone.

She and Christopher played for half an hour before he tired of the game. "It's getting late," she said, hefting him into her arms. "I'm hungry. How about you?"

"Hungry! Yes!"

After settling him down with a few toys in his room, she headed for the kitchen. On the way, she forced herself to stop in the front room. Edgar Marlowe sat on the cedar chest, looking utterly bored, and Callie had to wonder if the man had taken root there. Edna was seated on the settee busily working an embroidery pattern.

"Would you care to join Christopher and me for dinner?" Callie asked, though her stomach knotted at the thought.

"We've eaten," Edna said. "We had no idea how long you were going to be frittering away your time playing games, so we helped ourselves in the kitchen."

"Fine. That's fine. Wonderful." Though her voice dripped sarcasm, Callie was delighted. Now she wouldn't have to feed them. Her heightened spirits lasted only as long as it took to check the kitchen food supply. Between them the Marlowes had consumed the roast, carrots, and potatoes Deirdre had left warming in the oven, the meal that was to have fed the entire family this evening.

"A small price to pay," Callie murmured. On the counter she found a note from Deirdre. Her aunt and her new uncle had impulsively decided to drive to Rock Springs. *We'll be visiting with the Watsons at the Bar W,* Deirdre had written. *Perhaps not a honeymoon on the Continent, but if Riley is there . . . Oh, Callie, I am so happy. We'll talk when we get back. See you in a week or so. Love, Deirdre.*

For a long minute Callie stood there, trying to decide what it was she was feeling that seemed so odd. And then she knew. It was a sense of loss, a very real sense of loss. While she was happy for Deirdre, she felt hurt and abandoned, and maybe a little jealous, too.

"That's absurd," she snapped aloud. "If anyone in the world deserves to be happy it's Aunt Deirdre. I love her. Just because she's married now doesn't mean she loves me any less."

Yet ever since she'd ridden onto Shadow's Way things had been changing. Her relationship with Trace had so overwhelmed her that she hadn't even noticed Deirdre and Riley were in love.

"Aunt Deirdre was in love before we ever came to Shadow's Way," Callie admitted slowly. "God, how long have you been blind to anything but your own problems, Callandra Callaghan. You rope your aunt into helping you escape a man you didn't love, because you didn't have the guts to do it yourself. Then you hogtie her emotionally to come along on this god-forsaken gold hunt . . ."

She clutched the note tightly, a single tear tracking down her cheek. "I'm sorry, Aunt Deirdre." She vowed she would make it up to her aunt when she and Riley returned from Rock Springs. Then quickly she got busy fixing dinner for herself and Christopher. She tried to keep her mind on the potatoes she was peeling, but her thoughts shifted inevitably to Trace. If she had known Deirdre all of her life and still been blind to her aunt's feelings, how could she expect to understand Trace McCord's? More to the point, she thought bitterly, why should she? Life hadn't been pleasant to him from day one. Yet she had already learned to guard

253

against feeling any sympathy for the man. It had a tendency to turn back on her with a vengeance.

"Your papa can be a most exasperating man," she said to Christopher, as she settled him into his chair at the dinner table.

"Zass-rating?" he repeated curiously.

Callie shook her head. "Never mind. I think we'd best just eat."

After dinner, she settled Christopher into bed, annoyed to note that the Marlowes had already usurped the guest room. She had been hoping to sleep there herself tonight. Since Trace hadn't yet come home, it didn't seem important that she follow through on his edict that they maintain all appearances of a conventional, happy marriage and sleep in his bed.

Restless, yet not wanting to sit in front of the fire, lest the Marlowes decide on a late-night sandwich, she dragged the rocking chair from Christopher's room into Trace's. Slipping quickly into her cotton nightrail, she sat back, rocking gently, all too aware of how overwhelmingly intimate it felt just to be in his bedroom, let alone that she would soon be in his bed.

The motion of the chair soothed her, though she did not relax. Her thoughts were consumed by Trace. He would need her help more than ever to keep Christopher. But that only made her more uneasy. Because Trace was so desperate to keep the child, she couldn't trust anything he said, anything he did. When and if he returned tonight, it would likely be only to repeat his lies from last night—like telling her he loved her. And she still had to contend with the hovering specter of some dark secret in his past. A secret he considered so odious that he would resort to blackmail to get her to marry him before she could learn what it was.

As the night crawled on, her eyelids grew heavier until finally she dozed. She woke abruptly, disoriented, until she remembered she was still sitting in the rocking chair. She blinked, deciding it had to be near midnight. With a soft groan, she rose to her feet, her neck protesting having been so long in an awkward position.

Her gaze darted to the bed. She was still alone in the room. Unaccountably she felt a rush of melancholy. Trace was supposed to be going out of his way to maintain the appearance of a normal marriage for the Marlowes' sake. He wasn't doing a very good job of it so far.

Standing, she stretched tiredly, wondering if she dared lie down in his bed. Her stomach made the decision for her, rumbling in a most unladylike fashion. She hadn't eaten much at dinner. "Maybe a little bread and jam . . ."

She headed down the hallway, surprised to see the light of the fire in the front room still flickering brightly off the walls. She stopped dead, seeing the hunched figure on the settee staring into the flames.

"I didn't think you'd come back tonight," she said softly, unconsciously crossing her arms in front of her. She wished now she'd thought to slip into her robe.

"Now how would that look?" Trace asked. "The groom deserting the bride on their wedding night."

"The Marlowes are asleep. It doesn't matter how it looks." After all of her thoughtful musings, she was in no mood for his cynicism.

He climbed to his feet, stepping toward her, his eyes sweeping from the top of her tousled locks to the tips of her bare toes. "Ah, the nervous bride."

In spite of the heat of the fire rippling along her back, she felt a sudden chill sweep through her. "I beg your pardon? This isn't a *real* marriage. I don't want you thinking about me as a bride."

"I watched you sleep," he said softly. "You looked so fragile, so innocent . . ." He reached up with his right hand, gently rubbing the side of her neck with his palm.

"Watched . . . ?" She trembled. He'd been in the bedroom!

His thumb caressed her cheek. She longed to jerk away, but found she couldn't move. Why was he doing this?

"Did you resolve anything with Lyle?" she asked, trying vainly to slow the trip-hammer beat of her heart.

"Resolve anything?" His hand fell away, his voice taking on its accustomed coldness. "Just the usual course of events in my life. Now I find Jenny didn't trust me any more than anyone else ever has."

"I don't understand." In spite of his tone, he looked so lost, so achingly vulnerable. And yet she sensed any attempt to get him to reveal his true feelings would be met with all the instinctive savagery of a wounded animal. Instead she decided on an indirect approach. "I want you to tell me why you threatened to tell my aunt about . . . last night."

He looked away. "When I came to your room earlier today, it was my intention to apologize, to explain."

"And now?"

"Now it doesn't matter."

"I have a right to know."

"I've got nothing to say."

"I could ask the Marlowes . . ."

His head jerked up. There was no mistaking his

256

anger now. "Yeah. Yeah, I guess maybe you could."

Callie watched him, watched his face. When he wasn't aware of it, his eyes gave away so much. He had lowered his guard. She saw his pain. *Felt* it.

He walked back over to the settee and sat down. "When I was sixteen, I stole some money. A hundred dollars. From my father."

She almost blurted, "Is that all?" But managed to hold back. Obviously there was more to it.

"I ran away. Seth told me to come back when Pa had cooled down. I was gone four months."

"And when you came back . . ."

"He had me arrested."

Her eyes widened. "I suppose he thought that would teach you a lesson? Scare you?"

He swore. "Teach me a lesson? Scare me? I'm sure he had both in mind. In fact he wanted to make sure I'd never forget it. He testified against me at my trial."

"Trial?" she said in a small voice. Surely, Jeb McCord hadn't let it go that far.

"I spent five years in prison."

Callie gasped, stunned. "For stealing money from your own father? Five years?"

He didn't look at her.

She sank onto the settee beside him. "My God. That's what you didn't want me to know."

"I knew the Marlowes were coming. And that they were aware of my less than honorable past." His voice was now edged with self-disgust. "I arranged a dishonorable act to keep you from finding out about previous dishonorable acts."

"You made a mistake. You paid for it. You paid for it more dearly than some killers do."

He stood up. "I think I need some air."

She held up a hand, thinking to restrain him, but thought better of it. He had already said more than he intended. She said no more as he stalked out of the house.

Back in his bedroom, she couldn't think of it as *theirs*, Callie waited nervously for Trace to return. She knew he had had difficulties with his father. But this? What kind of a father could send his own son to prison for five years? Especially for something as petty as taking a hundred dollars?

The thought niggled at her that there was more to this story than he had let on, though even thinking about him locked away for five years tore at her heart. No wonder he was so cold, so hard.

The bedroom door opened, then clicked shut quietly. "You're still awake?"

She caught the note of surprise in his voice. Obviously he had stayed out until he'd been all but certain she'd be asleep.

"I was . . . worried. I know you don't like talking about yourself."

"You can bet I don't intend to do any more of it tonight."

She listened to the soft rustling of clothes in the darkness, her cheeks flaming as she realized he was getting undressed. He cursed when his toe stubbed into the nightstand, but he made no attempt to light the lamp.

She rose and struck a match, lighting it herself. "No sense fracturing your feet." She dared a glance at him as she spoke, wishing to heaven she had not. He was dressed only in the lower half of his drawers. The clothes, such as they were, looked almost humorously out of place. She recalled the night he'd stepped naked out of the bathing room. He'd said something then about sleeping in the nude. With this "arrangement" he would be forced to add the encumbrance of clothing.

Shaking from head to foot, she lay down, then stiffened as she felt the mattress give. Trace lay down. She shot out of the bed.

"I don't bite," he growled.

"I cannot sleep in the same bed with you."

"You knew this was going to be part of the bargain."

"The same room, yes. But not . . ."

He snapped back the covers. "I'll go out to the barn."

"No. It's your bed. I'll . . . lay a few blankets on the floor."

"The hell you will. I'm used to the ground." He got out of bed.

"Please, don't. Trace . . ."

But he was already yanking on his pants. She heard his soft curse as he stormed from the room.

Trace sat on the top rail of the corral, ignoring the night sounds and smells he loved. He was still trying to sort through the conflicting emotions that had roiled inside him most of the day. He wasn't used to dealing with most of them. Again and again he'd had to fight the all but overwhelming need to confide in Callie, to trust her, to believe he could tell her the truth and not have her hate him. In the end he'd told her more than he'd intended, but even that had not been half of what he'd longed to share with her.

Fear had stopped him. Fear of losing her cooperation at the custody hearing. Fear of losing what minuscule bit of compassion she might have left for his plight.

It didn't matter that he loved her. He did. Totally, mindlessly—even as he hurt her with his threat of blackmail. But for him, loving her was only another torment to be endured—as he'd endured his father's abuse, his years in prison, his fear of losing Christopher.

He hadn't minded leaving his bedroom. In fact, it had become imperative that he leave it. Even lying next to her for those few seconds had almost been his undoing. He'd wanted nothing more than to pull her close, make her his. But more and more he realized the futility of loving her. To spare himself the agony of her rejection, he would make certain that he never again be foolish enough to tell her how much he cared. After last night, he was certain she would never believe him anyway, and she could doubtless use such a weapon against him to exact a well-deserved revenge.

That he loved her and could still believe her capable of his own occasionally less than noble behavior seemed no particular contradiction. He'd accepted less than noble behavior in himself and others all of his life.

When he was a boy and things had gotten too tough with his father he had run away. Later, he'd called it drifting, going his own way, but it was the same. He'd run away. He had never faced down the old man, never fought that final battle. He'd just stayed gone until it was too late. And he had found it had resolved nothing at all, but only exacerbated a wound that had never healed.

The difference with Callie was that he couldn't run.

He had to consider Christopher.

He couldn't blame her if she didn't believe him about the trust fund. That the Marlowes would tell her something like that hadn't even entered his head. He had been too afraid of the other. But they hadn't even mentioned his prison sentence.

Why?

When he'd caught up with Lyle Morton this afternoon and demanded an explanation, the lawyer had avoided any direct answers, insisting instead that Trace had more important things with which to concern himself. "Your only way to diffuse the Marlowes' testimony is to tell Callie the truth yourself."

"I can't."

"Would you rather the Marlowes did it?"

"Lyle, she'll hate me." He'd said it as though she didn't already.

"Tell her. God help you if she finds out in the judge's chambers. You want to keep that boy. You'd best make certain that woman is on your side."

"Lyle . . ."

"Tell her."

Trace picked at the splintering wood of the corral rail. *Tell her.*

He let out a shuddering sigh as Kachina trotted over to him. Somehow he'd managed to tell Callie about prison. That she hadn't been as appalled as he'd imagined he hardly found heartening. It was just one more deceit to erode her opinion of him.

He stroked Kachina's silken neck. Nothing could make him tell her the rest of it. How could he tell the woman he loved that he had killed his own father?

Chapter Sixteen

Callie woke once during the night to find Trace nestled on the bed beside her. Sometime while she slept he had arranged a barrier of pillows between them, then lay down. She supposed she should be grateful. Instead she felt oddly rejected. By morning he was already up and gone.

Over the days that followed she settled into a routine that rarely brought her into contact with the enigmatic man who was her husband. Whether his absence was deliberate or necessary—he claimed to be checking on Reese's progress in tracking a rogue bear—she couldn't guess.

At least she hadn't had long to suffer the presence of the Marlowes. The couple left in a huff the day after their arrival, having made no headway at all in Christopher's affections. Nonetheless they vowed they would have their day in court, that they would have the child.

Six days after her wedding Callie stood at her bedroom window, the dawning sunlight bathing her face a sharp contrast to the bleakness of her mood. Somehow, she realized, she had expected these past nights to be different. She had actually dreamed that because Trace had shared a painful part of his past with her that it had been a beginning. Little by little he would trust her enough to share more and more of his life. He would pull her close, and she would hold him, tell him that his father was a rigid, foul-tempered man who'd been unforgivably cruel. With each passing night the ease with which Trace turned away from her cut more deeply.

More and more she found herself questioning why she had gone through with the wedding. If the pain was this great now, what would it be like when she would have to leave Shadow's Way forever, never to see Trace or Christopher again.

With a weary sigh she pushed the thoughts away. It would do her no good to dwell on them. Riley and Deirdre would be back any day now. Callie vowed to at least maintain a pretense that her decision to marry Trace had been the right one, if only for her aunt's sake.

Finishing the breakfast dishes, she settled herself on the settee, playing a distracted game of catch with Christopher while she attempted to write in her journal. She was surprised a short time later to hear a sudden rapping on the front door.

She opened it to the anxious, bespectacled visage of Lyle Morton. "You must have left the Bar W in the middle of the night," she said, knowing the lawyer used the Watson home as a resting stop between Shadow's Way and Rock Springs.

"I'm looking for Trace." The man was obviously not interested in small talk.

"He's out on the range somewhere. There's been a bear marauding the stock. Reese rode in last night to tell him one of the foals had been killed." The look on the man's face gave her pause. "What's wrong?"

"Has Trace told you about . . ." He stopped.

"Told me what?"

The lawyer strode into the kitchen. "Do you suppose I could trouble you for a cup of coffee, Mrs. McCord?"

"Call me Callie. And, of course, I'll fix one for you." She was grateful when Christopher toddled off with his rag puppy, indulging in his own version of *Treasure Island*. "Please, tell me what's going on, Mr. Morton."

"I wish I could. But I'm legally bound to maintain the privacy of my clients."

"I appreciate that. But you're also a citizen of this territory, are you not? And as a citizen you would undoubtedly come by certain knowledge just by living here."

"That would make an interesting argument in court."

"You care about Trace. I know you do. And whether he believes it or not, whether I want to or not, I care about him, too."

The lawyer searched her face for a long time before he spoke again. "You don't know how glad I am to hear that. Just how much has he told you?"

"That he spent five years in prison for stealing money from his father."

Morton seemed surprised, but pleased. "That's something anyway."

"You mean there's more?" Callie sank down onto the kitchen chair opposite the lawyer.

He ignored her implied request, saying instead, "He

didn't know about the trust fund. I want you to know that. And believe it."

"He feels Jenny betrayed him."

Morton sighed. "I knew that would be his reaction."

"Then why did she keep it from him?"

"It was Seth really. He wanted no part of Jenny's trust. He would provide for his wife and family himself."

"Even though the ranch was in financial trouble?"

"Especially because the ranch was in financial trouble."

"Trace said Seth lived for three days after he was hurt. Surely he would have wanted his pregnant widow provided for."

"Seth urged Jenny to look into the trust. But she'd spent the best years of her life here. The money didn't mean any more to her than it did to Seth. She decided to see to it that it was all given to her child."

"And you drew up the papers?"

"Exactly."

"That doesn't explain why she wouldn't tell Trace."

The lawyer looked uncomfortable.

Callie, too, felt a knot in her stomach. She remembered Trace's words *Jenny was the only person who ever accepted me as I am.* "It was her way of being certain he wanted the child for himself, wasn't it?"

"Trace hasn't exactly led the life of an altar boy."

"She was wrong to doubt him."

"For what it's worth, I'm on your side. But I was bound by ethics to do as she wished."

Callie shook her head. How could Trace help but be bitter, cynical? The people who should have loved him most always fell short of giving him what he needed

265

more than anything. Trust.

Jeb and Seth McCord had assured their self-fulfilling prophecy. By not trusting Trace he had in fact at times been untrustworthy. "Why did he steal that money?"

"Because Jeb hadn't said one word to him in three months. Not one word. He'd give orders to Trace through Seth. Trace figured that by taking the money he'd make Jeb so angry, he'd have to face him directly." Morton's lips thinned. "He was right. Too right."

They both turned at the sound of bootheels on the oak flooring. Trace filled the kitchen archway. Neither had heard him come in. Callie shifted guiltily. His face was a stony mask, but she was certain he had overheard at least part of her conversation with Morton.

"I'd like to speak with you, Lyle," Trace said, his voice much too even. "In the study. Now."

Morton gave her a slight shrug, as if to say it had to happen sooner or later. Then he rose and followed Trace out of the room.

Whether for her sake, or because he was already agitated, Morton made no attempt to keep his voice low as he spoke. "We've got a problem," he said. "Judge Lancaster is ill. I had the hearing set for a week from tomorrow, but it doesn't look good. The doc says he may not make it."

"Damn. He's a good man."

"And he's been unofficially on your side since the beginning."

"If Lancaster is too ill to decide the case . . ."

"Then we'll be starting all over again with whoever takes his place."

Trace raked a hand through his tawny hair. "We'll

266

just have to wait and see then."

"For now I've gotten everything moved back a week. If Lancaster is going to be on his feet again anytime soon, two weeks should tell the tale."

"And if he isn't?"

"Then we'll convince whatever judge we get that you're the best damned parent that boy could have."

Trace and the lawyer shook hands. "Thanks, Lyle." His gaze skated briefly to Callie, then back to the lawyer. "Even if you do have a big mouth."

"Like I said, you're going to need all the friends you can get in that courtroom. And that includes your wife."

Trace said nothing, following the lawyer as Morton headed toward the front door.

Callie intercepted them, facing Trace squarely. "I want to know what's going on."

"It's not your business."

"I'll show myself out," Morton interrupted, giving Trace an exasperated glance. "Remember what I said." With that he left the house.

Callie folded her arms in front of her, glaring at Trace. "If this has to do with Christopher and his happiness, it is my business."

"You're not his mother."

"I don't know why I bother."

"I don't, either." With that he stalked out the door, mounted Shoshone, and rode out.

"Someday I'm going to tie you to a chair, Trace McCord," she muttered after him. "And force you to finish an argument." Shaking her head, she headed toward the back of the house. She needed a distraction. She found Christopher in his room involved with his

267

toys. "How would you like to help me bake some cookies, young man?"

"Cookies! Make cookies."

Within minutes Callie's mood had lightened considerably. Christopher's idea of putting cookie batter in the pan would have produced one huge gingerbread cookie, instead of the six dozen the recipe called for. Sticking his fingers in the gooey mess turned out to have just as much allure as any mudhole would have had, and Callie found herself fishing dough clumps out of her hair with hilarious regularity.

Thankfully the last of the cookies came out of the oven at the same time Christopher was ready for other things. Callie settled him in his room with his toys, then headed for the bathing room. "I need to be de-cookied," she giggled, studying her reflection in the mirror above the basin. She had batter stuck to the top of one eyebrow. Still more batter had dried in the strands of her hair making them stand out like some grotesque sculpture. "A true vision of loveliness," she said, lifting an excess dollop of gingerbread to plunk it on the end of her nose. "The finishing touch."

She was just about to step into the bathwater, when she noticed she had neglected to bring a towel into the room. Throwing on her robe, she stepped into the hallway, only to find herself face to face with Trace.

"At least you're more discreet than I am," he drawled, his eyes trailing to the robe's revealing cleavage.

She clutched the robe together with one hand, the other hand fluttering to her throat as she felt her cheeks heat with embarrassment. "I didn't expect you back so soon," she stammered. *Especially after the way you left,* she added to herself.

"That's an interesting arrangement you've made with your hair."

She gasped, remembering the image that had peered out at her from the mirror. Stamping her foot with outrage, she fled back into the bathing room. Fuming, she flung off the robe, swearing she would use it to towel herself dry if she had to. At least she had remembered to bring in a change of clothes. The nerve of the man! Did he carve a notch in his bedpost for each time he embarrassed her? "If he does," she murmured acidly, "the bedpost should be a pile of splinters by now."

She took her time with the bath, hoping Trace would take the hint and absent himself. But as she scrubbed the cookie batter from her person, she found her hands unaccountably lingering on the sensitive flesh of her throat, her breasts. She swallowed convulsively, realizing she was imagining her own hands to be Trace's.

"No!" she half sobbed. "What's happening to me?" Furious, she scrubbed at her skin, nearly rubbing it raw before she slapped down the sponge and sloshed to her feet. Climbing from the tub, she used the robe as a substitute towel. She would rather die than call out to Trace to fetch her one. Dressing quickly, she squared her shoulders and flung open the door. Eyes front, she marched down the hallway.

Determined that he not know how deeply he affected her, she very pointedly ignored him as she crossed the front room and headed toward the guest room.

Christopher's happy shriek stopped her in midstride near the fireplace. She turned, seeing him trundle over

269

to Trace's outstretched arms. "Papa!" the boy cried. "Papa!"

She could almost feel Trace's heart swell with pride at the boy's word. No matter how heartbreaking these next few weeks might be, she had to endure them for Christopher's sake . . . and for Trace. They belonged together. She decided there was no sense hiding out in the guest room. "Do we get to finish the little chat you avoided when Lyle Morton left?" she prodded.

He looked at her, his eyes conveying none of his earlier irritation. "I was thinking that if you didn't have any other plans, we could take Christopher out to the south range for a picnic."

Callie grimaced. He was avoiding her questions as usual. And yet her heart skipped a beat. A picnic alone with Trace and Christopher? She could think of nothing she would rather do. Still, she kept her voice casual. "I suppose I could manage it."

"Pick-nee," Christopher shouted. "Pick-nee!"

"Then it's settled," Trace pronounced. "I'll bring the wagon around."

Feeling almost giddy, Callie scurried into the kitchen and threw together a quick meal. By the time she finished, Trace had the buckboard hitched and ready. She lifted Christopher up beside him, but Trace very deliberately scooted the boy to the opposite side of the wagon seat.

Callie considered outmaneuvering him by sidling the child right back, but the idea of sitting next to Trace was suddenly too exhilarating to resist. She sat down between them, noting with a mounting sense of excitement and unease that Trace made no effort to put even a whisper of space between them.

Against her will she recalled the sensual fantasies she'd conjured during her bath. Her mouth felt dry, her skin clammy. She had to calm herself. This was a picnic. Nothing more.

His arm touched hers, making her all too aware of the corded strength beneath the sun-bronzed flesh. His thigh caressed her thigh. She prayed he didn't notice her trembling, because try as she might to will it to stop, she could not. Except for Christopher's intermittent chattering, the road to the spot Trace had chosen for their picnic was uncomfortably silent.

Over an hour later, Trace reined the wagon to a halt beside a clump of cottonwood trees that lined the banks of a twisting, burbling creek. While Callie spread out a blanket and readied the food, Trace entertained Christopher. She could have called them to lunch then, but instead she sat for long minutes watching them— the tall man and the little boy standing side by side plunking pebbles into the creek. How much a part of her life they had become. How much it would hurt never to see them again.

"Trace! Christopher!" she called, unable to bear the painful thoughts any longer. "Lunch is ready."

Christopher scurried over and plopped in front of a plate full of food, attacking it with all the fervor of a starving coyote.

"You'd think he never eats," she said, laughing. Her mood darkened when she turned to Trace. He had that unreadable look on his face again. "Why did you want this picnic?"

"I wanted to be with Christopher."

She lowered her eyes, lest he see how his words had hurt.

271

"We used to do this a lot," he went on, "just he and I. Jenny was too sickly. It's just that lately . . ."

"Since I arrived?"

"No, it's not that. It's more that the custody hearing's been weighing on my mind. I didn't want Christopher to have to deal with my impatience." He tugged on a blade of grass, twining it through his fingers. "It's been a long time since he's been away from the house. I thought it would be good for him."

"It is breathtaking here," Callie admitted.

"Isn't it," he said, looking at her.

"You're very proud of your ranch."

He shifted. "My father started the ranch. My brother ran it. I've only had it for three years."

"In three years a ranch can fail, bankrupt. You've kept it going. Flourishing even."

His gaze shifted to Christopher, who'd snuggled next to him. Gently Trace stroked the boy's blond hair. "I think all of this fresh air and exercise wore him out."

She grimaced ruefully. "You just won't give yourself any credit at all, will you?"

His eyes never left Christopher. "What did you say?"

"Nothing." She shook her head. "It doesn't matter."

Trace lifted the sleeping child, carrying him over to the wagon, which he'd left in the shade of a towering cottonwood. "He looks a lot like Seth," he said, more to himself than to her as he settled the boy onto a blanket in the rear of the wagon.

Callie walked over to him. "You loved your brother, didn't you?"

"He was a stubborn bastard." The words seemed harsh, but they were said with affection.

"I have a feeling he loved you, too."

He twisted away, stomping back over to the blanket. Abruptly he lay down, staring up at the cloudless sky. For a moment she feared she had lost the tenuous link that had sprung up between them. But he continued. "After Pa died and Seth had the ranch, he decided it was his turn to tell me how to live my life."

"Surely your father meant the ranch for both of his sons."

"My father did exactly what he meant. Always."

"Riley told me about the two Indians he hanged for stealing horses."

"He used to brag about that quite a bit."

Though she winced at the renewed bitterness in his voice, she rejoiced at his apparent willingness to talk to her about what must be an unfathomable pain—to believe himself despised by a parent. "Why didn't you tell me he didn't speak to you for three months? I'd have done more than steal a hundred dollars. I'd have . . ."

"Remind me to fire Lyle Morton."

"Lyle Morton is not the issue. It's you. And why you're so hard on yourself, when it's your father who was wrong . . ."

"I don't want to talk about it."

She grimaced. *The hell you don't,* she thought. *You want nothing more than to talk about it, to draw out the poison that's been festering in you for so long.*

"My father hated my guts. Short. Simple. End of discussion."

She knelt beside him on the blanket, impulsively reaching out to squeeze his hand. Her heart leaped when he did not pull away.

His hand curled over hers. "If you think I'm pining

away over my father's despising me, I'm not. It was just something that was."

"You might be able to lie to yourself, but it's not working with me."

His lips thinned. Jerking his hand away, he stood up, stalking toward the creek. He stopped at the near bank, jamming his hands in his pockets.

She followed, halting a step behind him. "Do you know you never finish an argument. Never. You stomp out. You ride off. You just never finish it."

"I don't want to fight with you."

"I don't think you know how to fight. Not really. Maybe it's because you never finished things with your father."

"That's absurd. My father's dead. That's about as finished as you can get."

"But did you ever confront him about the way he treated you? Ever demand to know how he dare send you to prison for five years?"

"He was teaching me not to steal," he snarled, his voice heavy with sarcasm.

"You're not a thief."

"I stole the money."

"You were trying to steal his love, because he wouldn't give it to you."

"Shut up." His back was ramrod straight.

"No! Look at you! The way you hold yourself when you talk about it—like you expect someone to hit you . . ."

"Goddamnit, woman! Leave me alone!"

She lay her head against his back, curling her arms around his waist. "If I thought you really wanted me to, I would." She could feel his body trembling.

He arched his head back, then twisted to face her. "I can't talk about him. I can't. It does hurt. God help me, it hurts so much."

Her lips found his, his breath hot, wet, as he breathed her name over and over again. His tongue invaded her mouth, and her heart gave a rapturous leap at the seductive exploration.

She moaned softly, leaning against him, her legs no longer capable of supporting her. Eagerly, hungrily, she returned his kisses, craving the feel of his flesh on hers. Any thoughts she had of getting him past the bitterness that consumed him were lost in the sensual magic of his touch.

His mouth never leaving hers, his hands tugged open the tiny buttons of her dress front, his calloused palm skating beneath the fabric to cup her breast against the sheer barrier of her chemise. She reveled in the low growl deep in his throat as the soft mound swelled to fill his hand.

"Oh, God, Callie," he murmured, guiding her down to the lush grasses that lined the creekbank. "You are so beautiful. So damned beautiful."

He untied the silk ribbon of her chemise, easing the material to either side. His half-lidded gaze sent thundering waves of heat coursing to every part of her. Then his lips were trailing a path of fire along the exposed flesh of her breasts. When his mouth closed over one tender peak, she whimpered with longing, clasping her hands on either side of his head, holding him to his erotic task.

Instinctively her hips arched upward, her body ready, more than ready for his loving. He was tormenting her, a sweet, sweet torture she prayed would never end.

"Callie, I want you. I want you so much." His voice was ragged, rasping, throbbing with need. His loins were on fire, his body demanding that he bury his flesh in hers. *No!* The denial rose from nowhere and he fought against it. He had to have her, ached to have her.

He loved her.

Loved her.

With a savage oath he rolled away from her. Yes, he did love her. But he could never have her. If he took her now, it would only make losing her that much more agonizing. Better to torment himself now than to have the memory of their lovemaking haunt him for the rest of his life.

"Trace, what is it? What did I do wrong?"

He closed his mind to the trembling in her voice, a trembling that promised a need to match his own. Angrily, furiously, he told himself her need was based on illusion. She didn't know the real Trace McCord. If she did, she would never lie so wantonly in his arms. She would curse him, curse the day he was born. Just as his father had.

Shaking, he stood up, turning away so that he no longer suffered the sweet, sweet pain of looking at her and not making love to her. His attempt to regain control of himself took a heavy toll on his patience.

"Straighten your dress," he gritted.

Callie felt hot tears of shame prick her eyes. He made her feel like a harlot. All she wanted was that he make love to her. She was his wife! His rejection stung her to her soul.

"Trace." She tried and failed to keep the frustrated

longing from her voice.

"I'll tell you again," he rasped, "this marriage is in name only. And by all that's holy, that's the way it's going to stay." His shoulders heaved as he fought the surging tide of passion that threatened to sweep away the last vestiges of his self-control. He wanted her, longed for her, but he couldn't bear having her just this once. It was better never to have her, better if she hated him. His hands curled into fists at his sides.

She stood up shakily, adjusting her clothes. Stepping up behind him, she touched his shoulder. He jerked away as though she had burned him.

"For the love of Christ, woman, I'm not made of stone."

"Oh, but you're wrong," she said, feeling the same flood of bitterness that so often edged his words. "I think you most certainly are, Trace McCord. You most certainly are made of cold, hard stone."

He stiffened perceptibly. "Use your head. This marriage is a temporary arrangement. Why make things any more difficult than they already are? Neither one of us wants to face those kinds of consequences."

"Consequences?"

"Like pregnancy."

"Is that the only reason?" she asked unsteadily.

"Callie, I fully intend to get the divorce. I don't want you as my wife. I could take you as a woman right here, right now, but I wouldn't be very proud of myself afterward. Please, try to understand."

I don't want you as my wife. Those were the words that seared through her mind long after their conversation had ended. She didn't think she could ever forget the sound of them.

277

Somehow she managed to maintain her composure. She straightened her clothing, her hair, and it was as though their too brief closeness had never happened. She sank to her knees and gathered up the remnants of their picnic.

"I guess we'd better get back," she said, rising and hurrying over to the wagon.

He stepped up next to her, his strong fingers curving over her shoulder. "Callie . . ."

She stiffened, but did not turn around.

"Callie, you do understand? It has nothing to do with you. You're a beautiful woman."

She wanted to scream. How dare he patronize her? Did he think she would get on her knees and beg him to make love to her? That she couldn't live without it?

"You've made your objections perfectly clear," she said coldly. "Can we go now?"

His hand dropped away. Without a word they climbed into the buckboard and headed toward the ranch. In the brooding silence of the descending dusk she was left only with his words echoing over and over in her mind—*I don't want you as my wife.*

Chapter Seventeen

Callie bolted from the house, rushing toward the arriving buggy. The ten days Deirdre had been gone seemed more like a year. "It's so good to have you back!" she cried, clasping Deirdre's hand even before her aunt alighted from the carriage.

"My, my, what a welcome!" Deirdre's smile faltered slightly, her brow furrowing as her gaze locked with Callie's.

Callie shook herself inwardly. If her distress was that obvious, it wouldn't be long before Deirdre guessed its source. She didn't intend to involve her aunt in any depressing discussions about her deteriorating relationship with Trace. Forcing what she hoped was a convincing smile, Callie stepped back to allow the still hobbled scout to make a grand flourish of taking Deirdre's hand and assisting her from the carriage.

"How was your trip?" Callie asked, giving Deirdre a heartfelt hug.

"Just lovely," Deirdre said, her gaze softening. "Riley fussed over me the whole time."

Riley grinned, limping up the porch steps alongside Deirdre, helped only a little by the crutch under his right arm. Callie could scarcely believe this was the same trail-stained, rough-talking backwoodsman, who three weeks ago had lain in agony under a wagon in a mud-washed hollow. The scout's brown eyes sparkled, his clean-shaven jaw strong but gentle. He was dressed in a dark broadcloth suit that looked as at home on him as his buckskins.

"Now don't you go laughin' at me, Miss Callie," he said sheepishly.

"Hardly. In fact, maybe I'm a little jealous. It would seem marriage agrees with you both."

"And how is it agreein' with you?" Deirdre asked.

"Everything's just fine," Callie lied, pushing the front door open and heading toward the kitchen. "The custody hearing has been set for two weeks from today in Rock Springs."

"Trace should be happy about that," Riley said. "Where is he anyway?"

"He and Christopher are out together somewhere. He's been spending a couple of hours every morning with him."

Callie could see the unspoken question in her aunt's eyes—why wasn't she with them? To deflect her aunt's curiosity, Callie said, "Come on now, you two, let's hear all about your trip. Did you have a good time? How was Rock Springs?"

"Hmmph," Riley snorted, "'tweren't much more than a one-horse town."

"Bosh, Riley, dear," Deirdre said. "Everything was just fine."

Riley shook his head, easing himself into the chair at

the end of the table. "Ain't she somethin'? She makes Rock Springs sound like Omaha. It is growin', though, I'll grant that. In fact, Deirdre and I are even thinking of buying a mercantile that's for sale, maybe put down some real roots . . ."

Callie bit her lip, turning away. She suddenly couldn't bear to witness the genuine affection so evident between her aunt and Riley. She rejoiced for them both, yet their happiness seemed to magnify her own misery. She busied herself fixing a cup of coffee, hoping neither one of them noticed how much her hands trembled.

"Riley, darling," Deirdre said, "why don't you go on along to the guest room and lie down for a while. We've had a long drive and your leg could use the rest."

"Aw, I don't need . . ." He stopped, and Callie didn't have to turn to know the reason. Deirdre had sent him a silent plea that she be allowed some time alone with her niece. Callie's shoulders sagged as Riley rose and excused himself. "I guess I could use a little shut-eye," he said. "You be sure and wake me in time for supper."

"That we will, dear," Deirdre said. Then Riley was gone, and Deirdre was instantly at Callie's side.

"Don't make any excuses, Callandra," Deirdre said. "I want to hear it straight out."

Callie twisted away, marching over to the food pantry and making an elaborate display of straightening several rows of tin goods. "I don't know what you're talking about."

"Callie . . ."

"There is absolutely nothing wrong, Aunt Deirdre. I knew exactly what I was getting into when I agreed to this arrangement."

281

"So that's still what it is? An arrangement? I was hoping your having more than a week to yourselves would make a difference."

Callie frowned. "That's why you and Riley . . . ?"

"Not entirely," Deirdre said, blushing. "But it did cross our minds. We're not blind. We've seen the way you and Trace look at each other. It's like the fates were guiding you to Shadow's Way."

"Cruel fates they were, too." Callie slumped into a chair beside the oak table.

"I'm not sure the final tally is in yet."

"Please, Aunt Deirdre, I don't want to talk about this." She brushed a stray lock of coppery hair away from her face, steeling her determination along with her voice. "For a while I let myself believe there was some kind of destiny that led me here, led me to Trace. But not anymore. He meant it when he said he married me to gain custody of Christopher. Period."

"I can't believe that. He could have married anyone, if that's all he wanted."

Callie laughed, a short, bitter sound. "Trace McCord married me because I was the only woman in the territory who didn't know he'd spent five years in prison."

Deirdre gasped. "He did what?"

Callie told her aunt the story, finishing with, "Heaven only knows what other secrets the man has."

"I'm so sorry, dear."

"It doesn't matter. In two weeks it'll be over, and then we can all get on with our lives."

Deirdre's gaze showed clearly that she didn't believe a word of that, but her voice was gentle as she continued. "I just hope you haven't suffered all of this for nothing. The Marlowes aren't a couple to be easily denied."

"What do you mean?"

"They're staying at the hotel in Rock Springs, too. They didn't miss any opportunity to assure Riley and me that they would be taking Christopher back east with them."

Callie slammed a palm onto the tabletop. "Damn, I wish I knew how they thought they were going to get away with that. Jenny's will is very specific."

"They're intent on making Trace out to be an unacceptable parent. They think they stand a very good chance of breaking the will."

"The only reason they want that child is so they can get their hands on his trust fund."

"Edna Marlowe claims that to be Trace's goal."

Callie nearly muttered an oath. "Trace didn't know about that money."

"He told you that?"

Callie nodded. "He told me. And I believe him. Whether I believe anything else . . ." She blew out a long breath. "It doesn't matter."

"Oh, but it does," Deirdre murmured, "you know it does."

"What matters is Christopher. Trace loves that boy. The boy loves him."

Deirdre squeezed Callie's hand in her own. "It breaks my heart to see you hurting so. You love them both, don't you?"

Callie didn't answer. She didn't have to answer.

Callie stood in the bedroom, staring out at the

moon-shrouded Teton peaks, listening to the measured hoofbeats of Shoshone coming into the yard. Trace was later than usual. It was past midnight.

Deirdre and Riley had retired to the guest room hours ago. Christopher, too, had fallen asleep early, dozing off just after supper, worn out no doubt from Trace's efforts at teaching him to sit a horse this morning.

The sound of Trace's bootheels in the corridor sent Callie scurrying to bed herself. She didn't want him to think she'd been waiting up for him. Quickly she plumped up the pillow barrier, telling herself that just once she wanted to imagine that it was she who stayed away from him, when the reverse was so painfully true.

The door opened. She held her breath, seeking desperately to slow the sudden thudding of her heart. But her pulses only pounded harder as she caught the sounds of his clothing being stripped off, the mattress protesting slightly as he settled his weight on the opposide side of the pillows.

Then suddenly the pillows were gone.

Her back to him, Callie didn't move, her heart thundering so fast that she thought even in her prone position she might faint. She couldn't suppress a tiny gasp as he shifted closer, curving his body to hers. His hard-muscled flesh seemed to sear through the thin barrier of her nightrail.

She waited, not daring to speak, uncertain even of what she wanted from him at this moment. His breath was hot against the back of her neck, his arms tensing as they circled her waist. Strong, calloused fingers slid rhythmically along the soft skin of her arms.

He nuzzled the back of her neck, his warm, moist

breath fanning her cheek. "I want you, Callie. I can't bear being in this bed with you another night without having you." His hands slipped upward to cup her breasts, pulling her to him. She felt the rigid proof of his desire jab into the pliant flesh of her buttocks.

She writhed instinctively, her body undulating to the hypnotic power of his hands. Moaning softly, she allowed him to ease her onto her back. She looked up into his hooded eyes, moondust shadows dancing off the sharp planes of his face. "Trace . . ."

"Don't talk. Don't say anything. Please." He undid the ribbon fastening of her nightrail, easing the filmy material aside, his mouth trailing over the firm peaks of her aroused nipples. His breath caught, his loins burning with a white-hot heat that spread like liquid fire through his veins.

Take her. His body begged.

No. His mind pleaded.

He had thought about this moment all day, assuring himself he could at last give in to the agonizing frustration that tormented him night after night. That he could arouse her in the veiling anonymity of darkness and make her want him as much as he wanted her.

But at what cost? his conscience demanded. In the end he would only hurt them both. One day soon she would find him out. Find him out for what he was. And then she would despise him. He would be damned with the memory of loving her, sentenced to have her haunt his dreams for the rest of his life.

With a low curse he rolled onto his back, his frustration beyond a physical torment.

"Trace . . ." Her voice throbbed with confusion—

and more, the very longing he had hoped for, ached for. But he couldn't . . . didn't dare . . .

Without a word he jammed into his clothes and left the room.

For a long time Callie lay still, staring into the darkness. Why? Why had he done this? What sense did it make for him to hold her, touch her, tell her he wanted her—then storm from the room?

Obviously, he had changed his mind. But *why?* Surely, he had sensed her response. And though perhaps she should be, she was not the least ashamed that her body had so unmistakably revealed the desire in her heart.

"If only he would talk to me," she murmured to the empty room.

Had he aborted his lovemaking because he'd decided, however belatedly, to keep their arrangement strictly business? Or had he been the victim of a resurgent sense of honor—that he not compromise a woman he so adamantly wanted gone once the custody was settled?

Try as she might to sort it through, nothing fully explained his abrupt exit. All she really knew was that she'd never felt so alone. Better that he'd come in and ignore her as he had since their wedding night, than to entice her, excite her . . .

"Stop! Just stop, Callandra!" she muttered, slamming a fist into one of the pillows. "You've never given up on anything you wanted in your life. And you're not going to start now. You want Trace? Then you're damn well going to fight for him!"

She felt a little better then. It wouldn't be an easy battle. But he wanted her. He did. That was her edge and her hope.

She wasn't certain when she finally drifted off to sleep, but she woke before dawn, startled to find Trace in bed beside her. Though he lay still, she was certain he was not asleep. She studied him through half-lidded eyes, wincing at the haggard lines that marked his face.

"Why?" She hadn't meant to say the word aloud. But she hurt for him, hurt for them both.

He sat up, not looking at her. "It was a mistake." His voice was hoarse.

She let out a shuddering sigh. *I love you; that's not a mistake.* She couldn't say the words aloud.

"I'm sorry. It won't happen again."

"Not even if I want it to?"

He stilled, not even seeming to breathe for a full minute. But he did not turn to face her.

Impulsively, she reached toward him, sliding her fingers along the rigid flesh of his shoulder. She swallowed, her pulses leaping as his hand came up to curl lightly over hers.

"Why?" she asked again, wondering if this twilight world between sleep and wakefulness was what allowed her to be so bold.

"I don't know," he said, releasing her hand and turning to look at her.

She longed to burrow into his embrace, but sensed he was already regretting the lowering of his guard, no matter how slight. Yet just before the look of shuttered indifference took hold in his dark eyes, she could have sworn she saw her own want, her own hurt reflected in their depths.

"Trace . . ."

"I'm sorry, Callie. For more things than you know. Please, don't ask. Not now."

She averted his gaze as he flung back the covers, shoving into his clothes. Whatever had brought on last night was gone, buried, hidden from them both. His low curse hung between them as he stalked from the room.

Callie sat there, wondering how much longer either of them was going to be able to bear the sexual tension between them. But she did not give in to her own pain, reminding herself instead of her promise. "The battle has been joined, Trace McCord," she affirmed aloud. "And you've not been in a fight until you've scrapped with Callie Callaghan."

She rose quickly and dressed, flush with her new determination. Still she was grateful when Deirdre offered to entertain Christopher for the day. "You need some time alone, dear," her aunt said. "To sort things through. I know you'll do what's best."

Callie spent several hours in the meadow, recording in her journal as best she could the turbulent confusion of her feelings for Trace McCord. She loved him. She didn't trust him. She wanted him. She was afraid of having him.

If they made love, she would be bound to him heart and soul forever. She knew that, knew it as well as she knew the driving curiosity that had led her west in the first place. But she could accept the risk. What she longed for, but couldn't predict was whether Trace would ever accept it as well.

That night after supper she watched with an aching heart while he played with Christopher. If only she could truly be Trace's wife and Christopher her son. The spark of love that burned in Trace's eyes whenever he looked at the boy made her wish again that he would love her just a little.

She smiled wistfully as Trace got down on all fours and gave Chris a horsey ride. The boy sat astride the broad shoulders shouting, "Giddyap, Papa." Then they were wrestling on the floor, Christopher shrieking with delight, Trace laughing.

For once it was Callie's turn to retreat into the night, strolling in the moonlight until she was certain both Trace and Christopher had gone to bed. Still she waited another hour before she dared go back to the house, go back to Trace's bedroom.

She settled her nightrail over her head. His voice drifted to her in the darkness. "I was beginning to wonder if you were going to sleep in the barn."

"Damn you," she hissed, startled. "You could have told me you were awake."

"I thought my speaking to you would at least give you a hint."

"You know what I mean!" She hugged her arms against her, her skin tingling at the thought that he might have watched her undress, watched her slip the nightdress over her naked body.

"I did not compromise your modesty, if that's what you mean."

"You know full well . . ." She stopped, straightening. He was actually carrying on a conversation with her. She eyed him with a knee-weakening anticipation.

"I've been thinking," Trace said, his voice husky, its sensual quality playing on her heightened senses as surely as if it were his hands. "I need some time away to take my mind off the hearing. And I'm sure you could use the same."

She said nothing, holding herself still on the opposite side of the room.

"I want to show you the herd in the north valley."

"Why?" She blurted the word.

"I can't take you to Yellowstone yet. But I thought I could show you around more of the ranch. Maybe we could both relax a little bit. Your aunt said she would be happy to watch Chris. In fact, it was she who . . ."

Callie stiffened. Surely Deirdre hadn't gone to Trace.

"I didn't mean to say that. Don't be angry with her. I thought it was a good idea."

Callie didn't know when she'd ever felt more mortified. Deirdre had gone to Trace and arranged for this little outing? Yet even as her pride stung, the prospect of spending a few days alone with Trace could well prove worth the price. "Why do you think it would be a good idea?"

"I told you. To relax us both."

"Or to make sure I'm going to do and say what you want in court?" There was no anger in her voice, only a mild curiosity.

"That's not why . . ."

"Trace, we've hardly spoken to each other these past few days and now . . ."

"Then you don't want to go?"

"Not if you're only going to be angry and cynical and . . . a blasted sourpuss."

One corner of his mouth ticked upward. "Sourpuss?"

She straightened, eyeing him airily. "You heard me."

290

"And if I promise to be a good boy?"

"Then I'll consider it."

"Then I promise."

She smiled. "Then I'll go." She kept her tone matter-of-fact, not wanting him to see just how excited she was at the thought of the trip, the thought of being with him.

"Good." He pulled the covers back. "Then come to bed. You need to be well rested."

She lay down, praying he would take up where he'd left off last night. But though he pulled her close, his hands did not stray from her waist. She considered taking the initiative herself, but decided that to do so would be to risk his rejection—and, more, to risk his reneging on their upcoming trip alone together. No matter how much she longed for him, she would force herself to be patient.

The next day Trace was gone most of the day. Callie could only hope it was for the reason she suspected, that his self-control was nearly gone. She had felt the proof of his desire against the softness of her buttocks, but not once in the night had he made any attempt to assuage it.

All afternoon her imagination painted exciting scenarios of their upcoming trek. Even Yellowstone—her goal, her dream—had become secondary. Would he be able to hold back? Surely, even Trace McCord's self-control had a breaking point. Especially when she intended to do everything she could to see that he reached it. She settled onto the settee, dreaming of him making love to her under the stars. After weeks of denial, he would be tender, trembling with need. He would hold back no longer. He would hold her, touch her, kiss her . . .

The sound of Christopher's crying broke through her fantasies. He had been fussy most of the day.

"Mouf hurt," he whimpered, rubbing his cheek.

After considerable coaxing, Callie persuaded him to open his mouth. A new tooth peeked through near the back of his tender gums. "Poor baby," she soothed, hugging him close.

Books, toys, his favorite games—she tried them all. She was considering standing on her head when he finally fell asleep on the bearskin rug. Ever so gently she carried him into his bedroom, hoping fervently he would now sleep through the night.

Feeling exhausted herself, she fixed a light supper and ate alone in the kitchen. Deirdre and Riley had decided on an overnight outing of their own, promising to be back in time for Trace and Callie to leave early in the morning. Callie had to smile at how willingly Deirdre now camped out. Their first night on the trail out of Omaha had been a litany of fear and trepidation about insects, wolves, and assorted wilderness monsters.

Callie sat on the porch swing, watching the dimming ribbons of purples, reds, and oranges as dusk readied for darkness. As the night settled in, she couldn't help worrying. Surely Trace wouldn't stay away on the night before they were to ride out together. Just as her vision of him lying hurt somewhere was becoming frighteningly vivid, he thundered into the yard astride Shoshone.

She blew out a long, shuddering breath, though she did not leave the porch. She continued to rock the swing gently back and forth as she waited for him to bed down the stallion.

"You should have gone to bed," he murmured as he stepped onto the porch. "We'll be getting an early start."

"I'll be fine," she said, feeling her pulse quicken, helpless to prevent it. "You're very late tonight."

"Stuck filly," he grinned. "Silly female got herself tangled up in a treefall."

"I doubt if her sex had anything to do with her getting tangled up."

"Never can tell," Trace replied smoothly. "I considered it the better part of discretion to bathe in the creek before joining you." He sat down beside her, setting the swing into a gentle, rhythmic motion. "You look tired."

She told him about Christopher's tooth.

"You have my sincere sympathy. I went through the same thing with him a few months ago."

She gave him a tentative smile, her eyes unwillingly drawn to the hard, strong line of his jaw, the deep vee of his shirt. Abruptly she turned away, wishing he would go on to bed. The soft intimate light of the moon was suddenly much too dark, too suggestive to her heightened senses.

"Are you still looking forward to tomorrow?" he asked.

If only you knew how much. She was waging a battle with emotions beyond her understanding. Her moments of fantasizing this afternoon about what it would be like to have him make love to her were rushing back to her with alarming clarity.

"Of course I'm looking forward to it," she managed. "I want to see those horses of yours. They'll make a nice addition to my journal."

"I'm glad things have worked out for you here."

She turned to look at him, trying to discern in the dim light if he was mocking her. She decided that he was not. "Thank you."

"It's very important to you, isn't it? The journal I mean."

"It's what I've wanted more than anything in the world for as long as I can remember. To have my father publish my work in his paper . . . using my name."

She brought the swing to a quick halt. Standing up, she walked over to the top step of the porch and just as quickly sat down. She was surprised when Trace did the same.

"There are several things you'll need to bring with you tomorrow," he said. "I don't want to get there and find out you've forgotten something important."

"I know what to take."

"You never can tell when something of monumental import will happen."

She blushed heatedly, but said nothing.

He cleared his throat, rubbing his hand along his pant leg. If she hadn't known better, she could have sworn he was nervous. She cocked her head toward him, surprised to find his lips compressed in an agitated frown.

"Is something wrong, Trace? Maybe you don't really want to go on this little trip after all?"

"I want it more than anything." The words seemed to leap out before he could censor them. He took a deep breath. "I've been rough on you at times. I don't mean to be. Of all people I should . . ."

Her pulses raced. She knew how difficult it was for

him to be open about anything at all. His aloofness was a defense, a reaction to a lifetime of hurt. And now he was very deliberately lowering his defenses.

"Trace, you don't have to say anything."

"No, I want you to know how much I appreciate what you've done for me. I know I'm getting a lot more out of this bargain than you are."

Surely she could never love another man in her life the way she loved Trace McCord at this moment. Her heart was pounding so hard she wondered at his inability to hear it.

She held herself practically still as his hand reached out and cupped her chin. Slowly, deliberately he turned her head to face him. She longed for him to kiss her, and she did not resist when he pulled her close.

"You are so beautiful," he said. "So beautiful. I can't be near you without wanting you. And I want you now so much."

He held her, glorying in how her body quivered to his touch. He kissed the top of her head as she nestled against him, the soft jasmine scent of her hair, her skin, exciting him almost beyond bearing.

She opened herself to him, kissing him, loving him. Her heart soared. He was going to make love to her. She twined her arms around his neck, eager to learn how to please him, eager to be pleased herself.

His hands moving urgently along her responding body, his tongue trailing past her lips, down to the valley between her breasts. He undid the buttons of her dress, reaching to unlace her chemise. His usually deft fingers fumbled for a moment, not, she realized with awe, from clumsiness, but from his longing to see her, touch her. Her breasts spilled willingly into his

295

knowing hands. He kneaded the pliant flesh, teasing the nipples into twin peaks of desire.

"My God, Callie," he murmured. "I want you. I'm sorry. I want you so much."

He eased her down onto the porch, the rough boards strangely erotic against her bare back. His leg urged hers apart. His mouth explored her body with exquisite tenderness, suckling, nipping, delighting in her trembling need.

Quickly, he tugged off his shirt, then eased his weight on top of her. The soft mat of hair on his tautly muscled chest teased her nipples until she whimpered with longing. She felt the hard heat of him against her thigh as his excitement became her excitement.

The soft nickering of horses in the nearby corrals, the cool sweetness of the night air only added to the whirling sensations he was evoking in her body. She ached to know him, know him utterly, and would give him her soul if he but asked.

He freed her of her dress, then she listened to the soft chinking of metal as he unbuckled his belt. His mouth never left her, tracing the path of his loving from the tip of her breasts to her navel and below. She thought surely she would go mad from wanting him.

His eyes blazed, his body on fire. But just as he would have taken her, made her his, some long dormant conscience sparked to life. Where Callie was concerned he forced himself to give her one last chance to stop. "I promised you this wouldn't happen," he rasped. "I don't want you to hate me tomorrow. I couldn't bear for you to hate . . ." He swallowed the rest of his words, refusing even in his passion to be too vulnerable, too trusting.

She lay her hand along his lightly stubbled cheek. "You torment me only by making me wait," she whispered. "I want to feel you inside me, feel you love me . . ."

Her words sheared away the last vestiges of his self-control. With an animal cry of pleasure he buried himself in her satiny warmth, reveling in how her body arched to welcome him, reveling in how right it felt to be part of her. For a moment, at least, maybe for the first time in his life, he let go of the shadows of his past and gave himself up to the fierce and present joy of this woman, his wife—joy that spiraled outward as he felt her body convulse beneath him as she joined him in a world of sensual ecstasy.

Sated, happier than he ever remembered being, he rolled to one side of her. But somehow just breaking contact broke the spell. He lay there, waiting for the condemning words he was sure would come, no matter how much she had pleasured in the moment.

The sound was far away at first, imagined. It couldn't be. Then it came louder. A whimper, then a wail. Christopher!

"I should see to him," she said, pushing to her feet, shyly gathering up her scattered clothing.

He let her go, grateful for the reprieve. She felt his eyes on her as she hurriedly pulled on her dress. Her legs felt decidedly unsteady.

Inside the house, she hurried down the hallway. Christopher met her halfway, rubbing sleepily at his eyes. If anything, he cried even louder when he caught sight of her, holding out his arms.

"Mouf hurt," he sobbed. Callie scooped him into her arms and carried him back into his room, where she sank onto the rocking chair. Her own tears mingled with the child's. She was so confused. One minute she'd been so happy, the next she could almost feel Trace close a door between them.

Trace strode into the room. "A little whiskey on his gums might help," he suggested.

His concern for Christopher was evident in his brown eyes. But there was something else there as well. Regret?

Trace soothed the medicine over the fretful child's gums. He offered to take him from Callie, but Christopher would have none of it. "Call-ee," he cried. "Call-ee hold Christopher."

"He likes to stay with the first one who picks him up," she said quickly, afraid Trace would be upset by the boy's momentary preference for her. Instead his eyes registered only a mild surprise.

"I can tell when I'm a fifth wheel." He cocked a half smile at her. "Since we're going to be getting an early start in the morning, at least one of us ought to get some sleep."

"Maybe we should postpone the trip," Callie said.

"We'll see how he is in the morning." He rubbed the boy's head affectionately. Christopher was already struggling to keep his eyes open. It was a losing cause. He snuggled against Callie's shoulder.

She watched Trace stride down the hallway, again feeling a hot rush of desire. She longed to call out to him, but pride kept her silent. She rocked Christopher for another half hour before she was certain he was sound enough asleep to put him in bed. But as she carried him, he woke and began to cry again. It was another forty-five minutes before she could get him to fall back to sleep. All the while she sat in the rocking chair in his room, softly humming fragmented bits of long-ago nursery rhymes. She did not know that Trace watched her from the doorway for long minutes before retreating to their room.

"Good night, sweet boy," she whispered, brushing Christopher's soft cheek with her lips. She tiptoed from the room, hardly daring to hope that Trace had waited up for her. Her heart sank when she found him in bed, breathing deeply. Wearily, she lay down beside him.

Tomorrow they would be going on a four-day journey. He wanted her. She had proved that tonight. But risking a commitment was obviously not in his plans. More than ever, though, it was in hers. No matter what she thought of herself later, she would use his desire to her advantage when they were alone. She would do her best to force his hand—to have his loving and his love by the time they returned to Shadow's Way.

Chapter Eighteen

Callie woke with a start, instantly alert. Dawn was breaking, the first perceptible shadings of light beginning to filter into the room. This was it. The day she would set out on her five-day camping trek with Trace. She shifted nervously in the bed, turning toward the sounds of rustling clothing on the opposite side of the room. She was just in time to see Trace yanking up his drawers. A flash of exposed flank, sleek, hard muscled, sent a surge of wantonness through her. She started to look away, then caught herself, her eyes moving up to meet his as he turned to face her.

"Sorry," he murmured. "I tried to be quiet. Figured you'd sleep a little while longer."

"Don't apologize. If I haven't said it before, I love this place." She paused, then very deliberately added, "It has such a spectacular view."

She swallowed a smile as she watched his brows furrow in consternation, startled by her boldness. Though the dim light would not allow her to confirm her suspicion, she imagined a crimson blush creeping upward under his tanned face.

"I'll get the pack horse ready," he said, pulling on the rest of his clothes.

"I'll be right behind you."

He frowned, and she knew he was wondering if that was yet another reference to her morning view, but she kept her face carefully blank. Shaking his head, muttering to himself, he headed out of the room.

"Keep him on his toes, Callandra." She grinned. *The poor man didn't know it yet, but he had absolutely no chance of coming back from their trip with the walls between them intact.* If her erotic thoughts of last night had not driven her mad, her dreams had. Wonderful dreams, filled with passion and love. She wanted that man and she was going to have him.

All your life, whenever your da said no and you wanted it to be yes, what did you do, Callandra? she mused as she peered into the mirror above the basin in Trace's room. *You did what you damned well pleased, that's what. You're spoiled rotten, and you're too old to change now. You may have forgotten that for a time. But no more. Trace McCord thinks he married you only to keep his child, but we'll just see about that.*

Even so, she grew thoughtful. She would do her best, but for all her past methods of getting around her father's dictates, she had never come up against so formidable a challenge as this. She wasn't overcoming something tangible. How could she make a man love her? Trust her?

Maybe it wasn't possible, she admitted. But then, her quest for the Yellowstone treasure was no task for the fainthearted, either.

She dressed quickly, then headed outside. There she

found Trace lashing down the last of their supplies to a barrel-chested dun. Kachina and Shoshone stood nearby, already saddled and ready to go. Callie returned to the porch, skittering over to the swing. Somehow the idea of making idle chatter with Trace was just too overwhelming. She was too excited.

"You certainly look happy," Deirdre said, stepping out on the porch, Christopher trailing at her heels. The boy already seemed to have forgotten his discomfort of last night. The tooth had broken the surface of his gum, and he was his bubbly self once again.

"I am happy," Callie admitted, leaning forward to gather the child to her as he climbed onto her lap. She studied her aunt quietly for a moment then said, "Trace told me this trip was your doing."

"Are you telling me you wished I'd kept my mouth shut?"

Callie looked over at Trace, watching his broad muscles flexing beneath his shirt as he tied down the pack. "No," she said slowly. "I'm glad for the chance to be alone with him. I just hope it doesn't prove to be a disaster."

"You'll do fine. It's good to be together. The evenings Riley and I spent reading poetry . . ." She blushed.

"I'm glad you're so happy," Callie said, rising to her feet but keeping her hold on Christopher. Trace had finished saddling Shoshone and Kachina. It was time to go.

Trace took Christopher from her, giving him a tight squeeze. "I'm going to miss you, pardner," he said. "You mind Miss Deirdre now, hear?"

Christopher nodded solemnly, though his arms remained looped around Trace's neck.

"He'll be just fine," Deirdre said, holding out her arms. But before Christopher would go to her, he looked first at Callie. "Cal-lee, hug!" he demanded.

Callie gave the child another quick hug, loving the unabashed affection he lavished on her. "I'm going to miss you, too, sweetheart. But we'll be back in no time at all, don't you worry. And then we can play hide-and-seek, and I can tell you lots more stories. How will that be?"

Trace mounted Shoshone. "We'd better go."

She nodded, handing Christopher to Deirdre, then she mounted Kachina. Giving her aunt and the boy a final wave, she rode out, following Trace, feeling alternately exhilarated and terrified. Trace said little as they urged the horses into a ground-eating canter, the pack horse keeping pace on a lead rope tied to Shoshone's saddlehorn.

Callie gave little notice to Trace's silence. She was too immersed in the pleasure of the moment. The sheer vastness of the uninhabited land, after a lifetime among the thriving populace of New York, never failed to stir her. She felt a special kinship to this place, the snowy peaks of the upthrusting Tetons to the west, the tree-bristled basin through which they rode.

As the day progressed, though, the hours on horseback began to take their toll. Trace had allowed them only one stop since they'd left the ranch and that had been for nature's necessities.

Finally, near midafternoon, Callie could take it no longer. She reined Kathina to a halt, clambering gingerly from the saddle. Stiff-legged, she padded about, exercising her cramped muscles.

Trace dismounted, coming up beside her. "Tired?"

"A bit."

He shoved his broad-brimmed hat back off of his forehead, using his forearm to swipe at the sweat that glistened along the strong planes of his face. "We can rest for a little while, but if we're going to make camp by nightfall, we'd better keep moving."

"I'll be fine. Just give me a minute."

"A minute it is." He smiled, a tentative, uncertain smile. "I want you to enjoy this trip, you know." He stooped to pluck a daisy from the wilderness bouquet that skirted a nearby boulder. His gaze capturing hers, he tucked the flower behind her right ear.

Callie touched the flower with shaking fingers. "Why did you do that?"

He shrugged. "Felt like it."

She wondered if her feet were anywhere near the ground. She could only stare at him as he handed her Kachina's reins and helped her remount. Maybe the mountain air was affecting his mind, she thought giddily. Then more seriously she realized that this could be the first time in months that he truly allowed himself to get away from the pressures of the ranch and Christopher's custody battle.

"By the way, she's yours, Callie," he said quietly, patting Kachina's neck.

"I still can't believe you're letting me ride her," she said. "She's much too valuable."

"She's not just yours to ride now. I mean she's yours."

Her hand flew to her mouth. "Mine? Oh, Trace, I couldn't. I mean, that's crazy." He wanted to breed Kachina to Shoshone. The horse was worth a small fortune. Why would he give her away? And why to her?

"Of course," he went on, "you'll have to board her at Shadow's Way."

"I don't understand."

"Christopher's grown very fond of you," he said. "And I think you're fond of him." He hesitated, seeming reluctant—or was it unsure?—about what he wanted to say next. "Because of our arrangement, I thought you might be uncomfortable about coming back here. Kachina can be your excuse."

So it was Christopher he was thinking of. "That's very sweet of you, Trace," she managed. "But it's not necessary. I might have felt a little awkward after the divorce"—how could she speak of it as though it had already happened?—"but I would have come back one day to see Christopher." She stiffened. "Can we go now?" she asked, climbing into the saddle.

Trace mounted Shoshone. "Callie, if I've upset you, I'm sorry. It wasn't my intention."

She nudged the horse forward so that Trace would not see the sudden tears that rimmed her eyes. That he so clearly still intended to end the marriage tore at her. Why had he wanted this time together if he were not prepared to sort through their conflicting feelings? Did he merely want to prove himself made of steel, that he could turn away from her even in the isolated loveliness of this valley?

Toward early evening Callie again reined in Kachina. She made certain to keep her voice neutral. "If you don't mind, a certain part of my anatomy isn't used to all this saddle-riding. Is this place you want to camp much farther?"

He grinned, and swung down from the saddle. "I was

wondering when you were going to admit it."

She blushed. Did he have to notice everything? Casting an indignant scowl in his direction, she slid to the ground and hobbled off as fast as her stiff muscles would permit.

In an instant he was beside her, catching her arm, spinning her around to face him. "A bit testy, aren't we?"

She clamped her jaw shut to prevent a stinging retort. He was right. Her rump hurt, her legs hurt, her back hurt—and, as usual, her emotions were in a turmoil just being near him—all of which served to make her more than a little irritable. "I'm sorry."

He lifted her chin with his thumb and forefinger. "We've only got a mile to go."

"I'll be fine."

"I know."

The husky tone of his voice would be her undoing, unless she could distract him. She ducked away from him, stalking toward a carpet of blue wildflowers just ahead. Stooping down, she made a great pretense of examining them.

Trace hunkered down beside her. "Larkspur," he pronounced, his breath warm against her ear. "They grow like this along the bottomlands, where they can get moisture." He caressed a silky blossom. "They're actually wild delphiniums. In the spring when forage is scarce, cattle eat them and die because they're poisonous. This time of year, when grass is more plentiful, cattle don't eat them, but in one of Mother Nature's masterful ironies, when they're blooming they're no longer toxic."

What a perfectly marvelous way to get a botany

lesson, she thought, studying how delicately his long, tanned fingers trailed along the petal's edge. She did not resist when he turned her toward him. He placed a large hand on each of her shoulders, his thumbs stroking her throat. She closed her eyes.

"Behind you," he whispered, his lips against her forehead, "I can show you buttercups as bright as the sun."

She didn't open her eyes. She could feel the droplets of sweat above his upper lip as his mouth came down on hers. She could taste the salty sweetness of him. Then, just as she hoped he would deepen the kiss, he set her away from him.

"Why did you kiss me?" she murmured.

"Felt like it." He turned away, striding back to Shoshone.

Callie stared after him, dumbfounded. The man was impossible! His earlier moroseness had given way to an almost conscious determination to keep things open and light between them. His vacillation fueled her hopes about the night ahead. What would his mood be when the time came to share their first night under the stars? Would they make love again?

Her skin tingled at the thought. Then just as quickly she forced her mind elsewhere. If she'd learned nothing else, it was that she couldn't predict Trace McCord.

They'd ridden another quarter mile, when suddenly Trace reached out and gripped Kachina's reins, jerking both horses to a halt. He pointed toward the ridge a quarter mile to their left. Skylined against the backdrop of the setting sun was the most magnificent horse Callie had ever seen—a fiery red stallion with a mane of spun gold.

"He's beautiful," she murmured.

Trace didn't respond. She dragged her eyes from the stallion to see Trace sitting rigid in the saddle, his face ashen. "It's the first time I've seen him in two years. I'd almost convinced myself he was dead."

She didn't have to ask. This was the horse that had killed Seth McCord. For just an instant from the way Trace spoke, she expected him to draw his rifle from his saddle boot and shoot the stallion. But he just sat there watching the horse paw the ground. "Likely after some of the mares in my herd. Or maybe Kachina."

"Are you all right?"

"Yeah. Fine." He was still rigid as a stone.

"What will you do if he steals the mares?"

"Let him have 'em. Then I'll go after his offspring in a year or two."

Callie studied Trace closely, trying to discern some deeper meaning hidden in the words. She admired him for not killing the horse, yet wondered if he could really so casually dismiss seeing the animal again.

His voice continued to betray no particular emotion. "A wild stallion measures his worth by the number of females in his harem. The more mares the better the stud. After adolescence, his whole goal in life is acquiring females."

"I've heard some human males live by the same standards."

He snorted, and for a moment at least the grim mood was broken. They continued in silence for another half mile until they reached a section of the valley floor cordoned off by a stand of lodgepole pine. "We'll camp here," he said.

Trace dismounted and set about preparing the camp.

Callie made certain to do her share, brushing down the horses, while Trace started supper.

As dusk gave way to night, they ate quickly, both of them indulging hearty appetites after a day in the saddle. Finishing off her second cup of coffee, Callie lay back, groaning happily. It felt so good to be lying down.

Trace retrieved a blanket from their supplies, handing it to her. "You may not know it yet, but you're exhausted."

She was touched by his matter-of-fact consideration, and had to busy herself digging through her saddlebags, lest he notice. She lay there, wishing for the perfect ending to this first day of what she had dared imagine was her honeymoon, wishing for Trace to take her in his arms and make love to her, here in the mountains with only the stars and the horses as company. But it didn't happen. Instead it was as he'd told her. The sun had been gone barely an hour when her exhausted body drifted into a dreamless sleep.

She woke to a muffled curse. Disoriented at first, she sat up, noticing the campfire had burned itself out. The sound came again. Trace. He was twisting in his blankets, muttering nothing she could understand. Crawling across the five feet that separated them, she was about to wake him when the words came more clearly.

"Don't . . . horse . . . Seth. Don't, Seth . . ."

She touched his shoulder.

He was instantly awake. "Sorry." He didn't look at her.

"Are you sure you're all right?"

"Fine. Go back to sleep."

She knelt beside him. "You don't look fine."

"Please, Callie . . ."

Her heart pounding, she lay down beside him. His eyes bored into hers and she did not mistake the desire she saw reflected there. But there was something else as well, and that she couldn't read. So while he did not protest her presence, neither did he take advantage of it. His only concession to her snuggling close to him was the long, contented sigh that whispered through him as she fell asleep.

She woke to the dawn chill, shifting instinctively, seeking the warmth of Trace's body.

She was alone in the bedroll.

Trace was gone.

She was on her feet at once, looking around wildly. Kachina was gone, too. "Trace!" She shouted his name, even knowing he was nowhere near enough to hear it.

Frightened now, she struggled with Shoshone's saddle, dragging it over to the stallion. She was attempting to heave it onto the big horse's back when she saw him.

On the ridge barely a quarter of a mile from where she stood.

The red stallion.

At the same instant she heard the sound—pounding hoofbeats somewhere off to her right. She turned to see Trace, hatless, his hair whipped flat by the wind, astride a thundering Kachina. In his right hand he held a lariat, poised, ready. He swung the mare in a wide loop, bearing down hard on the ridge, on the stallion. He looked for all the world like some avenging spirit from another world. And in all of it, the stallion hadn't moved. As if he were waiting. As if he, too, were ready.

"No." Callie took an involuntary step foward, then stopped. There was nothing she could do. Yet she couldn't just stand there and watch. She let go of the heavy saddle, then gripped Shoshone's thick mane. Using the saddle as a stepping-stone, she flung herself onto the tall stallion's back.

As she rode, it was as though she were watching an outdoor theater—with Trace and the red stallion the only players. She had closed to within a hundred yards, when Trace's lasso whistled through the air, settling perfectly around the stallion's neck. Instantly he secured it to his saddle horn, even as the stallion's angry scream split the morning stillness.

The horse reared, pawing wildly, lunging at Kachina, who countered his every move. Trace slid from the saddle, shaking out a second rope. The stallion's ears flattened, his teeth bared, his eyes rolling back in his head.

"Trace!" Callie screamed. "He'll kill you. Please. Let him go!"

Trace let the second lasso fly. It, too, was a perfect toss, circling the stallion's angrily bobbing head. Trace wrapped the rope around his left wrist, whipping the trailing end behind his back and pulling on it with his right, using his back as leverage to keep the rope taut. The stallion was now trapped between the mare and the man. "Stay out of this, Callie."

"I will not stay out of it!" She jumped down from Shoshone's back, waving her arms to drive the gray horse back down the hillside, then started toward Trace.

"Callie, stay the hell away!" he roared, daring a

quick glance her way, then concentrating his full attention on the enraged red horse once again.

"What are you going to do?" she demanded, taking still another step toward him.

He didn't answer. But she knew. "Trace, he killed your brother. You told Seth that horse could never be ridden. Please. Don't do this."

He wasn't listening. He kept his rope taut as the stallion reared, pawed, trumpeted his fury. No matter which way the horse moved, the man and the mare moved with him, keeping the ropes wire-tight. Trace circled the horse like a lobo wolf closing for the kill. Callie made a wider arc around the battling trio.

"Trace, I beg you. Let the horse go."

The grim set of his features told her she might as well be talking to the stallion. He never took his eyes from the horse. When the stallion bent his neck low, scraping at the hard ground with his hoof, the decision was made. Trace let go of the rope. With lightning swiftness he leaped on the stallion's back, in the same motion yanking off both ropes. The horse reared again, seeking to rid itself of the man who now clung to his back. Using knees, hands, and an inner rage of his own, Trace held on.

Callie stared. Terrified, mesmerized.

The horse tore past her, bucking, kicking, twisting. Still Trace held on. Then suddenly the stallion stopped dead, his ears laid back, his eyes wild.

In one sickening, gut-wrenching moment the great red horse reared up on his hind legs, then fell back, rolling over in an attempt to free Trace from his back in the only way he could. Callie screamed, envisioning Trace being crushed just as Seth had been. Instead he hit the ground and rolled instantly to one side. Like a cat, he was up and on the stallion's back before the animal could regain his feet.

The stallion thundered across the valley floor, Trace clinging low, his features lost in the wind-whipped mane. Callie stared, the man and the horse seeming one being, a centaur, primitive, untamed, at one with the surrounding wilderness.

She lost sight of them more than once behind massive outcroppings of boulders. Each time she feared to see the stallion reappear without the man. Each time the man held on. Somehow guiding the horse, yet letting him run free, Trace set the animal on a wide, arcing path around the miles' long valley. They were a quarter mile away when the stallion stopped.

Callie held her breath, fearing the beast meant to repeat its crushing roll over. But the horse only stood there, trembling. He tossed his golden mane once, his great head still held high as he looked back at the man who sat his back.

For a long minute Trace didn't move, then very slowly he shifted his left leg over the stallion's back and dropped to the ground. He didn't look back as he strode toward Callie.

The horse took one step toward him, then whirled and raced to the top of the ridge. He reared high, pawing the air, took one last look at Trace, and raced away from the ridge's edge, disappearing from sight.

Only then did Callie shift her gaze to Trace, who now seemed absorbed in gathering in his lariats. "I thought you were going to die."

He fixed the ropes to Kachina's saddle. "It was something I had to do."

"That's the same reason your brother used."

He took up Kachina's reins and led the mare over to where Callie stood. "I know. Only now I finally understand it."

"You could have died, too," she repeated, her voice shaking.

"I didn't mean to scare you."

"Damn you, Trace McCord," she said, losing her battle to keep her tears at bay. "You had no right to play your rites of manhood games! You've never forgiven your brother for dying on you when it was so unnecessary. Yet you would have done the same damnable thing. For what?" Her voice rose. "For what?"

He reached a hand toward her, then dropped it back to his side. "Let's just get back to camp, shall we?" He started down the hill.

She glared at his retreating back, her voice now very soft. "What would you have wanted me to tell Christopher?"

He stopped abruptly, turning to face her. He seemed about to defend himself yet again, then his head sagged forward. He stared at the ground. "God help me, I never once thought of that. Never once thought I'd die."

"Neither did Seth."

"You've made your point."

For what seemed an interminable minute their eyes locked, neither wavering. Then Trace took a step toward her. "I'm sorry."

She let out the breath she didn't realize she'd been holding. "You won't do it again?"

The side of his mouth ticked upward, his gaze softening. "I promise."

"All right then," she said, a slow smile playing on her own lips, "you're forgiven. This time."

"Thank you."

She laughed, the last of the fearful tension that had gripped her since she'd awakened to find Trace gone draining away. "I really am glad you didn't shoot him."

"You thought I would?"

"A lot of men would have."

"I'm not a lot of men."

"I know." Her voice was low, throaty, tender.

He reached her in two strides, his arms circling her, pulling her against him. He brushed his lips along the slender column of her throat, tracking butterfly kisses up to her waiting lips. She opened her mouth to him, inviting, seeking, eager to give him whatever he asked, eager to accept whatever he gave.

"Oh, Trace," she murmured, "I was so frightened. I don't know what I would have done if that horse had . . ."

"Shhh, don't think about it," he whispered, kissing her cheeks, her eyelids, her mouth. "I'm all right. I'm all right." He tightened his hold on her, reveling in the feel of her, the taste, the scent. Glorying in the knowledge that she cared.

Long minutes later they headed back to camp, each quietly thoughtful. A new bond had sprung up between them—fragile, tentative, but real nonetheless. And for now at least, they were content to savor it, protect it, neither wanting to push too hard too fast, neither wanting to jeopardize the magic, even for the promise of a greater magic yet unknown.

The next two days passed with such speed and

wonderment, that Callie wished for the power to slow time. She could spend the rest of her life in this valley with Trace. For his part, he remained in high spirits and Callie marveled at how good it felt just to be near him. The only time he would withdraw was at night. He would brush down the horses, then lay out his blankets on the side opposite the fire from hers.

I still have two more nights, she told herself as they made ready to leave the camp on the third morning. *Maybe he's waiting for me to come to him. Maybe . . .*

"Callie . . . ?"

She started, turning away from her task of cinching down Kachina's saddle to find Trace standing directly behind her. "I didn't hear you," she stammered.

"Obviously. Is something wrong? You seem quiet this morning."

Nothing that making love to you wouldn't cure, she thought miserably. To curb his curiosity she blurted the first thing that came to mind. "I was just thinking about my father. One of these days he's going to find me, or have me found, and I haven't even made it to Yellowstone yet."

"I'm sorry. I know that's my fault."

She gave herself a mental kick. Now she had the man feeling guilty. That was the last thing she wanted. "No, no, it's all right. Even if he does find me, he's not going to stop me."

"The hearing is hardly more than a week away. You'll be able to make plans for your trip after that."

"Trace, it doesn't matter. My father is not . . ."

"July is one of the best months to be in Yellowstone anyway."

She grimaced. Now he probably believed she'd been

bemoaning her entire stay at his ranch, just itching for the day she could be off to continue her grand trek. Certainly, she still wanted to see Yellowstone, to make her personal search for the treasure, but the *when* of it no longer mattered. It only mattered that she go there with Trace. Convincing him of that at the moment, however, was highly unlikely. She opted for a change in subject. "What are we going to be seeing today?"

"More of the herd. There's a new colt I want you to see. Shoshone's son by one of my best mares."

"Shhh, Kachina will hear you. She'll be jealous."

He grinned, and she could believe the subject of her father and Yellowstone closed for now.

For the next hour they rode along the tree-lined border of a small forested section of the valley. Once Trace stopped, staring off a rocky ridge a half mile distant.

"What is it?" she asked.

He didn't answer right away, continuing to study the ridge. Finally, he shrugged. "Thought I saw a reflection. Must have been the sun playing tricks."

She frowned, unwillingly recalling the day in the meadow when she'd been photographing Christopher. She had no such feeling of being watched now. Yet Trace seemed more edgy than he was letting on. "Who or what . . . ?"

She was interrupted by his low curse. She followed his gaze skyward, spying a number of black specks soaring high against a blue sky.

"Buzzards," he said. "Must be something dead or dying." He kneed Shoshone in the direction of the birds.

Reluctantly, Callie followed. They reached the

clearing together.

"Son of a bitch!" Trace exploded, staring down at the bloody carnage staining the gentle green of the meadow. He dug his heels into Shoshone's sides, sending the stallion leaping ahead.

Callie hung back, striving with everything in her not to be sick, as Trace hunkered down near the all-but-unrecognizable carcass of a horse. She was grateful the breeze was blowing in the opposite direction. Not even that would help after another hour or two in the sun.

Trace stood, swearing softly. "The bear. That damned bear."

"The horse was part of your herd?" She knew the answer, but felt compelled to say something, anything.

"The mare I was telling you about. And her foal."

"Both . . ." Callie's stomach lurched. "Oh, God, Trace, I'm sorry."

"I should have made it my business to kill that bear."

"Isn't that what Reese has been trying to do?"

"I shouldn't have left it up to Reese. He forgets things, wanders off for weeks at a time." He looked back at the grisly scene in the clearing. "Damn. She died protecting her foal."

"If you want to take me back to the ranch so you can track the bear, I'll understand."

He looked up at her. "No. We still have two days. I want those two days."

Her skin tingled, her heart thudding.

"But you stick close to me, hear? There's something wrong with a bear that goes after horses. God knows what it'll attack next."

The discovery of the dead animals cast a pall over the rest of the day. By nightfall Callie was feeling more than a little melancholy. She sighed heavily, kneeling down in front of their campfire. The chances of Trace ever making love to her again seemed more remote than ever. She was just about to turn in, when she noticed him gazing fondly at a small photograph he pulled out of his saddlebags. "You miss Christopher, don't you?"

He nodded.

"I miss him, too." She poked a stick at the fire. "Maybe next time we can bring him with us." She stiffened, realizing what she had said. There would be no next time. She watched the smile on Trace's face vanish. He snapped the saddlebags shut.

"Get some sleep," he said, heading over to his own blankets.

She couldn't let the day end on a sour note. "That prairie dog town was really something today," she ventured. "Though I don't see why you wouldn't let me get closer to it on Kachina. Lugging my camera a couple of hundred extra yards was a bit tedious."

"We don't need the horses stepping into a dog hole. They can snap a leg like a twig. In case you don't remember, Kachina and Shoshone are blooded stock."

"Yes, Trace," she demurred, bringing her blankets over to his.

He looked at her blankets, looked at her. "I don't think . . ."

"If that bear comes down here . . ."

"I doubt a bear will come near the fire."

"You said yourself he's not acting like a normal bear. Maybe he's not afraid of fire, or people, or anything." She spread the blankets out, sitting down next to him. "I want to sleep next to you. Period."

He shrugged. "Who am I to argue with a pretty lady?"

A breeze sifted through the night air, bringing an unexpected chill with it. She shivered.

Trace's brow furrowed. "Are you cold?"

"I'm all right. It was just the wind."

His eyes held hers. She had no trouble reading his thoughts. He had spent one too many nights out here sleeping by himself. "Damn, Callie, I . . ." His hand reached out and gently caressed her cheek. She shivered again. But this time it was not from the cold. And he knew it. He leaned over and kissed her softly, searchingly.

"Let me warm you," he murmured.

She was shaking like a child. Wasn't this exactly what she had dreamed of—his desire getting the better of him. She couldn't take her eyes off his hands as he settled his body next to hers.

"I want you to be warm." He kissed her again. "I want us both to be warm."

As if they had a will of their own, her arms circled his neck, pulling him close, her fingers tracing lovingly along his throat and upward to explore his face. Ever so gently she sculpted his features, caressing the fine lines of his forehead, the arrogant arch of his brows, the straight line of his nose, the hard set of his jaw. He'd shaved early this morning, and the beginnings of a light stubble tickled her fingertips.

With a sudden movement he captured her hand in his and kissed the fingers that now rested ever so lightly on his lips. He held her hand prisoner, then shifted his mouth so that his kisses trailed upward to her throat. "I want you, Callie," he groaned against her ear, his teeth tugging at the sensitive lobe. "I want you so badly." His mouth went on seducing her, robbing her of her will, robbing her of everything but her overwhelming need for him. "I've never felt like this in my life. I need . . ." He stopped, amending the word, "I want you. Please . . ."

"You can need me, Trace," she said. "Don't be afraid to need me. I need you. I want you. I love you." She'd said it, half expecting him to bolt.

"Callie. My sweet, Callie. You don't have to tell me you love me. I don't want any lies between us tonight. I still want you, even if all you feel for me is passion. It doesn't matter."

"But it's not a . . ." He silenced her with a kiss. She wanted to assure him that she was telling the truth, but suddenly she couldn't think, couldn't speak. She could only feel. Feel, know, want.

His hands were firebrands, flaming her passion to equal his own. He was an expert. If she hadn't already known it, she knew it now. He knew exactly where to touch her, when to touch her. He played her body like a master musician. She was melting, floating, she wanted, no, craved him with every tiny part of her.

His voice trailed to whispers, love words that aroused her to mindlessness. He undressed her, undressed himself, his hands all the while continuing to work their magic on her body, her mind, her heart.

"Oh, Callie, see how your breasts fill my hands. They were made for me, Callie. Only for me. Tell me you want me, Callie. Tell me it's all right."

"I want you, Trace," she whimpered. "I want you to make love to me."

He pressed his naked length against her. "I will love you, Callie. I promise. I will love you."

She gloried in the feel of him, felt the hard heat of his sex teasing her flesh, an erotic contrast to the cool night air whispering across her breasts. "Please, Trace, please . . ."

"Say it, Callie," he begged. "Tell me again that you want me."

I want you to believe I love you, her mind screamed. But the demands of her body won out. Afterward, when they were sated, he would believe her, she would make him believe her. But now . . . now . . . there was no reality but the awesome power of her desire. "Now, Trace, now! Please!"

He thrust himself inside her, his cry sharp, almost pained, as the intensity of the joy that swept over him sent him past the edge of reason. He was part of her, part of this woman he loved. He began to move, his body powered by instinct and need. Yet even as he experienced the most exquisite pleasure of his life, a strange, surging tide of loss roiled and swelled within him, tormenting him, reminding him that it was all temporary, built on a foundation of sand. He would have her now, but he would lose her. And losing her would be worse than dying, worse than dying a thousand tortured deaths.

He forced the agony from his mind. He would think of nothing, nothing but loving her. He cried out his release, sparks exploding inside his brain, robbing him of the real world, spilling him over into a fantasy world where only he and Callie existed.

Long afterward, Callie lay there, hardly daring to give credence to the incredible wonder of her own body. How could anything feel so good, so right? She snuggled closer to him, instinctively craving his warmth. He kissed her hair, her ear, her cheek.

Tears stung her eyes. Only now did she realize how

deeply she had feared his regretting any part of what just happened between them. Could it be he was past regrets? Could he be ready to trust her? Almost of their own volition her fingers trailed across the heated flesh of his chest and lower.

"I love you," she murmured. Her own blood stirred as his body quivered its response to her tactile teasing. With a boldness she didn't know she possessed, she curled her fingers around his sex, the sticky evidence of their recent lovemaking igniting her passion anew.

"Have mercy, woman," he growled, but his blazing eyes put the lie to his wanting her to cease.

His hands joined the hunt, roaming along her sensitized flesh, until she shuddered with a fiery, primal need for this man's loving.

He was hard and ready again. She was wet and eager.

"Callie . . ." Her name was a choked whisper, his only rational thought. With a tortured groan he rose above her, crying out as her hands tracked a feathery path across his abdomen, capturing his manhood to guide his entry. He savored every sweet inch as he cocooned himself within her.

Still she approached the edge before he did, the tremors that rocked her body triggering a shattering release in them both.

Long before dawn Trace knew what he had to do. He had dared one last time to make love to Callie. He had had what he wanted, needed, ached for every time he looked at her. He couldn't *not* have her. She was his destiny. And like some godcursed fool, he had had her, even though he knew in the having, he could well

323

destroy himself. He would never be whole again, fully alive again without her. Yet once the custody was settled, she would be gone.

She would be gone, because she would never want to stay once she knew the whole truth. But he would not repeat his mistake by the hearth two weeks ago. He would not admit that he loved her. He would not burden her with that. Better that she hate him than to think him lost without her. A few scraps of pride were all he would have left.

He studied her, sleeping so peacefully beside him. God, how beautiful she would always look to him. His loins stirred just watching her. He shifted restlessly, ignoring his body's demands. Then ever so softly he laid his palm against the side of her head, being careful not to wake her. He would break his promise just this once. Just once. "I love you, Callie," he whispered, his voice shaking. "Somewhere in your heart one day, please know that I love you more than my life."

Callie opened her eyes to the rising sun. Streaks of purple, crimson, and gold played across clouds so low she imagined she could reach out and touch them. It would make a lovely picture, she thought. But she wasn't about to get up and take it.

She lay there, gazing lovingly at Trace, who was still soundly sleeping at her side. He looked so boyish, content, as though lovemaking agreed with him.

Surely he wouldn't divorce her now. A man had physical needs, but last night had been so perfect, it had to mean more than that. He would wake and tell her there would be no need for ending the marriage. Maybe he didn't quite love her yet, but in time he could. He had to. Because if her own love for him had been all-consuming before, it was beyond reason now. She couldn't bear the thought of leaving him.

She decided to let him sleep awhile longer. She would surprise him by having the horses saddled and breakfast ready. Quietly she slipped out of the blankets. She was pouring the coffee when she felt his eyes on her. She turned, smiling to find his gaze warm with remembered passion. Then his brows knitted together and a look of flinty hardness settled over him.

"I finally figured it out."

She stiffened, holding the coffeepot in front of her. "What did you say?"

"Your Catholic upbringing, remember? Consummation will likely make an annulment impossible. And isn't that just what you had in mind all along?"

She stared at him, her whole body trembling. What was he saying? What was he thinking? Where was the warm, tender lover who had taken her to undreamed heights of passion mere hours ago? His voice was hard, his words accusing, condemning. She forced her own voice to remain steady as she spoke. "Why are you doing this? Why are you saying these things? You can't mean them, Trace. You can't."

"Oh, but I do. It goes well beyond last night. I think you decided from the first to take advantage of my . . . situation."

"Trace, please . . ."

"Please, what? Please say I don't want the divorce? Let's not kid ourselves, Callie. Your body had my body last night. And can again tonight for all I care. Two can play this little game of yours."

"Game?" She wanted to scream, to cry, to run, but she could only listen as he went for her heart.

"No annulment, Callie. That means we'll have to divorce. And, of course, you'll expect some compensation for the resulting scandal to your family. So let's get down to reality, shall we? Just how much of Christopher's trust fund is your passion going to cost me?"

She stood stock-still. So that was it. He believed her guilty of seducing him to gain money from him after the divorce. His opinion of her was that low. Even after making love there was no room in him for trust. "You're despicable!" she shrieked. "How dare you!"

Blinded by tears, she stumbled toward Kachina, the forgotten coffeepot spilling from her hands. Sobbing, she leaped onto the mare's back and kicked the horse into a run.

She heard Trace call her name, but she only urged the horse to run faster, the spirited mare enjoying the freedom of the wild run.

The wind tore at her, her copper hair whipping behind her with the same frenzy as Kachina's mane. She bent low over the mare's neck, needing to feel at one with the raw strength of the sleek-muscled animal. Long minutes passed. Callie felt the anger flow out of her to be replaced by a mind numbing pain deeper than anything she had ever known. It was only when she saw the beginnings of the prairie dog town barely five hundred yards away that sensibility snapped back. She hauled back on the reins, but the mare had the bit between her teeth and did not slow. Callie pulled harder. The mare continued to close on the prairie dog town.

"No." Her cry was lost to the wind, lost to the sound of pounding hooves. "Kachina . . ." The horse would be killed.

Shoshone thundered up beside her, Trace urging the powerful stallion in a wider arc, forcing Kachina to turn. He held the stallion at a dead run, until finally the mare slowed, allowing Callie to take the bit.

Callie brought Kachina to a trembling halt, her own body shaking so badly she could no longer stay in the saddle. She eased herself to the ground, leaning hard against the mare. Trace was at her side instantly.

"You could have been killed!" His voice was harsh, but he pulled her against him, his arms wrapped fiercely around her.

She could feel the thudding of his heart, the trembling that matched her own. Her knees shook so that she couldn't have remained standing if Trace hadn't been holding her. He must have sensed that she was on the verge of collapsing, because he let her sink slowly to her knees, all the while maintaining his embrace.

"Is Kachina all right?" she asked.

He looked over at the mare, only now taking the time to notice. "She seems sound."

"I'm sorry. I would never hurt her, I . . ." Oh, God, why was *she* apologizing. After what Trace had done . . . She pushed away from him, getting unsteadily to her feet. "I want to go back to the ranch. Now."

He stood himself, his voice low, subdued. "We'll have to rest the horses for a while, break camp." He walked over and gathered up Shoshone's reins, watching to make certain Callie would be all right

327

remounting Kachina. He knew she would accept no help from him.

Never in his life had he expected her to react as she had to his cynical assertion that she would now want more money from the divorce. He had expected anger, disgust, even hate. But he had never expected to cause her such pain.

When he had seen Kachina barreling toward the dog town, the only image in his mind's eye was Kachina falling, Callie's body catapulting through the air to lie twisted, broken. Dead. He could still feel the effects of the hell-spawned terror that had shot through him.

He had had no right to hurt her, to say, do anything to upset her. He had done it to salvage his pride, because of his certainty that she would leave him after the hearing as arranged, leave him in spite of the fact that he loved her. Dear God, how could he dare to love her and be so cruel to her? His own selfish motives weren't worth one instant of her pain.

He kicked at a cloud of dirt, gouged out by one of the horses. What a fool he was. He'd hurt her so that he'd be left with his pride intact? Hell, he'd already lost it. When they got back to camp he would tell her the truth. All of it. About his father, about Reese, and about this morning.

They made the return trip in silence. Callie made no attempt to help him as he set about packing their gear. She sat on a small boulder, staring off at the ridge where yesterday Trace had done battle with a horse and won. Won with honor. Why had he no honor when it came to her? What kind of a man would . . . ?

"Callie?" She had not heard his approach. He was standing directly behind her.

"Can we leave now?" Her voice was cold, detached.

"No. I mean, not yet." He came around to face her. "I need to say something. To apologize . . . to explain . . ."

She held up a hand. "Save your breath. I don't want to hear."

"Please?"

She twisted on the rock, so that again her back was to him. "No." Blast the man! He sounded so pained, so lost. She found herself fighting her body's maddening response to his nearness. Even after all of the hurt he had heaped on her, she still loved him completely, hopelessly.

"I can understand," he said quietly. "I don't blame you for not listening. God knows I don't deserve it." He straightened, blinking savagely, grateful she wasn't looking at him. He took a deep breath. "Callie . . . when we go back . . . the marriage . . . Christopher . . ." Damn! That wasn't what he wanted to say.

She closed her eyes, her heart aching. He wanted to continue the illusion. "Don't worry, Trace. I'll be the perfect devoted little wife for the court. Despite what you think me capable of, I won't let you lose your son." He started to move away, but some sick desire to hurt him just a little for the endless agony he had brought into her life made her add, "Of course the divorce settlement will be . . . considerably higher."

He stood there, staring off into nowhere. "I understand."

She rose, striding off, needing to be alone. She was angry, furious that she had been made to feel guilty. Why should she? He had hurt her time and time again. Why? Why had he made everything so sordid? She searched her memory, going over last night in excruciatingly painful detail. So much pleasure, so much delight. Did such happiness require a full measure of pain as payment? Why was he forever hurting her? Hurting them both?

And then she knew. She whirled, stalking back over to him. She would have her say before her courage deserted her.

"I just figured it out, Mr. McCord," she said, planting her hands on her hips, glaring at him. "Why you hurt first and fast." He busied himself with their gear, but she railed on. "It's because you're so afraid of being hurt yourself. That's it, isn't it?"

She shook her head in disgust. "Don't even attempt to deny it! And as for your assertion that you didn't fully enjoy what we had last night, well, I may be naive, but I am not stupid. It wasn't your body and my body. It was you and me. And it mattered for me that it was you. And it mattered for you that it was me." She poked a finger into his back. "You can call me all the names you want. You can be a jackass, but it doesn't matter. Do you hear me? It doesn't matter. Because I love you."

If she could have seen his face, she would have seen the jolt of astonishment that ripped across it. But she didn't, and she gave him no chance to respond.

"You don't have to say anything, or even apologize, or explain. You see, I also figured out that loving you isn't enough. When the custody is settled I'll be gone. I have my writing. My book. There isn't a woman on this earth who could love you enough. Not until you love yourself. Not until you understand that you're not what your father judged you to be or your brother or the courts or your neighbors or God knows who else."

She stopped, clamping her mouth shut. She had already said too much. When he turned and took a step toward her, she jerked away, heading toward Kachina. "Let's go, shall we? I don't want to be out here any more with you. I want to go ho— back to the ranch. Now."

They rode in silence, ate in silence, set up a new camp for the night in silence. The tension between them was so strong it was like a living thing.

She lay down in her blankets, closing her eyes, but sleep wouldn't come. Trace had settled himself deliberately some sixty yards away. She would not think of him. In the night, despite the fire, her thoughts maddeningly drifted to the bear, a fierce, menacing presence that could be hovering anywhere, ready to attack, ready to tear the flesh from her body.

She swore. She was being ridiculous! Yet the only image that kept filtering through her mind was the savaged, bloody body of Trace's wild mare and her foal.

A twig snapped.

She sat bolt upright, hugging the blanket to her chest. Twisting around, she tried to pierce the inky blackness beyond the range of the firelight, but she could see nothing. She scrambled to her feet. Her pride be damned. "Trace!"

"Quiet!" He was already up, his rifle cocked and ready. "Don't move."

"But the bear . . ."

"Stay where you are, damn it! That's no bear."

"What then? I know I heard some animal . . ."

"Yeah, a human animal."

"Hello, the camp!" A deep male voice came from

somewhere off to their left.

Callie's brow furrowed. There was something disturbingly familiar about that voice.

He appeared out of the darkness, a formless silhouette that gradually took on substance as he approached the fire. Even in the middle of the wilderness his embroidered red uniform jacket and dark trousers were impeccably tailored. He flashed a bright smile as he swept his point-topped helmet from his blond head and bowed low. "Greetings, my dear Callandra." He made a sweeping gesture toward Trace. "I assume this is the temporary husband you've recently acquired?"

Callie could only stare in stunned disbelief.

Nicolas.

Chapter Nineteen

If Trace had hackles, Callie swore they would have risen as he prowled the camp while she spoke to Nicolas. But she had no time to worry about Trace's reaction. She was too busy dealing with her own.

"How . . . how did you find me?" she stammered.

"The how of it scarcely matters, my dear," he said, his voice as smooth, as silken as she remembered. Perhaps even more so.

She forced herself to take a steadying breath, daring a glance at Trace. He now stood, unmoving, his whole body coil-spring tight. She shivered. Whether or not this confrontation ended in violence, she realized suddenly, depended on how well or how badly she could defuse the volatile mix already evident between these two men.

"Please, Nicolas," she began uneasily, "I don't even understand why you followed me. Especially if you're aware that Trace and I are married." The man's presence pricked not only a feeling of weakness in herself that she despised, but her conscience as well. To

leave this pridebound aristocrat stranded at the altar—
without so much as a note of apology—had been, even
in her own estimation, unforgivable.

"There, there, my fiery Irish colleen," he said,
smiling indulgently, as he might for a precocious child,
"don't be so fretful. It's not like you."

"I am not *your* fiery Irish anything," she snapped,
though she was inwardly shaking. "And I demand to
know why you've followed us. You could have waited
until we got back to the ranch." She recalled Trace's
notion that he'd seen a reflection on the ridge this
afternoon. Had Nicolas been spying on them?

He stepped closer, his hand coming up to rest
possessively along the side of her neck. "I've missed
you."

She started. "You have?" She realized then that she
had envisioned Nicolas merely turning toward the
assemblage of New York's most prosperous families
right there in St. Patrick's Cathedral, flicking a finger
and obtaining any number of eligible, obsequious
young ladies to comfort him in his hour of need.

"I feel like such a fool," he went on. "I should have
understood how frightening a wedding day can be to a
woman of your delicate sensibilities."

Trace snorted. Callie sent him a quelling look.

"A sweet, untouched innocent about to be a part of
the social event of the decade—marriage to Count
Nicolas von Endenberg."

"The most sought after bachelor on two continents,"
she parroted, recalling the words of their wedding
announcement in *The Sentinel*. What was odd was that
she detected none of Nicolas's previous pomposity
about his favored status with the ladies. It was as

334

though he were merely reporting the facts, and unpleasant facts at that. He seemed genuinely hurt and
confused by her desertion.

"I behaved boorishly," he said, "but it was simply
that I was too proud to tell you how much you meant to
me."

Callie continued to stare at him, her initial shock
turning to wonder. He had spent these months
searching for her, not out of wounded . pride, but
because he truly cared for her. "I'm the one who
behaved badly, Nicolas," she said, waging a peculiar
battle between feelings of regret and embarrassment.
She didn't like Trace being a witness to this conversation. Still, she added, "Please forgive me.".

"Of course, my dear. And don't worry, I'll wait for
you."

"Wait?"

"I met a couple named Marlowe in Rock Springs.
They told me the whole sad tale. You only married this
man to help him gain custody of his brother's child. Or,
as they put it, until he loses custody of the child."

Callie watched Trace stiffen perceptibly.

"Maybe it would be better if we didn't have this
conversation right now, Nicolas," she said quickly.
"Perhaps we could talk privately later. You could come
by the ranch house . . ."

"No." Trace's voice was cold, implacable. He glared
at her. "Your *friend,*" he said the word derisively, "is
not welcome in my home. In fact," his gaze shifted to
Nicolas, "you can get the hell off of my ranch. Now."

For the first time there was a chink in the count's
cool facade. His shoulders squared ever so slightly.
"Come, come, dear fellow, there's no need for that

tone. We both know your marriage to Callandra is merely a legal convenience. It's hardly as though she's in love with you."

Trace started toward Nicolas. "Get on your horse. Or I'll put you on it."

"Trace, please . . ." Callie held up a restraining hand, though she did not touch him.

He stopped. With a low curse he stalked off several paces.

"Nicolas, go," she said. "Please go."

The count sighed. "Very well, beloved." He lifted her hand to his, gently pressing his lips to the back of her fingers. "I'll wait for you. However long it takes, I'll wait."

"You don't have . . ." She hesitated. How could she subject this proud aristocrat to a second public rejection? "I'll meet with you after the hearing. We'll talk then. I promise."

"If that's your wish." He released her hand, gathering up the reins to his mount. "For now, please accept my profound sympathies." His gaze shifted very deliberately toward Trace.

She tensed. Why couldn't he just leave? Why did he seem bent on baiting Trace. "I have no need of your sympathies, Nicolas."

"Don't you? Obviously this man tricked you into marrying him."

"What are you talking about?" She darted a glance at Trace. His hands were balled into fists at his sides.

"The Marlowes told me the man was a convict, a thief, a . . ."

"I know what he is," she cut in, frowning when Trace winced. He must have read a double meaning into her words. But she had meant no subtle insult.

Nicolas shook his head sadly. "You're too kind-hearted for your own good. But then, that's one of the reasons I was so drawn to you." Still holding the reins, he reached out, pulling her to him. "I have missed you, Callandra. I've missed you so much."

Callie was too stunned to move. But even as Nicolas's arms closed around her, she was jerked back. Out of the corner of one eye she caught the movement—Trace's fist slamming into Nicolas's face. The blow sent the count sprawling butt first in the dirt.

"Touch her again, and I'll kill you," Trace snarled.

Nicolas rose, dusting himself off. For just an instant Callie could have sworn she saw a murderous glint in those blue eyes.

Trace, too, was braced for an attack, seeming to be aching for it. Callie moved between them. "I won't let you kill each other. You can just get that through both your heads right now. Whatever I have to do to stop it, I will."

Nicolas clicked his heels together, bowing low. "Very well, my dear. For you, for now, I'll leave. But . . ." his gaze shifted to Trace, though he continued to speak to her, "I'll not give you up. This marriage means more to me than you know. I love you. I can forgive you anything, as long as you'll be mine." With that he vaulted into the saddle and rode off into the night.

For long minutes Callie stared after him. If it weren't for the pain she felt in her right arm from Trace wrenching her away from Nicolas, she might have sworn this past half hour was all some horrid nightmare. But the pain was real. And so was the rage still evident in her husband.

"He'd better stay the hell away from you."

"Until after the hearing, of course," she gritted. "After that, you couldn't possibly care less."

He seemed about to say something, but the usual cold mask settled over his features.

Callie rubbed her arms, unable to quell the chill that sifted through her body. She had viewed Nicolas as a man too self-absorbed to fight for a woman who displayed no interest in spending her life adoring him. But tonight she had sensed an undercurrent of something much deeper, something she might almost judge as threatening, if that didn't seem so ludicrous. Nicolas would never jeopardize his standing with her father. Then why . . .

"I can't believe you were going to marry that jackass," Trace muttered as he stalked back over to their blankets.

She was in no mood to be judged, and most certainly not by Trace McCord. Her voice acid, she said, "The fates have not been kind to me regarding a selection of mates."

He stiffened.

"My father chose Nicolas. The whims of chance chose you. How does one woman get so lucky?"

His shoulders sagged, the anger seeming to drain out of him. "I guess I deserved that."

She could tell by his tone he was trying to ease some of the awkwardness between them. But his cruel words this morning had cut too deep. She would need time to heal. She may have promised to maintain the illusion of the marriage to the court, but at times like these, when she and Trace were alone, she vowed there would be no more illusion, at least not on her part. She loved

338

him too much; she'd been hurt too badly.

She closed her eyes, her mind taunting her with the crushing contrast of tonight with last night. Trace had held her, made love to her, and she thought, hoped, that she had given as much pleasure back as he had given her. But it hadn't been enough.

Perhaps that hurt most of all. That what they'd had, what they'd shared these past days, hadn't brought them closer together, but rather seemed to have driven an unbreachable wall between them. She loved him, would always love him, but she had to be realistic. Though he had given in to the passion he felt for her, it went no deeper than that. When the custody was over, he wanted her gone.

She lay down, her mind drifting unwillingly to Nicolas, knowing she would now have to deal with him once the custody was settled. Deal with him at a time when she could be emotionally devastated should Trace shut her out of his life. She cast a furtive glance over her shoulder to watch him settle into his blankets barely two feet from where she lay. He didn't even look at her. Would he even care if she went back to Nicolas? She sighed. Once he had Christopher, he'd probably even help her pack. Feeling more forlorn than she ever had in her life, it was a long time before she fell asleep.

Callie woke to a curse. Disoriented, she sat up, peering around in the predawn twilight to spot Trace near the horses. He was bending over their cache of supplies.

Climbing stiffly to her feet, she settled the blanket shawl-like over her shoulders and hurried over to him.

"What is it?"

"We've had a visitor."

Her eyes widened as she spied the pile of shattered debris in the grass at his feet. "My God!" she gasped. "My camera!" Her photographs lay nearby, many of them ripped, shredded, pieces strewn everywhere.

A chill swept through her. "The bear?"

He looked at her, his brown eyes hard, bitter. "No bear. It was our human animal again."

She frowned. "You're not suggesting Nicolas would . . . But that's absurd. He'd have no reason."

"No? What about jealousy?"

Callie shook her head. "That would be even more absurd. Nicolas has nothing to be jealous of."

Something flashed in Trace's eyes so swiftly that she couldn't identify it. Then he twisted abruptly, stooping to sift through the torn photos.

"Why didn't we hear anything?" she asked. "How could anyone do this and not be heard?"

"I wish I knew. I'm a light sleeper, especially when that bear might be around." He poked at the camera bits with his boot. "There's just something about this. Something not right . . ."

"What are you saying?"

"That I think these things were taken away last night, smashed and brought back, then laid here, like some kind of sign, a warning."

"What sense does that make?"

"None. None at all."

She bit her lip, staring at the shattered camera, remembering her odd impression that Nicolas would not so easily give up on what he considered his. But she simply could not reconcile her impression of the man with images of him skulking about in the dark, destroying cameras.

"Nicolas did not do this," she said quietly. "He couldn't, wouldn't."

There was a moment of throbbing silence, then Trace's terse, "Well I wonder who that leaves as a suspect then."

Her head snapped up, her eyes boring into his. "I didn't mean . . ."

"Didn't you? Why don't you just say it straight out, Callie. Who better to do something like this than the resident ex-convict?"

She sighed heavily, not sure which she felt more at that moment, pity or disgust. "I don't need to suspect you. I swear to God, even knowing you didn't do it, your opinion of yourself is so low, you would suspect yourself."

He looked at the ground, saying nothing. She wanted to touch him, hold him, give him what he'd never had—a feeling that he was worth loving—but he wasn't ready to accept it, not now, maybe not ever. He'd been told too loud and too long by too many people that he was the one who didn't measure up; he was the one who was wrong, the troublemaker, the thief, and worse.

No one could ever love him enough to undo that kind of damage. Not until he loved himself.

She turned away, thoughtful as she walked back to the campfire. *Hurt first and fast.* Maybe she was even more right than she knew. Maybe it wasn't that he didn't care, but that it frightened him that he did.

It wasn't much. But it was something. And if she was right—if he intended to hurt, to keep from being hurt, she would have to be careful. Because the harder she pushed him, the more viciously he would lash out. And she intended to push damned hard. Which left her with only two possible outcomes. Either she would succeed, and he would know how much she loved him, how much he was worth loving. Or she would fail, and he would break her heart.

Chapter Twenty

For Callie the trip home gave the word *misery* new meaning. Trace was more distant than ever, his mood shifting from surly to surlier, as though their marriage were now a burden to be endured only because he needed her help in court.

"Just remember your promise," he said as they broke camp for the final leg of their journey back. "That you'll act the part of the loyal wife in front of Judge Lancaster."

"How can I forget," she snapped. "You've reminded me during every meal, every rest for the horses, every . . ." She stopped, hating how she had allowed his sour mood to affect her own. Mounting Kachina, she kept her gaze steady, her voice even, as she guided the horse over to where Trace already sat Shoshone. "I gave you my word. I can't make you believe that means anything to me. But it does."

"Like you gave your word to the count? That you'd marry him?"

She bristled. "You are insufferable, do you know

that?" Her words came through clenched teeth. "Not that it's in the least your business, Trace McCord, but I did not give my word to Nicolas about anything. I never agreed to his proposal." She shook her head in self-disgust. "Of course, I never actually said no either. My father and Nicolas arranged everything. I just sat back and let them."

"I find that hard to believe."

"When I think about it, I find it hard to believe myself. I've never been a person to let someone else make my decisions for me." Her shoulders sagged, her voice growing weary. "Haven't you ever been at a point where you were just tired of it all? Where you didn't have the strength to fight anymore?"

Something flickered across his features, but it was gone before she could identify it.

"We'd better hit the trail," he said, lifting the reins and turning Shoshone away from her. "I want to reach the ranch before nightfall."

She frowned. "You just can't stand it, can you?"

He twisted to look at her, his brown eyes instantly wary. "Stand what?"

"Any kind of open, honest conversation. You can ask me whatever you please, no matter how personal, but the minute I ask you anything, it's time to exit." She shoved her breeze-tumbled hair away from her face. "Dammit, Trace! Why don't you try it sometime? Say what you think, what you feel. Instead of keeping so much of it locked . . ." She shook her head. What was she saying? As much as she longed for him to admit that he cared, she was suddenly afraid of finding out that he didn't. "Never mind. Maybe I don't want to know what you think."

He stiffened. "The only thing I think about these days is Christopher. And if I badger you about that, I'm sorry. It's only that I can't imagine my life without him."

"I know. I just wish you could be as honest about other things as you are about that boy. I've never doubted for a minute how much you love him."

His gaze drilled hers. "You want honesty? Your knowing that is precisely what terrifies me."

"What . . . ?"

"Callie, you and I haven't exactly become great friends."

She winced inwardly, but allowed nothing to show in her eyes. "I don't understand what that has to do . . ."

"If you turn against me in that courtroom, or even stay neutral . . ." He didn't finish. He didn't have to.

His inference that she could use the child as a weapon to get back at him should have infuriated her. Instead she sensed the core-deep mistrust that fueled his fear. Mistrust that had its roots in a childhood shaped by a father who overtly favored his firstborn, who subjected his second son to months of silence, and who used a mistake to rob that son of five years of his life. When she spoke, her voice was soft, barely more than a whisper. "Whatever differences you and I have had, Trace, please don't think I would take them out on Christopher. You will never lose him because of me. On my life, I promise you that."

The muscles in his face seemed to tighten. He swallowed hard, his gaze clinging to her for just an instant before he averted his head. She could have sworn he was about to say something, but he only gathered up Shoshone's reins and set the horse into a gallop.

Callie held Kachina back. Her eyes burned, but she kept the tears at bay. Didn't he know how hard it was to constantly be the one to attempt to make peace between them? She had her share of pride, too. Did she mean so little to him that he couldn't even say thank you for something that meant so much to him?

They rode in silence for the next six hours, reaching the Shadow's Way valley by late afternoon. Trace reined in at the top of the ridge, Callie halting Kachina beside him.

"This whole trip was a mistake," he said, not looking at her. "I apologize."

"Don't bother," she said, a renewed surge of bitterness coursing through her. In his blanket apology she read his veiled wish that they had not made love. Against her will she relived the searing pain of wakening to his cruel words after a night of magic. "I never regret a learning experience."

He swore.

"My, my, an honest reaction." She took a vicious pleasure in knowing she had stung him back. They said no more as they rode through the valley to the ranch house.

Deirdre must have heard them coming. She was on the front porch, waving as they rode into the yard. Callie dismounted, rushing up to greet her aunt.

"How was your trip?" Deirdre asked, her eyes hopeful.

"Wonderful!" Callie lied, hugging her close. "Just wonderful." She crossed the porch and ducked into the house. "I want to make some last-minute notes in my journal. We'll talk later, all right?" She didn't wait for a reply. She was bolting for the bedroom, when she was stopped by a happy shriek.

Christopher came hurtling out of the kitchen. "Cal-ee! Cal-ee!"

With a happy cry of her own she gathered him to her, as he all but leaped into her arms. "Oh, I missed you," she murmured, burying her face in the soft lee of his neck. "I missed you so much." More even then she had realized as she held him close. The thought rocked her—she couldn't love that child more if he were her own. That he returned her affection made her heart soar with pleasure, even as the reality sank home—in hardly more than a week he would no longer be a part of her life.

A slicing pain ripped through her, a pain double-edged as she thought of her own loss, and more—what would her leaving do to the child? He'd only recently lost his mother. As he planted a wet kiss on her cheek, a tear trailed down her own. What had she done? It had never entered her mind that the child would regard her as any more than someone to fix his meals or tuck him into bed at night.

She was so absorbed in her own thoughts that it was a moment before she caught the troubled look on Deirdre's face. Her aunt was looking past Callie toward the doorway. Still clinging to the child, Callie turned to see Trace standing there, his eyes unreadable.

Christopher kept his small arms around Callie's neck as he peered toward the door. "Papa home."

"Yeah, Papa's home." His voice was as unreadable as his eyes.

Callie turned at once, carrying the boy over to Trace. "You give your papa a hug."

Trace held out his hands and the boy went to him eagerly, but Trace's eyes were on her. She tried and failed to meet a gaze that had grown steely. With a barely audible excuse she twisted away and headed toward the bedroom.

Once there she collapsed onto the bed. She could almost feel the ambivalent emotions that had been roiling through Trace. On the one hand, she was certain he wasn't displeased that the child liked her. After all, he would hardly want the opposite. Yet it must have occurred to him that Christopher would soon be without her.

But even more than that, as with the night Christopher had been cutting a new tooth, the child had gone to her first. Try as he might not to take it personally, Callie sensed Trace had been fighting a very real surge of jealousy. He was a man keenly acquainted with rejection. That he felt it now, no matter how unwarranted, likely stirred unwelcome memories of his father.

She closed her eyes, wondering if Christopher had unwittingly stirred other unsettling emotions as well. Did Trace have even more reason to regret his temporary marriage, suspecting the pain her departure might cause the child?

She bit her lip, refusing to shed any more tears for the man. Yet her thoughts continued to torment her. How Trace must now wish he had set aside his resistance to the codicil to seek out a woman he could truly love, a woman he could welcome as Christopher's new mother. Instead he had opted for expedience.

For that they would all pay the price. For herself and Trace they had gone into the marriage knowing that

348

its end was as predetermined as its beginning. But Christopher had no concept of wills, codicils, and legal custody. He would not understand her simply walking out of his life, no matter how she or Trace tried to explain it.

"Oh, Christopher," she murmured, "what have we done to you? What have we both done to you?" He was the innocent trapped in a web of adult machinations over which he had no control. Trace had been so absorbed in his own problems—battling the Marlowes, the will, his own past, that he had taken no time to consider the full ramifications of his marriage. Callie had been so drawn to the child, so in love with the man, that she had refused to look beyond the present. Neither had foreseen how badly Christopher could be hurt.

She pushed herself to a sitting position. "It's not going to happen," she said aloud. "He's not going to suffer because of me." Though her heart ached at the thought, she knew what she had to do. She had to make her departure as easy on Christopher as possible. And that meant beginning the break now. As much as it hurt, she would have to leave most of his care to Trace. She would cease the stories, the games. Trace would understand. She grimaced. He'd probably take it a step farther, encouraging her to have nothing at all to do with the youngster.

The last thought brought with it a flash of self-pity, which she angrily shook off. Trace wouldn't expect her to cut herself off from Christopher completely, not even after the custody hearing was settled and the marriage was over. Hadn't he given her Kachina as an excuse to return to Shadow's Way one day, making it clear that the gesture had been made for Christopher's sake? When he wasn't being tortured by his own self-doubts, she could believe Trace truly wanted her to remain a part of the child's life.

She would simply have to wean herself from Christopher gradually. That way he wouldn't feel the loss as keenly as when his mother had died.

Mother.

She remembered Trace's assertion that Christopher was as much his son as if he had been of his own body. Only now did she fully understand the depths of his feelings—because she felt the same.

With a forlorn sigh she wrested herself from the bed. She couldn't spend the day feeling sorry for herself. She'd hardly said hello to Deirdre, and she knew her aunt was worried. It was time to face her. Opening the door, Callie peered into the hallway to assure herself that Trace and Christopher were nowhere in sight. She intended to speak to Trace alone first before she began her withdrawal from Christopher's life.

The wondrous scent of cinnamon and apples wafting along the corridor coaxed a slight smile to her lips by the time she reached the kitchen.

Deirdre looked up from the cutting board where she'd rolled out several thin strips of dough. "Apple puffs," she said, grinning.

"My favorite." Callie tried and failed to match her aunt's cheery warmth.

"Do you want to talk about it?"

Callie sank into one of the oak chairs beside the table. "I don't know if I can."

Deirdre wiped her hands on a towel and sat down on the chair next to Callie's. "I'm so sorry. I was wishing it would work out for you, being alone with him . . ."

"I know." Callie's voice shook in spite of her efforts to prevent it. "I love him so much. But it's like he doesn't know how to be loved, doesn't want to be . . ." The tears came then—tears for herself, for Trace, for Christopher, any thoughts she might have had to couch her words in noble lies to spare her aunt, lost as Deirdre's arms swept around her.

"Callie, *ma chroi,*" she crooned, "I'd give all that I have to not have you hurtin' so." She kissed the top of Callie's head. "Don't give up on Trace, my darlin'. It isn't that he doesn't want you to love him. I just don't think he knows how to be loved."

"No, Aunt Deirdre, he doesn't want me as his wife. When the custody is settled, the marriage is over."

Deirdre patted Callie's arm, her voice soft, reassuring. "Maybe he's afraid to ask you to stay. After the business with the trust fund and his having been in jail."

"I don't know," Callie sighed. "Oh, Aunt Deirdre, I don't know anything anymore." She poked at a stray clump of dough. "What does it matter?"

"It matters very much, young lady." Deirdre gripped Callie's hand in hers. "I've never known you to give up on something you wanted. God knows, we wouldn't be out here in the first place if you didn't have this Yellowstone madness in your blood."

"Yellowstone is a place. Trace is a man."

"And you want him even more than you want to prove something to your father with Yellowstone."

Callie didn't answer that. She couldn't. Instead, she decided she'd burdened her aunt with enough of her problems about Trace. Very deliberately, she shifted the subject. "Nicolas found us."

Deirdre slapped at one of the apple puffs she'd been rolling out. "I chased him off as soon as I saw him. I begged him not to follow you."

"He said he knew everything. About Trace, Christopher's custody . . ."

"Yet he seemed determined to bide his time until the hearing. To wait for you, he said."

Callie sighed. "I knew his pride would be wounded that day at the cathedral, but I honestly never suspected that he . . . cared."

"He seemed quite sincere," Deirdre admitted slowly. "Still there's something about the man . . ."

"I know. But I did hurt him. And I apologized for it. Still, I don't love him. I tried to tell him that, but Trace was standing there. I'd embarrassed Nicolas enough already. I couldn't hurt him like that. Not when he was actually being kind."

"Oh, I'll wager Trace loved that."

"He couldn't have cared less if I'd gotten on my horse and rode after Nicolas, as long as I came back for the hearing."

Deirdre chuckled. "Oh, how you underestimate your effect on that man, my dear."

Callie shook her head wearily. As always, the subject had again drifted to Trace. "Maybe I'll make it easy on everybody and just go on to San Francisco and get a job on one of their newspapers when this is all over."

The scrape of a boot in the doorway made Callie turn. Trace was standing there, holding a dozing Christopher, the strangest look in his brown eyes. "Just make sure you're in the Rock Springs courthouse in five days. Then you can go to San Francisco or any place else you damned well please."

The chair scraped back as Callie rose abruptly. She didn't say a word as she skirted around him and headed down the hallway. All thoughts of discussing ending her relationship with Christopher fled her mind in the wake of Trace's unaccountable anger. To her aunt she called back, "Call me if you need help with dinner. I'll be in working on my journals."

"You should be able to fill up quite a few pages." Trace's voice.

She slammed the bedroom door. Blast him! Every time she promised herself he would not infuriate her, she allowed him to do just that.

Muttering under her breath, she gathered up the leatherbound book, slapping it open to the next blank page. But even writing did nothing to soothe her shattered composure. The words that flowed from her pen captured the aching emptiness in her heart. She stared at them through tear-blurred eyes.

Why is it I can feel *how much he hurts? How frightened he is of caring, and yet be so afraid myself of forcing him to face how much I love him?*

She thumbed back a few pages, to her entry the day after they'd made love in the valley. *He said I wanted to complicate the divorce. But the way he touched me, the way he held me last night told me he wasn't thinking about divorce.*

She bit her lip, seeing the three words repeated on nearly every page. *I love him.*

She shoved the book away. "I don't love him. I don't!" She cast a sidelong glance, her lips curving derisively at the liar who faced her in the mirror.

Grumbling, she stood up, slipping the journal beneath her folded undergarments on the bottom of the wardrobe.

It was getting late. She felt a twinge of guilt that she had let Deirdre do all the work preparing dinner. "I simply will not allow that man to affect me anymore." The liar in the mirror grimaced. Then she smiled in spite of herself. After all, who really knew what the future held? Maybe once Trace put the worry of the custody hearing behind him, he would have time to think about what they could mean to each other. With a new resolve Callie headed down the hallway.

A distinct chill pervaded the atmosphere in the front room. Deirdre was seated on the settee looking pensive, anxious. Only then did Callie notice the other woman, standing near the window.

"Callie," Deirdre said nervously, "it seems Trace has a visitor . . ."

"How lovely to meet you," the woman said.

She was beautiful, her sable hair hanging in thick, lustrous waves around the perfect oval of her face. Her luminous dark eyes projected a vulnerable look, a look Callie suspected would prove an illusion if she looked too closely.

"Perhaps my husband has spoken of me," the woman purred. "My name is Lanie. Lanie McCord."

Chapter Twenty-One

Callie didn't move. She stood there, staring across the room at Lanie McCord and tried hard not to hate her. But grand intentions did nothing to stem the instant, intense jealousy that welled up inside her. What was this woman doing here? What claim did she have on Trace? How dare Lanie call herself his wife. "Trace McCord is not your husband," Callie said. "Your marriage was dissolved, if it indeed ever took place at all."

Lanie smiled. "I see he's told you that story. Well, then I'm sure he's told you that if it hadn't been for Seth, Trace and me would've had ourselves an official ceremony." She paused, then added almost smugly, "eventually."

Callie's lips thinned. "Just what are you doing here?"

"You get right to the point, don't you?" Lanie said, stepping away from the window.

"Most of the time."

Deirdre rose from the settee, moving none too subtly to plant herself midway between the two women. "As I was telling you, Lanie," she said hastily, "Trace is out on the range with Christopher. I'm sure they won't be back tonight. Perhaps not even tomor—"

The door opened. Trace strode in with one dusty, giggling child in tow.

Lanie flung herself at him at once. Callie's heart twisted as Trace's arms closed awkwardly around her. "I missed you so," the woman sobbed. "Seth should never have split us apart." For long seconds he held her close, murmuring words Callie could not hear. Then he stepped back, but only to settle an arm around her waist.

"I take it you two have met," he said, looking at Callie.

Callie said nothing.

"I'd really like to talk to you, Trace," Lanie said, very pointedly adding, "alone."

He nodded, his gaze shifting between Callie and Deirdre. "I hope you ladies will excuse us. It's been a long time." He guided Lanie toward the door, Christopher traipsing after them. "We'll be awhile. I'm sure you understand."

"Of course," Callie managed. "Would you like me to take Christopher?"

"No thank you," Trace called back, the three of them disappearing out the front door.

Deirdre was at Callie's side in an instant. "Now don't go jumping to any conclusions."

"I don't have to. That little scene made a lot of things perfectly clear."

"Ach, the man's a fool . . ." Deirdre stomped into the kitchen.

Almost against her will Callie headed toward the

front door. Lips set in a grim line, she nudged it open. Her eyes burned to see Lanie on the swing with Trace, Christopher on his lap.

He looked up, his gaze clashing with hers, then very deliberately lifted his arm to curve it around Lanie's shoulders. "Is dinner ready, Callie? Christopher's getting hungry."

She turned on her heel and ducked back into the house.

In the kitchen she snatched a paring knife from the counter beside the sink and began to whittle viciously at a raw potato. "Blast it all anyway, why is that woman here?"

Deirdre set the last plate on the table. "She told me Trace sent for her."

Callie slashed a chunk off the potato. "Why? Why would he do such a thing with the hearing less than a week away?"

"I don't know," Deirdre said quietly. "Maybe you should ask him."

"Ask him?" Callie seethed. "I'll be damned if I'll . . ." She bit off the words, her tirade dying in her throat as Riley strolled into the room.

"How's my darlin'?" he said, giving Deirdre an affectionate hug.

Deirdre hugged him back, then shooed him a respectable distance away, glancing meaningfully at Callie.

"Aw, Miss Callie don't mind my . . ." His features grew solemn as he interpreted Deirdre's gaze. With a thoughtful frown he ambled over to the sink. Callie stood there gouging yet another potato. "I guess you seen the former missus, eh?"

Callie jabbed at a blemish on the potato's tip. "We met briefly."

"She don't mean nothin' to him, you know."

"Oh really?" Callie gritted. "No doubt you could tell that from the way they were cuddled together on the swing?"

"No," he said, rescuing the potato from her grip and beginning to peel what was left of it himself. "I can tell it from the way the man looks at you. A man don't have room in his heart to look at more than one woman that way. Ever."

Callie shook her head. "Thanks for trying. But it really isn't necessary. I couldn't possibly care less what the two of them are doing."

"Sure," Riley said, holding up the battered spud. "Whatever you say, Miss Callie."

She stalked over to the table and sat down, not sure why she didn't just flee to the bedroom. But she knew. Because she was not going to give him up without a fight. Still, she almost reconsidered when Trace strode into the room smiling into Lanie's adoring eyes. In mere minutes he had become more relaxed and animated with his former lover than Callie had ever known him to be.

All through supper, she glared at them. Trace fawning over Lanie. Lanie fawning over Trace. Even Christopher seemed to have fallen under the dark-haired woman's spell. He giggled every time Lanie trailed her fingers along Trace's arm. Their intimate murmurings were like a thousand tiny daggers piercing Callie's heart. Though Deirdre and Riley tried gamely to keep the conversation light, Callie could bear it no longer. She shoved her chair back and rose to her feet.

"I think I'll take Christopher into the other room. He's finished eating and so have I."

With an air of feigned indifference she took the child by the hand and left the room. Even her promise to ease out of Christopher's life did not take precedence over keeping her mind off of Lanie and Trace.

"Play horsie!" Christopher said.

Callie accommodated, dropping to all fours near the settee. Even so her heart was not in the game. She winced as Christopher clambered onto her back.

"Giddyap!" he bubbled.

She went through the motions, lumbering about the room on her hands and knees, being careful to match her movements to Christopher's as he bounced and squealed with delight. Several minutes passed, until in spite of herself Callie managed to relax, to lose herself in the joyous company of the child. Only then did she realize they were no longer alone.

Refusing to concede to the embarrassment that shot through to her toes, she peered over her shoulder toward the archway leading to the kitchen. Trace and Lanie stood there, he with hooded eyes, she with her arm preemptorily around his waist.

"Amusing little thing, isn't she?" Lanie said.

Callie twisted, gathering up Christopher as she shot to her feet. "It's time for bed, young man," she said. "Let's go, shall we?" She allowed the startled youngster no time to protest as she all but ran from the room.

In truth it was nearly an hour until his bedtime, and he seemed to know it. She perched herself on his bed and read to him from one of his Kate Greenaway books, paying little heed to the story, grateful only to be away from Lanie. She was certain her company wouldn't be missed anyway.

Only when Christopher had been asleep for more than half an hour did Callie venture back toward the front room. She had decided she would speak to Trace alone. Surely he would . . . She stopped abruptly. The only person in the room was Deirdre.

"They . . . they wanted to talk," her aunt said, obviously distressed.

"Of course," Callie said lightly, though her heart thudded in her chest. "It's only natural, after all. They've got a lot of catching up to do."

"Callie . . ."

"I've got work to do on my journal. If you'll excuse me, Aunt Deirdre." She turned quickly and headed back down the hallway.

Thankfully, her aunt did not follow. Slamming open the drawer that held her journal, Callie flung herself onto the bed, flipping open the slim volume to the next blank page. But no matter how she tried, she couldn't concentrate. Thumbing back through pages already filled, the words blurred before tear-rimmed eyes, her imagination conjuring a cruelly vivid image of Trace and Lanie alone together.

Finally, exhausted, she slapped the book shut. Too tired even to raise herself up long enough to return the journal to her wardrobe, she shoved the book under the mattress. Hugging Trace's pillow close, she closed her eyes.

Much later she woke. She lay there in the night-shrouded darkness and wondered what had disturbed her. And then she knew. She missed the comforting warmth she had grown accustomed to in Trace's bed.

She was alone.

Her lips trembled, forming a silent "no." She lay there, straining to hear the sound of his footsteps in the hall.

An hour later she still had not heard the sound. Bone-weary, she could stay awake no longer.

At dawn she woke again.

Trace had never come to bed.

Callie thought she might get used to it, but she did not. Lanie spent all of her time at the ranch with Trace.

"It's not right," Deirdre fumed as she stood at the kitchen table rolling out a layer of pastry dough. "I thought the man was a bit more sensitive than a goat. I . . ." She stopped. "Oh, Callie, dear, I'm sorry. My ranting is just making things worse, isn't it?"

"I'm all right. Honestly. I mean what else could Trace do? Lanie probably didn't have anywhere else to go."

"Bosh and nonsense. She's had other places to go for four years . . ."

Callie had no answer to that. Instead she busied herself around the house and with Christopher. Trace's absence at least had left no opportunity to speak to him about the boy and how her inevitable departure might affect him. As much as she told herself she should be strong for the child's sake, she was grateful just to be a part of his young life for however much time remained to her.

That meant she now viewed his nap time as an intrusion on their time together. Still she knew the boy needed his rest. And so, reluctantly, toward early afternoon she settled him in his bed. Too restless to

361

work on her journal and none too eager for another well-meant discussion with her aunt, Callie wandered toward the corrals. She had to keep herself occupied. Idle time meant thoughts of Trace.

Hooking her arms over the top railing, she called to Kachina, who promptly trotted over to munch on the handful of sweet-smelling hay Callie held out to her.

"Ain't workin', is it?" the male voice chided from directly behind her.

She cast a scowl over her shoulder at Riley Smith. "I don't know what you mean."

"Like hell you don't, girl."

"And I would appreciate it if you would have a care with your language, Mr. Smith."

Riley howled with laughter. "Miss Callie, you'd have the devil hisself blushin' that day the wagon broke down. Why I swear I learned a new word or two myself."

She grimaced, catching on to the cajoling tone in the man's voice. "I'm really not in the mood to be cheered up, Mr. Smith. So you can just go on back to my aunt and . . ."

"Now hold on, girl. Who said anything about Miss Deirdre sendin' me out here?"

"You deny it?"

He shook his head, looking genuinely wounded. "I know we was always battlin'. But I kinda thought of it as a friendly war. And now, well, since I married Deirdre, well . . ." He paused, seeming to grope for the right word, then shrugging and plunging on anyway. "You're family now, girl. And I don't want to see you hurtin'. It's that simple."

Callie stepped away from the railing, her gaze

shifting from the scout to the ground then back again. "I'm sorry. It just hurts too much, Riley." She sank onto a haybale, elbows on her knees. "I can't talk about it."

Riley plopped down next to her, his own arms on his knees. He didn't look at her. He just sat there, twirling a stray bit of hay through his gnarled fingers. "Knew a man once who kept a dog," he began slowly, his voice as rhythmic and reassuring as a heartbeat. "Sometimes that dog would be curled up sleepin' and that man would walk by and kick that dog as hard as he could. Other times—the dog never knew when—the man would lean over and pet 'im, just like the meanness never happened."

Callie threaded her own bit of hay through nervous fingers.

"The dog tried everything to please that man. But it never mattered. Kick him, pet him—the man had no rhyme or reason for either. Then there wasn't no more petting, just kicking. Dog got so it didn't trust nobody. Most people woulda just put a poor critter like that outa his misery. But the old man died, and a young girl took pity on the dog. Started leavin' him scraps of food. Tried to pet him, but he snapped at her. Dog was scared. He was just sure that girl was gonna kick him.

"Took real patience. But finally one day the dog just needed lovin' so bad that it took a chance. Let her pet him. And she didn't kick him. Lots more time and lots more patience and that girl had her a friend for life."

"Trace isn't a stray hound."

"No, but he sure has been kicked by those who should've loved him most. Jeb McCord was a hard, cold, mean man. A man like that could hurt a boy too

363

sensitive for his own good. I think maybe Trace got kicked one too many times."

"And maybe he just learned to kick back."

"When the custody's over, you're leavin'. That's the same as gettin' kicked. He loves you and it's gonna hurt like hell to have you gone. But it'd hurt a helluva lot more if he told you he loved you, and then you left anyway."

"So you think he's worth getting bit a few times?"

"Don't you?"

"Why do I more and more get the feeling you haven't been a scout all of your life. That your tales about single-handedly carving out the western wilderness are to cover up more civilized beginnings."

He grinned sheepishly. "Harvard. Class of '50. I quit after a year. I spent all my time readin' other men's tall tales about the West. Those men were livin' my life for me. Finally, I just figured it was time to live it myself. I come west and never once regretted it."

She reached over and squeezed his hand. "I'm glad you did. You're a very special man, Riley Smith. Thank you. For caring about me. And for caring about Trace."

"He does love you."

She said nothing, unwilling to engage in a no-win debate. Riley couldn't *prove* that Trace loved her. And she certainly had no wish to argue that he didn't.

The scout rose, stretching with exaggerated tiredness. "I think I'll take a little ride. Limber up this bum leg before supper." With that he headed toward the barn.

Callie stayed behind, quietly thoughtful. She recalled Trace's declaration of love the night he had tried to seduce her by the fire. She had thought the words merely a part of his despicable plot to trap her into marriage, but what if he had actually meant . . .

No, she was being foolish. Why did she want such a bitter, distant man to love her anyway? It was time she acknowledged the truth. That even if he did love her, he didn't trust her. And such a marriage could only wither and die. Better that it be done quick and clean than to continue the sham indefinitely.

And for all of Riley's web-spinning, the scout had had no tale to explain the presence of Lanie McCord.

"That's because the only explanation is the obvious," Callie murmured.

That night, again, Trace did not come to their bed. In the darkness she swore to confront him, that no matter what his feelings for her, he had no right to so blatantly flaunt his ex-lover to her face. But in the cold light of dawn, when he came in to change his clothes, the words that had come so easily in her dreams stuttered and died in the face of his indifferent brown eyes.

For the first time in her life she could not risk being wrong. No matter how she tried to convince herself that it was better to know the truth than to build hope in the shadows of a lie, she could not summon the courage to challenge him.

Instead, she lay there watching him dress, her heart aching with how much she loved him, yet trembling with fear that he should ever find her out.

"Lanie and I are taking Christopher out today," he said, tying off the blue bandana around his neck. "I'd appreciate it if you'd come along." His voice held no more emotion than if he were asking her the time.

"Why?"

He turned his back to her, peering into the mirror, seeming to study the light dusting of stubble along the curved line of his jaw. "I want Lanie to get to know Chris better. But we'll need you to look out for him, when she and I want to be alone."

Callie wondered at how she could lie there so quietly, when everything in her wanted to fly at him, rage at him, strike him. Instead she said, "I'll be ready in fifteen minutes."

In not many more minutes than that they were headed out in the buckboard, the four of them for the day. Lanie, dressed in an outrageously revealing lime silk totally inappropriate to the occasion. Callie's own choice of an old pair of Trace's trousers and a formless shirt had brought a look of disdain from the dark-haired beauty. "Such a little tomboy," she murmured, "maybe you and the child can make mud pies together."

"Nothing could please me more," Callie said.

Christopher clapped gleefully.

Lanie's glare turned icy. She nuzzled next to Trace on the wagon seat, while Callie and Christopher made themselves as comfortable as possible behind them in the wagon bed. Callie almost relished the slights. They added fuel to the flames of a fire that promised to burn out of control before the day ended.

When they stopped for lunch in a small clearing amid a thick stand of towering lodgepole pines, the fire burned hotter still as Trace and Lanie ambled off together, leaving Callie alone with Chris.

"Your papa thinks he's upsetting me," Callie said, chucking the boy under his chin. "And you know something? He's right. But real soon now, he and his lady friend are going to have a taste of Callie Callaghan's temper. And maybe they'll wish they'd paid a little more attention when their elders were teaching them manners!"

Christopher pouted uncertainly. "Cal-lee mad?"

"Callie is very mad. Very mad indeed."

"I sad for Callie."

She gathered him to her, taking comfort in the warmth of his small body, his arms twining round her neck. When Trace and Lanie returned over an hour later, Callie's patience with their abysmal behavior had reached the breaking point. "Which one of you wants it first?" she asked.

Trace's eyebrows shot up. "Wants what?" For once he seemed genuinely disconcerted, as though some plan had gone suddenly awry.

Callie very deliberately put her hands on her hips. "One of you is to take Christopher for a walk. The other is to stay here with me, and that person and I will have a little chat."

Trace frowned. "All right. If that's what you want."

He took a step toward her, but Lanie instantly held him back. "You go on with Christopher, darling. Let me stay and talk to her. The poor dear is obviously troubled. I think it's about time I set her straight on a few things. It's the only decent thing, after all."

"I don't like it," Trace said. "Let me stay. I'll . . ."

"No, no," Callie interrupted, "Lanie did speak up first. It's only fair that I talk to her first."

Trace's gaze shifted between the two women. He clearly didn't want to leave them alone together. Callie grew all the more determined that he do just that. "I don't want Chris to be upset. Please, Trace, I won't keep your lady friend long. I promise."

Something flicked in his eyes, but he quickly shuttered away whatever emotion it might have been. Most likely disgust, Callie thought, that she would demand this confrontation. But she didn't care anymore. There had been too many hurts, too many lies. Like Riley's apocryphal dog, she had been kicked a few times herself. She would have the truth. No matter what the cost.

Trace gave Lanie a long, unreadable look. "Remember what we talked about," he said.

She gave him a barely perceptible nod.

With that Trace gathered up Christopher and headed into the trees, leaving the two women alone.

The ebony-haired woman immediately advanced on Callie. "If you think anything you say is going to make a difference . . ."

"Oh, but it will make a difference. A difference to me. I don't know why I've kept my mouth shut this long. Trace is my husband. Mine. Legally. Morally. And I want you to keep your hands off him."

"Are you threatening me?"

"Take it any way you like. But hear this, when we get back to the ranch you're going to pack your things and get out."

The crimson slash of Lanie's mouth pursed with fury. "Trace will never stand for it."

"He will if he wants his son." Callie reveled in the brief flash of fear that sparked in those violet eyes.

And then the fear was gone, replaced by a cunning arrogance. "Your little bluff hardly matters. One more month and I'll have Trace back for good."

Try as she might, Callie couldn't quell the sudden chill that gripped her heart.

"Ah," Lanie said, "that made you a bit curious now, didn't it? Maybe I should be kind and put you out of your misery. You see, I know you love him. He doesn't know it, of course. But then he's never been very good at that sort of thing."

Callie winced, grudgingly acknowledging the woman's insight.

"The whole problem, darling, is that I've got another husband right now," Lanie said, her voice softer, somehow deadlier. "I couldn't get a divorce before that blasted deadline. In fact, it won't be all legal and proper for another month yet."

"What are you saying?" Callie could hardly breathe.

"You know exactly what I'm saying. Trace married you to get Christopher because my divorce wouldn't be final in time for him to marry me."

It was as though an iron hand squeezed the air from her body. "I don't believe you."

"I don't much care what you believe. But surely you *can* believe your own eyes. Has he even been near you since I've been back?"

Callie shivered.

"He's real good in bed, isn't he? Got a real way about him. Maybe it's because he doesn't give a damn. Always on the edge, never lets his heart get involved."

Hate. Like bile it rose in her throat. He'd used her. From the very first instant, he'd used her. Because Lanie wasn't legally available.

Lies. Nothing but lies.

She'd sworn she would never do anything to keep him from having his son, but now . . . now . . . She sank to the brown, brittle earth and imagined the look on his face, the pain in his eyes to match the pain in her heart, when she told him she would do everything in her power to take Christopher away from him.

Chapter Twenty-Two

For the first time in her life Callie fought the urge to physically attack another human being. Lanie's smirking assertion that Trace would have married her had she been legally free drove through Callie like a jagged-edged blade. She could no longer bear to even look at the woman, let alone speak to her. Very deliberately Callie turned away, staring off down the trail Trace had taken with Christopher some moments before. She stood there, willing him to return, aching to fling Lanie's claim in his face—aching for him to deny it. And should he not deny it, she would take infinite pleasure in denying him the one and certain truth in Trace McCord's life—Christopher.

For now the battle was over; Lanie had won. Callie had wanted to keep her pride intact, but this was too much. Hadn't Trace told her he didn't want her for his wife? Of course not, he'd wanted Lanie. Lanie whom he couldn't marry because of a legal technicality, so he had done the expedient thing and married the first willing woman who'd come along. And he had tried to keep it a business arrangement, she had to admit that. But she deliberately enticed his natural male attraction for her. She had damned herself.

But why hadn't he told her about Lanie from the beginning? Perhaps somehow she could have managed to block off her feelings for him, maybe not loved him as much? She gave herself a shaky smile. She might as well wish to halt the tides.

"What did she say to you?" Trace asked.

She whirled, startled, disconcerted further by the near anxious look in his brown eyes. She'd been so engrossed in her thoughts, she hadn't heard the sound of his approach. He and Christopher must have traveled in a small circle through the trees.

"What do you suppose she said?" she snapped, determined to hold onto her own anger, knowing it was her only defense against the devastating effect he had on her heart.

Trace handed Christopher to Lanie. "Watch him for a few minutes. I might as well get my little talk with Callie over with, too."

Callie thought she caught a suspicious glint in Lanie's violet eyes, but dismissed it to the waning light of early evening. While the ebony-haired woman moved out of earshot with the fidgeting child, Trace strode back over to Callie. "You have a right to be angry," he said. "But I can explain."

"Explain?" she said tightly. She wanted to shriek at him, assure him she intended to pay back his treachery with a vengeance, but something held the words back. Something wasn't right about this. This one last time she would hear him out.

"She told you she and I are supposed to be married

371

after you and I divorce, right?" His eyes searched her face, though she couldn't have begun to guess what expression he expected to find there.

"She took great pleasure in telling me."

"I'm sorry."

"Sorry?" Her temper flared anew. "That's all you have to say? You're sorry? For lie upon lie upon lie you're *sorry?*"

"I can't lose Christopher, even if it means losing . . ."

"Your self-respect?" she shot back.

"No," he said quietly. "I lost that a long time ago."

"You didn't lose it," she hissed. "You threw it away. Along with every other decent emotion. And then you sat back and blamed it all on your father. Well, he's dead. And you're alive. And you can't go on blaming him for every tiny misery in your life!"

She expected an explosive denial. Instead, he paced over to a massive treefall on the clearing's edge. Amid gnarled branches and uprooted stumps he blazed a narrow path to a limb-free space some ten feet square.

Annoyed, confused, she followed.

He hunkered down, clearing away several small twigs, then angled a glance up at her. "Sit with me. Please. I really do want to try and explain all this to you."

Not sure why she did so, Callie sank to the ground. He settled himself beside her. She did not pull away when his left arm pressed warmly against her right.

"Lanie and I are not going to get married," he said. "Ever."

"She said her divorce wasn't final, otherwise you would have married her instead of me."

"I wrote to her," he admitted slowly. "When I first

found out about the codicil." He shrugged. "She'd married me once. Or almost married me. I thought—what the hell?"

Callie grimaced. "So you did propose?"

"I asked her to come to the ranch. So we could talk." He picked up a twig, rolling it between his thumb and forefinger. "She never answered my letter. Until she showed up on my doorstep two days ago."

"So . . . now I'm in the way."

His hand slid over hers. "No. You're not."

She swallowed hard. Then she straightened, jerking her hand away. "What kind of a fool do you take me for? You've been fawning over her ever since she got here. It's as though I suddenly developed the plague. My God, you've even been sleeping with her."

"Lanie's been sleeping in the bunkhouse."

"I'm all too aware of that."

"I've been sleeping in the barn."

Her brows furrowed, her heart hammering hopefully in spite of the warning sounded by her common sense. "It's a very short distance from the bunkhouse to the barn."

"I can't force you to believe me."

Callie slapped at the ground with her palm. "You have lied to me so many times, Trace McCord. How am I supposed to recognize the truth? And what does any of it matter anyway? Whether or not you marry Lanie after you and I separate is of no consequence to me." She thought she might choke on her own lie, but found the fiction rolled almost too easily off her tongue. Lessons from a master?

He cleared his throat nervously, but his gaze remained steady. "When she told you we were getting married, what did you say to her? I mean, did you tell her the truth—that you couldn't care less?"

Callie didn't answer right away. She studied his face, wishing she knew where this was all leading. His evasiveness was driving her mad. "Actually I didn't say much of anything. I was too busy thinking how much I'd like to kill you."

"Oh."

Oh? That's all the man was going to say? *Oh?* She glared at him. "Was there something in particular you would have liked me to say? Perhaps if you'd spoken to me at all these past two days, I might have been able to taper my response to your needs."

To her astonishment, one side of his mouth curved upward ever so slightly. "You know, when you get really angry, you've got quite a sarcastic way about you."

"You find that amusing?"

"Not amusing, exactly. Fascinating would be a better word. Your eyes flash, your cheeks get all rosy . . ."

She raised up on her knees, planting her hands on her hips. "I do not intend to sit here with you and discuss my cheeks."

His grin widened. "You are one special lady, you know that."

"And *you* are trying to manipulate me. Again."

He sobered. "No. I'm making a mess of things. As usual."

Her fists clenched. "Damn it, I hate that! I just hate it when you run yourself down."

He blinked, genuinely astonished. Then seemed to consider what she said. "I guess my father had more

374

influence on me than I thought. Since he can't run me down anymore, I do it for him."

She sank back next to him. "Why do we fight so? I really think you and I could be friends, if you would just *talk* to me. Trust me."

He looked away. "I do trust you."

"But only to a point."

"No. I . . ."

"Never mind," she said gently, sensing how uneasy he had become. He didn't even realize how deeply his inability to trust went. "Just tell me about Lanie."

The tension in him eased perceptibly. "She's changed since she left. She's hard, bitter."

"Traits you should easily recognize."

He ignored that. "I want her to think I'm going to marry her."

"But it's just another lie."

"Dammit, I am trying to save Christopher."

"And how does lying to that woman help you do that?"

"If I don't agree to marry her, she intends to testify against me at the custody hearing."

Callie gasped. "What could she say?"

"That she and I were legally married, that in fact we never dissolved the marriage, and that I'm now a bigamist."

"Does she have any proof of that?"

"She showed me a Cheyenne newspaper clipping. Somebody thought our drunken marriage ceremony deserved two columns on the third page. Nowhere in the article does it mention that the man performing the ceremony had no legal authority."

"But you said Seth had everything taken care of."

"I have no idea if he ever got any legal documents. I've looked through his papers, but I didn't find anything."

"Would Lanie's word be enough?"

"With other things—like my prison record, it could be." He raked a hand through his tawny hair. "I'm going to lose him, Callie. I know it."

"You won't. You can't."

"If telling Lanie I'll marry her keeps her from testifying, then that's what I'll tell her."

"The lies have to stop somewhere, Trace."

His brown eyes mirrored the conflicting forces at war inside him. In that unguarded moment she could almost believe he hated the lies as much as she did. That he lied, not out of guile but almost reflexively as a defense against revealing too much of himself, of exposing himself to more hurt and rejection. But then the look was gone, its place taken by an almost sly cunning learned under his father's brutal hand. "I'll do whatever I have to to keep Christopher. And apologize to no one."

She threaded her fingers through a ragtag tuft of weeds. "How do I know you're not lying to me? Maybe you are going to marry her."

"That shouldn't matter to you one way or the other."

Her mouth tightened. What a fool you are, Trace McCord, she thought bitterly. That you can't see how much I love you. And what a coward I am. That I can't tell you and make you believe me. "Lanie loves you then?" she asked softly.

"Let's just say she's tired of mining camps and soldiers. She wants a home."

"She'd consider this home, when she has to

blackmail you to get it?"

"She's desperate."

"Like you were when you threatened to tell my aunt about our night in front of the fireplace?"

He grimaced. "If it makes you feel any better, I doubt I'll ever forgive myself for that."

She reached up, pressing her hand against his cheek. "I don't know why, but I believe you. Damn, why does all this have to hurt so much?" She leaned toward him, her lips brushing his. "I don't want it to hurt anymore. I just want . . ."

With a low oath he pressed her away from him. "Don't. Oh, God, Callie, don't."

"Why?"

He dragged in a deep breath, struggling for control. "For one thing, Lanie could be back any second. If she saw me kiss you, she'd know I was lying to her. For another, if I do kiss you, I don't think I'd be able to stop." He stroked her hair, twining a coppery strand behind her ear. "Don't you see, even if Lanie wasn't at the ranch, I'd still be sleeping in the barn. It's the only way I can keep my hands off you."

She captured his wrist, bringing his fingers to her lips. "I don't want you to keep your hands off me."

His gaze darkened, smoldered. "Don't say that. Please, don't . . ."

"This is crazy," Callie breathed. "We can take Christopher, go somewhere no one could ever find us." She didn't care what he read into those words. She only knew that she wanted him, loved him.

"I can't run. I've run from too many things all my life. This is too important. I have to fight it out. Legally. He's going to be mine, because it's right that he be mine." He trailed his fingers down her cheek. "Besides, I would never let you run off with me. I've caused you enough pain. When this is over, you've got another life to go back to."

"If you mean Nicolas, I have no intention . . ."

"Maybe you don't, but he does. I saw the way he looked at you."

"I don't want to talk about Nicolas. I'm sorry I hurt him, but I'm not going back to him."

Trace looked away. "Nicolas or someone else. It doesn't matter. Wyoming isn't New York and never will be."

She sighed, unwilling to continue the argument. It was obvious Trace believed her city upbringing wholly incompatible with his own. Perhaps it was his roundabout way of telling her that whether or not she loved him didn't matter, he didn't feel she would ever fit in with his life.

"Don't get me wrong," he said. "It means a great deal to me that you care."

Even though it will all end soon. He didn't say it, but she knew it was what he was thinking, because she was thinking the same.

And she was suddenly, desperately frightened. She couldn't lose this man, couldn't . . .

"You two finished with your little talk?" came an irritated voice directly behind them.

Trace stood up, instantly putting distance between himself and Callie. "I didn't hear you coming."

"Obviously."

"Where's Christopher?" Callie interrupted, looking past Lanie toward the stand of trees from which she'd come.

"He was right behind me."

"Well, I don't see him." Callie scrambled to her feet, retracing the woman's steps some fifty feet. Christopher was nowhere in sight. She called out to him. Her only answer was the soughing of the wind through the towering pines.

Trace caught up to her, Lanie at his side. He turned on the ebony-haired woman, his body rigid with anger. "Where is he?"

"I told you—he was right behind me. Don't worry, he'll be along."

"Along?" Callie said. "He's a three-year-old child. When was the last time you actually looked behind you?"

"I don't know. Not long. He was whining, saying he wanted you."

Callie willed herself to stay calm. It had only been a few minutes. Christopher couldn't have gotten far. She kept walking, calling his name.

Trace paced beside her, twisting in a full circle, scanning the forest. "Chris! Chris, answer me!" His voice rose to a shout, but still they heard no response.

Callie halted, staring off into the seemingly endless expanse of brown trunks. The overlapping upper branches of the lodgepoles allowed little light to reach the ground. Only a few isolated weeds gave any hint of color to the inches-thick carpet of brown needles beneath their feet. The dim light meant the descending darkness would come even more quickly in the woods. "He can't have gotten far," she said, trying as much to reassure herself as Trace.

"Christopher!" he shouted again. "Answer me! Now!"

Nothing.

She shivered. "Where is he? Trace, where is he?"

He looked at her. She saw her own mounting terror reflected in his eyes. "It'll be pitch-black in here in half an hour."

"We'll find him," she said. "We have to find him. And he'll be all right. He's a tough little kid. We'll find him." She stared at the darkening woods, feeling her control slipping away. "He's crying for us, I know he's crying. He wants us to find him. He's just a little boy, and he's all alone."

He gripped her arms. "To find him, we have to stay calm. You and me. Calm."

She swallowed hard, then nodded. "I'll be all right." She pulled free. "Let's don't just stand here. We've got to keep looking."

"We've got to be able to see where we're going. Wait here." He started back toward the clearing.

"What . . . ?"

"I'll be right back."

He returned carrying his rifle and a handgun, along with three two-foot-long pine branches he'd retrieved from the treefall. "Here." He handed her the pistol. "We have to spread out. Cover the most ground we can. If you find him, fire off two shots."

He then handed her one of the torchlike branches. "The ends of these are called pine knots. The pitch trapped in them will burn slow and bright for a couple of hours." He lit one and handed it to her, then lit his own. He handed the spare to Lanie. "Stay with Callie. When her torch burns down, use it to light this one."

"I want to stay with you," Lanie said.

"That wouldn't be a very good idea. If anything's

happened to that boy . . . He didn't finish. He turned to Callie. "Remember, if . . ." he stopped, correcting himself, *"when* you find him, fire off two shots."

She nodded. They stood there, torches raised, eyes locked, for long seconds. Somehow in that wordless exchange they were each trying to give the other hope.

"We'll find him," he said. "We will." With that he turned and headed away from her, choosing a deer path with less deadwood to block the way of a small child.

Callie kept moving in the direction Lanie thought she had come. Callie knew there was little chance the woman actually could tell one tree from the other, but moving forward in any direction seemed more useful than standing still.

For the first time in her life Callie experienced genuine terror. Except for the pale orange glow of the pine torch the surrounding forest was now as dark and foreboding as the belly of hell. And somewhere in that inky blackness was a towheaded little boy who she loved with all her heart. Somewhere, too, lurked twisting streams and hungry beasts.

"I don't like it here," Lanie said. "I'm going back to wait by the horses."

Very slowly Callie turned and faced the woman. "You're not going anywhere, except with me to find that child. If I hear one more word to the contrary, you're going to wish you never came back to Shadow's Way."

Whether it was her words or the promise in her eyes that backed them up, Lanie said no more, falling into step as Callie continued the search.

Over and over she had to fight the urge to panic, to

run blindly screaming Christopher's name. Instead she forced herself to move slowly, methodically, poring over every square foot of ground. He could have curled up and fallen asleep anywhere. She couldn't take the chance of passing him.

An odd shuffling noise from somewhere off to the right brought her up short. She stopped so abruptly, Lanie slammed into her from behind, nearly sending them both tumbling to the ground.

"What was that?" Lanie asked, her voice fearful.

Callie stood stock-still, listening, straining to hear the sound again.

Nothing.

"It was probably just a raccoon or something," she said at last. She held the torch high, peering into the void.

Still nothing.

"Let's get back to Trace," Lanie said. "We can't do anymore out here tonight. We'll just have to wait till morning."

"Christopher is out there somewhere. We are not going to stop looking."

The shuffling noise came again. Closer this time, but still indefinable.

"Christopher?" Callie took a step toward the sound, then nervously took a step back. She chided herself. This was no time to be afraid of the dark.

"What is that noise?" Lanie hissed again.

"I don't know," Callie said. "But we're going to find out. Christopher could be in trouble." She started toward the sound, then stopped, listening. There was nothing there.

She continued on, poking the torch toward any depression, clambering over fallen trees, looking in any conceivable place a child could fall or crawl into. Again and again she prayed she would hear the sound of Trace's rifle signaling he had found him.

She walked, stumbled, crawled herself, the torch flickering, the pine sap burning down. It had already lasted nearly two hours.

"Please, God," she murmured. "Please, help me. Help me find him. He's only a little boy."

Another half hour passed.

"It's hopeless," Lanie said. "We have to go back to the wagon. That is, if we're not lost ourselves."

"I have no idea where the wagon is from here," Callie said. "And I could care less. All I care about is finding Christopher." She held the dying glow of her own torch to the spare Lanie had been carrying. "We now have at least two more hours of light. Let's go."

Her legs ached from climbing over fallen trees, clambering over small streams. Her feet were wet. She was chilled to the bone, and still she staggered on.

"I can't," Lanie cried. "I can't do this anymore." She dropped to her knees.

"Get up!" Callie gritted. "Now."

"No." Lanie shook her head. "I don't care if you shoot me. I'm not moving."

"Fine. Stay here then. In the dark." Callie went on. She stopped after several yards, looking back. She could no longer see Lanie.

"Wait!" the woman called, obviously realizing that where Callie went, so went the light. "Please, don't leave me here. Wait."

Callie waited.

Lanie stumbled up to her. "Please," she sobbed, "can't we go back?"

"No." Straightening, Callie marched on, Lanie

stumbling to keep up as best she could.

Callie sensed by now that she was traveling in circles, but she didn't care. Christopher couldn't have gotten far from Lanie; the only question was in which direction he had gone. Somehow in her zigzag search, Callie hoped to cross his path. What worried her now was that she had not once crossed paths with Trace, nor had she seen the light of his torch since they had begun the search over three hours ago. How far afield had she gone? The thought that she could be miles away from Christopher by now sent a new terror coursing through her.

She stopped, blinking back tears. "Dammit, Christopher, where are you?" She sank to her knees, unable to quell the surge of hopelessness that swept through her. For long minutes she rocked back and forth, sobbing. If she was this frightened, what must Christopher be feeling?

Exhausted, cold, terrified, she struggled to her feet, the torch weighing a hundred pounds in her numbed fingers. "I'm coming, Christopher. Mama's coming." She gave bare notice to naming herself Chris's mother—her heart having made the transition long ago. She wasted no more than a few seconds trying to rouse Lanie, who sat slumped beside her.

Callie lurched on, ten yards, then twenty. "Just ahead," she murmured. "He's just ahead. A few more feet. Please. Just a few more feet."

She blinked, her mind belatedly registering something out of the ordinary in the forest terrain. A patch of color five yards back.

Red and blue.

Not wildflowers.

Red and blue. Christopher's jacket. Trace's red

bandana he'd so proudly tied around the boy's neck.

On the ground.

Five yards back.

Callie forced her flagging senses to respond. Turning, she retraced those five precious yards.

Her heart stopped.

Christopher.

He was lying in the maw of a hollow log, his tiny body dwarfed by the ancient pine. She fell toward him. He didn't move. She anchored the torch into a crack in the wood. Crying, praying, pleading, she pressed her hand against his face. He was so cold. So cold.

"No! No! No!" Screaming, sobbing, she dragged him toward her, wrapping her arms around him, hugging him, rocking him. It took a moment for the realization to sink in. The warmth against her neck. The warmth of Christopher's breath heating the chilled flesh of her neck.

She was laughing. Laughing and crying. "Thank you, God. Thank you."

It was she who was so cold, not him. Somehow the shelter of the log had protected him.

"Hide," he whimpered, shifting sleepily in her arms. "Hide from Lanie."

Callie kissed his tear-stained cheeks. "Mama found you. Mama found you. Mama loves Christopher."

"I love Mama." He wrapped his small arms around her neck.

For several minutes she just sat there, rocking back and forth, giving way to an awesome rush of relief.

"Can we get back to Trace now?" Lanie asked, limping up behind them.

Callie gasped, horrified. Trace still didn't know she'd found Christopher. "Here," she said, shoving the pistol at the bedraggled woman. "Go off a little ways and fire it twice. Hurry!"

Lanie stumbled away.

Callie sank back against the log, her eyes closed, hugging Christopher tight against her. She didn't think she could ever let him go. What was keeping Lanie? She should have fired those shots by now. Callie looked off toward the edge of the circle of light the torch provided.

Lanie stood frozen, the gun in the air. She was staring into the dark beyond Callie's field of vision. Callie was about to call out to her when Lanie screamed, a scream of undiluted terror.

Blood surged through Callie's exhausted body. Never had she heard such a sound. Instinctively, she shoved Christopher behind her. He clung to the tail of her shirt as she tried desperately to make out the huge black form moving out of night shadows toward Lanie.

She stared at the stuff of nightmares.

The grizzly.

Callie grabbed up the child, swallowing a scream of her own as the animal rose up on its hind legs, towering a full seven feet in the air.

Lanie threw down the gun and ran.

Callie scrambled toward the nearest tree with reachable branches. Lanie beat her to it. Grappling her way upward, the woman never once looked back.

"Wait!" Callie cried. "Wait! Take Chris up with you!"

Callie thrust the child above her head. "Lanie, for the love of God!" Christopher was screaming.

"Climb, Chris!" Callie commanded. "Climb! Now!"

The boy had a death grip around her neck. "Cal-lee!" She pried his fingers free. The bear growled low in his throat, lumbering, shuffling, favoring his left rear leg, but advancing ever forward.

"Lanie!" Callie screamed. "You take this child or so help me God I'll shoot you out of this tree!" Callie prayed Lanie was too addled to remember the gun was lying on the ground somewhere in the darkness. Lanie reached down, yanking Chris upward just as the bear swiped at the lower branch with his massive forepaw.

Callie ducked, ran.

"Climb!" she yelled back to Chris. "Higher! Don't come down from there till your papa comes, no matter what happens."

Callie threw a pine cone at the bear. She had to lure it away from Christopher. "Here. Here, beast."

Her gaze swept the ground in the dim circle of torchlight. There! She saw it. The gun. Her heart pounding so hard she feared she would pass out, she staggered toward it, the bear closing the distance between them. Grabbing up the Colt, she used both hands to lever back the hammer. Taking no time to aim, she squeezed the trigger. The recoil nearly ripped the weapon from her hands. Her fingers shook, but somehow she managed to fire it again. She was certain this time that the bullet had hit the massive beast, but it didn't stop, didn't even hesitate.

Saliva dripping from its gaping mouth, the bear continued its relentless advance, its soulless eyes reflecting the leaping flame of the torch.

Everything in her screamed at her to turn and run, even though she knew she had no chance. She was looking into the face of her own death. She did run then, but she could actually feel the ground shaking as the bear pounded after her. She could hear its labored breathing, smell its fetid stench.

Out of the corner of her eye came another vision, a

387

miracle conjured by one last desperate wish.

Trace.

Trace coming out of the night, carrying a torch and a rifle.

Callie heard Lanie screaming from her perch in the tree.

Callie stumbled over something, a tangle of branches, tearing at her, just as the bear would. She tried to keep her balance, but failed, collapsing, slamming into the ground, her chest on fire.

"Don't move!" She heard Trace shouting. "Callie, for God's sake, don't move!"

She didn't move. But the bear was still coming. Why didn't Trace shoot? Why?

The bear tore through the branches, its claws swiping at her. An agonizing pain slashed along her back. Still she didn't move. Didn't make a sound.

The rifle cracked.

The bear made an unearthly noise, and Callie had the sensation of the animal pivoting, roaring in pain and outrage.

Trace fired again.

The massive beast was falling, dying, but to Callie it all seemed terribly far away.

'Callie . . . Callie . . ."

She heard Trace shouting her name, but he too seemed far away. So very far away.

She felt herself being lifted, cradled, held.

Pain.

Such fearful pain.

Trace—so far away.

She gave herself up to the comforting shroud of oblivion.

Chapter Twenty-Three

Pain.

Callie had never felt such pain. Wave after wave of searing agony burned through her. She had fallen into a bottomless abyss, where the only reality was darkness mingled with the elusive twilight of near consciousness.

Where was she? She shifted a hand and had the vague impression of linens, but it was more than her tortured senses could absorb.

Time had no meaning. Her only measure of sensibility centered in and around an endless shroud of pain. Yet there were times just out of her reach when at the misty edges of wakefulness she was certain she was not alone. With her at her worst moments was a hovering, comforting presence, whispering loving words of encouragement. In the end that was the most cruel delusion of all, for she imagined her caretaker to be Trace. But Trace would never hold her so gently, rock her, soothe her, press cool, cool cloths to the inferno of her back.

Once she even imagined she heard him sobbing. But

he was so far away. So far. He was calling to her, begging her not to leave him.

Leave? Where was she going? She didn't know, didn't care. She only knew she couldn't tolerate this kind of pain much longer. More and more she welcomed the shadowy embrace of unconsciousness.

Trace sat on the bed, holding Callie's hand, too scared to even cry anymore. It had been three days. Three days since he brought her back to the ranch, and with each day she had grown worse instead of better.

"Please, Callie, don't leave me." He pressed her hand to his lips, kissing her pale, motionless fingers.

"She's lost too much blood." Riley rose from the rocking chair in the corner, coming over to squeeze Trace's shoulder. "You've done everything you can, boy. It's up to God now."

"He can't take her! She has to stay with me, with Chris. We need her. I need . . ." He closed his eyes, feeling the tears track down his cheeks. "Damn. She can't die."

"You just keep believin' that, boy."

The door to the bedroom opened and Deirdre strode in, carrying a supper tray. "I know you said you weren't hungry, Trace, but you're going to eat anyway. Starving yourself isn't going to do Callie a bit of good." She set the tray on the table beside the bed.

"Thank you." He swiped at his eyes. "You've both been very kind."

"Bosh and nonsense, she's my own flesh and blood. I love her like a daughter. You couldn't have kept me out of this room."

"I meant for what you've done for me and for Christopher. Especially since this is all my fault."

"You stop that. We've already been all through it. There was nothing you could have done."

"I should've stayed with her, not let her and Lanie go off alone."

"And then it might have been the bear finding Christopher."

Trace stood up, crossing over to the basin to moisten a fresh cloth. Returning to the bed, he pressed its coolness to Callie's overwarm forehead. "I'd like to stay with her alone for a while, if you don't mind."

"Of course." Deirdre and Riley started toward the door. Deirdre paused, returning to Trace's side. "You eat your supper now, hear?"

"Later."

"And you might try shaving, too. If Callie wakes up and takes a look at that face of yours, she's liable to faint."

He ran a hand across his three-day stubble and tried to smile, but failed. "I'll be all right."

Deirdre sighed. "You're not going to be any help to her if you make yourself sick."

"I'll be all right," he said again.

Deirdre shook her head, then quietly left the room with Riley.

Trace then did what he had done so often these past three days and nights. Though he remained atop the bedcoverings, he very carefully lay down beside Callie, nestling his face against her ear. "I love you." He said it over and over and over again. "I love you."

He kissed her cheek, wincing at how hot and dry it was. "Chris misses you, you know," he went on, speaking to her as though she could hear every word he said. "You've had quite an impact on that little boy. He even calls you Mama now sometimes." His voice broke. Clearing his throat noisily, he continued. "You know he wouldn't come down out of that blasted tree. I could hear Lanie yelling for him to jump down to her, but he wouldn't budge. He said Callie told him to wait for his papa, and that's just exactly what he was going to do."

He lifted her hand, squeezing it, aching to feel any kind of response. To keep his mind off the fact that there was none, he hurried on. "Did I tell you Riley went out and brought back the bear carcass? He dressed it out, then came in and told me he found an old arrowhead embedded in the joint of its left rear leg. The poor beast must have been in constant agony." He squeezed his eyes shut. "I should have gone after it when I found the mare and her colt. I—"

Callie moaned softly, her head shifting from side to side.

"Callie?" Trace said. "Callie, can you hear me?" He sat up, rubbing her arm, calling her name.

"The bear . . ." she murmured, her eyes still closed, ". . . have to run."

"Callie . . ."

"Stay in the tree, Christopher," she gasped. "Stay. Have to make the bear come toward me. Have to . . . The bear!" She twisted the sheets in her fists. "Run!" She cried out, then lay still again.

For a full minute he watched her, willing her to open her eyes, but she made no further sound. Maybe it was just as well. If she woke now, the pain would be excruciating. "Better if she sleeps through the worst of it," he told himself. Just as long as she came out of it soon. He and Deirdre did their best to force soup down her throat, but she wasn't getting nearly the nourishment she should.

The door opened. Trace turned, thinking Christopher might have gotten out of bed again. The child had been having nightmares every night since Callie had been hurt.

He grimaced. Lanie. "I thought I asked you not to come in here."

"I haven't seen you all day," the woman pouted, gliding over to the bed, undoing the top two buttons on the bodice of the green cotton dress she wore. "Besides, I wanted to tell you again that Callie's dresses are much too tight on my bosom. I just can't wear this thing." She unfastened a third button.

Trace stood up. "Don't."

"You always used to like it." She undid a fourth button.

Trace gripped her hand. "I said, don't."

"We're going to be married, silly. Why not have a little fun now?"

"Get out." Reluctantly, he added, "Please?"

Lanie's violet eyes took on a contemptuous glint. "Why do you bother with her?"

"She's my wife."

"You don't love her." Her brows furrowed. "Or do you?"

He turned away, walking over to the basin and picking up his shaving soap. "What I feel for her doesn't matter. She's been hurt because of me, because she was kind enough to help me when I needed it."

"So you're grateful. That doesn't mean you have to

spend every waking moment in here with her."

"How would it look to her aunt if I didn't?" He lathered up the soap and smoothed it along his jaw, wishing fervently Lanie would just leave. Callie's influence was weighing heavily on him at the moment. He was getting damned tired of lying—even to Lanie. Even though to do so was to improve his chances in court.

Strange how he hadn't even thought of the custody hearing these past three days, except to send word to Lyle Morton that it would have to be postponed. Having Christopher's custody settled once and for all had been the only thing on his mind for months, and now any delay could be tolerated as long as Callie got well again.

Lanie came up behind him and slid her arms around his middle. He stiffened abruptly. "I can't shave very well with you doing that."

"Then don't shave. I don't mind a little stubble."

He took a swipe at his cheek with the razor. "I'd like to get this done without slitting my throat . . ."

She took a grudging step back. "You could let me shave you."

"I can manage, thanks." He continued to scrape at his beard.

"I remember you let me shave you once. It was after we spent the whole night—"

He turned to face her. "Don't you think it's time you went to bed? It's getting pretty late."

She frowned. "It's lonely out in that bunkhouse all by myself."

"Maybe you'll be lucky, and Reese will show up."

She planted her hands on her hips. "That's not

funny. You know that man always gave me the willies."

"Reese has never been dangerous around me."

"He killed a man! You told me that yourself."

"And I also told you why. He saved my life in a prison riot."

"I don't care, he still makes my skin crawl. I didn't even think he still worked for you. I haven't seen him."

"He comes and goes as always."

She trailed her hand down his arm. "Can't you at least come out and tuck me in? I can make it worth your while. I know what you like in bed." She glanced toward Callie. "I'll bet she doesn't."

His lips thinned. "Don't say one more word about her." When she made as if to continue he held up a hand. "Not one more word."

"All right. All right. I guess I'll just have to be patient. We'll be reliving all our old memories soon enough. After the hearing is over. In fact, I don't know why you had the judge postpone it. I'm sure you could have gotten everything taken care of, even without Callie."

"My lawyer said her testimony could be important." Besides, he couldn't imagine going into court without her at his side. "I need all the advantages I can get."

"Why? Jenny's will spells it all out, doesn't it?" Her dark brows furrowed above her violet eyes. "Do these Marlowes know about your father?"

He stood very still. "What about him?"

"How he put you in jail."

He let out a long breath. "I suppose they know." He wiped the leftover soap from his face, hoping Lanie didn't notice how his hands shook. As far as he knew, neither Seth nor Jenny had ever spoken of Jeb

McCord's death to Lanie. But if she'd found out some other way . . .

"Mmmm, so handsome." Lanie stroked his freshly shaven cheek with her long, slender fingers. "I always did like your face." She wrapped her arms around him, pressing her breasts into his chest.

He reached up to put her away from him.

The door swung open.

Deirdre.

His eyes locked with hers. He watched first the shock, then the anger, and lastly a bitter disappointment that tore at his insides. But he couldn't say anything, didn't dare. He just stood there, while Deirdre condemned him with her eyes. Without a word she turned and left the room.

"Better that she knows the truth," Lanie said. "That her precious little niece hasn't got much longer to be your wife."

It took everything in him not to betray the sick feeling in his belly.

"Since she knows," Lanie went on, oblivious to anything Trace was feeling, "you can feel free to come on out to the bunkhouse now, can't you?"

"I'm not going to add adultery to the Marlowes' ammunition in that courtroom. I would appreciate if you would get that through your head."

"Who would tell? Certainly not me."

"Deirdre Callaghan wasn't too pleased with what she just saw in here. Just remember, if I don't get Chris, I'm not going to want to be married to anybody."

She trailed her hand past his crotch. "We'll see."

He gave her a withering look. "I wouldn't touch me like that again."

Lanie shook her head. "You certainly have changed. You used to be a lot more fun. Wild. You didn't care what anybody thought."

"Maybe that's the difference. These days I care very much what some people think." He stole a glance at Callie. "I care very much indeed."

Callie stared into the slavering jaws of a massive grizzly. The huge beast rose on its hind legs, towering over her like a malevolent demon. She tried to turn and run, but her feet were caught up in a tangled maze of branches and pine needles, jabbing, stabbing. She couldn't break free. Bloodied claws slashed at her.

She flailed at them, screaming.

She opened her eyes.

"There, there" came a soft voice. "You're all right now. You're safe."

Deirdre.

"What . . . ?"

"Hush, child," her aunt soothed.

"Trace . . . Christopher . . ."

"They're fine, darling, just fine. Don't worry now. Hush. Go back to sleep."

"The bear . . ."

"Is dead," Deirdre assured her. "Rest now, sweetheart. Rest."

With great difficulty Callie managed to focus on the room—Trace's room in the lights and shadows of late afternoon. "My God, the hearing. We have to start toward town to be in time for the hearing." She tried to rise, but cried out as a blade of fire shot through her back.

"The hearing's been postponed," Deirdre said.

"Postponed? No. Oh, please, no, not because of me."

"Mr. Morton sent word Judge Lancaster put it off until Trace notifies him you're all right."

Callie closed her eyes. "How long have I been—?"

"A week."

Tears tracked down her cheeks to dampen her pillow beneath her head. "It could've been settled. Trace must be furious."

"The only thing he's been thinking of is you."

She felt so weak. It was hard just to think. "Where is he?"

Deirdre looked away. "The poor man's been beside himself with worry and guilt. He's blaming himself for what happened."

"If it hadn't been for Trace coming when he did, I'd be dead. Please, Aunt Deirdre, where is he? Where's Christopher?"

Deirdre came over to sit on the bed, taking Callie's hand in hers. "You need your rest."

"Why are you avoiding my question? Please, they're not hurt, are they? The bear. Trace did kill the bear. Please . . ." She struggled to sit up.

Gently, Deirdre pressed her back. It didn't take any real strength. Callie had none to spare.

"The bear is dead," Deirdre said again. "Trace is fine. I promise you."

"Then where is he?" Had she only imagined the gentle hands? Or was there another, more likely, explanation? "It was you, wasn't it, Aunt Deirdre? It was you in this room all the time I was sick. Trace never came at all, did he?" The room wavered in front of her. She had to fight to keep from passing out.

"See? What did I tell you? You mustn't excite yourself."

"He's with Lanie, isn't he?"

"Hush now. Trace will be in to see you later. This is just about the first time he's been away."

"He is with her, isn't he?"

Grimly, Deirdre nodded. "I don't know why he even lets her stay." She frowned. "I'm sorry. I say I don't want you getting upset, then I tell you Trace is with that woman."

"I asked."

"I'm sure it's not what you're thinking."

"And what am I thinking?"

Deirdre stood up. "I'll bet you're hungry, aren't you?"

She smiled wanly. Obviously her aunt would tell her nothing more about Trace. "I'm famished."

"Well, that's certainly a good sign" came the husky male voice in the doorway.

Callie's heart leapfrogged in her chest. He was holding his black Stetson in front of him, his gray chambray shirt open at the throat. Even in her weakened state, just the sight of him set her pulses pounding. To cover her feelings she asked, "Is Chris with you?"

"I might have known I was second fiddle." He stepped aside, allowing a certain small boy to catapult into the room. "Cal-lee!" The child crawled gingerly onto the bed, as though he had been roundly cautioned to have a care for her injuries. Gleefully, he hugged her neck.

"I missed you, too, sweetheart," Callie said, holding him close, aware that Trace had crossed the room and was now standing at the foot of the bed. She looked up at him, giving him a tentative smile. Why did he look so ill at ease all at once?

"Welcome home," he said, though he continued to twist nervously at the brim of his Stetson.

Home. She liked the sound of that. "It's good to be back. Deirdre said it's been a week."

"One helluva week," he said. She had the strangest impression he had tried to make his voice sound light. Instead it was hoarse, uncertain.

Deirdre moved in, holding her arms out to Christopher. "Let's you and me fix Callie a nice welcome-back dinner, shall we?"

Reluctantly, the child let go of Callie. "Please, let him stay," Callie said. "I want him to stay."

"We'll be back in just a few minutes, dear," Deirdre said, her gaze shifting to Trace, then back to Callie. "All right?"

Bewildered, Callie nodded. She had seen the contempt in Deirdre's eyes when her aunt looked at Trace. But Callie managed to mask her confusion as she called to the departing child, "You make me something real good to eat now, all right, Christopher?"

"Oatmeal," he said solemnly.

"That sounds wonderful."

The child blew her a kiss, as Deirdre carried him from the room. "Cal-lee home."

Callie's smile faded as she turned her attention to Trace. "What was that all about?"

"I think your aunt figured I'd like to be alone with you for a few minutes." He sat on the bed. "You don't know how happy I am to see you feeling better."

"Deirdre told me about the hearing being postponed."

His gaze grew dark. "I was not referring to the postponement. I was talking about you."

She swallowed, disconcerted. "Oh." Why was everyone so on edge?

"I'm sorry. Sorry for so many things." He slid his hand over hers. "I was so afraid I was going to lose you."

The pain in his eyes was genuine, and for a moment her heart soared with hope. Then she realized what her death might mean to Christopher's custody. "Surely, the judge would have considered the codicil conditions met if I hadn't pulled through."

He shot to his feet, his face a mask of fury and pain. "Goddammit, Callie, I am talking about your life! Not the hearing! I was nearly out of my mind." He paced the confines of the small room, alternately angry and hurt. "When I heard the two shots, I knew you'd found Christopher. And I was so happy. I was running toward the sound. I knew, *knew* he was all right, because he was with you. But when I got there and saw that bear, saw him . . ." He stopped, his voice shaking.

For herself she couldn't speak.

"What a monster I must seem to you, that you can think all I cared about in your living or dying was any inconvenience it might mean to the hearing."

"I didn't mean it that way."

"Not that I don't deserve it. What have I ever brought you but pain?"

"The bear was not your fault. Please, don't blame yourself for that." She patted the mattress beside her. "Sit with me?"

401

He sat.

"Is Lanie still here?"

He nodded.

Her mouth twisted ruefully. "No wonder Deirdre's upset."

"It's more than that. She came in here the other night and found Lanie with her arms wrapped around me."

Callie stared at her hands. "Oh."

"It's not what . . ."

"Don't explain," Callie interrupted. "Please, don't explain."

Trace slapped a hand against his knee. "See? There I go, hurting you again. This time with the truth."

"You told me you haven't been sleeping with her. I doubt you'd start up again in this room, especially when I was taking up most of the bed." She threaded her fingers through his, knowing she was about to take a dangerous risk with her heart. But somehow having been so close to death made such a risk easier, even necessary. "It's Lanie who wants you, isn't it? Not the other way around."

He could only nod. She felt him trembling. Could he at last be ready to take a risk of his own?

He reached up and smoothed back her hair, gently tracing her eyebrows with the tips of his fingers. He spoke very slowly, his voice tight with emotion. "I am very much afraid of what I feel for you, Callie. I suppose that's why I keep trying to drive you away. But this past week when I didn't know if you were going to live or die, I realized what a fool I'd be not to at least try . . ."

She caught his hand in hers. "Kiss me."

He leaned forward, his lips brushing hers, once,

twice. Her lips parted. She welcomed the intimate exploration, reveled in knowing the pleasure she gave him, gloried in the delight he aroused in her own body. Why had they wasted so much time?

He groaned deep in his throat, his hands moving up to capture either side of her head. "I love you, Callie. God help me, I love you so much."

She threaded her fingers through his hair, pulling him close, cradling him to her. She closed her eyes, her heart filled with so much joy she could hardly bear it. Gently, she kissed the top of his head. "I love you, Trace McCord."

The door slammed open. "I knew it," Lanie said. "I knew it was all a lie." Her voice rose hysterically. "I saw the way you looked at her. But I couldn't believe it." She stalked across the room, waving a finger in Trace's face. "You'll be sorry. You'll both be sorry. We'll see what the judge has to say when I get through testifying."

Trace was on his feet. "Don't even think about it."

"Is that a threat?"

His voice was deadly soft. "Yes."

Callie watched Lanie swallow nervously. "You're just like Seth. You think I'm dirt. Not good enough for you anymore." She blinked back tears. "Well, you'll see. You'll both see. There're bigger fish than you out there, Trace McCord." She whirled, storming from the room.

Callie's heart hammered against her ribs. "She can't really stop us from having Christopher, can she?"

"No," Trace said. "She won't stop us."

The next morning Lanie was dead.

403

Chapter Twenty-Four

Callie paced the width and breadth of the sparsely furnished Rock Springs' sheriff's office seeking vainly to control her mounting anxiety. Her still healing back throbbed, but she took little notice of her physical discomfort. More important issues were at hand, issues whose resolution could well affect the rest of her life. Across from her in front of the jail's only cell two men escalated what fifteen minutes ago had begun as a polite conversation.

Lyle Morton was angry, and he was letting Rock Springs' lawman Lem Douglass know it in no uncertain terms. But Douglass was not a man easily intimidated. At six five the sheriff towered over the wiry lawyer, his height seeming all the more imposing to Callie, because what the lawman so vehemently debated was what he considered his legal obligation to put her in jail.

"Jealousy is one helluva motive," Douglass said. "Lanie came riding back into Trace's life, and this little lady"—he gestured toward Callie—"didn't like the idea of sharing her new husband."

Morton snorted his disgust. "How many times do I have to remind you that the night Lanie was murdered, Callie was flat on her back recovering from wounds received in a bear attack."

"She looks pretty healthy to me."

"Lanie's been dead a week, for God's sake." Morton slapped a fist at one of the cell's iron bars. "Do you want me to have Callie show you her back?"

Callie watched the lawman's mouth tip upward in a lascivious smirk. "That might not be a bad idea."

"Come on, Lem," Morton said, his voice taking on a placating tone. "You know me. I'm not a man to obstruct justice."

"This woman is your client's wife. And, frankly, I have to be a bit suspicious of your having Trace McCord as a client in the first place. I wasn't around when he had all his troubles with the law, but—"

"He was a wild kid," Morton broke in. "He's paid for what he did. Maybe more than most. If you put his wife in jail now, you could destroy any chance he has at Chris's custody hearing this afternoon." He crossed over to the sheriff's desk and perched himself on one corner. "You've been a good friend, Lem. I think I can speak confidentially."

Douglass frowned, then slowly nodded. "All right."

"You know as well as I do, as well as every gossip in this town, that Miss Callaghan's marriage to Trace was not exactly a love match. There was nothing for either her or Lanie to be jealous of."

Callie marched to the window that faced the street. She couldn't take much more of this. How had everything gone so wrong? She'd been lying in her bed, holding Trace, hearing at last the words she'd longed to hear—that he loved her. And then Lanie had burst in making threats. Callie tried to shut out the menace in Trace's softly spoken reply, but the warning in his voice rang over and over in her mind. He would not allow her to jeopardize Christopher's custody.

And now Lanie was dead.

Strangled.

Riley had found her body in the bunkhouse the next morning. For most of the rest of that day Trace—with Riley's blessing—had given serious thought to never reporting it, intending to concoct a story for Deirdre and Callie that Lanie had left for parts unknown. But conscience had prevailed over expedience and report it they had.

"Don't have too many suspects," Douglass had said as he strolled methodically about the bunkhouse two days later, looking for clues.

"Are you going to arrest me, Sheriff?" Trace asked.

"No. I figure if it was you, no one ever would have found the body."

"What does that mean?" Riley demanded as Deirdre clutched at his arm.

"It means that maybe there was someone else on this ranch with a real strong motive to kill an ex-wife who's come back to live with her ex-husband."

"Don't be stupid." Trace stalked back and forth, his hands jammed into his back pockets. "Callie isn't capable of murder."

"Just the same, as soon as she's able to travel I want her to stop by my office in town."

"She'll stop by, but you aren't going to harass her."

"Don't tell me how to do my job, McCord."

Deirdre couldn't listen anymore. She left the bunkhouse, coming to Callie's bedside to assure her at least that Trace had risen to her defense.

"My God, Aunt Deirdre," Callie whispered, "does Trace know I didn't do it, because he . . . ?" She couldn't finish. It couldn't be true. Trace was desperate to have Christopher, but not to the point of committing murder. "Maybe Reese came back," she said hopefully. "Lanie startled him. Or . . ."

"There, there, dear," Deirdre soothed, "you can't be fretting about all this now. You've got to concentrate on getting well."

"You don't believe he did it, do you?"

Deirdre patted Callie's hand, but did not meet her gaze. "Of course not."

"You're humoring me."

"Callie . . ."

"You don't trust him. Not since you think you saw him in Lanie's arms."

"I don't want to see you hurt anymore. That man has brought you nothing but pain since the moment you met him."

"I love him. I can't help it. I just do." She took a deep breath to keep the tears at bay. "Why did this happen? I can't believe Lanie's dead. I just can't believe it." She sagged against her pillow. "That woman and I would never have been friends, but I never wished . . ."

"Of course you didn't." Deirdre leaned forward to give Callie a hug. "I think you'd better try to get some rest. You're still not completely well."

Deirdre left her then, but Callie couldn't sleep. Over and over her own words came back to her. *It's a very short walk from the bunkhouse to the barn.* If Trace hadn't killed her, had he honestly slept through the commotion of whoever did? And why hadn't he come in himself to keep her apprised of what was happening with the investigation?

In fact, over the course of the week Trace was conspicuous by his absence. He'd declared his love, then all but disappeared from her life. And she could draw only one conclusion from that. He made certain he was never alone with her, because he knew she would ask about Lanie. Whether he avoided that confrontation because he feared the question suggested doubts of his innocence, or because his answer would be yet another lie, she couldn't have said.

She leaned her forehead against the warm glass of Lem Douglass's office window.

"It's been quite a day for you so far," Morton said, coming up behind her.

She turned. "Is the sheriff going to arrest me?"

Morton shook his head. "No proof. I think I've got him considering Reese, though. As a suspect."

"Reese hasn't been back at the ranch for weeks."

"Maybe he came back one night, then left again."

Callie shivered. "It sounds terrible, but . . ."

"You hope I'm right?"

She didn't answer.

"Trace didn't kill her, Callie."

She blinked back tears. "Can you promise me that?"

Morton looked at the floor. "If I thought he did, I wouldn't be trying my damnedest to win him custody of that little boy."

"Then why isn't Trace here? With me. Now."

"More than likely he's off stewing about the hearing. Now that it's finally going to happen, he's likely scared to death."

"I'm a little nervous myself."

"You'll be fine. Judge Lancaster is a good man. I've known him since he was territorial marshal years ago."

"Lancaster is feeling better then?"

"Sometimes I think he's only been hanging on for this hearing."

Callie excused herself and headed for the hotel, her earlier anxiety about facing the sheriff gone, replaced by an even greater fear—facing Trace. The hearing was about to take place at last. Her uneasiness about the event itself—her terror that Trace might somehow lose Christopher—was matched only by her uncertainty that even though Trace now professed to love her, he would still find a reason to end the marriage once the hearing was over.

Whether the man liked it or not, they had to talk.

She took a deep breath, then strode into their second-floor room. He was standing near the window, staring down at the dusty street below. He did not turn to look at her. "How are you?" she asked softly.

Stiff-backed, he crossed over to her. "Just great."

He couldn't stand still, pacing from one end of the room to the other. "I wish this was over with."

Callie sat on the bed. "Don't you think we should talk? I don't want to say anything wrong in court."

"What would you say that was wrong?" he snapped.

"Nothing. Not deliberately. But . . ."

"Just say whatever you think."

"Dammit, Trace, you're not being fair. I'm in this, too."

He sank down beside her. "I'm sorry." He dragged a hand across the back of his neck. "I can't even think. For the first time in my life I am absolutely terrified."

She pulled his hand onto her lap. "I know. So am I.

Thank heaven, Deirdre and Riley have Christopher. The poor kid wouldn't know what to think seeing us like this."

His arms swept around her. "Hold me. Just hold me."

She clung to him. "We won't lose him, Trace. We can't."

His mouth came down on hers, his kisses fevered, desperate. His hand cupped her breast, the soft mound swelling to his touch beneath the thin fabric of her dress. She returned his kisses eagerly, wantonly, aching for even a moment's respite from the fear that threatened to swallow them both.

Her hand fumbled with the buttons on his shirt. She was being swept away by a need to feel safe, protected, even as she wished to give him the same. Her fingers glided across the soft mat of hair that spanned his chest. He groaned, allowing the erotic exploration, then just as suddenly he gripped her waist, putting her away from him.

"We can't. Not now."

She kissed him. "We can. We need each other. Trace, please . . ."

"No. No. Not like this."

Why did he have to have scruples now? All she wanted was to love him.

His eyes blazed with the passion he still felt, but he seemed determined to hold it in check. "Before this goes any farther, I need to know something. I've been trying hard to avoid it, but . . ."

"What is it?"

"I think you know." His gaze held hers. "Do you think I killed her? Do you think I murdered Lanie?"

In just that instant before he'd said the words, she'd

known the truth. It was only because he had so scrupulously avoided her this week that she had ever doubted. "No, I don't believe you killed her."

He continued to study her face. "But you weren't quite sure, were you?"

"Trace, please . . ."

A stony mask settled over his features. "A moment or two of doubt, perhaps? When you thought your ex-convict thief of a husband had graduated to murder?"

"I'm not going to fight with you. Not now."

But he was relentless. "Were you in the bunkhouse when Lanie died?"

"Of course not."

"Then how do you *know*, exactly, that it wasn't me."

Her lips thinning, she shot to her feet. "This doesn't make any sense. We have to be in that courtroom in an hour, a happily married couple wanting custody of their child."

"*Their* child? Yours and mine?"

"Yes," she hissed. "Mine! I love him, too."

For a full minute he glared at her, then suddenly he closed his eyes. "Damn, I don't even know what I'm saying anymore." He pulled her to him. "Forgive me."

She buried her face against his chest. "Lyle is right. We're going to need each other in that courtroom. We have to remember we're on the same side." She took a deep breath. "Which leads me to an unpleasant question of my own."

His gaze grew wary, but he said only, "What is it?"

"You haven't always been . . . open about your past." A muscle in his jaw jumped. Quickly, she continued. "I only mean that you haven't leaped at the chance to tell me the Trace McCord story. Like your having been in prison, for example."

"What's your point?" His voice was tight.

"I want to know if the Marlowes are harboring any more of your secrets."

"I hope not."

"Hope not? Trace, if there's something I should—"

A knock sounded at the door. Before either of them could respond, an agitated Lyle Morton burst into the room.

"What is it?" Trace asked.

Morton looked positively ill. "Craig Lancaster died half an hour ago in his sleep."

Trace paled visibly. "Damn."

Callie looked from Morton to Trace. "I don't mean this to sound callous, but does that mean the hearing's postponed?"

"Unfortunately, no."

"What do you mean?" Trace said. "There isn't another judge."

"It seems that after the last postponement, when Callie was hurt, the Marlowes' attorney took it upon himself to have another judge waiting in the wings. It was no secret Lancaster was seriously ill."

"So what's wrong, Lyle. Dammit, tell me."

"The judge," Morton said. "The judge is Fenton Thompson."

"Oh my God." Trace looked as though he'd just been shot.

"What is it?" Callie cried. "Who's Fenton Thompson?"

Trace stared straight ahead, his gaze focused on nothing, yet most certainly locked on some past agony she couldn't see. "He's the judge who sent me to prison."

412

Chapter Twenty-Five

The first thing Callie noticed about Judge Fenton Thompson was his eyes. Opaque blue eyes that seemed to look right through her. Silver hair and a ramrod straight spine exacerbated her image of a man whose mind was already made up, a man who'd already condemned Trace and, by association, the woman he had chosen as his wife. Annoyed, she shook off the notion. This was no time to indulge fearful fantasies. Christopher's future hung in the balance. No matter what her concerns about Thompson's biases, she intended to make certain nothing she did or said in the man's courtroom today would tip the hearing in favor of the Marlowes.

They were all here, all who had a hand or an interest in Christopher's fate. Callie, Trace, and Lyle Morton sat on one long side of the rectangular mahoghany table in the judge's chambers. Edna and Edgar Marlowe sat on the other, along with an obsequious-looking man in his late fifties. Edna Marlowe had introduced him as they'd taken their seats, bare minutes before Thompson's entrance.

"Ashley Warren," she'd said. "Our attorney. The man who will see to it that justice is done here today, that Edgar and I are awarded custody of Jennifer's child."

But before Morton or Warren could square off, Thompson showed them all who would be in control of the proceedings this day. "We'll dispense with formalities here. This is not a court of law, but a forum of justice to decide the best interests of a three-year-old boy. I have written statements from both sides. Though you may worry that my coming into the case late puts me at a disadvantage, let me assure all parties concerned that I have read all of these documents quite carefully."

Morton stood. "I have a few opening remarks I'd like to make, Your Honor."

"That won't be necessary, Mr. Morton," Thompson said.

Morton sat back down, chagrined. Callie shifted uneasily. Things were not starting off well at all.

"This is all bull—" Trace said, his gaze drilling Thompson's. "These people," he swept a hand toward the Marlowes, "only want Chris because of the trust fund Jenny's parents set up for her and her child."

"That will be the last unsolicited comment from anyone in this room," Thompson said. "Is that understood?"

Trace's jaw tightened, but he said no more.

"You'll each have your chance to speak," Thompson went on. "Even you, Trace. Maybe you'll even convince me that five years in prison mellowed you, made an honest man out of you."

"Objection!" Morton said. "Prejudicial."

"I'd better not hear that again, either."

Callie sank back, feeling useless. After all she'd gone through could they just be going through the motions? She stiffened. No, she couldn't think that way. Didn't dare think that way.

"All right, McCord," Thompson said. "Let's hear your side of it first, shall we?"

"Ask me anything you like."

Callie relaxed, if only a little. Trace seemed more at ease now. Perhaps having some definite questions to speak to, definite points to make would help ease the mounting tension in the tiny room.

"Mr. McCord," Thompson said, "are you suggesting to this court that you met Miss Callandra Callaghan on a Monday, fell in love with her on a Tuesday, and married her on a Saturday without any thought of the deadline set in Jennifer McCord's will? That you would have married this woman anyway?"

"Yes," Trace stated. Callie was startled at how easily he spoke the lie, but then Christopher was at stake.

"And you have no intention of divorcing her as soon as this adoption is finalized?"

"No."

"If I haven't said so previously, you realize that you're all considered to be under oath for any and all questions asked. Is that fully understood?"

"It is."

"And you still insist that you love your wife and intend to stay married to her even if this proceeding should not be decided in your favor?"

"Yes."

"Your Honor," Warren interjected, "you have

before you affadavits signed by two women of Rock Springs, both of whom were approached about marriage to this man."

"That's a damned lie!" Trace snapped. "I don't know how much the Marlowes paid . . ."

"McCord," Thompson cut in, "I'll not warn you again."

Morton gripped Trace's arm, whispering urgently. "Take it easy. We'll get our chance. Don't ruin it."

"Each woman states separately," the Marlowes' attorney continued, "that McCord assured them the marriage was temporary and that they would be paid well for their time and inconvenience."

"I read their statements, Mr. Warren," Thompson said. "And when I want your input again, I'll ask for it."

Warren's smile was polite, his eyes angry.

"And now, McCord, shall we delve a little further into your fitness as a guardian for this youngster. Like your past, perhaps?"

"Objection," Morton said. "Mr. McCord's past is not at issue here. We're here to act on the last wishes of Jennifer McCord."

"We're here to decide the best interests of Christopher McCord." He eyed Trace. "Mr. McCord, why were you in prison?"

Morton again tried to object. Trace waved him off. His voice was expressionless. "Theft."

"Thank you." Thompson's eyes registered no emotion whatsoever, yet Callie shuddered. This wasn't fair. Nothing was happening the way she had imagined it—that they would walk in, assure the court they'd fulfilled Jenny's last wishes, and then, in accordance with those wishes, they would be awarded full and legal custody of Christopher.

The judge then turned his attention to the Marlowes. "Mr. Marlowe," Thompson said, "I'd like to hear in your own words why you feel you would make a better parent to this little boy than Trace McCord would."

"Well, for one thing, Your Honor," Edgar Marlowe replied, his obsequious tone grating on Callie, "Edna and I have a wonderful home back in upstate New York, servants, the best schools would be available. I was always so fond of Jenny. She was my brother's only child, you know." He extracted his kerchief from his vest pocket and dabbed at his eyes.

"Why do you suppose Jenny picked McCord to be Christopher's legal guardian—in the event, of course, that he should marry within the stipulated time? Why wouldn't she simply state that the child should go to you and your wife?"

Edgar shifted uncomfortably. "I think it's sadly obvious, Your Honor. Though I'm loath to say."

"What's that?"

"Jenny lived at the ranch with McCord. He had access to her, could easily have intimidated her . . ."

Morton slammed to his feet. "Objection!"

"Since he knew full well about the trust, no matter what he says . . ."

"Objection! Your Honor . . ."

"And God knows how else he may have intimidated her, all alone out there in the middle of nowhere."

"Your Honor!" Morton shouted. "This is an outrage. I—"

"Sustained," Thompson said.

"You cannot allow these blatantly hearsay remarks . . ."

"I said your objection was sustained, Counselor," Thompson said. "Sit down."

Morton slapped at the papers in front of him on the table. Callie caught his muttered, "Travesty."

"Mrs. Marlowe," the judge said, "I'd like to hear from you regarding why you want custody of the youngster."

"Oh, Your Honor," Edna said, batting her ample eyelashes, "Chrissy is just the image of his grandfather. He's such a darling child. I've always wanted several of my own. But the good Lord didn't see fit," she sniffled, "to bless us. Perhaps this is His way of guiding us."

Callie was glad she hadn't eaten any breakfast. She would have lost it.

"Now you, my dear," Thompson said, "I have a question or two."

Trace nudged her. Callie gasped, startled, only then realizing the judge was speaking to her. "Yes, sir . . . Your Honor?"

"Mrs. McCord," Thompson said, "could you tell this court how you could fall in love with a man you'd only just met."

"Who can explain love, Your Honor?"

"I don't believe that was the question. You are in love with your husband, are you not?"

"Yes," she said in a small voice.

"What was that? I couldn't hear you."

"Yes, I love him," she snapped.

"According to statements I've been reading from Mr. Warren and his clients, they suggest that the marriage is in name only. Mr. McCord is a young man, strong, no doubt possessed of a man's wants and desires."

418

Callie held her breath. Surely, the judge wasn't leading where he seemed to be . . .

"Tell me, Mrs. McCord. How do you love a husband and hope to continue a marriage that has never been consummated?"

Callie gasped, crimson staining her cheeks.

"That's enough!" Trace grated, shoving to his feet, his chair making scraping noises on the wood floor. "Leave her alone, damn you."

Morton grabbed Trace's arm. "Trace, if you have one ounce of sense left, you'll sit down. Now."

"Yes, you will sit down, McCord," the judge warned, "or I will have you taken out of this room."

Trace sat grudgingly, glowering at Thompson.

"I'll make my point clear, Mrs. McCord," Thompson went on, "this marriage of yours is no marriage at all. It's a business arrangement. You're to help McCord fulfill the codicil of a will he found distasteful and you—what will you gain, Mrs. McCord? Money?"

"There's a word for a woman who exchanges favors for money," Edna Marlowe put in.

"That's enough," the judge said. "Look at me, Mrs. McCord."

Callie did so.

"Now, I'd like to think you're an unfortunate young woman caught up in unfortunate circumstances. Is this marriage in name only? Are you doing Mr. McCord a rather large favor? Or have you taken it a step further?"

Callie wrung her hands. How dare this man humiliate her like this? And then, just that suddenly, she grew angry. How dare he impugn her character? He didn't even know her. Perhaps it was time he did. "My husband and I have a normal marriage in every way,

419

Your Honor. I find your intimation that it would be otherwise not only offensive, but embarrassing as well."

"You've consummated this marriage?"

Trace swore explosively. This time Morton couldn't move fast enough to restrain him. Trace stopped inches from Thompson, only some last shred of control preventing him from ripping the man to pieces with his bare hands. "You will apologize to my *wife*," he said, his voice deadly soft.

Callie put a hand on him. "It's all right." He jerked away, stomping over to the door, seeming ready to bolt. The room grew very still. Callie waited, knowing that if he left the room, he took any chance of getting Christopher with him. But he had to make the decision himself. At last he straightened, coming over to sit back down. He looked at no one.

She faced the judge squarely. "Our marriage has most certainly been consummated, Your Honor. Not that it is in the least your business. But I would like to tell you something that is, if I could."

Thompson gestured broadly with his hands. "By all means, Mrs. McCord."

"I'm not certain what your intentions are. But if it's to intimate that I am prostituting myself with Trace McCord for some personal gain, you couldn't be more wrong. I'll say it again. I love him." She was amazed at how easily she could say the words here in this room before strangers, when it was so often so difficult to say to Trace when they were alone. Taking a deep breath, she plunged on. "I don't know if you're a father or not, but if you could see Trace with that child, you would know that we're not just talking about breaking Trace's heart should you take them away from each other, but Christopher's as well."

The judge stared at her with a new respect. "The court offers its sincere apologies to you, Mrs. McCord. I think you are indeed in love with this man. And yes, I do have children. Three, as a matter of fact." His voice grew gentle as he continued to question her—on her upbringing, her reasons for journeying west, her own feelings for Christopher. When he'd finished, he looked Trace squarely in the eye. "You've got one helluva woman there."

His voice was steady, strong. "I know."

"I would've wanted to punch me in the nose for questioning her character myself."

Trace's jaw remained set in a stubborn line. It was apparent he trusted nothing this man said.

The judge scratched his chin thoughtfully. "I've said it before, but I want all of you in this room to understand that my paramount concern here today is the child."

Callie waited. She, too, wasn't certain where the judge's sympathies lay.

"Mrs. McCord, are you aware of your husband's past?"

"Of course." She knotted her hands together, remembering her plea that Trace warn her if he harbored any more secrets.

"And yet you married him anyway?"

"Trace isn't perfect. But I've never met anyone who is. He can be moody. Right now he's terrified, scared to death you're going to take away the most important person in the world to him. But he's also capable of the most unselfish love. Something he himself was denied by his own father, yet which he freely gives to Christopher."

Thompson frowned. "Jeb McCord was a friend of mine. Perhaps you haven't been fully enlightened about Trace's relationship with his father."

"Don't." Trace's voice was ragged.

The judge ignored him. "You say you know this man, Mrs. McCord?"

"I do." Yet she trembled.

"Do you know then, that Trace McCord killed his own father?"

She was glad she was seated. She might have collapsed otherwise.

Trace slumped forward, his head in his hands, looking for all the world as though he'd just received a mortal blow.

"Care to enlighten your wife, McCord?" the judge prodded.

Trace said nothing.

"I can tell by the look in your eyes, Mrs. McCord," Thompson said, "that this is the first you've heard about this particular incident in your husband's past. Am I right?"

She didn't answer. She didn't have to.

"After his father had Trace arrested for stealing, he and Jeb got into a fight, a fight in which Jeb was shot."

Callie willed Trace to deny it, but his silence condemned him. Why hadn't he told her, prepared her, shared his side of the story? She had not been able to hide her shock from the judge.

"I don't have to recess to consider the disposition of this case," the judge said. "I have to consider first and foremost the best interests of the child. And, unfortunately, an ex-convict who would show the poor judgment of marrying a woman merely to fulfill the conditions of a will, giving no thought to the maternal needs of the child, does not suggest the type of person who should raise that child to be a decent, law-abiding citizen. Trace McCord is an unfit parent and I have no choice but to award custody of Christopher McCord to Edna and Edgar Marlowe."

Callie expected Trace to explode, to attack the judge physically. Instead he just sat there, staring straight ahead.

The Marlowes were on their feet, clapping their attorney on the back, offering their profuse thanks to the judge.

"I'm not finished," Thompson said sternly. "Sit down. All of you."

Reluctantly, the Marlowes did so.

"As I said," Thompson continued, "my interests here are for the child. Since I'm setting aside Jennifer McCord's will anyway, I'm also ordering that Edna and Edgar Marlowe receive a monthly living allowance to meet Christopher's basic needs. The bulk of the trust is to be held in escrow and awarded to the child on the occasion of his twenty-first birthday."

Edna's face purpled, but Warren gripped her hand, his eyes silencing any protest.

Trace was on his feet, heading for the door. He paused only long enough to whisper something to Lyle Morton. Callie followed, fighting a feeling of despair so profound she thought she might die of it.

Deirdre and Riley were standing in the hallway with Christopher. The child looked bewildered, frightened, as though he could sense something was going on.

Edna Marlowe grabbed Christopher's hand. "Come

along, child."

"Papa!" Chris shrieked.

Trace's eyes blurred. He stepped up to the woman. "I'd like one minute with him. Please?"

Edna relented.

Trace hunkered down, perching Christopher on his knee. "I want you to show your papa what a big boy you are and go along with these nice people. They'll be better for you. You'll have a better home, go to a better school . . ." His voice shook. "I love you, boy. I've got to go now." He gave the child a fierce hug, then lifted him up and handed him to Edgar Marlowe. "Bye, pardner."

"Cal-lee! Papa! Home! Home!"

Trace walked away, not once looking back.

Callie sobbed, glaring at Lyle Morton. "You can't let them take him! You can't!" She started after Trace. The lawyer caught her arm. "I think it's best to leave him alone for now."

"How could this happen? Doesn't that judge know what he's done?" She felt as if she were suffocating. Though the Marlowes had already left the building, she could still hear Christopher screaming for her, for Trace.

"I'll appeal the decision," Morton was saying. "I promise you. We've got good grounds for it. Thompson was prejudiced from the outset."

Callie sank onto a long bench seat that abutted the wall. Deirdre came over to grip her hand. "You'll get the child back, Callie. You will."

"Trace never had a chance," she murmured, looking up at Morton. "Did he?"

Morton's shoulders slumped. "He would have. If

Judge Lancaster had held on one more day."

"I want you to tell me what Thompson meant about Trace killing his father. I don't believe it. Not for one minute."

Morton sat next to her. "I should have made him tell you."

"Then you did know."

He nodded.

"Damn you. My not knowing might have cost Trace his son."

"No. Don't even think that. In fact, with Thompson in there you gave Trace the only chance he had."

She swiped at her tears. "No more secrets. I want to know about his father. Now."

"All right." He patted her hand. "Actually, it was Jeb who tried to kill Trace."

"My God," she said softly, already knowing this ultimate horror had been the final blow to Trace's ability to believe anything good about himself.

"Trace came back after he'd stolen the money. He thought everything had been straightened out by Seth. It wasn't. His father nearly beat Trace to death before he sent for the law.

"Jeb testified against him at the trial. Trace was awaiting sentencing, when Seth decided to try one last time for a reconciliation. He got Thompson to release Trace to his custody. Seth convinced Trace to go home with him, to face Jeb, to ask his forgiveness.

"Trace didn't think much of the idea, but Seth finally talked him into it. There was a fight. Jeb pulled a gun. The bullet ricocheted, hit Jeb in the back. Paralyzed him. He spent the last six years of his life flat on his back being cared for like he was a baby."

"The whole time Trace was in prison, then, his father was an invalid."

Morton nodded. "That was why Trace didn't go near Shadow's Way when he got out. But then Jeb took a turn for the worse. Seth tracked Trace down, sent him a telegram, told him it was his last chance to make peace with his father. Trace did start home, but he was too late. Deliberately so, I think. Jeb was dead when Trace got home."

Callie sobbed brokenly. "Why didn't he tell me? Why?"

"He thought you'd hate him."

"I could never hate him. He hates himself enough for us all."

Assuring Deirdre and Riley she would be all right, Callie headed back to the hotel alone. She tried to tell herself Trace would pull himself back together, as he had so many times before. Lyle would renew the legal battle. They would do whatever they had to to get Chris back, and they would win.

But the brutal reality kept playing in her mind. Chris was gone. Gone. Though she wanted to fly apart in a million pieces, she was determined to be strong for Trace.

In their room he was already packing. He didn't look up. "You can come back to the ranch with me and get your things," he said, his voice all the more chilling because there was no emotion in it at all. "There's no reason to continue the marriage. I've already told Lyle to start whatever procedures are necessary."

"Procedures?"

"For our divorce."

Chapter Twenty-Six

Callie woke to the sound of Christopher crying. Instantly alert, she flung back her bedcovers, reaching over to rouse Trace. She stilled, reality washing over her. Trace was not in the bed. She was sleeping alone in the guest room. She listened again for Christopher.

The ranch house was silent.

Christopher was not crying. Christopher was gone.

She bit her lip to keep from crying herself. Six days. Six empty days and nights had passed since the Marlowes had taken Christopher. She had spent four of those days alone at Shadow's Way with Trace. Time and again he'd told her to pack her things and leave, to go back to Rock Springs, back to Deirdre and Riley.

"I wouldn't abandon my worst enemy to the kind of pain you're suffering," she'd railed at him. "I'm certainly not going to leave you."

"I don't need you. I don't need anybody."

"Well, I need you. We need each other. We both love Christopher. We both hurt to have him gone."

Again and again, he'd raged at her to get out,

reminding her he'd already set the wheels in motion for their divorce. But she saw through his anger. He lashed out at her, praying she would leave, because he didn't want her to see his pain, didn't want her to see him break down completely.

He had been gone most of the last two days, and she'd had to wonder if perhaps he'd gone after the Marlowes, stolen the child and left for parts unknown. She hoped he had. But he'd come back this morning looking haggard, lost, alone. And he'd been drunk. Dead drunk.

When he'd sobered up a little she had played her final card. "You still owe me a trip to Yellowstone, Trace. There was never anything said about winning or losing custody. If I married you, you would take me to Yellowstone. Period."

He'd glared at her. She was certain in that moment he had hated her. But he'd relented. "Fine. If that's what you want. We'll leave the day after tomorrow."

The day after tomorrow.

She lay on the bed, listening to the quiet, trying to focus on the sound that had disturbed her. But whatever it was was not repeated. The haunting silence only served to amplify Christopher's absence. To spare herself the hurt she forced her thoughts elsewhere. To Yellowstone. Her dream. A goal that had obsessed her for more than half her lifetime. Now it was within her grasp—and she didn't care.

Yellowstone didn't matter. Nothing mattered now that Christopher was gone. Her only reason for haranguing Trace into making the trip was her certainty that such a diversion was necessary to keep them both from going mad. Morton had told her the paperwork to appeal Judge Thompson's decision could take weeks. She couldn't allow Trace to spend those weeks drunk and alone. If taking her on her damned treasure hunt kept him busy, then, by God, that's what they were going to do.

What saddened her most was that Trace had given up. He refused to even discuss the possibility of getting Christopher back.

"It's for the best," he'd said on the ride home. "I don't know who I was trying to fool. I'm no father. I—"

She'd wanted to shake him, but mostly she'd wanted to hold him, to let him cry out the anguish he held so tightly dammed inside himself.

In the darkness the sound came to her again. Muffled, indistinct. Brows furrowing, Callie rose from the bed. Slipping into her robe, she padded across the house toward Christopher's room. She stopped in front of the closed door, suddenly nervous. Pushing past the smooth pine, she peered inside. At first she could discern nothing out of the ordinary. Then, as her eyes grew more accustomed to the familiar shapes and shadows, she noticed the silhouette on the floor beside the bed.

She crossed to the hunched figure, her heart breaking as she stared down at Trace. He was trembling violently, holding Christopher's puff puppy crushed to his chest.

She almost turned and fled, fearful that he would permit no visitors to intrude on his private hell. But she needed to be with him. Sagging to her knees, she drew him to her, cocooning him in her embrace.

He didn't say anything, didn't curse, didn't cry. He

just slumped against her, staring straight ahead. But if ever she could *feel* someone else's pain, she felt it now.

"He's gone, Callie," he said at last, his voice lifeless. "He's gone and I'll never see him again. It's like he died."

"He isn't dead. And neither are you. We'll get him back. We will."

"They took him. They took him away from me. I wasn't good enough. I wasn't a good enough son to my father. I wasn't a good enough father to my son."

She made no effort to check the tears that streamed down her cheeks. Huddled together in the darkness, she held him until he fell asleep.

The next morning he rose before she did. She woke to find a blanket settled about her. But if she thought it signaled a turning point, that Trace was breaking through his stone wall of misery, she soon discovered how wrong she was. There was a new hardness, coldness in him, a bitterness beyond anything she'd seen in him before. When a letter arrived that morning from Lyle Morton, Trace refused even to look at it.

Callie opened it instead. Her brows furrowed at the short terse message. Lyle wanted Trace to go through Seth and Jenny's things, looking for any correspondence the two might have had with each other. Perhaps Jenny had written something about the Marlowes that would give Lyle something to go on.

When Trace refused, Callie conducted the search herself. She found nothing in Seth's effects. But Jenny was more the sentimentalist. She had tied a satin ribbon around several letters Seth had written to her. The first suggested Seth had sent her back to her parents for several months during the final, fateful trouble Trace had had with his father. Only after Trace had been in prison for several months had Seth again written and asked her to return to Shadow's Way.

One by one Callie read the letters, touched by the occasional bursts of emotion Seth McCord showered on his wife. *The flowers are blooming in the fields now,* he had written, *but it will never be spring in my heart until you're with me.* Most of the time, though, he wrote of more mundane things—livestock purchases, feed prices, the growth of the ranch. He told Jenny little of Trace in the first four letters, saying only that he worried about what prison would do to him.

In all of the letters never once did Seth complain about caring for his by then paralyzed father. In fact, he went so far as to tell Jenny she had every right to reconsider his proposal, knowing the burden caring for an invalid would put on their relationship.

Later, in a letter obviously written after their marriage, when Jenny had gone east for a visit, Seth wrote: *Trace has been in jail four years now. He doesn't show the remotest sign that it's changed him in any way. A letter last week—his first in over a year—tells how some hulk named Reese saved his bacon in a prison fight. I told Pa about it. He said he wished this man Reese had minded his own business.*

Callie's fist closed reflexively on the letter. "You were a vile, sick man, Jeb McCord," she gritted. "Thank God Trace didn't make it home to have you spit in his eye one more time before you went to the devil."

Though she found more references to Jeb McCord's seemingly limitless hatred for his younger son, she found no mention of the Marlowes in any of the letters.

With a resigned sigh she retied the ribbon and settled them back into the cedar chest. She was about to replace the linens that had been on top of them when she caught sight of a bit of paper sticking through a board at the bottom of the chest. She poked at it, astonished to discover that the board moved. A false bottom. Lifting the board upward, she tugged on the paper, pulling it free. Another letter. A letter deliberately concealed, kept separate from the others.

Frowning, Callie opened it. Her eyes widened, her pulses pounding as she read. For long minutes she sat there, stunned, as she considered its implications. Then, quietly thoughtful, she returned the letter to its hiding place.

She strode out to the corral to find Shoshone gone. Trace had ridden off as usual. He didn't accomplish anything, except to stay away from her.

But he would be back tonight. He had to be. He'd promised they would start out for Yellowstone tomorrow.

She turned at the sound of a horse approaching, surprised Trace had deigned to return before nightfall. She stared at the rider in disbelief.

Nicolas.

He dismounted, striding over to her. "Callie, my dear, so good to see you again."

"What are you doing here, Nicolas?"

"Always so subtle. That's what I love about you."

"Nicolas, please . . ."

"I know," he said, his voice soft. "I'm sorry about the child."

His sincerity disconcerted her. "Thank you," she managed.

He stepped closer. "Please don't take this the wrong way. I understand that you have a certain loyalty to the man in this distressing time, but even you must admit that your reasons for staying married no longer apply." His voice had grown husky, his eyes clinging to her face.

Callie turned away. She supposed Nicolas meant well, but she could tolerate no emotional exchanges right now. "Perhaps we can discuss this when Trace and I return from Yellowstone."

His eyes lighted. "You're leaving soon?"

"Tomorrow."

"It would be quite a feather in my cap if I helped you find that treasure. Your father would be in my debt for life."

"Trace and I are going alone."

He nodded reluctantly. "I understand." His gaze held hers. "But I will be waiting for you when you get back. I want to return to New York with you in triumph."

Callie marveled at his sensitivity. She had to wonder if he had been so those many months ago in New York, how different her life might have been.

"You're thinking that I shouldn't have been such a pompous ass during our courtship, aren't you?"

She toed the ground sheepishly. "It's like you're two different people, Nicolas. I mean . . ."

"It's all right. Maybe it wasn't until you left me that I realized what a fool I'd been to take so much for granted. Your father, I'm afraid, took your departure much more personally than I did."

"How is he?"

"He encouraged me to find you."

"And drag me back kicking and screaming?"

"No. Quite the contrary. He decided if you made it this far—to Yellowstone, that is—I was to give you my fullest cooperation in helping locate the stolen payroll."

"I appreciate that, Nicolas. Truly. But this is something I have to do myself."

"I understand."

"I do want to thank you for—"

Trace thundered into the yard aboard Shoshone. Sliding from the saddle, he reached her in three strides. She had the definite suspicion he'd been somewhere nearby. He was not surprised to see Nicolas.

"I believe I told you once you weren't welcome on Shadow's Way land."

"Just passing through, my boy, I assure you. I wanted to remind Callandra that I'm still waiting."

"Get on your horse."

"Whatever you say . . . for now." He marched over to Callie. "Best luck in Yellowstone, my dear. Best luck." He captured her hand, raising it to his lips. She felt the warmth of his breath on her flesh. She did not pull away as he kissed the back of her hand. He bowed low, then, turning, he mounted and rode out.

Callie shook herself. Something wasn't right. But she couldn't quite put her finger on what it was. Instead, she turned to Trace. "You didn't have to be so nasty. He doesn't mean any harm."

"Then go after him. Go to bed with him, see if I give a damn."

She took a deep breath. His outburst was typical of the insults he'd been flinging at her since they'd returned from Rock Springs. The only time he'd been decent was last night in Christopher's room. He'd

434

simply been too exhausted to fight with her.

Over and over she told herself he was trying to drive her away before she made the choice and left him.

"When we get back from this damned trip," he said, "Lyle should have the divorce finalized."

The words were like the slash of a knife. "I thought you might have reconsidered hurrying it through. Lyle is still working on your appeal to get Chris back."

It was as if she hadn't spoken. "I know you'd prefer an annulment, but since we did, unfortunately, consummate this union . . ." He didn't finish, saying instead, "I thought things might get pretty messy with your church."

"A divorce will be fine." She didn't recognize her own voice.

"Good. Then if you want your fancy Count Nicolas, you're free to go to him."

"Free." She nodded. "Free."

"Anyway, it doesn't matter to me. I'll be selling the ranch come spring. I guess I'm just a born drifter. No roots. No ties."

She said nothing, striding alone toward the house. Damn the man. How much was she supposed to take? Maybe she was a fool. Maybe he really did hate her.

In the guest room she slapped open her journal, pouring out words as fast as she could think. And when she was finished, she threw the book across the room. No words counted now. Only her heart, which she held together on the flimsiest of hopes.

Yellowstone—her dream.

Yellowstone—her last chance to be with Trace.

Yellowstone—where the treasure she would now seek was Trace McCord's love.

Chapter Twenty-Seven

"We ride where I say, when I say, for as long as I say," Trace snarled, glaring at Callie.

She sat Kachina, waiting for him to finish tying down their extra gear on the pack horse they would take with them to Yellowstone. They hadn't even left the ranchyard and already he was trying to pick a fight with her.

She murmured a polite response, unwilling to rise to the bait. If it was her dream to draw out this man's love during their journey, it was patently obvious he was dreaming the exact opposite. As they rode out, she assured herself it was his bitterness talking, but the ensuing miles of moody silence made her wonder if she was being a fool. To the west the majestic shadows of the Tetons only exacerbated the bleakness of her mood.

For five hours she put up with the rugged pace Trace set, but by midday her aching muscles could take no more. "I need a few minutes," she called, reining

Kachina over to a stand of lodgepole pines.

He shifted in the saddle, glowering at her. "We keep riding," he said. "Or I leave you here."

"I need a few minutes," she said again.

He nudged Shoshone into a gallop, the pack horse keeping pace on the lead rope tied to Shoshone's saddle horn. Callie swore. The war of wills was on. She wasn't going to take a month of this. Slamming her heels into Kachina's sides, she put the mare into a hard run. Coming up alongside the stallion, she leaned over and grabbed hold of Shoshone's reins.

Trace pulled up, his eyes blazing with fury. "Don't ever do that again."

"Then don't leave me alone in this wilderness."

"You do what I tell you, and you'll be fine."

"Dammit, Trace!" she hissed. "I didn't lose Christopher! The judge took him away. And you can just damned well stop taking it out on me!"

He was off his horse and moving toward her. Without a word he dragged her from the saddle. For a moment she feared he meant to strike her. Her terror then was greater than any she had ever known, for it went beyond fear for her safety. If Trace dared harm her physically, he would destroy in an instant any chance they had to overcome the agony that lay between them. She could never forgive him.

But he only gripped her arm, propelling her toward a nearby tree stump. "Sit."

She sat, arms folded across her chest. She felt a renewed hope that no matter how much anger and pain he unleashed on her verbally, somehow she could overcome it—if she only had the time.

"I want you to get something straight," he said.

"I'm listening." She met his angry gaze without flinching.

"I'm taking you to Yellowstone, because I made you a promise. That's all. It means nothing else. Absolutely nothing. The marriage is over. Done."

"I know."

"When we get back Lyle will have everything in order. All we'll have to do is sign the papers, and our lives will go on as though we'd never met."

"I know."

"And nothing you say or do during this little treasure hunt of yours is going to change that. Do you understand?"

"Yes."

He slapped a hand against his thigh. "And don't think your little submissive act is fooling me one damned bit."

She nodded. "Whatever you say, Trace."

He swore viciously, storming over to Shoshone. The horse shied as Trace snapped up the reins. "Easy," Trace said, though his voice was charged with irritation. The stallion was not fooled, pawing the ground nervously. Trace threw off the pack horse's lead and vaulted into the saddle.

Callie remained on the stump, waiting. She had to know if Trace really could leave her out here alone. She was still close enough to Shadow's Way should she be forced to find her own way back.

Trace drove his heels into Shoshone's sides, sending the stallion thundering away. Callie made no move to follow.

A half hour passed. An hour. Then two.

She built a small fire and made herself some coffee. Three hours later Trace rode in.

"Get enough rest?" he gritted.

She betrayed not the slightest hint at how grateful she was to see him. Another fifteen minutes and she would have conceded defeat and headed back to the ranch, knowing any chance they had together was gone. No matter how much the initial burden of salvaging their relationship fell to her, she could not succeed without his ultimate cooperation. If he couldn't bear to be with her for even one day, the outlook for their trek was all but hopeless.

But the very fact that he'd agreed to the trip at all had been the first real thread of hope she'd had to cling to since the custody hearing. He could have refused, sent her packing, and she could have done nothing to stop him. But he had agreed. Consciously or unconsciously, he had committed himself to being alone with her for at least a month.

He would initiate nothing personal between them, of that she was certain, and in fact would likely counter any such gestures on her part with cynicism and rejection. But if she'd learned nothing else these past months with Trace, it was that she possessed a heretofore unsuspected reserve of patience. That he would test that patience to the limit she had no doubt. But she had prepared herself for that challenge and would not be undone their first day on the trail.

"Get on Kachina and ride," he grumbled.

"I think we'd best address a few ground rules about this journey first."

"No. I set the rules."

"I am not going to spend the next four weeks being

bullied by you, just because you know the terrain and I don't. We can stay on this very spot until the snow flies for all I care. I'm not moving until you promise you're not going to be a jackass."

His jaw set in that stubborn line she knew so well. "You want polite, I'll give you polite." He raised his hat in a mock salute. "If madam would be so kind as to mount up and accompany me?"

She swallowed a biting retort. "I'd be delighted, sir." It was going to be a long month.

They headed north, Trace holding the pace to less bone-jolting canter. Callie held no illusions that she'd made so much as a chink in his defensive armor. Rather she worried that she'd widened the breach between them. Trace was polite all right, insufferably polite.

On their third day they crossed the southern border into Yellowstone. She slowed Kachina to a walk, reveling in the exhilaration of simply being there. "So many years of dreaming," she murmured, turning to Trace. "Thank you."

He shrugged. "Just paying off a debt."

She ignored his sarcasm. "It feels almost sacred," she said, staring out at mile after mile of pine-bristled slopes—lodgepole, Douglas fir, ponderosa, and more. "Like I'm in a church. God's very own cathedral."

He looked at her, his eyes unreadable, then seemed to shake himself. "Let's just keep moving. We've got plenty of daylight left."

"In a minute. I want to show you something." She reached behind her, opening her saddlebags and pulling out the worn photo Willliam Henry Jackson had given her in his hotel room that long ago day. For the first time since her wagon broke down she felt a flush of excitement at the thought of searching for the stolen gold.

She handed the photograph to Trace, watching him study the picture she knew by heart. Five men—four of them members of the Hayden Expedition—were standing to the left of a huge spherical rock. The fifth, wearing a military uniform and standing a full head taller than the others, stood off a pace, as though he had been about to bolt. She shivered, recalling Jackson's description of the demented soldier.

"Private Jeffrey Burns," she told Trace. "He was moving away while Jackson was taking the picture. That's why his features are so blurred, though he still looks like he's snarling."

"Obviously he didn't like having his picture taken." Trace gave the photograph back to her. "Do you really think you're going to find a wagonload full of gold?"

"It was always my intention," she grinned. "Somehow Yellowstone wasn't quite as vast in my imagination as it seems to be in fact. I thought we could start by looking for the rock in that picture. That's where the Hayden Expedition crossed paths with Burns and Mason."

"I remember the stories," Trace said. "I was fourteen when it all happened." He scratched his chin, remembering. "Mason was the lieutenant in charge of the shipment, right?"

"Right. He was shot by the thief, a Sergeant Hogan."

"Who also killed this man Burns's brother."

Callie was pleased that Trace's version so closely followed the one she'd heard from Jackson. Legends had a way of twisting and turning according to the whim of the tale-spinner. "Burns went berserk after seeing his brother murdered."

"And he went after Hogan . . ."

"Killing him before anyone found out where Hogan had hidden the money."

Trace shook his head. "There's always something that bothered me about that. Hogan had less than a day's head start. How could he 'bury' a wagon full of gold?"

"You told me once you thought it could have gone to the bottom of one of the hot springs."

"Maybe."

"Jackson told me Burns is still supposed to be out here somewhere—looking for the money, or maybe haunting the place."

"We'll just look for his ghost then. I figure it'll be easier to find than that wagon." He gigged Shoshone into a trot, effectively ending the longest conversation they'd had since leaving the ranch.

She kept pace, asking questions about the park as they occurred to her. Trace was brusque but informative—surprising her with his knowledge of the park's geological beginnings.

Days and nights blended together in an awe-filled journey of discovery. Callie was struck by the contrasts of the country's first national park. Nature ruled here—wild, untamed. Geysers, plains, marshlands, forests, sulphurous mud holes and pristine lakes coexisted over two million acres of virgin wilderness. A rainbow array of wildflowers dappled the hillsides, while nearly everywhere she looked she saw a different variety of bird or animal. Sounds rivaled sights as she delighted in the shrill, musical rattle of the sandhill crane, the bugling of a bull elk, the mournful cry of a coyote.

She was feeling a little mournful herself as they made camp one night, their twelfth in the park. Finished with a supper of cornbread and beans, she poured herself a second cup of coffee and settled into her blankets across the campfire from him. Things were just not progressing between them.

"I want to thank you again for bringing me here," she said. "Riley was a fine guide, but you seem so at home here."

He looked up from his side of the fire. "I should. I spent a lot of time here when I was a boy."

She had expected no more than a grunt or a nod. Heaven knew she'd received little else these past two weeks, whenever the topic shifted to any kind of personal level. "When you . . . left home?"

"Ran away," he corrected dispassionately.

"You came up here alone?"

He nodded.

"How old were you?"

"I think the first time I was eight."

"My God." She looked around, feeling the very vastness of the park suddenly press in on her. "You were alone in this wilderness when you were eight years old? How could your father allow . . ." She stopped. "I'm sorry."

"He never followed. Even Seth would only track me so far. I guess they figured if I didn't get myself killed, I'd come back on my own eventually. Or maybe they hoped I wouldn't."

Callie winced. Even when he didn't realize it, he was telling her how much he hurt.

From somewhere off to the right she caught the unmistakable grunt of a bear. She felt the blood drain from her face.

Trace was around the fire in an instant, rifle in hand, settling himself beside her. "Don't worry. Nothing's going to hurt you. I swear."

She managed a shaky smile. "I'm all right."

The shuffling noise receded into the night. Still, Callie did not relax. When Trace's arm curved around her shoulders, she burrowed into the crook of his arm. "I'm sorry. I don't mean to be a coward."

She felt the warmth of his breath on the top of her head. "You're the bravest woman—hell, one of the bravest people I've ever met."

Still, she couldn't relax, the memory of claws tearing into her back too fresh, too real. "Don't leave me tonight. Please."

She felt him stiffen, but didn't withdraw her plea. She was battling an all but irrational terror. If he hadn't been holding her, she couldn't be certain that she wouldn't already be hysterical.

"All right," he said, his voice oddly strained.

His arms surrounding her, they lay down. Gradually her fear subsided, to be replaced by a spreading contentment. She snuggled against him, taking pleasure in his ragged moan. Her hand glided along his shirt-sleeve, feeling the rippling play of muscles as he tensed, then relaxed.

"Don't. Callie, please, don't."

Reluctantly, she ceased. She wasn't being fair. But then her heart didn't care about fair. Touching him like this, all she wanted in the world was to recapture the magic of that night in the valley he'd been able to subdue his private demons and truly make love to her. With a heavy sigh she allowed herself to drift off into a restless sleep.

In the morning he was once again cold, aloof, as remote as the snow-capped peaks in the distance.

There's still time, she told herself as she saddled Kachina. He couldn't keep the walls up forever. If she couldn't get him to take them down, she would just plow right through them.

She tightened the cinch. "Maybe it's time to escalate the battle."

He'd held himself in check last night, but she sensed it hadn't been easy for him. If she had her way, it would become more difficult still. His stoicism only kept his pain trapped inside him. Until he gave vent to the hurt, his withdrawal from her, from the world could only grow worse. Like the geysers that bubbled and boiled below Yellowstone's surface, the pressure would build in him until it reached intolerable levels. She intended to force the inevitable explosion. She only prayed she wasn't making a mistake, that the resulting catharsis would heal him—not destroy him.

Trace perched himself on a weathered log across the camp from Callie. It had been all he could do not to make love to her last night when she had been frightened by the bear. He sat there now, watching her sleep, cursing himself to hell and back for ever agreeing to this blasted treasure hunt. What difference would one more lie, one more broken promise have made? He should have refused to go along with her and spared himself the torment.

He ached for her, physically—with a need to hold her, bury himself inside her; emotionally—with a gut-wrenching longing that threatened to split him in two.

445

More and more he sensed her need to draw him out, to make him face his feelings for her, for Christopher. Her prodding was subtle, gentle—and agonizingly painful. Today when she'd suggested they send a present for Christopher's fourth birthday coming up in two months, his response had been an angry curse, but instead of putting her off, she had seemed almost pleased.

"Damn!" He raked a hand through his tawny hair. Why couldn't she just leave it alone? Why did she seem determined to provoke him—one way or the other?

He studied her slender form huddled under her blankets, his gaze caressing the gentle curves. God, how he wanted her. He swore his poor besotted body had been in a near constant state of arousal ever since he'd first laid eyes on the woman. The irony was that he knew she would be willing should he but ask. But he was also certain she would be willing only because she would feel sorry for him.

He stood, pacing, frustrated, shoving off the bitter-sweet fantasy of going to her, kissing her awake, taking whatever surcease he could in the sweet warmth of her body, no matter what her reason for allowing it.

Instead he stalked off several yards, twigs snapping under his feet in counterpoint to the gentle soughing of the wind through the moon-shrouded pines.

His thoughts leapfrogged from Callie to Christopher and back again. How had everything gone so wrong? If Judge Lancaster had lived just one more day . . .

Had he won Christopher he might have believed in himself enough to risk courting Callie, risk asking her to stay. But Thompson had declared him unfit to raise the child he loved more than his own life. Unfit to be a parent to Christopher, unfit to be a husband to Callie.

He cursed again, hating his own cloying self-pity, yet feeling so confused and lost that he couldn't begin to bring himself out of it. To face his feelings to allow them free rein was to be open, vulnerable, exposed—something he had not allowed in his life for a long time.

"Even from the grave you twist my life, Pa," he murmured, remembering that final, fateful fight . . .

"Pa's willin' to forget you stole the money," Seth had told him. "Come back home with me, you'll see."

Trace shook his head, pacing nervously near his Appaloosa stallion. He'd stayed away from the ranch for four months now, ever since his father had threatened him with prison for stealing a hundred dollars. "You know he's lying, Seth. I don't dare go back. He'll have the sheriff on me in a minute."

"No, he promised me."

Trace faced his brother squarely. "I'm sixteen years old. Pa has hated my guts every one of those sixteen years. Nothing could have changed that in a month."

"It isn't going to be perfect," Seth said, "but he won't have you arrested. He swore."

In the end Trace relented, returning to Shadow's Way, some tiny spark of hope still burning somewhere inside him that he could at last make peace with his father. Terrified, yet determined, Trace had insisted Seth wait in the ranchyard, while he went in alone to face his father.

The elder McCord stood in front of the fireplace. He waited until Trace was less than three feet away from him. Trace hadn't even seen it coming. From nowhere his father raised his right hand, a three-foot leather strap hissing through the air to crack into the left side of Trace's skull. Trace went to his knees, pain lancing through him.

"Thief! Scum!" Jeb McCord raged.

Trace groaned, raising a hand in self-defense. Jeb brought the strap down again. Trace rolled away. "Pa, please. Don't do this." He tried once, twice, to rise, then sagged back to the floor. He tasted the salty sweetness of his own blood, only vaguely aware when Seth burst into the room.

"Pa, what the hell have you done? You swore you'd talk to him."

"Talk to him? He isn't fit to breathe the same air as decent folk. He should never have been born. God's curse, that's what he is!"

"He's your son."

"He put your mother in her grave." Jeb McCord talked to his oak desk, yanking open the center drawer. He raised the long-barreled Colt.

"Pa, for God's sake!" Seth shouted.

Trace pushed himself to his feet, swaying drunkenly. "Go ahead, old man. Put us both out of our misery!"

"Pa, you can't do this!" Seth said. His voice grew desperate. "Think, Pa. Think. If you really want to punish him, send him to jail."

"I'll send him to hell!" He lunged at Trace. Trace side-stepped, bringing up his arm instinctively as Jeb brought the gun to bear. The shot echoed, deafening in the small room, slamming into the iron hasp hinging the door.

Jeb's eyes widened with surprise and pain. Without a sound he slumped to the floor.

Trace stared at his father, at the spreading red stain across his middle.

"Jesus," Seth said, leaning down, "the bullet ricocheted. Help me with him."

Trace backed away.

"Trace, help me."

"They'll hang me."

"Don't be stupid. It was an accident. Besides, he's not dead. Help me with him."

Trace continued to stagger back. "What did I ever do? What did I ever do to be hated so much . . . what . . ." Whirling, he ran from the house. It took a posse just two days to track him down.

Trace rose, shaking off the unsettling memories. He would sell the ranch, drift, maybe build a shack in the mountains, hunt, trap.

Run away. The voice was Callie's. He looked at her. She was still asleep. *Run away, that's what you'd be doing. It's what you're doing now.* The words were as clear as if she had spoken.

"Don't let me run away, Callie," he murmured. "God help me, I don't want to run anymore."

Callie shifted in her blankets, coming awake slowly, wondering what had disturbed her. She sat up, rubbing awareness into her chilled limbs. Her brows furrowed, her gaze skittering across the camp to Trace. He was staring at her, the darkness preventing any true impressions of his shadowed features. "Did you say something?"

"No."

She climbed to her feet, settling the blanket shawl-like over her shoulders. "What is it?"

"Nothing."

She moved toward him. "Want to talk about it?"

"Dammit, leave it alone. Leave *me* alone."

"If you really wanted me to do that, you wouldn't have come with me on this trip." She could see his face now, his eyes reflecting an odd mingling of fear and hope. Fear that he might appear foolish in front of her, hope that she wouldn't turn her back on him, no matter how hard he tried to push her away.

"Just go back to sleep."

"I would, if I thought that's what you really wanted." She longed to touch him, but feared he would retreat back inside himself if he did. "I think you want to talk. And I happen to be here."

He shook his head. "I'm not worth the trouble."

"You're worth everything." She kept her voice low, soothing, as she crossed the camp to sit on a log not far from where Trace stood. "I think you're a very special man. You've been hurt by the people who should care about you most. And maybe you were too sensitive for your own good. You kept getting hurt so you turned it all inside. You made yourself the bad guy. Well, you're not. Look at what you've done with the ranch. It's a success, because of you. Look at Christopher."

Raw pain flashed across his face.

"Yes, I'm going to talk about him. He's not dead. And one day you're going to have him back."

"Just leave it be. Dammit, I shouldn't have . . ." He didn't finish, tramping over to the log instead. "Go back to sleep, Callie. Please."

She sighed heavily. "You really don't understand, do you? I can't let it be. I can't let you be. When you hurt, I hurt." She swallowed, then plunged on before her courage fled. "I love you. I love you, Trace McCord.

And there's nothing you can do to stop me. No matter how you run yourself down, or yell at me, or spend your time being a jackass, I'll keep right on loving you."

"You don't know anything about me."

"Don't I? Your mother abandoned you by dying, your father rejected you for living, you were never sure where you stood with your brother . . . Personally, I don't know how you turned out as well as you have.

"You crave closeness, yet sabotage anyone's attempts to be close to you."

"I don't need anybody." His voice shook.

"That's all right. Because someday you will." She patted the log beside her, waiting until he relented and sat down. She didn't look at him as she continued to speak. "You're a man who needs other people in his life, people who you can care about, people to care about you. I know you can't deal with that right now. But you see, I love you enough for both of us, and I'll wait. For as long as it takes, I'll wait.

"Until you believe what I tell you is the truth. That I love you. With all your faults, all your flaws, I love you. Not in spite of them. But because all that you were, all that you've been through is what makes you Trace McCord, the man I want to spend the rest of my life with."

"You don't deserve a man like me."

She smiled. "I suppose not. I'm opinionated, stubborn . . . Heaven knows what kind of man I do deserve. But since I love *you* . . ."

He pulled her into his arms. "Hold me, hold me."

She could feel the desperation in him, and she knew he would make love to her tonight. For a brief moment

451

she worried about what would happen afterward, if she let him. Would he be angry, embarrassed, ashamed at having let down his defenses, no matter how briefly?

But as his hold on her tightened, his need transferred itself to her, and she knew she would be strong enough, no matter what the morning might bring. She loved him.

"Callie . . ." His words were broken, fragments. "They took him . . . they took my little boy . . . oh, God, Callie, it hurts so much . . . it hurts . . . I can't . . . I need somebody, I need you. But I'm afraid . . . afraid . . ."

He tried to turn away, but it was too late. His body was fire, and she was fuel to his flame. He cried out, his fingers working the buttons of her shirt. "Callie, Callie, love me. Please, just for tonight, love me."

She uncinched his belt buckle, slipping her hand inside the waistband of his jeans. She reveled in his throaty moan as her fingers closed around the throbbing core of his sex. She couldn't take away the pain of his losing Christopher, couldn't take away all the lifetime of hurt he'd suffered at the hands of his father, but for now, for this tiny space of time she could make him forget everything, everyone in the world but her.

"I love you, Trace," she murmured. "Right here. Right now. I love you."

Her hands slid upward, gliding across his chest, teasing his nipples.

"Don't talk," he rasped. "Don't promise. Don't say anything. Just take from me. Let me take from you. Hold me. Let me hold you."

He bore her down into the carpet of soft grasses,

peeling away her clothes and his o
both naked, ready. His lips roved h
denied him nothing. He found the t
her passion and stroked her to madr
his mouth, all that he was.

She gasped, whimpered, pleaded,
ing in his hair, holding him to his sensual task. For long
minutes her body quivered in the aftershocks of her
release.

His body was primed past endurance just watching
her. If he held back another minute he would shatter
apart. But when he sought to enter her, she gently
pressed him back.

"It's my turn to pleasure you," she murmured.
"Whatever you want, whatever you need, tell me and
I'll do it for you."

He lay back, trembling, not daring to give voice to
the fantasy that filled his mind. He couldn't ask it of
her. Though she was bold and eager and passionate,
she was no courtesan, practiced in the art of fulfilling
erotic dreams.

"Tell me," she whispered again, "I want to please
you."

"You please me by being here, by . . ." The words
wouldn't come. There were no words adequate enough
to tell her what she meant to him. And in the next
instant it didn't matter, as her mouth tracked across the
taut muscles of his belly, nipping, biting, licking.

"Maybe if I did for you what you did for me," she
said, her mouth exploring lower still.

"I can't ask you to . . ."

Her hand captured the rigid core of his sex, her
mouth tasting, testing, teasing, until he thought surely

being could endure such excruciatingly
torment.

a cry of animal need he raised up, gripping her
and forcing her beneath him. In one powerful
unge he made himself part of her. An undescribable
joy spread outward from the center of his soul. She was
his. For this time, for this place she was his. He would
give her all that he had because in his heart he believed
he would never have her this way again.

Her own passion surged out of control, her body
bucking upward, her legs twining round his hips to
snare him to her. "Love me," she cried. "Trace, love me.
Now."

He gasped, shuddered, plunged, his thrusts rhythmic, savage. He gloried in the feel of her fingernails
raking the sweat-drenched flesh of his back. She was as
free, as wanton, as driven to please and be pleased as
any fantasy he could ever have dreamed.

Primal, fierce, awesome, the power of their passion
consumed them, until they both surrendered to the
swirling, blinding light of their loving.

The next morning she woke to feel his eyes on her.
His regret was already all too apparent. Pressing her
fingers to his lips, she whispered, "Don't apologize for
needing me last night. I needed you just as much."

His eyes were overbright. He twisted away from her.
"I'm sorry. I want so much to love . . ." He stopped.
"Never mind."

You do love me, she wanted to say but didn't. So
many old wounds had been opened, many still
bleeding. He would need to curl up inside himself for a
while. But she had all the patience in the world now.

He rose to his feet, no longer meeting her gaze.

"We'd better get after that treasure of yours."

As they rode out, the silences between them at least were less awkward. She knew Trace was still smarting from revealing too much of himself, but he wasn't taking it out on her. In fact, she suspected if he were given a choice he would change nothing of what happened last night.

Toward noon she reined to a stop, peering off toward a ridge to the west. "I've had the strangest feeling this morning," she said.

"What's that?"

"That we're . . . being watched."

"That's because we are."

"What?" She looked around wildly. "By whom? Why didn't you say something."

"It's only your fiancé, the count."

She grimaced. "He's not my fiancé. And how long have you known he was there."

"Since about dawn."

"Why do you suppose he's keeping his distance?"

"You know him better than I do."

She thought about that a long minute as they continued to traverse a tree-studded slope. "Actually, I don't know him well at all. My father introduced us. Da was impressed by Nicolas's social position, and Nicolas always seemed to know the right thing to say."

Trace said nothing, and Callie had the impishly pleasant sensation that the man was jealous.

"I suppose Nicolas's self-assuredness wasn't so odd," she went on. "I met him while he was indulging 'a whim,' as he called it. He was part of a repertory company. An actor. I thought it peculiar that a man of his noble lineage should choose such an avocation, but

455

he relished the theater."

"My God!" Trace nearly set Shoshone back on his haunches. "Look!"

Callie followed the direction of his finger—a tumbling waterfall next to a peculiar-looking spherical rock.

Trace was already off Shoshone, scrambling along the rock-strewn slope, sidestepping boulders, breaking into a run.

Callie hurried after him. When she caught up to him, she was gasping for breath. "This is the rock in the picture, isn't it?"

Trace was running his hands along the seemingly solid wall of rock to the right of the sphere. Up close there was a fissure that ran the length of two side-by-side gigantic boulders. She and Trace had to scramble to the top of the one on the left before they could find enough space to maneuver through.

"It's pitch-black in here. I'd better go after a couple of torches." He retreated, returning in minutes with two knotty pine firebrands.

The flames split the blackness with an eerie, guttering light. The dank, closed-in smell of the place permeated even the rocks. The cavern snaked back more than a hundred yards. They walked along, their feet making a squishing noise.

"Be damned careful," Trace warned. "There's a dropoff here. A fissure that may not hit bottom till you hit hell."

Callie clung to Trace, ill at ease in the closed-in dampness of the fissure. When Trace halted abruptly, she stumbled into him. "What . . ."

He held the torch high. Callie gasped. Just ahead sat

the remains of a wagon, its canvas top rotting, moss covered. The black letters U.S. ARMY were stenciled across the side boards.

Trace let out a long, low whistle. "I don't believe it."

They took a step toward it. Out of the corner of her eye Callie noticed something in the shadows. "Trace, over there. Hold the light . . ."

Lying six feet left of the wagon, a boulder smashing its left leg was what was left of a uniformed skeleton.

"The late Sergeant Hogan," Trace pronounced.

"It was here all the time. Right under their noses. How could that be?"

"I don't know. I can't even figure how that wagon got in here. Unless there was some kind of tremor . . ."

Callie's brows furrowed as she searched her memory. "Of course! Jackson said there was a tremor the day before they came upon Burns and Mason. Hogan could have already driven the wagon in here." She clapped her hands together. "Bang! Earthquake and it swallows him up before Burns and Mason can . . ." She paused, frowning. "But that can't be."

"What?"

"The legend, the story Jackson told me. Hogan didn't disappear . . ."

"He was supposed to have been killed by the demented Burns. Tossed into a hot spring as I recall. Lieutenant Mason told Jackson the whole story."

She stared at the tattered sergeant's uniform, the skeletal hand curved around a gold bar, as though the man had been caressing it when the quake hit. "But Hogan died with the money. Why would Mason tell Jackson that he'd seen Burns kill Hogan?"

"Why else?" came a low, menacing voice from

directly behind them.

Callie whirled, stunned. "Nicolas!" Trace had been right. Her eyes widened as he pulled a gun from beneath his jacket and leveled it at her. "Nicolas, for the love of God, what—"

"Don't hurt her." Trace's voice was a deadly whisper.

"I'm giving the orders, horseherder," Nicolas said. He chuckled, looking at Callie. "Count Nicolas von Endenberg—perhaps my best part ever. After all, I've been playing it for a very long time." The studied, polished veneer dropped away. "Almost as long as I've been looking for that wagon."

Callie felt a chill bone deep.

Trace swore, taking a menacing step forward.

Nicolas leveled the gun at Trace's middle.

"You're well schooled in the Yellowstone legend, are you not, Callie darling?" Nicolas asked, his grin somehow malevolent in the torchlight.

"You know I am."

"Then you must recall the leader of that ill-fated troop."

"Of course. It was Mason. Lieutenant Mason. But I hardly see what that—"

He levered back the hammer on the Colt, bowing ever so slightly. "Lieutenant Everett Thaddeus Mason to be precise."

Chapter Twenty-Eight

Callie stared at the gun in Nicolas's hand, its barrel seeming more illusion than real in the flickering light of the torch. "Nicolas, what are you talking about? Mason is dead. He was shot. He died of his . . ." She stopped, trembling suddenly at the sight of blue eyes now glittering dangerously.

"Mason is not dead, Callandra, my dear," he said, his voice strangely soft, silken. "Didn't you hear what I said? *I* am Mason."

She shook her head. "That doesn't make any sense." She took a hesitant step toward him. "Listen, I know you're angry about my marrying Trace."

He laughed, an eerily indulgent laugh. "I couldn't possibly care less whose bed you share, my dear."

Trace stiffened.

"All I've ever cared about was that wagon and what's in it."

"Then what—" She stopped again, thoroughly confused.

"Take the money," Trace put in. "And let Callie get

on her horse and ride out of here."

"I believe I'm the one holding the gun," Nicolas said. "That means I give the orders."

Trace took a sideways step, positioning himself between Callie and the count. "I said let her go."

"We had it all planned," Nicolas went on, as though speaking to himself. "Burns, Hogan, and I. Down to the last detail. But Hogan got greedy. Drove off with the wagon after he shot me."

Callie still wasn't convinced this wasn't some elaborate charade Nicolas was playing out to pay her back finally for humiliating him at the altar. "This is all absurd, Nicolas. William Henry Jackson told me Mason died."

"An honest mistake. It was widely reported that I had passed on. In fact, it was six months before I was even out of my sick bed."

"I don't believe you. If this wagon was your goal, what on earth were you doing in New York?"

"I searched for the money for over a year actually. Then I spent another five looking for Burns. I was certain he knew where it was, that he'd found it while I was out of my head with fever. But I couldn't locate him either. I just gradually moved east. In New York I heard through various social circles that you were interested in the Yellowstone legend. Your father had even sponsored successful treasure hunts in the past. If I could ingratiate myself to Fletcher Callaghan, to you . . ."

"But you're a wealthy man!"

"I have nothing. A title bought and paid for. A pittance really. I lived out a fable of my own making. People invited me to their estates. I can't remember the

460

last time I had to pay for anything in New York."

"Isn't living the life you want the same as having it?"

"No. I killed for this." He gestured toward the wagon. "I want it. I intend to have it."

"Even if it means killing for it."

"Whatever it means."

A dawning realization stole over her, terrified her. "Then the story you and Burns told Jackson was a lie. Burns didn't kill Hogan. In fact, he never found him."

"We had to tell the Hayden people something. We didn't want them looking for the gold."

She shivered. "Then you and Burns are . . ." she stumbled over the word, "murderers."

"We all have our little quirks, darling."

"Was Burns even crazy? Or was that for the explorers' benefit, too?"

"Oh, he was crazy all right. Burns threw his brother into a geyser pool. I think that's what sent him over the edge."

He cast an expansive glance around the dim chamber. "This is a perfect place, really. I can shoot you and have your bodies remain hidden another twelve years. Maybe forever." He rubbed the barrel of the pistol along the side of his cheek. "Keep our greedy Sergeant Hogan company. However, a short reprieve might be in order. After all, I don't want to do a lot of heavy work myself. Both of you can start carrying the money outside."

Callie followed Trace over to the wagon. He hefted one of the heavy chests, whispering urgently. "I'm going to distract him. I want you to get on your horse and ride out of here as fast and as far as you can."

"I won't leave you."

"Dammit, don't argue with me. Not now. He's going to kill us."

Nicolas kept the gun on them as they carried their burdens out into the sunlight. "Put them over there by that tree," he said, gesturing toward a massive cottonwood whose gnarled roots extended halfway across the creek.

Callie started toward the tree, then stopped, gasping at the sight that greeted her. A body lay slung across the saddle of Nicolas's horse.

Reese.

She watched Trace's fists clench, his body go rigid with rage. "Why the hell would you attack a simpleton? He couldn't hurt you."

"Oh, how wrong you are." Nicolas dragged the body from the horse. It fell heavily. "A hard man to kill, I must say. Finally I found a pit of rattlesnakes this morning. So appropriate."

"Why?" Callie cried. "What threat was he to you?"

"How twisted together our lives have become," he murmured, almost to himself. "Don't you see? Reese was the one who wrecked your cameras, my dear. Though I stole your pictures hoping you had made some notations."

"But why would Reese . . . ?"

"Reese wasn't his real name. It was his brother's name. Reese Burns."

Callie stared at the crumpled figure, recalling the blurred image in her photographs. A large man, dark, demented. "Reese is . . . ?"

"Private Jeffrey Zachariah Burns," Nicolas supplied. "Though he hasn't been aware of that fact for about twelve years now. When I found him wandering

462

on your cowboy's range I nearly went out of my mind. I was sure he'd found the gold while I was recovering from my wound, and just hadn't told me where he hid it."

"Reese was like a child," Trace gritted. "He wouldn't harm anyone. In fact, he saved my life in prison."

"Maybe now he's docile," Nicolas said. "But the day of the robbery he was anything but. Now he claimed not to even remember it. He couldn't even remember why he'd been sent to jail, though he did recall that he didn't like having his picture taken. Thought it was some kind of way to steal his soul."

Callie suddenly knew who had made her feel uneasy that day in the meadow when she was taking Christopher's picture.

"I stole your photographs," Nicolas said, "looking for this one." He held up the Jackson photo that had led them to the cavern. "I was too sick to have any recall of where I was the day Hayden and his group overtook Burns and me. I should have known you'd keep it in a special place. Signed by Jackson himself." He laughed, a strange, sick sound. "To think we were on top of it. If not for that damned quake . . ." He shook himself. "Back to the chamber, both of you. Now."

Callie and Trace went inside, Nicolas following, anchoring the torch between two closely spaced rocks. Even so, the light barely reached the back of the wagon. The yawning abyss ahead of them looked more like a portal to hell. "I'm going to jump him," Trace whispered. "Be ready."

Her heart pounded, the very real possibility that Trace would be killed suddenly slamming home. "Let me try again. I could reason with him."

"You can't reason with a snake."

Nicolas stayed on their heels. "I always wondered where Hogan could have gotten in such a hurry. Such a large wagon, so bulky, weighted down with the gold."

"So now you've got the money," Trace said. "Let us go."

"No, no, I've spent too much effort establishing this identity. I like being royalty. I have the look, don't you think? And now I'll have the money to go with it."

Trace carried out another strongbox. "You can't get it out of here without a wagon."

"I've taken care of that eventuality. I'll merely bury all this, then ride back to your ranch for a wagon." He jerked the gun toward the fissure. "Back to work. Both of you."

"Don't hurt her, Mason."

"Oh, of course not, my boy. At least not yet. Why spoil my fun?"

"Have you ever killed a woman?"

"As a matter of fact, I have."

Callie's blood ran cold.

Trace stared at him. "What woman?"

"I think you know. It was such a shame, really, that your late wife recognized me as a former . . . customer, shall we say, from her Montana fort days."

Trace lunged at Nicolas. "You son of a bitch!" he roared. Nicolas leaped aside, bringing the pistol barrel down behind Trace's ear.

"No!" Callie screamed, rushing to Trace's side. "Nicolas, stop. Please."

Trace was on his hands and knees. Callie put her arm around his shoulders. "Don't fight him anymore,

Trace. Please."

Rubbing a hand across the rising welt along the side of his head, he climbed groggily to his feet. "Why would you kill Lanie, you bastard? She never meant anyone any real harm."

"She wanted to blackmail me. Very unwise." He waved the gun at them. "None of that matters now anyway. I have more important things at hand. Like which one of you wants to be first? Which shall watch the other die?" He shifted the gun toward Trace. "After that sentimental display of marrying this convict for the sake of the child, darling, I think I'll allow you the pleasure of watching your husband die first."

"No, I beg you."

"Callie . . ." Trace didn't want her pleading for his life.

"Whatever you want, Nicolas. Please."

He gave her a derisive look. "It's too late for that offer, my dear."

Trace used the distraction to slam into Nicolas, sending both men sprawling.

Callie bolted for Trace's gun. Nicolas tore free of Trace, firing at Callie. Trace cursed, heaving himself bodylong at the blond aristocrat. They grappled, fought, rolled. Nicolas rammed his fist into Trace's face. Trace went to one knee. As Nicolas sensed the kill, Trace drove himself upward, launching himself at Nicolas's middle.

The count stumbled backward, collapsing against the rusted iron rim of the wagon's rear wheel, his rifle clattering to the rock floor. Nicolas dove for it as Trace scrambled after him.

Callie grabbed up Trace's pistol, bringing it to bear

on Nicolas. She waited for a clear shot, the torch offering precious little light as the two men fought their deadly battle. She only vaguely noted an odd, scraping noise coming from the direction of the fissure opening.

"Stop, Nicolas!" she cried. "Stop or I'll kill you."

"You won't stop me from having what I deserve!" he cried. "I've waited too long." He swung the rifle toward her.

In that instant Callie fired. She missed.

"No!" Trace threw himself between Nicolas and Callie just as Nicolas squeezed the trigger. Trace's body jerked, his momentum catapulting him forward. He seemed to try to catch himself, then toppled over the abyss. Callie watched him disappear, her eyes wide with a horror such as she'd never known. She screamed, a mindless, keening sound that drove her to her knees.

Nicolas straightened. An evil leer split his face. Slowly he levered another cartridge into the rifle's chamber. Callie couldn't move, didn't want to, as she stared at the edge of the pit.

Nicolas leveled his gun at her head.

A strange, guttural noise caught her ear. Even in the depths of her torment, Callie turned to look. Her heart stopped.

Reese. Huge, lumbering, wild-eyed.

Insane.

The bear-sized man heaved himself into the chamber.

Nicolas squeezed the trigger. Reese's body slowed only for a second, a red stain spotting his chest. Nicolas shot him again. "Dead!" he shrieked.

He shot again.

Reese's hands closed around Nicolas's throat. The two men stumbled back. Nicolas's high-pitched scream slammed off the walls of rock. Together they went over the edge of the precipice.

The silence of death. Callie sat there alone in the darkness. It was a long time before she moved, then finally she knew what she had to do.

Crawling, sobbing, she made her way to the rim of the abyss. Shaking violently, she peered over into nothingness.

She sat on her knees, screaming, screaming Trace's name until she could scream no more.

Chapter Twenty-Nine

Callie had no idea how much time had passed. She sat on her knees in the darkness, sobbing, the rush of water outside the fissure the only break in the awesome stillness of the cavern. It was because of the water that the other sound did not register at first. She quieted. From what seemed a long way off, she heard a low groan.

Again crawling to the rim of the dropoff, she stared into the blackness. She saw nothing. Dizzy, she leaned back. "Trace. Oh, God, Trace . . ." She bit her lip. He couldn't be dead. Couldn't be.

Groping for the torch, she held it over the opening. Her heart stopped.

His body lay twenty feet below her on a jutting ledge that began and ended in a six-foot-long, four-foot-wide outthrust of rock. If he'd fallen to the left or right . . . "Trace!" Again and again she called to him, willing him to wake up. She lay on her stomach, holding the torch down into the pit as far as she could reach.

She squinted, watching him. His head moved,

shifting from side to side. Her whole body shuddered with relief, until a new terror gripped her. If he awoke, not realizing where he was . . .

"Trace! Don't move. Trace, do you hear me?"

He groaned, moving his arm, his hand flopping over the side of the ledge, dangling above the gaping maw of the abyss.

She lay down the torch. "Do not move."

He shifted, groaned again, started to sit up.

"Lie still, damn you!" she shouted, uncertain how much of what she said penetrated his semiconscious mind.

His eyes opened, comprehension coming slowly. "Damn." He started to rise. "Callie! Callie, where are . . ."

"I'm all right. Nicolas is dead. Lie still, please."

He lay back. "My leg hurts. I must have landed on it wrong."

"I'm going out to get a rope. Be still. Promise me."

"Promise," he mumbled.

She clambered out of the chamber, gathering up the lariat and tying off one end to Shoshone's saddle horn. Hurrying back to the pit, she tossed the rope's other end to Trace.

While she held the torch, Trace maneuvered the rope around his middle. "All right," he called up. "Get me out of here."

In minutes the stallion's strength pulled Trace free of the chasm. He lay on his back, his breathing ragged, his left leg twisted at an unnatural angle.

"Broken," he pronounced unnecessarily.

"This is where I came in," she murmured, the irony washing over her in an odd, *déjà vu* sense of relief.

Trace was here and he was alive. That's all that mattered in the world right now.

Outside in the grasses, she eased him onto a blanket. He sucked in his breath, swearing broadly as he lay back. "You're going to have to set it," he said.

"No. Oh, Trace, I couldn't." She'd watched Deirdre set Riley's leg, but watching and doing were two entirely different things.

"We're over a week from the ranch, maybe longer. There's no one else. If you let it go, I'll be a cripple."

"Trace, please don't ask me."

He gripped her hand, his brown eyes boring into her. "You can do it. You can." He paused, then added, "I trust you, Callie."

She swallowed hard, wishing he trusted her in matters of the heart as easily as he seemed to with his injured leg. "All right," she said. "I'll do it."

Shaking so badly she could hardly draw a breath, she cut away the denim covering his leg and eased off his boot. Though the break was apparent in the ridge of flesh midway up his shin, at least the bone had not broken through the flesh.

She breathed slowly, deliberately, calming herself as Trace twined his hands in the thick grasses on either side of him.

"Do it," he said. "Quick."

Callie wiped the perspiration from her hands. Lifting the leg, she gave herself no time to think about it. She yanked—hard, her skin crawling as she heard the bone snap into place.

Trace's only response was a low grunt, though it was a long minute before any color came back into his face. She fashioned a splint, then sat back to survey her handiwork.

"You did a good job," he said.

"I hope so."

"I won't be able to sit a horse, though. You'll have to make a travois."

While she did so, he slept. She checked on him frequently, fearful that he would develop a fever. She lugged the lost payroll shipment back into the cavern. It had been safe enough there for twelve years. It would be safe again until she could return for it.

She made a supper of beans and biscuits. Trace ate little, falling back to sleep almost at once. Callie watched him, musing on the twists and turns her life had taken since that fateful day she'd seen the wood-burned letters—*Shadow's Way*.

The Yellowstone gold had been so important then. It was her way to make her father take notice of her, recognize her grit and her writing talent all in one package. Now none of it mattered. It wasn't a golden treasure she sought after all. It was this man, Trace McCord, and his son. It was a treasure of the heart that she ached for, would always ache for, until it was hers in the only way it could be—when Trace believed in her love enough to ask her to stay.

She lay down beside him, snuggling close, yet taking care not to interfere with his movement should the leg bother him. She thought he was asleep, but he reached out, twining his fingers with hers. He didn't say anything, but neither did he loose his hold on her as they both drifted off to sleep.

The next day they started back. She helped Trace hop over to the travois she'd rigged up behind Kachina, Shoshone being too high-strung to tolerate the transport device. Callie kept the pace slow. Trace tried not to show it, but Callie knew he was in considerable pain most of the time. She expected him to withdraw inside himself, but instead he seemed to try very hard to be a good patient. His agreeableness continued even after they'd arrived back on Shadow's Way.

Night was falling as she helped him into bed. "Don't fuss," he grumbled. "I'm all right."

"I'll fuss if I want to. Are you hungry?"

"A bit," he admitted.

"I'll just bet." They hadn't eaten since noon. She left the room, heading for the kitchen. As she went about preparing a pot of chicken soup, she paused a long minute simply to rejoice in being home.

Ladling a bowl of the steaming soup, she returned to the bedroom. Trace was sitting, propped up against several pillows. She set the bowl on the bedside table, then sat next to him on the bed. She had to smile. If he could've bolted away from her, he would have. Their trip home had been abysmally platonic. And she feared it would have been so, even if he hadn't injured his leg.

But no more. Their relationship was everything to her. She would do whatever she had to to save it. And if that meant forcing him to once again face emotions he'd rather ignore or bury, then so be it. "It was you holding me when I was sick after the bear attack, wasn't it?" she probed softly.

He looked uncomfortable. "You were hurting, what did you expect me to do?"

"You did just fine." She linked her hand to his. "People like to be held when they hurt."

He looked away. "I should be on my feet again in a few days."

472

"Are you going to want me to leave then?"

He winced. He had tried not to, but she hadn't missed it. It was a feeble thing on which to pin her hopes, but it was all she had. "I'm tired," he said at last. "I'd like to get some sleep."

"We have to have this conversation eventually. I'm not leaving until we do." She stroked the back of his hand, the warm roughness sending a gentle tide of sensual pleasure through her. "If you want me to go right away, I could send for Aunt Deirdre. I'm sure she and Riley could get away from their new mercantile in Rock Springs long enough to look out for you."

"I can take care of myself."

"Uh huh, you've done a great job so far." She drew in a deep breath. She might as well get it said. "We have to talk about us."

"There's nothing to talk about. It was decided before we ever married, that the marriage would end."

Her heart thudded. "Do you love me?"

"It won't work."

"Do you love me?"

"Chris is gone."

"I'm going to keep asking it, until I get an answer. Do you love me, Trace McCord?"

His eyes grew overbright. His voice was ragged. "You know I do."

She kissed his hand. "Then why do you want me to go?"

"I told you. It won't work."

"Then it's me you don't believe. You don't believe *I* love you."

"I blackmailed you into marrying me. I've been in jail, I've been . . ."

473

She rose to her feet. "I don't give a damn what you've been! I care who you are. The only person who won't forgive you for any wrongs—real or imagined—in your life is you." She paced back and forth at the foot of the bed. "I don't care if you've been in jail. You're not there now. I don't care if you were a thief. You're not a thief now." She planted her hands on her hips. "I love you. And you love me. Yet you want me to leave. Does that make any sense at all?"

"It does to me. I don't want to be hurt again, Callie. Not by anyone. Ever." He slapped at the mattress. "Damn! You couldn't do this to me if I weren't stuck in this bed."

"You aren't above underhanded stunts," she said, coming around the end of the bed to sit beside him again. "Why should I be?"

He didn't answer.

"You're not fooling me, you know," she said gently. "You don't want me gone, any more than I want to leave." She curled her palm over his forearm. "Say it. Damn you, say it."

He twisted the sheets in his hands, not looking at her. He said it then, one word. A word to make her heart soar with hope. A word to terrify her with its potential for failure.

"Stay."

Callie lay beside Trace, taking sweet pleasure in just listening to him breathe. She had held him for hours, long after their mutual need to be in each other's arms eased, and he surrendered to sleep.

They had made love—sweet, tender love without

barriers, without defenses. Because he dared, however tentatively, to trust her with his heart.

Her own body ached from holding his weight for so long. But she would not let go. Not yet. Not yet.

She refused even her own need for sleep that would steal her away from this man she loved. *Stay*—that single word, echoed in her mind. Trace had asked her to stay.

She kissed his forehead, taking care not to wake him. "That's all I've ever wanted," she murmured. The rest could be taken care of—the building of trust, the sharing of feelings, the understanding. Time would make it all right, as long as she had his love and his wanting.

They could begin to be a real family now. She and Trace and . . . Christopher. Thoughts of the child as always were like a knife to her soul. They would get him back. They had to.

But how? Trace had given up, because for Trace even to hope was to plunge himself into despair. They had already waited two months for Lyle Morton and the legal system with no results. It could be months, even years before Chris would be back with them. And what would be happening to the child in the meantime?

Even now he was living with people who didn't love him. The Marlowes would provide him shelter, food, but there had been no hint of love in their desire to gain custody of the child.

The thought that Christopher would grow up even for the tiniest space of time without love—as Trace had done his whole life—tore at her. How long before Chris began to build walls of his own?

Her mind raced. She had to get him back where he

belonged. Now. If Trace was right and all the Marlowes wanted was money, they couldn't be very happy with a small allowance from the inheritance. Maybe, she could buy them off . . .

She shivered, the thought for a moment repulsing her, as she equated it with buying Chris. But that wouldn't be true. She would merely provide the Marlowes with what they had wanted in the first place, while rescuing Christopher from a loveless home.

Callie peered over at Trace, his features shadowed by the moonlight filtering into the room. He slept more peacefully tonight than he had since he'd broken his leg. She wanted to credit that to the fact that she lay beside him, that he'd reached out to her tonight, dared trust her.

She longed to kiss him awake, to make love to him. Fierce, passionate love. But she let him sleep on, oblivious to her growing resolve.

At last the decision was made. Quietly, she crept out of the bed. She had no choice. She had given the law its chance. But her troubling thoughts of Chris tonight, coupled with no news at all from Lyle Morton, gave her no recourse.

She had to go to New York. To her father. He would help. She was certain of that. He would be ecstatic over the story of Nicolas and the treasure. It would sell newspapers by the thousands. Her payment now would not be the byline she had dreamed her goal. Rather it would be her father's power, his influence, his money. Fletcher Callaghan would pay off Edna and Edgar Marlowe and end their claim to Christopher forever. She would have the child home before the autumn leaves had fully turned.

Dawn wasn't quite ready to make its appearance, when Callie finished packing. She swiped at the tears that stung her eyes as she folded the note she'd written Trace, then tucked it in the door of his wardrobe.

He wouldn't understand her going alone. She knew that. And yet he couldn't accompany her, either. His leg would never stand the trip. And if by some horror of fate she should fail to gain custody of Christopher, she could never survive watching Trace leave him behind a second time.

Shrugging into her beaverskin jacket, she turned up the collar against the early fall nip in the air. Hurrying to the barn, she quickly saddled Kachina, then led the mare back to the ranch house. There she retrieved her valise and hooked it over the saddle horn. She mounted, deciding to stop in Rock Springs, tell Deirdre and Riley what she intended to do. They would come out to the ranch and look in on Trace. It would still be a couple of weeks before he was mended well enough to sit a horse.

She was about to ride out, when she thought again of how hurt and angry Trace was going to be when he woke up. She wanted to do whatever she could to ease that pain. Flipping open her valise, she extracted a leatherbound book. Her journal. Her most private thoughts, her most private yearnings. Nearly all of them to do with Trace McCord.

She drew in a deep breath. She wanted him to trust her completely She had to be prepared to do the same with him. Dismounting, she crossed the porch into the house. Padding softly, she headed down the hallway and stole once again into Trace's room.

Her heart ached to see him, his sleep-tousled tawny hair brushing down into his eyes.

"I'm doing this for you," she murmured, "Please know that." She lay the journal on the nightstand, then turned at once to go, fearful her resolve would desert her should she linger. Her leaving would not be painful only for Trace.

Outside she mounted Kachina, the dawn chill seeping into her bones. She didn't look back as she nudged the mare into a canter, leaving the ranch house behind—leaving Trace and Shadow's Way.

Chapter Thirty

Trace scowled darkly as Deirdre set the breakfast tray across his lap on the bed. "I'm not hungry," he said, "I thought I told you that."

"You mentioned it," Deirdre said cheerfully. "But you have to eat. Callie is not going to appreciate coming home to an emaciated husband."

He stiffened, shoving the food tray away from him. "She won't be back. We've already been through that. Just like we've been through my asking you and Riley to leave."

"My niece was adamant," Deirdre said. "Riley and I are to take care of you until you are on your feet."

"You have your store to run in Rock Springs."

Deirdre sighed. "I'll leave the breakfast and be back later. Try and eat, Trace. Please."

Deirdre left. Trace lay there, tormenting himself yet again with the memory of waking a week ago and finding Callie gone. He had hobbled about the ranch grounds for over an hour, shouting her name, believing she might have somehow been hurt. Certainly she wouldn't have left, not after she'd gotten him to admit he wanted nothing more in the world than for her to stay.

Then he'd found her note, reading and rereading the parts that said she loved him, *but* . . .

He swore, flinging the tray and its contents halfway across the room. Why hadn't she talked to him first? Why hadn't she asked him to go with her? *Your leg wouldn't hold up to the journey,* her note had said. But he didn't accept that. He was convinced she had made the trip alone for reasons far different than his injured leg.

It wasn't that he didn't believe *she* believed she was coming back. But once she was there, back with her father, back in New York, back in the big city excitement she had grown up with . . .

He shoved back the covers, swinging his legs over the side of the bed. His leg ached and it was still annoyingly weak, but if he hunched down a bit he could get around well enough on Riley's old crutch.

As he dressed, his gaze fell often to the leatherbound journal on the nightstand. He had yet to open it. He wasn't about to do so now.

He turned at the sound of the door opening, frowning when Riley Smith strode into the room. "I already told your wife I don't need a nursemaid,"

"You still don't believe Callie's comin' back, do you?"

"Get out." He was tired of being polite. He just wanted to be left alone.

"If you'd seen her that day in Rock Springs, you'd know."

"I said get out."

"Not until I've had my say."

Trace took a wrong step, sucking in his breath as a lance of pain shot through his leg. Swearing, he limped over to the rocking chair and sat down. "Get it the hell over with then," he snarled.

"She wanted to spare you the pain."

"My leg doesn't hurt that much."

"It wasn't that kind of pain she was thinkin' of. If she somehow can't get the boy . . ." He paused, frowning, as though wishing he'd chosen a different tack. Then he straightened, pointing a gnarled finger at Trace. "There's only one thing you need to get through that thick head of yours—and that's the fact that that woman loves you." He turned on his heel and left the room, leaving Trace alone with his thoughts.

The days passed. His leg healed. But his uncertainties turned again to fears when he heard no word from Callie. He told himself he was a fool for having trusted her, for allowing himself to be vulnerable one last time.

Yet night after night he stared at her journal. Why had she left it? Why did she so obviously want him to read it? No doubt she had made some keen observations about Yellowstone and her journey west, but he was in no mood for a sightseeing tour.

He reached over, touching the smooth leather, then jerked his hand back. It was as though Callie had touched him. With a vicious curse he heaved the book across the room.

In the end, though, it was no use. It was as Callie must have known it would be. He couldn't resist, couldn't resist knowing what part he had played in her innermost thoughts.

It was past dusk and he was pacing restlessly in front

of the fire. Deirdre and Riley had left for Rock Springs that afternoon. The journal lay on the settee, where he had most recently tossed it unread. But as usual it was calling to him, beckoning him to learn its secrets. The quiet, the solitude contributed to his odd melancholy. He was alone in the house, truly alone, for perhaps the first time in his life. He sat down, opening the journal to the first page and began to read. The daily entries began just after her wagon broke down in the ravine near Shadow's Way.

I swear I have never met a more arrogant cowboy in my life than Trace McCord. He all but threw me bodily off of his precious ranch today and he didn't like my name either!

An unwilling grin tugged at one corner of his mouth. He read another entry.

Trace is up to something. I'm not sure what, but I am sure it has something to do with me. Damn, if only he weren't so blasted handsome. He has a most unsettling effect on me sometimes, just by the way he looks at me.

His throat tightened, his need to have her in his arms suddenly overwhelming. Damn, but he missed her! He stopped reading when he reached the entry dated for the night he had first tried to seduce her, then forced himself to read on.

He even arranged to have Aunt Deirdre catch us, but by luck she twisted her ankle. How can anyone be so despicable? And yet, and yet . . . Why do I feel how he hurts? Why do I know how desperate he is? What he did tonight was all but unforgivable. Yet I forgive him. And—heaven help me—I love him. He glided his fingertips over the words, tears streaming unheeded down his cheeks.

"I love you, Callie," he whispered. "God, how I love you."

He was alternately touched, astonished, and amused by what he read. Not once did she condemn him for his past, for anything.

The second to the last entry told again of why she was leaving, beseeching him not to think she was rejecting him. She loved him, would always love him. She loved him enough to spare him the pain of losing Christopher twice. Loved him enough to risk his never wanting to see her again should she fail.

He stared then at her final entry. These words, too, were written directly to him.

Trace—I don't know if what I'm doing is right. I know you're angry and hurt that I've gone. But hopefully when I come back with Chris, you'll forgive me.

I could fill page after page with reasons why I love you, but I worry you would find a reason to disbelieve each and every one of them. If only I could make you see yourself the way I see you, not the way your father did. Jeb McCord was a twisted, pathetic man. I just pray that what I'm about to tell you will help more than hurt you.

Trace's brow furrowed as Callie's words directed him to Jenny's cedar chest. *You must decide whether to read the letter or not. For me it made no difference. I loved you before I read it. I love you still and always. Callie.*

His heart thudding against his rib cage, Trace walked to the chest. Sifting through its contents, he easily found the false bottom now that he knew to look for it.

He sat there, his hands trembling, as he opened Seth's letter and began to read.

Dearest Jenny,

Pa told me something awful last night. If I don't share it with someone I think I may die of it. But you must promise me never to speak of it to anyone.

Pa was drunk. The doctor had been out earlier and told him what Pa already knew in his heart—that he'd never walk again. Pa started raving about Trace. About how much he hated him.

Trace paused, pinching his eyes shut as his vision blurred. He took a steadying breath and read further.

Pa was rambling, blaming Trace for everything bad that's ever happened to him, going on and on about how Trace never should have been born. That's when he told me the rest of it. Oh, Jenny, swear you'll never tell, please.

Pa told me my mother slept with another man—he was a territorial marshal then, named Craig Lancaster. Pa found out about it. Ma swore it was only one time, one night. But Pa couldn't forgive her. He called her all kinds of terrible names.

But he still loved her. Thought it was God's way of testing him. When Ma turned out to be in a family way he went out of his mind wondering if the babe was his or Lancaster's. There was no way to know.

Pa raged about how he hated Ma, yet he loved her, too. Her death tore him apart. And even though Trace was most likely Pa's blood son, it didn't matter. Ma had sinned. Every time Pa looked at Trace, who so favored Ma in his looks, he remembered it all. Remembered her unfaithfulness, remembered his own sin of still desiring her even though he thought her a harlot.

I know I've been indelicate, Jenny dearest, and I beg you to forgive me, but it weighs on me so. I wonder if I should write Trace at the prison and tell him. He's always been so desperate to know why Pa hates him . . .

Trace's hand now trembled so badly he had to will it to stop. His gut was on fire. Never had he felt such fierce blinding hate.

He crumpled the letter in his fist, tossing it into the flames, watching it be consumed by them. Ignoring the throbbing of his still healing leg he stalked into the night, saddled Shoshone, and rode out.

He drove the horse mercilessly, as he drove himself, pulling up only when he regained his senses enough to know that he would kill the stallion if he didn't stop. He slid from the saddle, collapsing as his leg gave way. Stumbling, struggling, he gained his feet.

He stood on a moon-shrouded knoll, gazing up at the star-blanketed sky, alone in the night, in the silence. "Goddamn you, old man!" he raged. "Goddamn your self-righteous hide! I hate you! Do you hear me? I hate your damned guts!"

He sank to the ground, sobbing. *I hate you.* He said it over and over and over again. Until finally he heard the words and knew that he had been saying them to himself for years, living his father's vengeance out on himself.

I love you still and always. Callie. He could hear her voice in the wind. And he knew why she hadn't told him until now. *You needed to accept yourself for who you are inside, not what your father said, or your brother, or me, or the letter, just you.*

485

When hours later he started back toward the ranch, he felt—believed—for the first time in his life that all the years his father hated him weren't his fault after all. That maybe Callie really did have a reason to love him.

"Ah, Callie, it's so wonderful to see the child again," Deirdre said, brandishing a featherduster at the shelves of canned goods lining a quarter section of wall space in the Smith Mercantile. "What I do not understand is why you want Riley and me to take him to Trace. That's your place, not ours."

"I'll go with you to Shadow's Way," Callie said, "but I will not see Trace. Not yet." She looked around for Christopher, smiling to see him animatedly discussing how to procure a pickle from the barrel in the front of the store. Riley was failing miserably at driving a hard bargain. "I can't face Trace right now. He'll have enough to absorb having Chris back. He'll need time."

"He will? Or you will?"

Callie paced to the back of the store. "The longer I put it off, the longer I can delude myself that Trace will still want me." She'd been back in Rock Springs for less than an hour, having brought Chris most of the way cross-country by train. Deirdre had already assured her that her letter announcing Chris's return had made it to Trace three days before. She hadn't wanted to give him too much notice, lest he try to intercept them somewhere along the route and they miss connections. At least that was the reason she kept telling herself.

"The man loves you," Deirdre was saying.

"I can't be sure about that. Not anymore. My leaving had to have hit him hard. But I didn't see any other way. He still needed to work through a lot of pain and anger. And I think he needed to do that on his own."

"Did you know he has the ranch for sale?"

Callie gasped. "He could never sell Shadow's Way."

"Well, he sure has me fooled."

"He'll change his mind when he sees Christopher. Chris is the ranch's future."

The youngster sauntered over to her, his face bright and alive, so different from the way he'd looked the day she'd taken him from the Marlowes. Callie lifted him into her arms, hugging him close, then let him go off to wrangle another pickle from Riley.

"Your letter said your da helped you get him back," Deirdre said. "I'm glad you and Fletcher made up."

Callie smiled. "So am I. Da didn't care about the Yellowstone story nearly as much as I thought he would. He was actually just happy to have me home." Her smile turned rueful. "He wasn't especially over-joyed, however, when I mentioned I had acquired a husband, as well as found the gold. But after I explained everything, he did his best to accept it all. Eventually." Callie picked up a can of peaches, gazing distractedly at the label. She knew full well if it hadn't been for her father, Christopher might well still be with the Marlowes. How different her encounter with Fletcher Callaghan had been from the one she had conjured in her mind.

"My grandson?" he'd boomed. "You name the figure, you'll have the money. We'll free him from those wretched people at once."

"Is this my real father?" Callie had asked, "or have gypsies spirited him away to have him replaced by a twin of a less temperamental nature?"

"I'm just so happy to see you," he said, and for the first time she noticed the new lines around his blue eyes. "You tell me what you need," he went on, "and I'll see to it it's done."

When she had detailed her troubles about Chris's custody, it had taken her father no more than two days to contact the Marlowes, a day more to discover they had stolen most of Christopher's trust, and less than five minutes to convince them that it would be in their best interests to give up the boy or go to jail. To seal the arrangement, her father had them sign papers giving up any claim to the boy—forever.

Chris had been fearful, shy, and, she suspected, angry when the Marlowes surrendered him to her. And he had every right to be. But she had been showering him with love and attention ever since. Gradually he had believed she was truly back in his life.

And always, always she had told him how much his father missed him. That Trace couldn't wait to see him again. That Trace had hurt his leg or he would have come with her to fetch him.

"I'm going to give Papa a big hug," he'd said, as they'd stood in the train depot ready to depart for home.

Callie hadn't missed the note of uncertainty in the small voice. She gave his hand a reassuring squeeze. "Your papa will like that very much."

"You write to me, hear?" her father had said as he tipped the porter who was loading her luggage.

She nodded. "And don't you forget your promise to come visit us next spring."

She had been determined, then, not to even consider the possibility that things wouldn't work out between her and Trace. But now that their reunion was so close . . .

"Come with me to Papa's, Mama!" Chris pleaded.

Her heart swelled. He never called her Callie anymore. "Of course I'll come with you."

An hour later she was sitting in the backseat of the carriage Riley had hired to transport them all to the ranch. When they reached the Shadow's Way valley, though, no amount of cajoling by either Riley or her aunt could get Callie to go down to the house.

"Mama, come with," Chris said, his wide blue eyes growing anxious, fearful. "Mama's not going to leave me alone?"

She gathered him to her. "I'll be there a little later, sweetheart," she said. "Mama has to get herself all prettied up first for your papa. It's been a long time since I've seen him, too."

Still a bit dubious, Christopher stayed in the carriage with Deirdre and Riley, while Callie covered the last half mile to the ranch house on foot. She was thankful it was past dusk. She didn't want to risk any chance that Trace might see her. Crossing the porch, she peered into the window, just in time to see Trace come out of the kitchen to spy Christopher for the first time.

Her heart caught as she heard his whoop of pure joy. In two strides he closed the distance to the child, scooping him into his arms, weeping unashamedly. "I love you, Chris," he said over and over again. "I love you. I missed you so much."

"It's all legal," Deirdre reminded him, wiping tears from her own eyes. "He's your son. Forever."

Trace grinned, looking expectantly toward the door.

"Where's Callie?"

"She stayed behind," Riley said quickly. "She didn't want to intrude."

"She didn't want to see me?"

Riley cleared his throat, none too subtly changing the subject. "Lyle Morton told me to tell you a buyer was coming out in the morning. You might want to spiff up a bit. Some easterner." Riley gave Deirdre a sly wink, which Trace could not see. "You know the type."

"I still can't believe you'd sell the ranch," Deirdre said.

"This place hasn't felt like home without Chris, without Callie."

Riley chuckled. "There's hope for you yet. I do believe you're admittin' out loud you're in love with that little lady."

Trace said nothing.

Deirdre swatted Riley's arm. "Don't embarrass him."

"We're going out to the bunkhouse," Riley said. "It's late. Besides, you and Chris have to get reacquainted."

"You're welcome to stay in the guest room."

"No, no," Deirdre said, smiling, "the bunkhouse will be fine. More private, you know."

Trace managed a half smile. "Whatever you say."

They refused Trace's offer to walk them to the bunkhouse. After they'd gone, Trace rejoiced in giving one hundred percent of his attention to Chris. He made him supper, gave him a bath, told him stories of fair maidens and dragons until his voice caught.

"Mama tells me those stories," Chris said. "Mama loves me."

"She loves you very much."

"Mama loves Papa, too. She told me."

"I love your mama," Trace said. "And I miss her a whole lot."

Chris thrust his small chin out confidently. "Mama will come see me."

His heart hurt. "I'm sure she will." Trace picked up another slick-paper book and read to Chris until his blond head bobbed sleepily against his arm, then he carried him to his room. He tucked him into bed, nestling his puff puppy under his chin. For a long time he sat at the foot of the bed, just watching Chris sleep. It was so good to have him home. So right. Eyes stinging, he swiped at new tears, then quietly left the room.

Why hadn't Callie brought Chris herself? She said she loved him. He'd told her he loved her. Then where was she?

He strode out to the fire. Wherever she was, if she wasn't here with him, she was in the wrong place. He swore. He was going to do something about that and damned quick. He would take Chris to Rock Springs. They would catch her before she left.

His mind made up, he wasted no time hurrying to his bedroom, where he immediately started to throw some clothes into a valise. It was then he remembered a buyer was coming out in the morning. He threaded his fingers through his tousled hair. At this point he'd sell the place for fifty bucks, if it meant tracking down Callie a minute sooner. Whipping off his clothes, he crossed into the bathing room and took a quick bath. When he'd finished, he recalled leaving Callie's journal on the settee. He wasn't about to leave that behind. He hurried down the hallway, a towel thrown carelessly around his neck.

"I do love the way you do that," Callie murmured.

He stared at her, taking an involuntary step toward her, then stopped, jerking the towel to a more discreet position on his anatomy.

She smiled. "Dry your back for you?"

"What are you doing here?" he stammered, though the answer didn't matter, only the fact that she was here.

"To tell you the truth I heard the ranch was for sale."

"So?"

"So it happens I'm in the market for a piece of land."

His heart hammered in his chest. "I don't know," he said hoarsely. "I'm asking a pretty steep price."

"How steep?"

"The buyer has to live with me, love me. The buyer has to be my wife, be mother to Christopher."

"You drive a hard bargain, Mr. McCord." She walked up to him, circling her arms around his neck, reveling in the feel of his warm, damp flesh through her shirt, her jeans. The towel dropped from his grasp. "A very hard bargain indeed."

His pulses throbbed. "Those are the terms. They're not negotiable."

"Promise?"

"Promise."

She feathered her lips across the strong line of his jaw. "Deal," she whispered.

His arms swept around her, his mouth coming down on hers, hungry, fevered. "I thought I'd die when I found you gone."

"I thought I'd die when I had to leave you, but I

couldn't see any other way."

"I was so angry, so . . . hurt, that I didn't dare believe you'd come back. Then I read your journal."

Callie flushed. Though she had wanted to share her private thoughts with Trace, she felt suddenly vulnerable, exposed. "And?"

"And you're a damned fine writer, as well as a damned incredible woman."

She kissed his cheek, his lips, then leaned back to capture his gaze. "Are you all right? Your father . . ."

"I'm just fine," he cut in gently. "Better than I've ever been."

The kiss deepened. "I love you, Callie McCord."

"I love you, Trace McCord."

He linked his hand with hers, bringing it to his lips. "It was always so hard for me to believe that."

"Not from where I'm standing. And I'll have you know it is going to be my sincere intention to make you see yourself as I see you—then you'll know exactly why I love you."

He pressed her down onto the bearskin rug, his eyes searing into hers. "I remember the first night I lay with you on this rug. I was so sorry afterwards about . . ."

She pressed her fingertips to his lips. "It's gone. It doesn't exist. There's only now. Only you and me—and our little boy, our son."

He made love to her, sweet, sweet love, delighting in teaching her more of the wonders of her own body. And when his own need was beyond bearing, she was the one who urged him with her words, her hands to bring surcease to their mutually exquisite torment.

"Love me, Trace," she murmured. "Love me now."

He couldn't speak, could scarcely think. All he

wanted, ached, long for was to join his body to hers. Staking his arms on either side of her, he cried out, driving himself inside her, reveling in her need, her love for him, knowing that that love had made him whole.

Afterward, Callie lay staring at the ceiling, her hand curled in the crook of his arm. "Not that it matters, but are we ever going to go back for the gold?"

His mouth curved in a lazy grin. "Why spoil such a great legend?"

"I couldn't agree more," she giggled. "Something else just occurred to me, too." She hoped she didn't betray the sudden impishness she felt. "I hope you won't take it wrong."

"I doubt I'll ever take anything wrong again."

"Let's not press for miracles, shall we?" she said. "I was just thinking about how isolated it is out here. That Shadow's Way isn't exactly on the world's beaten path."

"You'll be lonely. I knew it. I—"

"I'm so glad you're never going to take anything wrong again," she said dryly. "Actually, I was thinking about Christopher. He'll need someone to play with closer to his own age." She grinned. "Maybe a brother or sister, maybe two or three."

Trace's smile lit up her heart. She opened her arms to a new beginning.